The
Lightbearer

To:

Juliet Burton, who glimpsed a spark nearly 40 years ago when I was a Nobbut Lad.

Jane McGregor who has promised to keep the original grossly over-written manuscript locked away for at least a thousand years to save me embarrassment.

Margaret Haffenden for her radiance on all levels and her endless patience at the endless rewrites to create this final version.

And Storm Constantine who helped the characters quit the night and enter the day, as McGregor Mathers might have said....

The
Lightbearer

Alan Richardson

IMMANION
PRESS
Stafford England

The Lightbearer
By Alan Richardson
First edition © 2017

ISBN 978-1-907737-76-3

IP0127

Cover design by Danielle Lainton
Interior layout by Storm Constantine
Edited by Storm Constantine

Set in Garamond

An Immanion Press Edition
http://www.immanion-press.com
info@immanion-press.com

What bears light? Darkness bears light.

William G. Gray

How you have fallen from heaven, Lucifer, son of the dawn! You have been cast down to the earth...

Isaiah 14: 12

I am fire and air; my other elements
I give to baser life.

Antony and Cleopatra

There is light and dark within us all. But the dark is not necessarily evil, nor the light inevitably good.

O.J. Wales

Although it can and should be read without any knowledge of arcane topics, *The Lightbearer* is a magico, gnosticky thriller-cum-love story (if that's not too pompous a description). It contains adequate levels of varied sex, appropriate violence and a discerning range of heavy weaponry for the non-mystic.

But it also has an occult 'game' within the text. Thus the reader is challenged to find all the imagery of the Major Arcana from the Rider/Waite Tarot and then fit them onto the kabbalistic Tree of Life – about which you need to know nothing.

You're not supposed to have an Appendix in a novel, but please have a glimpse at the final pages before you start.

Alan Richardson, Nov 2016

June 6th
1944

1

Father Gilles Fournier cried out and sat up in his narrow bed. Trembling, soaked in sweat. It felt as if a thin knife had been jabbed upward into his solar plexus, and twisted. He clutched at himself, crossing his arms tightly around his midriff to stop his guts spewing out. His nightshirt was soaked with blood or sweat or piss. He couldn't tell which in the pitch blackness of the windowless room.

This poor priest knew nothing of the momentous events in the sky above which heralded the D-Day Invasion. Or of the paratroopers plummeting onto French soil. But he did sense that something terrible had just exploded into his world: a nemesis he had been expecting all his life. And which he dreaded but could no longer avoid. This was his own supernatural sense of destiny that was tied in with horrors of his past. From the sharp, sick feeling in his gut he knew that his own Day of Judgement was about to creep up and seduce him.

Shaking with fear he swung out of bed and reached blindly for where he kept matches.

*God God God...*he gasped, prayed, through chattering teeth. The index and middle fingers of his right hand were fused: he seemed to be giving a permanent benediction to the world; simple tasks became difficult. He shook so much the matches scattered everywhere. But he found one and struck it. Then lit the candle, which stood before the skewed picture of the Virgin on a corner shelf.

All Latin exhortations and calls for help fled from him. *God god god...* was the best he could manage. The soothing face of Our Lady emerged from the darkness and flickered in the light. "Sainte Marie, Mère de Dieu..." he said to the picture. Said to himself. The nightmare had come back and taken another leap into a new realm of terror. It – whatever *It* was – no longer existed only in his head. *It* was now out in the world.

When it first happened he had been a little boy of three, sharing a bed with his *maman*. Sensing that there were...*things*...outside the window. *They* peered and sneered, waiting for him to let down his guard. As he grew older, alone in his own bed, he had the same nightmare: walking down a dark, descending corridor with a large wooden door at the far end. Dull red light like rancid blood seeped out from underneath. And through cracks in the wood. The sense of there being something behind that door, which was utterly evil, was palpable. Something that wanted to emerge and crawl across his skin, licking with a forked tongue. Something that was profoundly dirty, and without conscience. Something that did not belong on God's good earth. He never wanted to approach that door. Felt he was being pushed from behind, a hand on each trembling shoulder. And somehow *It* knew him. Lurked behind him daily. He called it, for lack of better term, *Le Noirceur* – but it meant, to him, more than just 'the darkness'.

God help me God help me... he whispered now.

In lieu of windows there were two mirrors, one on either side of the corner shrine. In the light of the candle which flickered under his heavy, panicked breathing, he could see his own two profiles. There, to the left, was the *bonshomme*, the frightened, simple, middle-aged priest with the thinning, greying hair. But to the right, where the lightning bolt had struck him years before, was the scarred, seared and wasted face with the scraps of hair, and remnant of an ear.

He was afraid to look at either. Afraid of the darkness behind.

"*Mon ami...*" said a quiet voice; a cool hand touched his shoulder.

"*Mon Dieu!*" swore the priest, who then remembered. Felt a surge of relief that he was not quite alone. "Luc...I'm sorry. I forgot you were here. I...I..."

The young man took a towel and wiped the priest's face, gently, both sides.

"What we did is not wrong."

Father Gilles closed his eyes. In the darkness of his thoughts, before his brow, the Door to Hell closed again.

"You don't understand. Something...something terrible has

come."

"It was an aeroplane. It flew very low above the house. That's what woke you."

The priest frowned, and sat on the edge of the bed, with the young man's arm around him.A welcoming touch. It reminded him that he had fallen from a state of grace. Fallen a very long way.

"An aeroplane? No, it was not that."

The young man didn't understand. How can you explain about demons?

"Come back to bed," said Luc. "You are safe with me. No-one will see. No-one will know…"

2

At the very moment that Father Gilles Fournier cried out and sat up in his bed, paratrooper Michael Horsett was flying through hell in the skies above. The twin engines of the C-47 had filled his head with their droning on the long flight from England: *Ahmnnnn Ahmnnn Ahmnnn...* The sound drilled into his brain. He found himself rocking back and forward to their rhythm like a rabbi in prayer. The other guys in their bucket seats kept looking at each other, their faces broken into angry camouflage patterns of green and black. Some of them forced hero-smiles through their masks. Some of them stared blankly into their pasts and scarcely dared think of their imminent futures. At one point they were flying so low that the prop blast blew cold spray from the English Channel in through the door. It cleansed them before they'd even committed any sins on the battlefield. Most of them were smoking, hardly able to move because of the quantity of kit in the narrow space.

These were all Screaming Eagles of the 101st. Airborne. The 101st had no history, as their officers kept telling them, but they sure as hell would have a destiny. They hung onto that notion and pulled on it as they needed, like the risers on their 'chutes. It kept them going, like the Benzedrine that many of them had taken.

Out in the dark, flittering on either side, were the other C-47s from 506th Parachute Infantry Regiment. They were tasked to land first on French soil at 0048 and light up the drop zones for the airborne assault to follow. As a signal-light man, Horsett's duty was to set up a 'T' of panels and lights to guide the rest of the ships.

Many of them were guys who had screwed up in some way. Their first outfits got rid of them by transferring them to the Pathfinders or ordered them to volunteer. Horsett's unit was stationed just outside Nottingham. When they got into trouble in town, Captain Quinn would bitch about the calls from the Sheriff of Nottingham to come get his present day hoods out of jail. No fines, no punishment just get them the hell out of here. English justice at its finest. It was the least they could do for what everyone knew was a suicide squad.

If they were screw-ups they were proud as Lucifer. They trained hard. The previous week they had done seven jumps, two of them at night. These guys were the best. Up until now they had all been acting at being killers, but now they were heading for the real test. They were the good guys in this war, Michael had told his mother. And even when he did kill it wouldn't make him bad. What could go wrong?

The C-47 seemed to gain height. It tilted sharply. He tried to look out of the small window but just turning was difficult: a glimpse of moon over a white sea. Sat back and breathed deeply. The pressure of all his belts and straps, the tightly-laced boots made him feel as if he was wearing armour. Oddly secure. He didn't need the bennies.

To his right hand, his buddy Tommy Woods took a deep, slow drag on a Lucky Strike before crushing it under his boot. To his left was Harry Spark, clutching a vomit bag. They called themselves the Three Kings, but the guys in the other sticks wouldn't bite. Their sarge called them the Three Stooges. He loved them really. As they nodded to each other now, the back of Horsett's helmet scraped against the fuselage, nails on a blackboard. Then suddenly, over what must have been the French coast, he heard a cheerful male voice as clearly as if he had been in a quiet room: "*Bienvenue!*"

His eyes widened, he looked around. Assumed one of his buddies was reading out from the phrase book they'd been issued with. Why would any of them say 'Welcome'? But no, they were engrossed in their own thoughts. Shaking his head, he tried to prepare himself. Really, with all the training they'd had, what could go wrong?

Ahmnnnn Ahmnnn Ahmnnn... ah ah Ah Ah AH AH!

The whole plane rocked when the flak hit. One engine died and then Tommy's head burst into flames. They licked down from under his helmet and curled back up in little flicks, like the blonde hair of Shirley Temple. Tracer had come through the fuselage and into his skull. He never made a sound. And then something punched a hole clean through the chest of Harry on Michael's other side, and *he* didn't do more than gasp as his guts filled the puke bag. But when a third guy opposite had his feet blasted off, *he* screamed just as loud as you might expect. Everything then – the whole mission – just slithered on down into a burning void that was darker and deeper than anything a guilty priest might imagine.

The plane started swerving and rocking. It veered and twisted like a fairground ride. Snaking red lines of tracer, and comets of blue and green flak, burst around it or fingered their hot ways into the long sheath of the fuselage.

The jumpmaster's face was glistening wax. He started hollering "Clear the ship! Clear the ship!"

Michael heard his sergeant shout "Hubba-hubba!", so they stood like robots – long months of training did that – hooked their static lines to the overhead cable and lurched toward the door. Then, in an act of mercy which no priest would ever have to administer, the guy drew his automatic and shot Tommy in his burning face.

Another hole appeared in the fuselage opposite as raw metal peeled back like petals, with a great surge of orange flame in the middle. Air was sucked from Michael's lungs as the shell punched out again next to his head with a great *woo-whooosh!*

The others were taking hits, screaming, two of them for their Moms. One cried out, "Please, please, oh please!" The C47 was rammed with the stink of roasting pork, of burning electrical circuits, smouldering rubber, paint, leather and webbing. Shit and vomit. Then the ammo started to pop and bang and the plane lurched again.

He must have blacked out, because if there had been a green light when they got to the Dropping Zone he never saw it. If he had made his way to the door he had no memory of doing so. Then the plane or his head took another hit and the next thing he knew he was plummeting through the night. And if it wasn't strings of tracer scorching past like meteors, it was real stars and a full moon as he plunged to earth. He tried frantically to release the leg pack containing his equipment, or else his contact with the ground would be at a zillion miles an hour. Then he was smashing through branches, when he should have had at least a few seconds of descent left.

They had dropped him too low – Christ it was far too low! Less than the three hundred feet any para needed. Every part of his body was raked and ripped. It felt like his balls were pushed up into his body by the harness and his face was being shredded.

Not me, he willed. *I ain't gonna die tonight!*

And so he didn't.

Instead he found himself hanging upside-down in a huge tree, one leg bent and trapped behind the other. Scarcely able to move because of the parachute rigging and the branches. He swung slightly so his helmet clashed against the trunk like the clapper in a bell. The big cargo pockets on his jacket and trousers were ripped open and a fire-storm of contents fell to the ground past his head: K rations and D bars, writing paper and pen, gum and condoms. A flashlight and cigarettes, ammo and sewing kit.

Now his whole body arched in agony as he hung there, speared by some sharp branch in his back. Draped and blinded by the canopy. It took long seconds before the urge to move kicked in. He had to do his duty and team up with what was left of his buddies. Then get the whole war over with in a few days. That's what it was all about.

Ptah... he spat, for there were small twigs and oak leaves in his mouth. Blood leaked out over the camouflage cream and into his eyes, making them sting as much as his palms did from the rigging. His agonies were mute: if he screamed, he didn't know who might hear him.

Bizarrely, the sky was clear again. No sign of the plane or the flak he had flown and fallen through. No sound of the *Ahmmm* in his brain, just a breeze making the leaves click. And the tilted grin of a yellow moon. So there he was, come to save the world, but now just hanging in the darkness in a big old oak tree. He suddenly felt a very long way from Detroit.

Somewhere below him a stream gurgled. He couldn't tell how far, but he could hear little gloops when his blood dripped into it. Head pounding, he used the trench knife strapped to his thigh, and started to cut himself free. They had talked about this in training in Fort Benning, and shown how it should be done. Never thought he'd have to do it.

Saw, hack, saw, slash...

Christ! he thought, as the harness was cut through and he swung even more wildly, 90 degrees, his boots smashed against the trunk, branches snapped like breaking teeth.

Shadows in the starlight, movement in the nearby field – Krauts searching with flashlights? White claws scraped at the ground, then scythed in great arcs, before they were switched off.

The headlights of some monster vehicle swung away, as it growled off and left him in silence, dangling from his tree, head exploding.

Cut cut, saw, hack…Pain, pain, pain…

Jesus! Jesus Fucking Christ! he hissed as he swung upright, released what was left of the chest harness, and fell the last six feet, into the stream. He got to his knees and hauled himself onto its bank to collapse face-down, shaking, on the sodden earth of Normandy.

It was one helluva way to visit France…

His right leg was ripped from ankle to knee. Bleeding and hurting badly, though it missed the arteries. There were cuts around both eyes which blinded him until he staunched the blood, although he couldn't quite straighten his head. Then there were spiky fragments of shrapnel, like bits of stars, poking through his jump suit into his arm and chest. He plucked some of these, making himself bleed more. The morphine syrette, which every trooper carried, had fallen from his ripped pocket and was gone, probably swept downstream. *Damn damn damn.* But he still had the sulpha powder, which he poured into the wound, and a field dressing with which he bound his leg as best he could.

I can do this, he thought. *I **have** to do it.*

After a minute of deep breaths, he hauled himself up, left the trees, and limped into the field in which he had seen the witch-fingers of the flashlights, as they had groped and splayed around, searching.

He had fallen to earth – but where? There was nothing to see, just outlines of poplar trees waving sinister shadows in the near distance. And a surge of low hills beyond. Soon, the main Airborne invasion force would be above and looking for his lights and florescent panels and the T-shape marking the dropping zone. But there he was making high-pitched noises of terror inside himself, like a bat and as blind, listening for echoes. Hobbling lamely on the ground. Useless.

He knew the angle of fall, and from his jump number could figure out the direction to search for the other twelve guys in his stick. Far off, he heard a burst of automatic fire – very rapid, not American. One of the German burp guns they'd practised with. It confirmed his calculation. He looked all ways, from the damnedest of angles on account of his damaged neck. Checked his Tommy gun, checked his ammo and limped off in the likeliest direction into his new world

Before he got to the edge of the field he found something. It looked like a small rippling pond amid a silver cornfield. Moonlight turned the scattered poppies into constellations of black stars. As he drew nearer, he saw it was a parachute spread limply over the stalks, a shroud for the body beneath. He peeled it back and took long, sick seconds before he recognised Sergeant Topper Burns. An hour ago that guy had stood in the open door of the C-47 to piss: it had blown back inside over them. "You're gonna get covered in worse than that where we're goin'!" he'd shouted. They'd forced out a few laughs to show that they were Airborne.

Now here he was, his limbs smashed into twisted rags. The heavy Eureka Beacon that would send out a homing signal to the others had punched itself neatly into the guy's chest. His innards snaked out of his mouth. This should have been released on a line to dangle below, so its great weight would hit the ground first, slowing the final few feet of descent. Michael Horsett's own leg pack had been severed by shrapnel, probably, and that had saved him.

He threw up as silently as he could.

The moonlight showed the beacon's big red button clearly marked DEST. This would blow up the device and stop it falling into enemy hands. But he daren't press it. He couldn't hobble far enough away in time. He daren't risk alerting the Krauts. Their job was not to fight, but illuminate. Yet he couldn't do either.

Everything, *everything* was going wrong. In the simple sort of life he had had so far, this sort of thing didn't happen. It struck him then: the pilot had messed-up, the flak had scared the shit out of him. So it made him lose his target and drop his load – shit and men – wherever he happened to be.

He hated the Air Corps.

The sky was pure. There was a bright orb shining just above the eastern horizon which he knew was Venus. In a few hours, the sun would rise and avengers would be unleashed. But at the moment it was still and calm. So he sat back, cold with horror, his injured leg straight and stiff in front of him. He couldn't give a wooden nickel for the officers, but he had idolised his tough, foul-mouthed, heavy-drinking sergeant: the finest fighting man who had never fired a shot in anger. Even if he was a guy who, in real life, sold garden furniture.

Here, in France, after long months of training and acting at War, Horsett felt like a performer on stage who had forgotten his lines. His best buddies were dead before their mission had even begun. His selfish bastard sarge had deserted him. And although Michael's own father had always called him a darned mummy's boy, in truth he had never known true fear. For the first time ever, after the sunny places from which he had come, he did now.

3

Colette was another soul who had been troubled by the pathfinder's fall from the heavens. She'd been up at first light, woken in the night by a low-flying aircraft that had growled and stuttered above the crooked chimneys of her home. She was seventeen plus a day, and felt old. Feared that she might *rester vieille fille* as she heard in her head. That is, remain single, left on the shelf. Other girls got married at fourteen. Other girls were not trapped. They did not live in a large house that was deliberately hidden from the world in general, but the Nazis in particular.

She had been told when she was little that shooting stars were really souls falling to earth to be born. She had no idea that her destiny had already arrived in this way.

Yet at that moment her hair was in a mess. Her bloodied hands full of the eviscerated bits of two large owls. She fumed at her own bad luck and timing.

A young German motorcyclist with an empty side-car had come past the sagging gate that was secured with string. It was *very* hard to find the road past their house at best of times. No-one came by accident.

The whole area of the *bocage* was a maze of narrow roads and dirt tracks. High hedges on either side. You knew where you were or you didn't. Locals, to create shortcuts, fashioned gaps in the hedges but made false gates of stout branches and leaves. You would have to look closely to see these. One of the fools in the next farm must have been drunk again and left one open.

Was this guy bringing Trouble? Were they about to be raided again, as had·happened a few years before?

She had nodded to him on his first transit, when she had gone from her house to the old stables, empty-handed, to fetch some straw. He was young, looked bewildered and harmless. German or no, courtesy costs nothing, and this one was young. There he was, bouncing past, cheerfully wrestling with the steering, trying not to let the ruts guide him into the hedgerows or ditches. Eyes had locked. Youth had called to youth and she knew there'd be no Trouble from him. If her heart didn't exactly leap, it did something akin to giving a *hmmmm*, overlaid with a hint of *ooh!*

He passed, she sighed, but then he came back again, heading in the opposite direction this time. The matte-green bike threw out smoke and kicked up dust. The machine was rattled badly, the emptiness of the side-car was enormously tempting. One leap into the unknown and her world would change.

"Good morning!" he shouted in a thin, high voice, with a lovely smile and a bold wave.

"*Au 'voir!*" she cried back, grinning, watching him disappear around the bend. She swished the air with her hands to clear the dust.

Hmmm, she sighed for real this time. The fact he was a German didn't trouble her. On the few times she had seen them, *ordinary* Germans had always acted correctly. The fact that he wore a uniform that was too large, had teenage boils, was hardly to his detriment. He was young, and there were so few young men in her world just then. Only grandfathers, cripples and priests. Most were doing forced labour for the Third Reich. Or hiding down in Vichy France. Or with that Free French Army in England she had heard rumours about.

"Colette!" cried a familiar voice behind her.

"*Grand-mère.*" She said it without inflection, almost as a soldier might say *Yes sir.*

The older woman, stood silver-haired but straight-backed. Prim as a young girl. Her hands full of something that seemed to glisten, drip and slurp in the sun.

"Did someone just drive past?"

"Only those idiot brothers in their tractor," she lied.

"Whatever you're smiling about, stop it. You know what happens when you get too excited. Now, here…take this. Dispose. Go!"

This was the innards of the two huge owls the other woman was in the process of embalming. She dumped the mess into Colette's cupped palms, wiped her own hands on her thick, leather apron. Then turned back into the house, and her hobby, with a spring in her step.

Colette heard the motorcycle returning yet again, for the third time. Three times along such a hidden lane was no coincidence. He drove up too quickly for her to dispose of the mess. The oozy bits began to drip and slip between her fingers. She was caught with her hands full of it, in the No Man's Land between the house

18

and the midden, next to the broken gate. He stopped his engine and came towards her, carrying a large map.

What could she do but stand there like an idiot, giving an idiot's grin?

He looked at her and smiled – it was a very nice smile, she thought. It helped drive away the *cafard*[1] that she often had to wrestle with. She that felt this was caused by boredom, loneliness, being stuck out here in the middle of a friendless nowhere. The other women spoke of it like a disease.

"Bonjour, *m'amselle. Ça va?*" he said softly, in excellent, confident French. "We meet again as you prophesied – one minute ago!"

Colette gave an awkward smile; the entrails in her hands were disgusting. She could almost imagine they were moving.

"Can I help you?" she asked, giving a little motion from one side to the other, as if she were about to go somewhere meaningful.

He stood on the bottom bar of the gate to get height, and leaned over to look. It creaked and groaned.

"Mmm. Is that going to be some delicious Norman dish? A pie perhaps?"

He was teasing. She smiled. She would have to tell him the truth. It was so absurd that it would take away her feeling of stupidity.

"This used to be two owls. My, er, grandmother, she does embalming. This is what she does *not* want. You might have seen her work in various places around Neuilly. The town hall has a very fine black dog."

"I know it! It has black pebbles for eyes – slightly crossed."

They both laughed.

"*Alors*…she could not get her usual glass eyes. The war you know."

He lowered his head. "I know."

Colette whistled and two dogs came lolloping from around a corner. "Nu, Geb…have this," she said, and threw it onto the ground where they dived upon it. Free of the mess, she wiped her hands on her pinafore, looked at the map he carried.

---

[1] Literally a cockroach. Used as a common term for depression or apathy

"You are lost."

"Oh I am, so *very* lost," he said, and she knew he meant in more ways than one.

He rested the map across the top bar, leaning over with his elbow, fussing it into shape. The dogs fought and snarled, but neither human noticed.

"Where do you want to go?" she asked.

He hesitated. "I…I am not allowed to say. Orders from on high. But if you would just show me where I *am*, I would be grateful. There are no sign posts."

"The war, of course."

She leaned forward, on tippy-toe. Her left breast touched the side of his arm. She knew from his brief swallow he felt the contact. She felt wicked, delicious. "*Eh bien*…where are we? Er er er…Here. This little dot, I think. It does not show our road. It does not show much."

"It is a French map," he said, with a hint of scorn.

She looked up from the map but kept her breast exactly where it was, and if anything, increased the pressure. "Perhaps we French know that some things should be kept hidden."

She saw him blush. His eyes widen.

"Well," he said, looking at his watch. "So, we are here. If I wanted to get to this big road, am I in the right direction?"

She pulled away, feeling rather pleased with herself. Tried not to get too excited as *grand-mère* was always saying. "Go down there. Do not take any side roads. This will curve around for a kilometre. When you come to a junction turn left, then first right. Another kilometre and you will be on your road, going to your secret places."

He folded the map up slowly, very carefully. "*M'amselle*…if only…I would have liked…"

"I know. The war."

He looked around. "It is so quiet here, so lovely. You would never think…"

"Think what?" she asked, to string him out. "What do German soldiers think in places like this?"

"I am not a soldier. I am a policeman, a *Feldgendarme*."

"And what do *Feldgendarme*s do?" she asked, genuinely curious.

But he straddled his motorcycle and started the engine. *Duty* was suddenly all over his face.

"The war is coming nearer. In fact it is very near. That is all I can say. But some day it will end, and perhaps you and I might, well...?"

"*ALLEZ!*" screeched the *grand-mère* who came up behind them both. They turned to see the woman standing on her right leg, making a fist of her left hand. The index and little fingers pointed at the young man's heart, like two horns. She was breathing heavily and hard, as if sending evil out through those fingers into the target, intoning: "*Zazas, Zazas, Nasatanada Zazas...*"

"Pardon, Madame?" he said to the older woman, then looked at Colette for explanation.

"She is cursing you."

He gave a smile. "Half of Normandy has cursed me."

"And the other half?" she asked, in a whisper.

He mounted his motorcycle again, looked at the *grand-mère* and spat into the dust of the road. To Colette: "My name is Dieter," he said.

"I am..."

But he roared off, more noise than speed. She watched him go. He gave a little reverse wave with his gloved hand and was lost behind the hedgerows within seconds.

4

The day edged up. Whole armies were roaring toward Normandy by sea and air but there was no sign of that here. The sky became pale and white – and empty. Michael hoped that the other pathfinders would have been successful and illuminated the dropping zones for the 101st Screaming Eagles and the All American 82nd Airborne.. Maybe it was all done and dusted. Maybe he could go home!

Shit shit shit. He should have been a part of it, doing his duty. Instead he limped along the edges of cornfields. Poked his bent head around and squeezed through the endless hedgerows of the Normandy *bocage.* He was no more than a blackened face bobbing up and down through qualities of light.

Back in England, at their base at North Witham, near Nottingham, he had spent days studying maps, aerial photographs and three-dimensional scale models of the land. He knew all about St. Côme-du-Mont, Vierville and Ste. Marie-du-Mont, which formed Drop Zone C. He had stared down upon that artificial world until he knew every church, road, field and river. Every fake sparrow on every fake tree. But nothing here in the real world made any sense. He had a small compass and an unmarked map in his escape kit, plus seven dollars in French money. But there was nothing around to give him a bearing.

Lord, but he was alone! No buddies, no people, no war, no invasion. Just clouds of unknowing, an empty world and a hurting body. He could do this – he had to do this! He was born with a sense of being special. His Mom always said so! Plus he had something to prove to his late Dad, who was probably up in his Heaven sneering at him, and calling him a 'two-faced little shit'.

He blacked out. When he came to again, he was on his back. The sun had risen and pinned him out flat, a new species of butterfly. His leg was bad but it could have been worse. Out of habit he pulled out a cigarette, dragged himself to hide amid a tangle of bush, and lay there smoking. He cupped the tip in his shaking hands in case it gave him away.

When he had volunteered to be a Pathfinder, it hadn't been because he wanted to be the bravest of the brave. In fact he had joined the Army Specialized Training Program. This allowed enlisted men to attend universities and study subjects such as physics, chemistry, engineering, mathematics and languages. He'd thought that the great overshadowing entity known as Uncle Sam (which he'd always imagined as a huge bearded face seen in profile), had made him a promise. A promise to keep him out of the hazards of actual war. For a time, as entrant no. 93, he'd even worn the insignia of the ASTP, which consisted of the Lamp of Knowledge, on which was super-imposed the Sword of Wisdom. And he felt smug – insanely smug. Though he knew enough to hide the fact.

But after one month the whole program had been closed and he'd been sent toward full infantry training. Totally betrayed by that big face in the sky. Plus it had become clear to anyone that the only way the Nazis could be beaten was not by air or sea power alone, but soldiers on the ground. They needed infantry more than they needed scholars.

Yet when he'd got the chance to divert into the Paratroops he hadn't hesitated. His reasoning had been that they were elite. If he had to fight, he didn't want the guys around him to be ordinary. He was nearly eighteen and already a snob. So he'd signed a document, which stated that he would hereby volunteer to jump from a plane while in flight and land on the ground via parachute. Then he'd got his jump wings at Fort Benning, all the while sticking one finger up to the ghost of his father who was afraid of heights.

Simply, the chance to volunteer for the even more elite Pathfinders had been pure logic: land silently, unexpectedly at night, in a big open space. Less chance of being seen. Set out the lights on the dropping zone and then the whole of the Airborne would follow and do the fighting. He would sit himself under trees and bask in glory. Plus this group lived better and were paid better than the rifle companies. They were spared KP. Once their training with the holophane lights and Eureka beacons had been completed, they could pretty much come and go as they pleased. The alternative, joining the infantry and doing a daylight sea-borne assault on beachheads had disaster written all over it, as far as he could see. And on his good days he felt he could see very far indeed. Though he kept that part of himself pretty much hidden.

Besides, he was afraid of water, couldn't even swim. Being a

Pathfinder suited him. He was a natural athlete. Nothing to do with being brave, all to do with air and fire.

He shuddered, took another deep drag on his cigarette. Tried to misdirect his thoughts away from the pain. For a brief time in ASTP he'd had a pal called Mel Brooks, who told him that one day he planned to make crazy movie about the war in which nothing would be as it seemed. It was almost as if he were in this movie now.

Then he saw his first Kraut.

His first Kraut was an off-duty German military policeman. Another, older, *Feldgendarme* from the same troop as Dieter. If Dieter had been lost, this one was trying very hard to hide. The man was well-fed and under-exercised, bulging inside his standard field grey uniform, cap slanting jauntily over his brow. In one hand he pushed a bicycle, the handlebars cutting a swathe through the ripening corn. His other hand held that of a woman. She wore a floppy sort of straw hat with flowers in the brim, from which flowed lank black hair done in pig-tails, ending in red ribbons. All this setting off a dowdy green dress and the silk stockings, which told of their relationship, and what was in it for her.

He could hear their voices – gulls of sound, which dipped off into the distance. There was a sense of urgency about the guy. He kept looking around, causing Michael to sink back into cover and push his cigarette into the soil. She walked under a cloud, and scarcely looked up from the ground.

The man dropped his bicycle and walked her on a few paces toward Horsett, forcing him to slip even further back into the bushes, gun ready, the couple less than twenty yards away. After a sweeping look that took in their watcher but failed to spot him, the German fumbled with his pants and dropped them around his knees.

Horsett watched. He had never seen a man and woman doing *it* before. He could see everything – the fat pumping cheeks of the soldier's spotty ass. The jerking of the woman's legs as she tried to cleave around a too-great bulk. The red garter she wore on her upper thigh. Even the taut brows' momentary peace at climax. She didn't even take her hat off. Then the wiping of her private parts with a handkerchief from her dress pocket.

She sat for a moment, lost in thought, smoothing wrinkles and the future from her stockings. As she adjusted her suspenders her lover heaved his lower body back into uniform.

"Uli…" she said, pulling at her pig-tails like a little girl. "Je suis—"

"Ssh! Not now Juliette," he said briskly, angrily, peering back across the fields to whatever it was he was avoiding.

The girl sighed, looked at the ground again. They left as quickly as they had come, losing themselves to Horsett's secret gaze.

The American sank back into his cover, revolted by the flabby white flesh and their sordid hygiene. The act had been pathetic. He was eighteen and still a virgin. A situation he planned to rectify when he got to Paris, where all the girls would be begging for it. If – *when* – he got to this stage, he wanted better than that.

But most pathetic of all was the knowledge that the mere proximity of this seedy old wreck from another race, who had done no more than waggle his fat ass at Horsett, had scared him. Though for sure he couldn't have said why.

Must have been the blood loss.

5

Not far away from all of them, Dieter stopped his motorcycle, switched off the engine and marked a small cross on the map. This marked not where he was, or where he had to go, but where he must return: to that girl. He hadn't quite caught her name. He felt sure that something had passed between them. He wanted to create a future for himself that would not involve war.

The mad old woman behind her had spooked him. That was why he had driven off so quickly. To blot out the image of the hag, he started singing quietly a Kreigsmarine song, which had been all the rage four years before. This had inspired him far more than his father's impassioned commands. *Wir Fahren Gegen Engelland.* We're going against England. As a boy he had listened to its catchy tune on the radio as the Germany Army had swept through Poland, Czechoslovakia, France, Belgium, Denmark and Norway. England was the final stop. And in those days he'd wanted to be part of that advance.

"Wir Fahren Gegen Engelland," he sang, but the irony was not lost on him that, on the beaches of Normandy, England was now coming against him. He ended every line this time with a scathing *Scheisse!*[1]

He looked at the cross on the map. Under that cross was the most perfect girl. He had orders from 'on high', to drive far inland on a secret mission. Yet he wanted nothing more than to strip off his absurd uniform and go back to that girl who had seemed so welcoming. Dieter had never fired a shot in this war, and had no aptitude for police work. He just wanted some sort of a home.

Unknown to him, as he searched for his true home in the world, he was being watched.

Horsett had seen the old army motorcycle wavering along the rutted dirt track, and he pulled back into cover as it stopped. The guy wrestled with a map, folding it into a manageable square, taking a pencil to mark a particular spot with a cross.

---

[1] Shit

Some sort of a dispatch rider. A skinny little guy with a big stupid grin on his rat-like face, as if he'd just found a hundred dollar bill. And a uniform too big, so the collars came up over his chin, and the sleeves near down to his knuckles

Michael Horsett needed that map. God but he needed it!

He watched from behind the hedgerow, within the unreal silence of the *bocage*. He was sweating. Each heart-beat burst like flak, frenzied by the sense of being lost

In his training, in the months before, the other guys thought him fearless. His sergeant knew it was an act, a face he could pull. He had caught Horsett once, sitting under a tree, reading. Snatched the book away, looked at it, frowned.

"What is this shit?"

The private sighed, found out. "It's called *L'Etranger* by Albert Camus."

"You can read this?"

"My Mom is French."

"You're not what you seem."

"Is anybody?"

"You could have been an officer."

"No, sarge. I am what I am."

"You're dumbing yourself down for these guys. And for me."

"No, sarge. Really. I love them all. I love everybody!"

"Bull. So why you doing all this – *really?*"

"Destiny sir!"

"Listen you little sucker, remember your 'destiny' and what role you're playin' when a Nazi opens up with his zip gun. Now gimme twenty-five you freak. Hell no, make that fifty!"

He tried not to smile as he did the push-ups. Sure but the sarge loved him really.They were great guys. No-one pulled rank. *Forward as One!* they would cry. So God and the whole of the 101st Airborne was on his side.

That was weeks ago. It was aeons ago. In a different world. On the other side of the sky.

Scheisse! said the young German rider as he flattened the bulged paper against the motorbike's tank, frustrated by something that made him look up into the sky, close his eyes and take deep breaths.

Horsett swallowed and pressed his head down, his heart pounding the ground so hard that it and not the wind might have rippled the corn. He wanted that map: his own had been blasted into space. He needed to know where he was. He wanted that map *so* badly. He *had* to know where he was.

Sure, it had all been easy in training. With his buddies around, egging him on, supporting him and covering his ass – easy. A stealthy approach from behind. Cover the guy's mouth. Pull his head back and slit the throat... But they had all been using wooden knives. Acting. Now... he found himself trembling again. Hell, considering the state he was getting into, he *owed* it to himself to waste this guy! So, egged on by ghost-memories of his buddies, and the endless scorn of his late father in heaven, he started a countdown. From ten to zero. At zero he would rise, creep, clutch and slit.

But he could hardly walk by now, never mind sneak up, so he decided he'd blast him instead.

At zero, he started another countdown

At zero again he started from eight.

The rider was refolding his map, fumbling with something in his pocket. He would be off within a moment.

8, 7, 6, 5... Chance to let him go, he was an innocent looking kid, they could have been pals.

Scheisse! said the kid again.

4, 3... The kid revved the engine and straightened the bike. But as he looked back over his shoulder he caught a glimpse of Horsett's greeny-brown and blackened face peering at him between the leaves. So when his eyes widened, and he started to reach for his Luger, then it just had to be done.

Nothing stealthy or elegant. Ignoring the pain Horsett jumped up from cover, hopped forward and emptied a magazine into the boy's side and back. An endless burst which smashed the map into flecks of thistledown. Blood and bits poured over the machine and made the rider's arms jerk like flags. Bullets hit the gas tank. The paratrooper was hurled back into the hedge by the explosion. His victim was blasted sideways, immersed in flames, flapping at them, screaming.

So much for the map. So much for the kid.

Shit...

Horsett hurled himself back into the cornfield. There was a long piece of wood there, nearly his height, two inches in diameter. It might have been a post of some kind. He slung the

Tommy gun over his shoulder and used the pole as a crutch, hobbling as fast he could, clenching his teeth against the pain. He muttered low weasel cries until he reached the deep shelter of a copse. *Forward as One!* – but there was only one of him, and he didn't know forward, back or sideways just then.

He looked back: there was another crump of an explosion, probably the kid's grenades. Smoke shot upward, waggling ornate patterns and fanning out, a totem to his achievement.

He had to get as far away from there as possible. There'd been twelve in his stick: some of the others might have made it. But they would just have to fend for themselves. Now he needed shelter, somewhere to try and fix his leg and neck. As he swayed from side to side, trying to find some landmark other than high hedges, he saw the cat.

It was a flat-faced, ugly critter which seemed to be waiting for him. It sure wasn't a wild cat. There had to be a home for it somewhere. Then it turned and set off, slowly, along the edge of a field. It turned at intervals, as if to make sure he was still following.

He was.

This is crazy, he thought.

But that's how he found the three women who were to have such impact upon his life, and turn him – a good-natured sort of fella – into a kind of demon…

6

Hours later. Dusk. Bats were flitting above the roof in the light of the rising moon. Somewhere in the woods a fox was making a noise like a woman in pain, while Colette still thrummed with thoughts of Dieter.

She had no problem with with him being a German, despite the hatred of the *grand-mère* and *maman*. Ordinary Germans had never caused *her* any trouble. On the rare occasions when she had gone into town, they had been unfailingly polite. Dieter wasn't a Nazi, he wasn't even a soldier. He was a young policeman. Something inside her was alive, and singing: *Dieter Dieter Dieter...* She wondered how soon he would take her to Germany. Time was slipping away.

And then it all stopped. Dieter's memory became as thin as an exorcised ghost when she glimpsed the soldier lying there in the darkest corner of the crumbling stable.

Colette stifled a cry, and only came closer when she saw the man was sleeping deeply. She put the bucket down amid the rotting straw and manure, edged the lantern forward. Brushed her long black hair from her brow with the clean skin of her wrist. Peered at where he lay at the edge of her light. It looked as if the man wore a black and green mask of some sort, and a spurt of loathing rose within her. Why be so stupid? Who and what was he?

As her eyes grew accustomed to the thick treacle of the darkness she saw it was paint, or polish on his face. The exhausted angle of his head had twisted his features into a scowl. Underneath the helmet he had a long, oval face with a pronounced nose, a gash of a mouth with swollen lips that looked as if he had been punched. Both his bare flesh and uniform were raked in lines, like claw marks. He seemed to be weeping tears of blood.

The whole uniform was filthy, sodden and blood-stained. His right trouser leg was torn open in a long gash from the top of his boots to beyond the knee. A bloodied tongue of bandage poked out from the tear. From the high boots and style of the uniform she thought he must be one of the strutting parachute soldiers –

they called themselves *Fallschirmjagers* – she had seen during a rare weekend in town. A deserter?

Then she saw the fat, Persian cat they called Matagot sitting calmly in the shadows, near the man's head, as if waiting for him to wake up. Her eyes widened. The Matagot never did that with anyone. The Matagot was more than just a cat, as anyone from Normandy or Brittany could have told you.

Outside, hens were squabbling, pigs squealed and grunted. The wild cries wrapped a cocoon around the cracked timbers, entrapping the moment. Nearer still, heart pounding, she almost squealed herself, thinking him to have been watching after all. His left eye was not quite closed: it had a strange hieroglyphic twist to the upper lid so that a two millimetre strip of whiteness and pupil peered through, always.

She took up the bucket carefully. Closed the broken door and tried to scurry as silently as her wooden shoes would allow, determined to be furious at this invasion of their property.

Ahead of her, coming through the gates, was the battered tractor of the grizzled brothers from the next farm. Visitors in this place were rare. Shrivelled old Armand Allumage was driving, while the hatless long, balding head of his younger brother Jules hung out from the side window. They were shouting above the faulty silencer for her mother.

She was surprised, it was late; as neighbours they only came when they wanted something. What could they want now? They would have no time to return before the 8 o'clock curfew.

The two men got into the house only seconds before Colette. In that brief time the whole building exploded. They were all shouting, with lamps being lit, bottles being popped. Whatever the reason, she was annoyed that her own news would once again be brushed aside. Made to seem silly. Yet when she got there she found even normally dour '*maman*' Selene, and '*grand-mère*' Astrid dancing around like dervishes, helped by the two yelping dogs. They seemed intent on using up a lifetime of grins within minutes. She had never seen them like that before.

It all made sense to her then. She should have guessed from the loud droning of aircraft in the distance, far to the north-west. She should have sensed it from the brooding, which lay over the whole French sky and which had made the bones ache for so long, like damp mist. For on that morning, at the very moment when the sun rose, the Allies had begun to spill against the Normandy coastline like acid.

And best thing of all, one of them, she realised now with blinding certainty, was sleeping in the stable like a baby.

7

Colette said nothing. The men slugged as much as they could of the 1942 Saumur kept for dubious visitors – possibly their only reason for coming to break the news. Then they staggered out to their tractor, murdering the gear changes before lurching out of the gates and down the lane to tell others.

"*Au 'voir, Mesdames Cachette!*" Jules shouted above the engine noise. In passing, he made vulgar *you-know-you-want-to* signals to Colette, when he thought the other women weren't looking.

"They'll get shot..." said Astrid cheerily, her thin arms making wings of her shawl, waving them away like an Angel of Death.

"Many times, I hope," added Selene, with even greater jollity as the pair of them made their own obscene gestures to the disappearing men. They'd been invaded and occupied before, in many ways, by too many men.

"The brothers Allumage are good for nothing but burning. Kindling by name, kindling by nature."

They went indoors. Colette put logs on the fire, one by one, very carefully.

"You have something to say," stated Astrid, warily. She had seen a shining in the girl's face, and it wasn't good for her to get too excited.

Selene, who had high regard for the older woman's insight, put the lid back on the simmering pot and gave a look which could only mean: *Well? What trouble are you in now?* The pair of them stood before the girl, arms folded, eyebrows raised in question.

For Colette, it was almost a shame to reveal her secret. She asked for more wine; it was given. She looked at them both over the brim of the glass. She might have dragged the game out longer but one of the dogs was barking and the revelation had to come from her, not some stupid beast.

"There is a soldier asleep in the stable. He is not German. I think he is a parachutist."

Eyebrows were raised; lips pursed forward like beaks to form an astonished *Quoi?* And then the three of them dashed for lanterns, for shoes, and for the door. They stumbled in a knot along the narrow passage and burst out into the evening.

8

At the same moment, back in Neuilly, Father Gilles Fournier sat alone in the empty classroom. The last rays of the sun slanted in through the windows. It reflected off the glass domes which contained the stuffed squirrels. Bounced off the face of the big old clock with the loud implacable tick. The children had long since put their chairs on their desks and said their Amens. Then waved solemn good-byes to the scarred and scary priest who taught them. They had heard rumours about the events on the distant beaches, where many of them had never been. And though they couldn't name them, they had seen portents in the sky: Typhoons and Hurricanes, Thunderbolts and Lightnings – aircraft of every nation. The priest had tried his best to distract them, but in truth his own head was constantly full of…Things.

When the children had gone he closed and bolted the double doors and crossed himself. As if this act would also seal up a portal within. But still the demons – for that is what they had to be – hammered at his consciousness. *Let us in, let us in…* they seemed to whisper. *We want you to meet Someone…*

He knew what Jesus must have felt like in Gethsemane. But had Jesus been wracked with innumerable guilts? He half-closed his eyes against the sunlight, his lashes breaking it into innumerable rays. Taking deep breaths he tried to suck his fears and his monsters into a space deep within. Tried to seal them into a place as dark and secure as his windowless bedroom.

Then he heard, above this internal din, the unmistakable noise of weeping from the next room.

Sighing, he summoned the energy to go through the small door at the far corner of the class. This led him into the sanctity of the church where a young woman was crying, twisting the ends of her pig-tails, her head bent to her chest. She wore an old coat over a cheap dress and a silly hat that donkeys might wear at the seaside.

He touched her shoulder. "And you are...?"

"Ju… Ju… Juliette," she sobbed, waving him away without looking up.

The priest sighed. He had hoped to say his own prayer, for

himself, from the Act of Contrition, which went:

O my God, I am heartily sorry for having offended Thee and I detest all my sins because of Thy just punishments, but most of all because they offend Thee, my God, who art all good and deserving of all my love. I firmly resolve, with the help of Thy grace, to sin no more and avoid the near occasions of sin.

If he said it hard enough, and dug his fingernails into his palms, then it might keep that door closed in his dreams. Which weren't dreams at all. He, the priest, needed help himself. His Bishop should have been here to supervise his work, as had been agreed. Or even perhaps his Deacon. He needed someone to look after *him*, pray for *him*, try to heal *him*, in this god-forsaken place. And at very least keep the Devil away.

So he knelt before the altar and prayed, but knew that the woman behind was calling silently for his help. He really should approach her again. The last fragments of sun glinted on the faux-gold cross and the blurred figure of the crucified Christ, who could forgive all things.

He pulled the sleeve of his soutane down to cover his right wrist. She mustn't see that part of him. His forearm was permanently scarred with what a doctor had described as Lichtenberg figures: fern-leaf patterns of painless cutaneous marks on his right arm, back, buttocks, and right thigh. They had appeared after the lightning strike, which had also fused those two fingers of his right hand into the sign of papal blessing. These were deformities, testaments to his shame. God's mark.

A few months before, the bolt had struck him suddenly. It exploded from a heavy sky in a field outside Paris. He had felt his hair stand on end, then a shock wave. And the sort of nausea that came to him in the nightmare. When he came to, he had been blasted some four metres. Deaf and disoriented. The right side of his body singed and smoking. In the field next to him a large, brown ox was looking at him with doleful eyes, its long tongue rolling out of its mouth, drooling.

If there was ever a true Act of God, a divine punishment, he had received it then. His parishioners there, who knew about him and the teenager, had had the most unholy glee when they heard about the heaven-sent strike. It even strengthened his own Cardinal's faith as he transferred Fournier to the distant backwater of Neuilly-sur-Fronds. Here, this spoiled and now deformed priest was given another chance. How are the nearly-mighty fallen, he once allowed himself to think.

"Father…" said the woman's voice from behind.

He ignored her. He was thinking of the same old quote, which rose in his mind like a song which wouldn't go away: Luke 10:18-20: *He said to them, I watched Satan fall from heaven like a flash of lightning.* Did St Luke have the same dreams? Did he have the same sins? Had Lucifer fallen to earth near St. Luke and come pounding on his door?

"Father, I need to confess."

There was a desperate whine in her voice. It needed no heaven-sent inspiration to guess what she would say. If only she knew how much *he* had to confess, and how little it had helped.

With a deep sigh he rose and turned to face her. She had taken one of the ribbons out of her hair and was wringing it between her hands. It was almost a garotte. Her face was red with tears. He had not seen her in church before, but then again he had only arrived in Neuilly a few weeks ago. Perhaps it was just early days. Perhaps it was not the most Christian of places. So few people came to Mass that he wondered if they knew about the Paris workings.

There was still light coming into the church through the stained-glass windows. One of the images was of St Ywi, a 7th Century Breton, who could heal eye problems and who was looking down on Gilles now. The reds and oranges of the saint's mean face glowed, as the long body dissolved into darkness. Was it a glow of anger or embarrassment at his servant?

Père Gilles didn't want to go into the Confessional with this woman. Not yet. Not until the monstrous creature, which lurked and grew in the back of his head like a cancer, had been dealt with. There was an odd, coppery taste in his mouth – or was it sulphur?

"You should wait until Saturday," he said, but her face fell even more. He sighed: a priest with as much sin as himself could hardly withhold succour. "All right…You can confess now, here," he said. "No-one will come in."

Looking back at the door, she made the Sign of the Cross. Her face was pale, it seemed like a sneer. The way she twisted the ends of her pig-tails irritated him. And he had that familiar, terrifying rising feeling in his gut, as if he was going up a level – or even plummeting.

"Bless me, Father, for I have sinned," she said, using the time-old words.

"How long is it since you have confessed?"

"Many years, Father."

"What is your sin, mademoiselle?" he asked, though he already knew, and had added the 'mademoiselle' deliberately. She was pregnant. By a German soldier. How many times had he heard this in Paris?

"I am going to have a baby. The father, Uli, is a German policeman. He does not know. I tried to tell him but…"

Aeroplanes flew low above. The whole church rattled. St. Ywi quivered in his frame. The air felt heavy and his arms and legs had started tingling. Fournier had the intense feeling that these events had happened before. Soon, the fear would come. Or was it *Le Noirceur* – daring to approach him even in the sanctity of his church?

Another baby coming into the world, thought Gilles. Would this one also grow to be another doe-eyed teenager who would taunt and tempt, corrupt and destroy?

Outside, on the main street of Neuilly, large vehicles thundered past. The vibrations made dust-motes dance on the pews. More aircraft roared overhead. The sun was going behind clouds and leaving the windows. A tide of darkness rose in the church, and in himself. "Will you tell him?"

"If I see him. But the war has begun."

Stupid, he thought. *The war began years ago. Here in the backwater of where supernal powers have dropped me for my sins, it has only just erupted.*

Outside, above, there was distant thunder – or was it cannon-fire? Dreadful things were coming into his head: a dark and dismal kind of annunciation. Dark spots floated into in his field of vision, broken with zigzag lines. He felt nauseous. The altar seemed tiny, no bigger than a sugar cube. While around, in all the old cracks and gaps in the church where evil lurked, came a sort of growling. That was aimed only at him. He looked at his fused fingers. God had done this to him to punish the sinful things he had done with that hand.

Things were pulsing and blurring before his eyes more rapidly. Fearing the fire-bolt again, he curved himself inward, like a leaf, to avoid its blow. His thoughts raced at a million miles an hour. They made no sense.

"Father?" asked the young woman, annoyed at being given short shrift. She might not be a good Catholic but she knew her rights. "Father?"

Father Gilles was having one of his seizures He fell off his chair and curled up in the aisle, twitching like a trapped rabbit. His jaws chewed madly as his whole body stiffened and twitched. His mind entered another place entirely.

The woman pulled a face when she saw the weird patterns on his skin. She knew there would be no succour in this place of God. Her life would require more than some Hail Marys and an Act of Contrition. Though she dreaded the next option she knew of two women – ex-nurses – who lived in the old former asylum some kilometres away, who would help her in a more practical way.

She straightened her hat and stepped over the writhing priest, holding her skirts primly. Then hurried out into the relative sanity of the Wehrmacht-infested town. The harsh noises outside jabbed her. Although she didn't want the thing in her belly, she found herself covering it in protection. Along the narrow road was a string of horses pulling field artillery, jolting toward her over the cobbles and pavements. The long barrels of the cannon known simply as 88s were jerking like fingers of reproach.

9

Those two ex-nurses, who would soon offer their practical help to the woman in the church, were annoyed with Colette.

"Is this a joke?" asked Selene.

"He was here!" the girl hissed. She strode to the very spot and hefted the light high and into the corner. Then poked one foot into the old straw as though he might have been underneath. "Truly *maman*, he was here. The Matagot sat with him…"

The other women were convinced. That cat – which was more than a simple cat – never went near men. So he had to be hiding within the vast cave of the decrepit stables. He must be watching their lanterns shimmer, expand, and then contract into tight knots of light as they swung them in search.

All three walked the length, slowly, silently, peering into empty compartments. They stared up between cross-beams and rafters, shoulder-hard against each other, suddenly afraid of this presence – this *parachutist*.

The very name was charged with menace. It invoked so many warnings, and brought to mind the rash of propaganda after the Fall of France about these people who might fall from the skies.

These parachutists, they were told by the authorities, were not ordinary soldiers. They were recruited from the ranks of convicted killers, rapists and child-abusers. Many of them had murdered their parents. They were the nastiest underclass from the slums, incapable of mercy. Anyone who had any information about parachutists of any kind should contact the nice Gestapo immediately.

"*Zut!* Where is he? You speak some English, Colette," said the oldest woman, shivering.

"This creeping around is nonsense. Call him," urged the other, her arms crossed firmly under her breasts. "Tell him we are friends."

Colette tried to remember. Words almost forgotten bubbled in her mind, most of them popping in the heavy air of the occasion. Her throat almost dried up. "We…we are your…friend." The lantern swung like a censer. "Please, we wish for you…er, we wish…" She clenched her fists in annoyance at her forgetfulness.

"Come please, we wish for you," she managed finally to invoke in a small voice.

A long silence. Until even she began to doubt his presence. Perhaps he had fled?

But there came a sound of scraping above them to the right. Their scalps tingled. They lifted their lanterns still higher.

"*Mon Dieu…*" gasped Selene, when she saw him.

Astrid caught her breath, clutched the other women's arms in her bony fingers. She gave a little bow with her head and added almost reproachfully: "*C'est **notre** Dieu…enfin.*"

He – the *dieu* in question – was crouched upon a cross-beam, his body wedged against an angle and secure against the recoil from his machine-gun. His face merged and re-emerged in the darkness as the lanterns flickered. The camouflage paint more like a mask, accentuating his glistening eyes.

Colette, of course, was plummeting into love as quickly as this man had plunged through the skies. Dieter had been a brief dream, a silly little boy with boils and a map. *This* was what she wanted. No less.

"You are English?" she asked, shy of her small stock of words.

"English? English, *non*?" They were expecting English armies to land and the English were – she had heard - always sending spies.

The soldier grinned, a dazzle of perfect teeth. Yet from the odd angle of his head it was almost a leer.

"*Non*, honey. No," he added very loudly. Then flicked on the safety catch of his weapon and sat on the edge of the beam with his legs dangling down. Blood dripped from one of them. The oldest woman caught some in her cupped hands, and seemed thrilled. Smearing some on her index finger, she dabbed little crosses on Selene's palms. The two women giggled like girls.

"He is wounded," said Astrid, the *grand-mère*. "Look at his leg. He has the wound! The Lame One! Tell him to come with us."

They beckoned, mimed food and drink. He edged along from his perch and winced as he made his way across, down the wooden steps, using the staff as a crutch. His right leg was in agony. The women made to help but he snapped: "I can hack it! You bet." So they stepped back and formed a half-circle before him.

Colette understood now. A door had opened in her mind. She was radiant. She could see her man more clearly now that he had

40

come from the shadows. He swayed before them in the brightness of the three lanterns. She turned to the other women and smiled, and then to her man again, brushing the flop of hair away from her brow. On another night the drama in her voice would have been absurd, embarrassing. Now it was charged to the point of being sonorous, as she turned to them both and told them:

"*Il n'est pas Anglais. Il est...*" and she paused, a priestess intoning the Word: "*...Americain!*"

She saw a small wrinkling around his eyes, like the faintest of nods.

"*Americain,*" she whispered, totally enchanted by this man who had come from nowhere.

They kissed him, on each cheek, very formally, but faces alight.

"*Notre Dieu...*" said Astrid the *grand-mère* firmly, eyes shining even brighter than hers. "He has come at last."

10

Some little distance away across the fields, brothers Armand and Jules were also marvelling at what had arrived in their own world. They made sure their old green curtains were closed and would emit no light, or let prying eyes look in. Especially German eyes. They stoked the fire against the cold of the evening and prodded it into life with the black iron poker. Sparks showered onto the stone hearth. Then they lit a second lamp, which sputtered with a weak yellow flame. Together they stared at the long, grey container on their table, on top of the dirtied white parachute that billowed down like a vast tablecloth.

"Where is our precious nephew?" asked Jules. "Luc should be here."

"He is doing some work for the priest. Painting, decorating. He will be back tomorrow."

"Luc is too kind," Jules muttered sourly, then turned his attention back to what they had found in the woods.

Armand, almost reverentially, removed his felt cap and brushed the long hair on one side of his head over the bald patches. He told others they were scars from the mustard gas of the previous war. They both knew it was impetigo.

There were simple catches at both ends and two on the side, but for a long minute they hardly dared touch them. Hardly dared imagine what it might contain. Jules' face was covered in sweat. It made his brow glisten, his balding head shine. He rubbed the palms of his hands together, and then on his trousers.

"You open it," said Jules.

Armand, who had taken on such responsibilities all his life, looked more quizzical than usual. He had been damaged by a grenade during the First World War and his right eyebrow arched higher than his left one. "It might explode."

"It's not a bomb! Bombs don't have catches."

"It might contain gas," explained Armand, who had also been gassed in that other war. Not too many kilometres from Normandy.

"Courage! *On les aura!*[1] said Jules, somewhat teasingly.

His brother grimaced, took a breath, then flicked the spring catches one by one. Each catch gave a little metallic twang. As he did the last one, the iron poker they used to prod and stoke the fire slid along the wall and clanged down against the stone hearth.

"*Merde!*" they both cried, and laughed nervousl Then turned their attention back to the box.

"Perhaps it is Nosferatu," joked Armand, referring to the vampire they had seen in the cinema at Caen.

Slowly – with a great show of courage – the two men lifted up the top half of the container and laid it gently on floor.

"You were right, Jules. That man you saw watching us from the stables. He must be an American. Look at the stars." He pointed at the Army Air Force symbols emblazoned upon the equipment.

"A parachutist," Armand added, flicking at the billows of silk. He rubbed the texture between his fingers, thinking of what he could earn on the black market.

"An American parachute soldier. The landing really has begun."

"Did I not tell you?" Armand preened. "I know the way of war."

"You said they would land in Calais!" Jules retorted. He was annoyed by the way his brother would always draw upon his experience of the Great War. Sometimes he would talk about the monstrous battle of Verdun in a monotone, almost a whisper. As if it were some huge feminine spirit he both hated and loved for making him a man and yet damaging him. "He is a long way from Calais."

"And he is a long way from Cotentin. Perhaps he is a spy?"

They picked up the smaller items, held them up to the light to stare at every aspect and then replaced them exactly. "You are *sure* you saw him."

"I am sure. In the stables. He was peering out when Madame Riche waved us *adieu*. Am I not known far and wide as Jules the Eagle-eyed?"

"Actually, no. Not at all."

---

[1] Marshal Petain's famous Order of the Day for the endless Battle of Verdun: *Courage! We'll have them!*

"*Merde!*" hissed Jules as a thought struck him. "*Merde Merde Merde!*"

"What?"

"He will have Colette before me."

"*You* would never get her."

"I wanted her virginity."

"*You* would never get her! Look at you!"

"If I had some American cigarettes or silk stockings I would."

"But she is mad. All three of them are mad. You know that."

"But Colette, how shapely, eh?"

"You would be better off trying Astrid."

"Never?"

"You used to want her."

"That was before she increased the rent. But Colette..."

Armand snorted and picked up some flares. He felt too old for lust. "What do you think these are? Hey? Hey?" *He* knew what they were; he was taunting. His younger brother had never known the trenches. Never known Hell. "Or this?" – being a long device which looked like a rifle, but which was obviously a flashlight of some kind.

Jules would not rise to the bait. He looked at the treasure trove and sighed. "I think they are keys."

"Keys to what?" snorted his brother, irritated by Jules' tendency to be cryptic.

"I am not sure. But I think we can use them against the Boche."

Armand put the items back carefully. He pulled the lid closed and fastened all the catches. "That would be good," he mused, remembering so many things he had never avenged from *La Guerre du Droit*[1]. "That would be *very* good..."

---

[1] The War for Justice – ie World War 1

11

While Jules and Armand hatched their plans in their little cottage, the three mad women in the big house took their American into a room lined with dirty windows on one side and dusty wooden shelves on the other. On these was an array of old pans, two kettles, some jars and pots. With sad gaps between them where items had been sold over the years. The doorway at the far end of the room had a big key in the black iron lock. Large stuffed owls stood guard on little perches at either side.

Horsett sank down on a chair next to the long, broad and battered table. He let his Tommy gun clatter onto its surface. Around him, the women busied themselves with lamps, and a few candles. As with the brothers, there was a ritual of curtain-closing to keep out the darkness and keep in the light. There were daubs of camouflage paint on all the women's faces where they had formally kissed Horsett on his cheeks. Astrid placed a large earthenware basin of warm water on the stone floor next to his foot, indicating the wound.

The man's eyes drooped. His silence was absolute. He didn't know what to say. Plus his head was doing weird things from the exhaustion, the killing and the pain. For months he had trained for combat with airborne hosts of around him. He didn't know how to react to gentility.

"He is very tired, very tired, that is all," Colette said defensively, owning him. The other two nodded.

"Ask him what his name is," said Astrid.

"Ask him if he wants to remove his helmet," offered Selene.

Collette asked the first question with words, the second with mime.

Her mime was good; he seemed to know exactly what she said.

In fact he knew damn fine *everything* they said; but if he pretended ignorance it might give him an edge.

"Michael. Michael Horsett," he muttered.

"Pardon? Ah, Michel. Bonjour Michel!"

"Not Michel. Michael. Mi – Kel. Get it right, okay?" He didn't mean to snap, but he was suffering.

The two older women nodded. No mistaking his tone. They exchanged an *Oo-la-la!* expression, as if it confirmed something.

"*Est-il seul?*" Astrid commanded the girl to ask.

"Are you... er, alone?"

The paratrooper ignored the question. He didn't know how safe he was, plus he didn't know the answer. They jumped in sticks of at least ten because it was believed there would be an eighty percent casualty rate.

Shrugging, Colette unlaced his right boot and pulled it off with difficulty, causing him to wince.

"Hey, watch out for the other leg. Don't touch *this!*"

This was the small, compact Hawkins anti-tank mine strapped above his left boot which could blow the track off a tank.

"Bof!" grunted Astrid, who stepped in to cut away the makeshift dressing. She rolled the trouser leg up beyond the knee, removing the bloodied sock and then pulled the bandage free of the clotting. The gash was jagged and deep. He winced. She *sssshd* him. As she knelt at his feet, he saw the black roots of her hair in the crown, spiraling outward.

"*La foudre...*" Astrid muttered wonderingly.

He didn't need to look. He didn't care if it looked like lightning. Tried to console himself that if he'd got that wound in combat it would have been honourable. Plus they'd have shipped him on out, back home. With a medal. No shame, then, being here, down among these women? He fumbled in his pocket and brought out another sachet of sulpha powder, indicating that she sprinkle it on the wound.

Astrid looked at it scornfully. She and Selene raised their eyes and tuttted.

"*Nous avons mieux!*" Astrid said, triumphantly, and Colette struggled to remember the English.

"Eh er, better. *Oui* – yes – *better.* We have better!"

Astrid went into the next room and returned, wearing a white, knee-length tunic of the sort that doctors might wear. She pulled from her pocket what was obviously a surgical sewing kit with curved needles of varying sizes. "Patience," she said, and sterilised one of them in the flame of the nearest candle, then produced an evil-smelling bundle of herbs that had been wrapped in thick greaseproof paper.

"*C'est l'herbe d'or. L'herbe d'or,*" she repeated, as if it were somehow precious, or as dangerous as his anti-tank mine.

"Listen ma'am, I don't think…"

"Silence!" the oldest woman insisted. "*Je suis infirmière!*" which he knew meant she was a nurse, but he rolled his eyes wide as if he didn't understand. "*Buvez…*" she said more softly, offering him something from a test-tube.

Ah, what the hell, he thought, figuring he'd rather die of poisoning than gangrene. So he buvezed, gulped, gasped. Waves of calm seemed to flow up through his body. Oh that was good!

Expertly – so it seemed to Horsett – Astrid and Selene worked together, the latter massaging his neck, humming as she did so, caressing, soothing. Maybe it wasn't broken! Oh god it was a relief to feel it straighten again.

Selene cleaned the wound by dabbing it with the herbs, and then the oldest woman set about sewing it up. Horsett didn't look, just closed his eyes and thought of Detroit and his Mom and tried to remember what he was really here for. Then they used clean, new bandages, very tight and white, he could have been a mummy. These two women were good!

"Thank you," he said, when they had finished, and he meant it.

Standing up to see how it felt, he towered above the pair as they knelt at his feet. He removed his helmet for the first time and placed it on the table. "Ah my *head…*" he sighed, rolling it back and forth, and running his hands over the narrow mohican strip of hair between the blue-shadowed halves of his skull.

They gawped. As if he wasn't even human.

"Don't touch those," he advised, as he placed the gun and combat knife on either side of the upturned helmet. He did thiscarefully, as though they were sacred objects. Bending awkwardly, he took an unbloodied part of the old bandage and dipped it into the basin. Without looking at anyone he scrubbed the camouflage from his face. When he threw it into the low fire he watched the damp cloth sizzle and hiss on the logs.

Horsett turned and faced them then, leaning against the table. At the top of his brow a knot of veins glowed and writhed beneath translucent skin. His whole face was aglow with the vertical scratches which told of his descent. There were burn marks on his palms. Swollen eyes. He was able to turn his head again, slowly side to side.

"*L'œil droit est le soleil, et l'œil gauche la lune,*" said the oldest woman.

Right eye sun, left eye moon? What are they talking about? But he said nothing, showed no reaction. They had never seen anyone like him. That felt good too.

"Ask him where he came from?" asked the *maman.*

"Where? *Où?*" Colette used facial expression and little gestures.

He gave a thin smile, and pointed upward.

"Pah - I knew *that!*" said Astrid. "Where else, heh?"

"Down there, perhaps?" shrugged Selene, pointing in the opposite direction.

They both laughed. The cat came into the room and rubbed itself against his injured leg. He noticed how they gave little nods to it, as if the cat were more than a cat, and stood back deferentially as it made a regal path out of the room again. The two dogs cowered to either side, and wouldn't look at the creature.

"This is all too crazy," he muttered, blinking rapidly, not able to think straight. "Where am I?"

Colette gathered her words, delivered them with an air of minor triump. She inclined her trunk forward as she spoke, bouncing back on her heels like a school girl. "By Neuilly-sur-Fronds."

To him, that might have been the dark side of the moon.

Then: "*Connaissez-vous* Neuilly? Er er…Know you Neuilly-sur-Fronds?" She spelled the name on a scrap of paper with the stub of a pencil. He looked at this and then pressed his eyes with the thumb and middle finger of his right hand, slowly shaking his head.

Taking the stub and trying to grip it properly in his larger hand, he made a sketch of the Normandy coastline and the Cotentin peninsula, dotting where he should have been. "Where? *Où?*" he asked again.

Colette drew a tiny cross quite some distance to the south-east, about as far from the Dropping Zone as you could imagine. He couldn't have got deeper inland, or further from the Normandy beaches if he'd tried. The pilot must have hedge-hopped in and hedge-hopped out, avoiding those areas near the coast where he knew the flak would be heaviest. He sighed and slumped back in the chair.

The other women were enthralled. This little scrap had become an important key in the whole strategy of the Second Front. They looked to their visitor but his face remained impassive. He sighed through clenched teeth then rolled the paper along its length, twisting it into a stick. Pushed this into the last embers between the smoking logs. Watching as it burst into a tiny flame, blue and failing.

"God… they dropped me in the wrong place. I knew it."

Shivering with cold, or shock, Horsett took his gear and slumped down in the corner of the room, next to the fire. He cradled his machine-gun on his lap and leaned back against a wall. Bandaged leg straight in front of him. Staff close to hand. Whatever it was they had given him made him feel like he was entering la-la land. Which wasn't a bad place to be just then.

"What did he say?" asked the *maman* as they hovered uncertainly, watching as he sat with his eyes closed, head supported by the angle of the walls.

"He said…God. He knows God. Something like that."

He opened his eyes and glared: they stepped back, startled. Hell, the whole situation was insane, with these women staring at him with shining eyes, and that big, nasty old cat. Yet he couldn't hold their gazes for long, he felt so guilty. He should be out there with his buddies! So he closed his eyes again and pretended to sleep, feigning exhaustion. Maybe when the women had gone to bed he'd scoot, hole up somewhere else.

Astrid inched nearer, careful not to make a noise. She looked at the Screaming Eagles - the talismanic little badges sewn on each arm. "*Ça alors!* It is a hawk. He is certainly the one. He has come to us at last."

The *maman* nodded, and added: "And he has come today, *Mardi* – the Day of Mars." She smiled at Colette who hadn't followed the drift of their comments at all.

"I will get news to the women – our women. He has come a long way. And we have been waiting for him for a very long time…"

12

If people's lives were already revolving around Michael Horsett like planets, one more soul was taking up its orbit at the bleakest limits.

Hauptmann Heinrich Schimmel of the *Feldgendarmerie* hardly dared look toward the blackened, mangled corpse. Or the still-smoking burnt-out motor-cycle known as a Green Elephant. This was not what he had trained for at the Technical Police School in Berlin. This was nothing to do with his usual duties: traffic control, overseeing the populace, rounding up enemy stragglers, deserters and guerrillas. And then – to use the old *Feldgendarme* joke – hanging them after a fair trial. Not to mention guarding captured booty, and making sure that civilians handed in all weapons.

This was the worst moment of his life. The *worst*.

One of his men held up the remains of an American cigarette that he had found next to the scene. Schimmel noted it, and a tide of wrinkles broke above his specs and faded out under his peaked cap. He noted the blood in the long grass next to it. What he didn't *want* to note was what lay a few metres ahead of him, spread across the dirt track that served for a road. But he had to. It was his duty. And more than that.

"Stay here," he said to his men.

The other men stood back and watched him approach the scene. There was little brotherhood among this lot. A couple of them sneered when they saw him nervously clutch at the silver, crescent-moon gorget that he wore on a chain around his neck. This device showed his authority. It glinted in the sun; it was luminous; it would also shine in the dark.

"The *kettenhunde*[1] looks worried." said a gawky private, Gunther Funkeln, to no-one in particular.

"Let him shit himself," said Uli Erde – Fat Uli, as they called him. He took out his own cigarettes, lit one and puffed away. His aim was to keep as far away from the invasion – if that was what it was – as possible. And if he had to stay here and be mocked by

---

[1] 'Chained dog'. A reference to those who wore the shield and chain gorget as a mark of rank.

the regular soldiers as one of the *feldmäuse*[1], then so be it.

The rest hung around watching the sky. Although they all wore the uniform of the German Army, two of them were French, loyal to the Nazi cause. The first proper paid job they had ever had.

Schimmel reached under the silver moon and his fingers fumbled through his shirt to clutch at his crucifix. He felt its sharp outline and the awkward squirl of the little figure that was fastened to it. The officer valued this symbol even more than the *ringkragen*, as the gorget was called.

*Please no…*he prayed silently. *Let it not be him. Anyone but him.*

Messerschmidts and Heinkels flew over in the distance, too far away and too high for their engines to be heard. They might have been geese.

"I hope it is him," said Fat Uli, hitching up his trousers for the *n*th time. "No-one gives *me* extra duties."

"You were out fucking that whore!"

"She's not a whore, Funkeln," he mused, thinking of that short romp in the corn, which both felt might be their last.

"You could have gone to the brothel where you know they're clean."

"Well, not really. I quite like her. I think she loves me…"

"I hope you used a gummi."[2]

"Don't be so –"

A Focke-Wulf 190 roared so low overhead that they all ducked. The sound exploded around them and shook leaves from the trees. It seemed to fly faster than its engine noise, and left a guttural growling that echoed around them before it curved up and away toward its pals.

"We should be at the coast. Helping the lads out."

"Teufel! You don't mean that," said Uli. "Until Kaiser Heinrich there gets his precious orders from above we'll do exactly as we've always done. Anyway, they'll soon drive that lot back into the sea. The *Panzer* Divisions will be on their way. Nothing can stop *them*."

They watched as their *Hauptmann* approached the body.

It could have been a piece of blackened timber, propped

---

[1] Field mice. A scathing term for the Feldgendarmerie.
[2] Rubber

against the burnt hedge. What used to be legs were shrivelled tapers. What were once arms were black, evil-smelling branches frozen into a praying position. The head was little more than an oval, with depressions that had once held eyes.

Yet it moaned, through the motionless slit that had once been a mouth.

The *Hauptmann* swayed, made as if to grab the thing, paused, then drew his Walther PPK and shot the creature through the head. Once, twice, until the whole body toppled into the ditch.

They watched as their superior bent over the body, stooped ever lower, and ended up on his knees. His hands made hesitant, waving motions toward the still smouldering dead thing. As if he wanted to cradle it, but couldn't bring himself to do so.

"Go on, touch him..." muttered the oldest of the men, Der Bomber, who had seen far worse than this as a veteran of a Rollbahn convoy, which had supplied Stalingrad. He understood his officer's dilemma without being touched by it. After all, *Hauptmann* Schimmel had probably never cuddled his son Dieter when he was a child. Or shown him much warmth when he was living flesh, and in the same troop. How could he do so now that he was a piece of burnt wood?

The officer sobbed, unashamedly.

"He's human after all," said Gunther, and worried again about his own children back in Munich.

"I never want to have children," sighed Uli, waving them all away for a little while, to give the man some privacy.

13

Astrid's neighbours were *not* stupid. They came back the next day. Their ancient tractor rattled into the yard and slewed through the mud and manure. Luc, the nephew of Jules and Armand, was twenty going on fifteen and had the doctored papers to prove it. His hair was washed and parted neatly on the left side. His shirt was buttoned neatly and his blue tie was tightly knotted. This old school uniform was part of the disguise, although the worn trousers didn't quite reach his ankles. Yet he looked smug, sitting preciously in the trailer on some bales of hay.

The three women came out to meet the men. They stood in a line, smoking, making both a point and a human barrier. Their faces showed that their neighbourliness, like their wine, was not infinite.

Armand let the engine run for a while, as if he might turn and drive out again, but he switched it off. Very wary, the men got down from the tractor and removed their hats, as if in church.

"We are not stupid, Astrid," said Armand, the elder brother.

Astrid looked astonished. She gripped the cigarette deep in the V between her second and third fingers and turned her mouth into a perfect and tiny O. "*Non?!*"

"We know you are hiding someone. A parachutist."

The three women looked at one another. They puffed heavily on their cigarettes as if to make a smoke cloud. *Who had blabbed?*

"I saw him last night, as we left here," said Jules, nodding to where he had glimpsed Horsett

"I saw him before that!" boasted Luc, giving a huge and silly grin that showed his teeth. He jumped down from the back, tilting a shepherd's crook over his shoulder like a rifle. In his free hand he twirled a white flower that he gallantly offered to Colette. One of the dogs snuffled at his heels but he kicked it away.

"Saw who?" Selene persisted.

"The American, of course!" snapped Luc. "I followed him from field to field. He killed a Boche – just like that!" he added, snapping his fingers. "And then he came here."

"You're a fool," snarled Selene. "Just like your uncles."

"Pah! But remember that his grandfathers too were *complete* idiots," added Astrid, with a sharp nod of her head. "And his grandmothers were known to…"

Luc bristled. He leapt up into the back of the rickety trailer and threw aside the hay. Underneath was the long, grey container that they had found.

"We found this," said Armand.

"Is that a bomb?" asked Colette, dropping the flower.

"Leave that!" The voice came from above, through one of the many holes in the planking. They didn't need to know English to understand that bark. They couldn't see where, but they knew he was watching.

Horsett had slept in the stables that night, refusing the offer of a bed, thinking he might need to escape. In her poor English, Colette had almost made the offer sound indecent. He was watching them down in the farmyard, his Tommy gun at the ready.

"Wait there…" he muttered, and they heard his boots clump across the timbers of the upper floor.

"Attendez," Colette explained.

The men gave little gasps as Horsett limped out into the light, clinging to the pole and glowering at them like Moses come down from his mountain. The scars spoke to them of many battles. They had never seen a soldier like this before, or a gun like that. The women gave little possessive smirks. He was *their* man, and he had come to *their* house.

Horsett ignored them and went straight to the battered, familiar box. His leg was too painful for him to climb up and see, so he indicated that the men should bring it down and drag it into the stables.

"That is not a bomb," said Luc, implying he had already seen inside.

Horsett took a lantern from one of the women, held it up as the boy undid the catches with a sort of *Ta-da!* They looked inside with widening eyes. This was treasure. There could be money in it for them. The Allies might be fighting for the liberation of France, but here in this remote place there were still bills to pay.

"What is this?" asked Jules, picking up a large, black gun-like object, which had wires trailing from it, and making very sure he avoided the trigger.

Horsett put the lantern down, slapped the guy's hand, and took it from him.

"Light," he said, knowing it was useless now the Airborne had landed – whatever the result. "If you must know, it's an M-227 Signal Lamp. It's for sending messages by Morse code. And that other one, the small one – that's an Aldis Light. Ditto."

He was saying it to himself, sadly, as if describing a former girlfriend. They all looked at him blankly.

"*Lumière*," explained Luc, who got the gist of it. He had learned a lot of English from the m'lords starting their Grand Tours in St Malo. There, through choice, he had been one of the dozens of rent boys known as '*petits jésus*' until 1940.

"*Ça marche?*" asked Colette, not wanting to be left out.

"Does it work?" Luc translated.

"You bet." Horsett pressed the trigger and a thin shaft of silver light punched down the length of the old stables and they all went *Oooh!* He clicked out the Morse code he should have used to summon the gods of war onto his own Dropping Zone A: dot-dash; dot-dash: A.A.. But this time onto the rotting wall of an old barn rather than piercing the stellar dome of night.

There were other things in the canister: a few stick magazines for the machine gun, holophan lights to summon the Dakotas, bright red ground panels which unrolled like carpets, K rations, black and orange smoke grenades... Jules reached in, but its owner pushed his hand away, slapped the lid shut, fastened the catches and sat down on it to rest his leg.

The older men nudged Luc. All eyes were on him now as he clasped and unclasped his hands, swallowed hard and tried not to look as if he stood on the edge of a precipice. Finally, the prepared speech:

"*Monsieur*, my family are honoured, very much. They are happy to protect you. The Allies will be here soon. We hate les Boches. They murdered my mother. Now we are ready to help you fight them. We men hate them, truly."

When he said that last, he gave a quick sideways glance at the women, as if their attitude toward the foe was somewhat different.

Horsett sighed. There were no 'explosives' in the canister: nothing more than flares and smoke canisters. No way could you make them go bang. He said nothing, staring into the far distance

– a real paratroopers' thousand-yard stare. He wondered if he should take some more of that stuff the women had given him.

"What is this place?" he asked. "A barn?"

"Er...stables," said Colette. We have, before, many horses, er small horses. The Germans, they er, take them."

He stared into the darkness, trying to think.

The silence was too much, it had to be filled. Luc spoke up: "We have been thinking your job is to look at the enemy, yes? And to start resistance? To attack les Boches from behind, yes?"

Horsett hauled himself up using his staff, and indicated that they should drag the canister into the darkest corner and cover it. As the men burst into willing action, he figured this might be his chance of redemption. He would say nothing of the disastrous drop; he would forget the slow simmering of cowardice in the moments after landing; plus the explosion of his nerves when he had gunned down the kid. Maybe he could use their esteem to restore to his own. He still had a tincture of destiny, even though he had no idea of how that might manifest itself here.

What had General 'Slim Jim' Gavin said before they set off? *You will have only one friend: God. Avoid trouble at all cost. The mission depends on speed and stealth.*

Well now he had a whole room full of friends, he was in deep trouble, incapable of speed or stealth. God was conspicuous by His absence. He had to think carefully before he spoke, in case he gave away his fluency in their language. "I am here to do what I have to do. But I stand alone!" he insisted, quoting the motto of the 101st Airborne Division. It felt corny saying it there, then, like that. Back home, his buddies would have been around him whoopin' and hollerin' and punching the air. "You all understand?"

For sure *he* didn't, but they all nodded.

And it really bugged him that the two older women kept raising their eyebrows as if at some secret joke, and the young one kept smiling as if she was in on it – yet clearly wasn't.

"And if you really want to help me, then get me a good map. Mine got burned. You must understand how important a good map is to me. And you tell no-one about me, huh? Unnerstand? No-one!"

No-one, *jamais, ne personne*, never...

14

Père Gilles also stood alone, in the shadow of his church. He watched while the German policemen dug a grave some distance away from the others. Their little spades chomped into the soil. They had neither sought his permission to use his graveyard, nor acknowledged him. Just pushed through the gates carrying a simple coffin on their shoulders. As they stepped past they sang their doleful *Ich hatte einen Kameraden*, which, even with his lack of German, he knew must mean *I had a comrade*.

The sun was shining through the ancient yew trees at the edge of the graveyard. It sent shrapnels of light onto the faces of the men who lowered the coffin into the hole. It was a shallow grave, the priest noted. As if they had planned to come back at another time to retrieve it, and bury it somewhere better, somewhere Deutsch.

From the north-west came a faint but unrelenting growling thunder, the sound of a giant beast approaching. That would be the Allied war machine – everyone was whispering about it.

The officer who was leading the ceremony draped the coffin with a flag, which had a crucifix and swastika in the middle. It looked rather chic, Gilles thought, despite his inner torments. In fact he had seen this before, in Paris. There, his friend and protector Cardinal-Archbishop Alfred-Henri-Marie Baudrillant, had made a wonderful speech about Hitler's War being a noble undertaking in defence of European culture. He, Father Gilles Fournier, might have applauded as heartily as did the French audience, but his own storm clouds were already gathering. To him, the Cardinal-Archbishop was a source of succour rather than inspiration.

The men around the grave, Fournier noticed, were dutifully solemn. The officer was like a bomb before it exploded: a hard casing holding powerful forces in check.

He knew such things. It made him feel better when he came across someone worse than himself. How he would love to hear *that* man's Confession! He was surrounded by a tangible force-field of guilt. It flowed over the tilted crosses, the un-named humps in the green earth, over the cracked grey stones with their ancient, worn epitaphs, rippling through the dying flowers that sagged on many of the plots, left by unforgetting relatives.

The officer spoke some words over the coffin, which were carried away by the wind. But the unified and sharp *Heil Hitler!* and the *Feuer! – Laden! Feuer! – Laden! Feuer!* as they volley-fired in the air made him jump.

The grave was filled-in; a simple wooden cross was pushed deep into the earth at its head. The men filed out. He, Fournier, saw what their officer did not: some of the men were smirking. Was their officer, who was now straightening his cap, The Thing that his dreams had foretold? He would have to see the man's eyes; he would have to know.

The men left their officer alone with his thoughts, pushed through the broken gates of the sad little church and squeezed back into their two vehicles. Fournier heard the engines cough and stutter into life before being revved; he never took his gaze from the lonely man before him.

The officer was wrapped into his heavy coat, eyes hidden by the peak of his hat. The man's long shadow touched Fournier's feet first; the priest felt no shock, no chill, so that was a good Sign. Still, he had to see the eyes.

"What are you looking at?" demanded the German, for the first time raising his gaze from the ground to look at this tilted priest in his path.

Father Fournier said nothing, but bit his upper lip which made his lower jaw thrust forward in a vaguely simian way. The German's eyes narrowed; Fournier couldn't *quite* see into them.

Schimmel grabbed the priest by his coat and looked at him with disgust. "I have buried someone very important in there. When this war is over, I will move him from this shit-hole. Until then, tend his grave…"

He pushed the priest aside and wrestled with the gate, becoming increasingly angry until it cracked open. Inhaling deeply he suppressed his rage as officers must, then strode briskly to his staff car.

High above, in the gaps between the gathering clouds, two *schwarms* of Messerschmidt 110s hurried over like steel wasps.

15

Colette was sitting in a café in the town square, less than two hundred metres from that scene in the graveyard. If Dieter had been buried in the ground yet now loomed huge within his father's conscience, he was already ashes to ashes and dust to dust within this young girl's life.

It was drizzling. Huge green-brown, heavy vehicles scraped between the jumbled, gray, fieldstone buildings of Neuilly-sur-Fronds. Their vibrations on the cobbled streets rattled the windows and the bottles of cheap wine that stood on the café's counter. The whole of the high-beamed smoke-blackened place shook. There was even a continual ripple in the barley coffees, which Colette and Jules drank from small blue cups, as they pretended to relax in the straw chairs.

She ate stale croissants and glanced at the newspaper that was spread out on the dark wooden table. It mentioned nothing of the Allied landing. In truth, she was seeking all the while to count, memorise, analyse.

After sending Luc off on the mission for their unexpected guest, Jules had whispered to her that he, Jules the Bold, had been working with the Resistance in Morbihan all along. She must tell no-one! Actually, he had taken so many risks that his leaders had sent him back home for a rest.

The news had surprised her. He seemed to be telling the truth. But then again he always *seemed* to be telling the truth. And giving himself grand titles.

"Colette, there are many things you don't know about me, your handsome neighbour."

"That's what *maman* and the *grand-mère* keep saying."

"Hah! Your '*maman*' – pah! And Astrid still calls herself *La Grand Mère* does she? They are insane. Them and their 'coven'. They have not dragged you into that yet, have they? Wise Jules can tell you things, Colette."

He leaned across and squeezed just above her knee, trying to get eye contact and enter an 'understanding'. Jules the Goat was always trying it on. She pushed his gnarled hand away before it tried to go further. He gave his usual shrug, slurping loudly at his drink.

Colette was confused. The '*covine*' was just a group of lonely older women who used to work for Astrid and Selene. They met occasionally, talked about politics and the Occupation, moaned about men – or the lack of them – got drunk and a bit silly. Colette was too young to join in, although now she was seventeen they implied her time would soon come. She could think of nothing more boring.

More large vehicles rolled past, squeezing down the street, screeching back the street signs in passing: nails on a blackboard. The lights in the café swung on their frayed cords.

"Twelve. That's twelve. Now remember that number and their shapes, and we will draw them for him on our return, but not now. Security!" Jules hissed from the corner of his mouth. "Security. Commit all things to memory."

Colette was impressed, despite herself. So much was happening in her life now that Michael had arrived. The depressions which sometimes gripped her, *les crises de tristess sombre*[1] had dissolved. Truly, he was heaven sent! There seemed to be a great choir hymning within.

A white-haired, slim, middle-aged man walked past the window, his face almost glowing with suppressed delight. Jules rapped on the glass with his knuckle to get his attention. As the man turned from the convoy and glanced within, Jules gave him a stupidly exaggerated wink. More for Colette's benefit than the person beyond the glass.

"*Bonjour,* L'Étincelle! *Ça va?*" he said, through the glass. "Where are your fishing rods?" he asked, miming holding one on each shoulder. Then he broke a match in two, put it in a V shape on the table and pointed to it, whispering through the glass: *ba-ba-ba-bom...*

L'Étincelle gave him a look of pure hatred and hurried on.

"What did you mean by all that?" asked Colette.

Jules gave her an arch look. "In 1940, he was one of many who carried two fishing rods down the street to the war memorial."

"So?"

"*Deux. Gaules.* Say it fast: *de gaulle.* He was showing his support

---

[1] Crises of black melancholy

for General De Gaulle. Of the Free French! Do you know nothing? The Germans never guessed. And the match – V for Victoire. *Ba Ba Ba Bom* – the Morse code for V. Do you not listen to the BBC?"

Colette looked around anxiously, but no-one else was listening. "Who is he?"

"An old friend," said her companion, with a hooding of his eyes.

Colette looked at the clock on the town hall. "We must have that map," she whispered. "*He* really needs a map. He told me that."

Jules tapped his nose. "Luc…he will provide."

Luc had gone on, and would rejoin them soon. He knew of a map in the old school where he was doing some work for the crippled new priest, good Catholic that he was.

In the lulls between convoys, Colette glanced at the two blowsy women sitting beneath the huge ornate mirror, who had stared so rudely when they came in. Their blouses seemed too small, their hair stacked too high. They looked bored, and painted their nails from a communal varnish pot.

Colette rubbed her own nails with the edge of her thumb, conscious of her callused hands.

"They will be sorry when the Boches go, those ones," Jules said.

"But why?"

He gave his man-of-the-world smirk and looked out to the street again. A troop of the German policemen, which served the whole area, was heading eastward, back to camp, in their angular, scarab-like *Kübelwagens*. Their officer had a face like death, grey and frozen, not even wearing his helmet. As the lead vehicle stopped at the junction, one of the Frenchmen in the second car recognised Jules sitting in the café and waved. Jules pulled his hat down over his brow and turned away, as if he had not seen. Colette was too busy pretending to be at leisure to notice.

Minutes later the bell above the door rang madly as it burst open. The two French *Feldgendarmes* that they had seen go past earlier swaggered in and sat at the table with a clearly discomfited Jules. The handful of other customers, all very old men, sighed and reached for their identity cards. The older of the two policemen gave a cheery wave: that was not necessary, he was one of the Good Men. Any number of loyal Frenchmen wore German uniforms! The patron came over and took their orders for two large glasses of Calvados.

"Yohan..." said the younger one.

"We are off duty, Henri," the older man insisted. "And we have just been to a funeral. Drink."

"*Alors*, should you not be fighting?" asked Jules, deciding to brazen it out. It might cause trouble to be seen with two Frenchmen who served with the Germans.

Yohan le Blanc gave an insouciant shrug combined with a *bof*. His hands shook as he took the glass and gulped. "That is half a world away. Everyone knows they will be driven back. The Atlantic Wall is impregnable. Rommel said so himself. Behind that he ordered the fields to be flooded, so all the paratroopers drowned or lost their equipment. And soon the Panthers and Tigers will set loose. Nothing can stop *them*. Their armour is like your skull: nothing can penetrate. Besides..." this said conspiratorially, "what is happening at the coast is only a diversion. For us, here in Neuilly, life goes on."

"Diversion?" asked Colette, determined to soak up information in her new role as spy and *resistant*.

"*Bien sûr* ... the *real* —"

"Yohan, you talk too much!" whispered the younger man, who sat stiff and awkwardly in his chair.

"Shut up, Henri. I say what everyone knows. It is Calais where the *real* landings will happen. Those Allied fools at the beaches and drowning in the marshes are just human sacrifices."

The two whores came over and slung their arms around the uniformed men. Colette marvelled at their perfume. She didn't know enough to decide if it was cheap or not.

Yohan squeezed the ample waist of the one who had targeted him,. "Hey Jules, you have any money?"

"To pay for a traitor? *Non!*" He bit his lip.

That *non* was like a button. Once it was pressed the smiles disappeared.

The woman bent toward Jules, glaring. "A traitor? Listen, old man, my heart is French, but my *chatte* is international..." Then the two women bustled out in search of richer prey.

They seemed so jolly, so confident, that Colette was fascinated. She was learning so much! When she was older, perhaps she'd be happy to be a *putin!*

Yohan downed his drink almost in one, and ordered another, all but panting with relief. He looked appreciatively at Colette. "Your father and I went to school together. I could tell you some tales about him!"

She was about to explain that Jules was not her father, but Jules nudged her arm and nodded outside, where they saw Luc coming down the street. He had something under his arm, wrapped in newspaper.

"We have to go, *messieurs*," said Jules, standing up quickly. They left without ceremony, as quickly as the prostitutes.

"Peasants," said Yohan, loosening the top buttons of his uniform. "Always was, that one, always will be. At least we've made something of ourselves, eh Henri?" he added, fiddling with the Eagle-and-Swastika arm badge whose stitching was coming loose.

16

Horsett sat in a high corner of the stables, looking out across the yard toward the lobster-coloured brickwork of the main building. His damaged leg was throbbing. Thin light poured through the cracks like swords in a magician's cabinet. A few feet away, the damned cat was staring at him. Just sitting on its haunches and looking. It wouldn't scare. What was it Colette had said, before she went into town to get a map? That it was a 'Matagot', a magic cat that would bring good luck to its owners. Who had to feed it well and treat it with respect. Did they really believe that?

When she'd brought him a simple meal of cheese, eggs and a glass of milk, he had shown Colette the little blue primer he'd been issued with: *Technical Manual 30-602 – French Phrase Book*. It was one of the things that hadn't been ripped from his pockets. He planned to go through this piece by piece, hiding the fact that, thanks to his French mother, he was already pretty damned fluent. So he sat close to her. learning the *mercis* and *bonjours* and all those basics that the US Army felt would enable him to survive in another world.

"You are very good," she said.

He paused. His Dad had served with Pershing in World War 1 and done bold things (which he would never talk about) in the St. Mihiel salient. Then married a girl he met on a furlough in Paris. Took her back to Detroit, and took up his old trade of carpentry. As a boy, Michael would watch him planing rough timber with a curious intensity, as if the curls of wood were memories that he was trying to get rid of. Slowly, seemingly unaware of his son's presence, he turned gnarly, rough-sawn lumber into something beautiful. Yet there was a part of him that was still in that battlefield. In fact his Dad spent all of Michael's childhood acting trapped and resentful, whether by his memories of the war or the presence of his wife. From the way he spoke, he seemed to hate the French who he had once 'saved'. Got angry when he heard mother and son speaking the language. Resented the special bond they seemed to have. Michael grew up knowing that speaking French in public caused trouble. He wasn't going to reveal himself now.

"I learn fast. Learned the whole book: '*Avez-vous huile de machine?*' That means...Thank you."

He chickened out. He wanted to deliberately twist it and say it meant: *Can I kiss you?* but figured it might have been a leap too far. He might have spent the last year becoming a fighting machine, a trained killer, but he was also shy.

Fact is, he'd never had a girl before. He spent all his spare time studying. He would take things apart and improve them, so that he could take up that entry into the ASTP scheme as an engineer. Then when his Dad had a stroke and became a vegetable around the time of Pearl Harbour, he had helped his Mom look after the guy. Duty, not love. One morning – Michael was sure – she had put a pillow over her husband's face and killed him. The duty of love? He couldn't say. That had been the first dead body he had ever seen. When they stood over his corpse, it was still smelling of shit. As the only begotten son he felt obliged to try and cry, started to whisper *Dad...* but his *Maman* shushed him and said: *He never touched me. Never.* And reached out to close his cold eyes.

So he'd never even had much opportunity with girls before. Kissed two back in Detroit. Both lost interest when he told them he was joining the Airborne. They wanted regular guys, guys who would work on the auto-mobile lines and get rich. Later, after some warm beer on leave in England, he got one to sit on his knee and kissed her too but sorta passed out. He'd never even got to first base.

All these brief flickers of memory crossed the scars of his face.

Colette laughed, then looked solemn. "You have worries."

"Sure do."

In fact his conscience told him to get on out of there, ignore the pain in his leg and find his buddies. But they were fifty miles away, maybe more, and the whole German Army was between him and them. Hell, what could he do? It was easy acting tough among a band of tough brothers. It was easy just to take orders from above and act things out. After The Fall, as he now thought of it, ('cause he sure as hell hadn't jumped), being alone, without a map or knowledge or valid orders, was terrifying. He had never felt like that in his unit, or in the whole Division. Maybe his sarge was right. Or worse, maybe his old Dad had seen right through him when he had beckoned him over and whispered: *When I was your age, I could have torn you apart...*

Dad... he had tried to say, but the old man pushed him away, muttering, *Don't call me that, huh?*

Michael sighed. There were some mysteries that would never be explained. Not least how to rejoin his unit.

Besides, his whole body ached, he could hardly walk, although his neck felt normal again. So he made himself just sit there and stare out over the place, until they came back with a map, until he could work out a plan. *Lighten up Michael, lighten up...* he kept telling himself. The guys in training always looked to him for that. No matter how grim things were, he always had a smile or a joke, nothing was ever that bad or serious. Yet when needed, he had the best war face of them all.

But now, here in France, he was still alive and wondering what in god's name he was going to do with his life.

Now that Michael could see it in daylight, the place where he had found sanctuary was much bigger than he realised. Just behind the little building where he had been stitched up, was a large but very run-down house, connected by a long brick passageway. It was like an English manor, he guessed, but with holes in the red earthenware roof tiles. The shutters on many of the windows were askew, moss thrived on the exposed stonework. Something was growing out of one of the chimneys. It needed a good injection of cash and a whole lot of builders to work hard for a summer.

And beyond that, in a kind of fold between little hills, was a dense wood with a single trail through the long deeply green grass leading into it, and the conical top of an old tower just poking out of the trees. Crows seemed to like the place and he could hear their cries clear across the fields.

The two older women were out in the front yard, waving their arms about as if they were gathering something from the air. And singing – he didn't know what. This was the first chance he'd had to really study them. The *grand-mère*, who was clearly the boss, and the *maman* could have been sisters. They were both slim, neat, with long, black-but-faded, lace-trimmed dresses and little lace-up boots.

Astrid, the older of the two had long eye lashes and silver hair pulled tight back in a sort bun. Fastened into place with two little sticks like a geisha girl that he'd seen pictures of. She seemed to be all elbows and sharpness, both in her movements and speech. Plus she always carried, slung on her left hip, an old leather pouch which contained a large bunch of keys that jangled as she moved.

Selene, who didn't seem to be more than a few years younger and who was slightly taller, had long, dark hair that hung in a single plait down her back. Tight, disapproving lips, and the palest of blue eyes. These showed sadness when she thought no-one was looking, and pure coldness when she knew they were.

Together, Selene had the air of one who had lost something important; Astrid, that of a woman who damned sure was going to find it.

Their wooden shoes clattered on the cobbles and they sang as they danced. To Michael they just looked like a couple of crazies. Though the more he studied them, the more he realised that they weren't as old as the names *grand-mère* and *maman* might suggest.

His leg throbbed; he winced and shifted his position, trying to make out the pattern of the women's dance. They seemed to step, hand in hand, as if they were tracing out a crescent moon on the ground beneath. Every now and again they shouted out what seemed like *Haw!* Or maybe it was *Whore!* It came from the back of their throats, as if they were coughing up phlegm.

That startled him at first: that was what the other guys at school had called him: *Hor* – short for Horsett, sure – though they liked the dirtier connotation too.

Colette, on the other hand, now *she* attracted him. Every bone of his body might still ache, all of his training might still want to propel him toward meeting up with his unit... but he sure noticed *her*. And the way she looked at him, and the way she had waved to him before setting off into town.

She had black jet hair which was threatening to curl, parted to flop over one eye, and left to float free down to her shoulders. Her brown eyes were lop-sided almost imperceptibly out of true, and seemed to give her a vision that was angled differently to others. Her face was narrow but carefully chiseled. When they had sat in the kitchen last night, she had sprawled upon the chair, one leg cocked over the arm She was saved from impropriety by her long skirts, but to his eyes the very soul of come-and-get-me. All this would have drawn him to her out of any crowd. She was a lightning-tree endlessly exposed and drawing bursts of electricity from the storm. Brown-eyed, droopy-eyed, laughing, oh god but she drew him!

He might not have much of a plan, as yet, but he sure as hell knew that sometime soon he would have to have her, scary as that thought running through his virgin's mind might be.

Hor! came the cries from below.

His Mom had always spoken softly of France as being a kind of demi-paradise and the women so *gentil*. Maybe this was just a charming French custom but they looked pretty damned crazy to him…

The broken silencer, the nearest thing to gunfire that he could hear in this tranquil realm, alerted Horsett to the old tractor's approach. He peered through the slats on the stable wall as it chugged into the yard. Colette, Jules and his nephew. No sign of the other guy, Armand. That worried him. Was he blabbing to the Nazis? And how did they have a tractor? Why hadn't it been requisitioned or smashed up? Were they all collaborators?

Colette was out of the vehicle first, scanning the area around the stable's outside wall. At one point she stared straight at him without knowing and, more than ever, he liked what he saw: lively and trim, animated and springing.

His buddies had all swapped yarns about French girls, how they were all gasping for it, and how they sure as hell were gonna get it. Though first, the guys all agreed, they would deal with that bastard Hitler. He'd kept quiet during all this joshing: in some ways they were talking about his Mom.

Hauling himself up with his staff, he took a few deep breaths to master all the aches and twitches from his other wounds, and limped down to meet them at the door of the stables. Michael Horsett, Screaming Eagle, wanted to flutter his wings and be big for them.

Jules snatched the map from Luc and offered it to Horsett. *"Mais les Boches…"* he said, giving a little mime with lots of arm movement, which tried to show the mighty German Army pushing the Allies back into the sea.

"What…?"

Colette reached for the dictionary. She looked for the right words.

"Michael, the Germans they… they are… to win. And also, *le vrai* – the true – war is at Calais."

The American gasped. He knew that things had gone on before D-Day to make the Germans think that Calais would be the invasion point. Had it all been a double-bluff? Is that why he and his buddies had been dumped where they had – as a diversion? Was he really just a sacrifice?

"How do you know?"

Jules tapped his nose. Rubbed his palms together.

"Jesus…"

Colette touched him gently on his arm. He winced: he still had tiny bits shrapnel in it. Looking around at their faces they all seemed so damned pleased! Didn't they want to be liberated?! Had he come all this way for nothing? Had his own government just used him as bait?

"Get me some coffee, will you?" he ordered, gripping the staff and limping off with the precious map into their old kitchen. He'd done with stables. He was a Screaming Eagle first and foremost and had a war to understand.

The three women looked at each other and beamed.

17

As Michael limped toward the kitchen to start planning his war, the German officer who would sell his soul to find him was at his desk in what had once been the town hall of Neuilly-sur-Fronds. The room had high walls and triple aspect windows, which looked over the square. Although he could not have known it, not long before he had stared out, mindlessly, as Luc walked anxiously past clutching the one thing – the map – which united them all. Now he was slumped in his chair and felt as if nails were being driven into his head.

At the back of the room, in a glass case, was a stuffed black dog with slightly eerie eyes. This was one of Astrid's creations, although he didn't know that woman any more than he knew Luc. On one of the walls was a silver-framed picture of his beloved *Fuhrer*, dressed as a Teutonic Knight, which made it seem as if his head radiated light. And to the right of that was a gold-framed painting of his equally beloved and perfectly Aryan Jesus Christ, with his blonde hair and blue eyes, his chest opened and his all-loving heart bared to everyone in the universe except Poles, Russians, Roma and Jews.

But Hitler and Jesus weren't helping him now. On Tuesday June 6th he'd had a son. Now, a day later, he had none.

Hauptmann Heinrich Schimmel slumped in his chair and downed another glass of Schlichte – the fierce North German schnapps – then threw up into the waste bin. He sank his head upon the desk. As he rested his forehead against the cool wood, his whole body was still shaking, it made his crescent gorget rattle. He had hoped to save his son by sending him on a *druckposten* – a cushy, rear-area job – but he had sent him to his death instead.

Every time he thought of Dieter he remembered him as the young, fair-haired boy he had once taught to ride their small pony in the fields bright with sunflowers. He had been so tiny that Schimmel had had to prop him up on the creature's back. They would trot along, within the walled garden, laughing. And those many times watching Dieter and his little twin sisters standing next to the piano, arms raised high, singing about their lovely *Fuhrer*.

But now the image of that blackened shell popped up and obliterated everything.

He. Had. Shot. His. Own. Son.

It was the greatest act of love any father could have shown.

His chest rose and fell. There wasn't enough air in the world. He had lost his son, but there was a war on and he was a good German. The orders on his desk had just been put there by his Generalleutnant, who knew nothing of his tragedy and wouldn't have cared anyway.

Duty, Duty, Duty... He tried hard to be a just but compassionate leader of men, wielding the sword of truth and protection, in the name of justice. But sometimes he felt like a snake, with poison in his head. Anyway, this was war, and he was defending the Fatherland. He would do what was necessary. Pouring the last drops of the Schlichte, he licked them from the glass, upturned the bottle into his mouth, and tried to think.

Everyone knew that the unbeatable Waffen SS would quickly throw the Allies back into the sea. No-one could get through the Atlantic Wall – Goebbels had promised that! Meanwhile the role of his *Feldgendarmerie* was even more important than before. His tasks at this time, the Generalleutnant emphasised, were particularly clear. In fact the kind man had written down what he must continue to do:

> Maintain order and discipline; disarm, search, collect and escort prisoners of war; supervise the civilian population in occupied areas; check papers of soldiers on leave and in transit; apprehend and hang deserters; control evacuees and refugees during retreats; plus all aspects of border control and anti-partisan duties.

He read that again and again. The words kept going hazy.

Schimmel took out his pistol and put it on the desk. He unfolded what was left of the map that he had given his son, which was punctured with bullet holes and burnt at the edges. This must have been the last thing the boy had looked at before being shot and then immolated.

Although he hefted the pistol from hand to hand, the thought of suicide never entered his head: he had a wife and two daughters back home. How to break the news to them? But he knew that he would have revenge. He owed it to his son to track down the killer. He owed it to himself and all Germany. He knew that, technically, he should pass this over to the Geheime Feldpolizei – the Secret Field Police – whose duty it was to deal with such events. But they were idiots, who would never understand.

Measuring the holes against the bullets of his own pistol, they were obviously .45 calibre. There were too many of them in both the map and the remains of the motorcycle to have been the action of anything but a machine-gun.

Resistance? There had been almost no activity in his area. For one thing the rural peoples made various kinds of living from their occupiers. For another, the Milice Francaise were very active and totally loyal to the German cause. Some of them were more Nazified than the ordinary German soldier. They had kept a lid on any kind of resistance so far. A parachutist? Too far from the beach-heads, surely. Yes, there was the butt of that American cigarette next to where Dieter had been murdered. Yet any number of his own men had those sorts of cigarettes, from all sorts of sources.

His stomach was churning; his mind was rolling like the sea. He threw up again.

Hauptmann Schimmel no longer cared about what was happening on the Normandy beaches. Up until now, for him, Normandy had been the *butterfront*, where everything was plentiful, where life was quiet and safe. But now he would change all that: he would take advantage of the chaos that would inevitably ensue, and use everything at his command to find his son's killer.

As a good Christian and a good Nazi, he knew there were great forces of evil loosed within his world.

And he would find and fight them.

18

Horsett, who saw himself as a cross between a lost soul and a liberator rather than a great force for evil, sat at the head of the table, the large map spread out in front of him. Two dogs gnawed happily at bones somewhere around his ankles. He had the hots for the girl, sure, but he didn't know if he even trusted her. Or any of them. The two older women were nutcases, who looked as if they wanted to eat him; the old man Jules was somewhere between a slimeball and an oddball; and his nephew, Luc, walked and acted like a faggot.

But along with the other one, Armand, they were all he had. He lit a cigarette and scoured that map like it was a crystal ball. He never realised how important such things were. He needed to know where he was in the world.

It was Luc who broke the silence. "Oh *Monsieur*. We know nothing, *rien*. We want for you to make *un réseau*, a, er, *group* for resistance. You will er, you will teach us, yes?"

"Don't you have any young men in this country? I mean, older than you, but younger than him. Young. Men?"

There was a gap of comprehension. Colette tried to explain. Her voice was warm honey. "We lost many, beaucoup, in the last war. Then, er, 1940, all our men – our soldiers – were, for to work, sent to camps in Allem – er - Germany. To make roads, to make the factory, to work on the farmings. They did take… all the horses, aussi, too."

"They weren't all Jews?"

"Jews? *Non! Ordinaire* French men. Old men and boys left, only," she explained, her eyes moving between Jules and Luc respectively.

"Gee…"

"But you will form a resistance to the Boche, *oui*?" persisted Luc.

Resistance? Horsett's whole head was turning and twisting; he didn't know whether he was up down or sideways. He'd been buffeted by fire and air before coming to earth in a stream. Didn't know what to think, what to feel.

He opened his mouth to say something smart, but then shut it again. Truth is, he didn't know *what* to do. There were three wooden cups on the table, stacked inside each other. He shook them apart, turned them upside down and put them in a line, throwing a small black grape under one of them.

"This is what we gotta do," he muttered and did the old Three Cups trick. He had learned this and other conjuring tricks as a kid and sometimes amused the guys in the platoon this way. "Watch carefully. Watch..." He moved the cups quickly, scraping them back and around, in and out. "Now show me where the grape is."

Jules pointed. Wrong! Horsett did the trick again. Luc pointed. Wrong again buddy!

They enjoyed the trick but they all frowned. They assumed this must be something that would make sense to any American. They didn't begin to understand what his plan might be. Nor did he, but he liked performing. Plus he had his war face on and that both inspired their confidence and hid his bewilderment. He even allowed Jules to steal one of his cigarettes.

Luc pushed the map forward. He'd have to watch that guy.

"Here, show me exactly where we are on this damn thing."

The boy dived forward and made to point out, but he brushed against Horsett's arm and Horsett shouted with pain.

The two older women looked with interest. This was their sort of thing.

"Shrapnel," he said to them. "Tiny bits. Ain't had time to remove it all yet. I got it from..." He pointed upward.

They looked confused.

"*Obus à balles*," translated Luc, looking very smug.

Astrid and Selene glowed. This really was *their* sort of thing.

"You children play your silly games with your map," said the *grand-mère* to the others. "*You* come with us..."

They beckoned him to follow into the next room, gesturing to his arm. He figured they'd done a pretty good job with his leg, which was a whole lot better than it had any right to be, so he followed – still carrying his Tommy gun.

"*Nous savons...*" the pair said almost in perfect unison. *We know...* as they shut the door after them and led him down long dusty corridors, through many locked doors, up a chaos of staircases, into a room that had long been closed.

Once Horsett and the older women had gone, and the kitchen

door had clicked shut behind them, Jules edged onto the bench next to Colette.

"Jules the Wise thinks you do not really want to fight the Boche," he said to her, licking his upper lip. His hand edged along toward her leg once more, ignoring his sister's son at the other side of the table. "Truly, you do not want the Allies to free us because then you will lose him. If they are driven back, he can stay here, forever, with your mad 'mother' and the 'grandmother'."

The two males were looking at her for a response, so she studied the map intently, though with no idea of what she was looking at, or for. Luc, she knew, wanted to fight the Germans with all his heart to avenge his mother. Armand had a true hatred of the Boche going back to the last war; he was probably off somewhere organising his battle even now. But this brother Jules, well, he was just a blancmange.

Yet what he had said was perfectly true. She would be happy enough to see the Boche go – well, they all had to say that. But there was a side of her which thought, in order not to lose her man, she wanted them to crush this landing of the Allies like beetles.

19

The two women took Michael into a large room at the back of the house, locking the door after them with a big brass key from the ring in Astrid's pouch. Whether this was to contain him or keep others out, he wasn't sure. The room was in total blackness until they hauled back the heavy curtains, and then creaked open the white internal shutters of the high windows, one by one. Dust was sent flying up into the sunbeams that punched inside.

The walls were panelled with dark timber up to shoulder height. Above that the terracotta paint had long since faded into the colour of old blood. The wooden floors had once been polished, but were stained with the globs of wax that had dripped from a chandelier. This dangled from the high ceiling, filled with the stubs of old candles. There were many solid-looking cupboards around the walls, which were all padlocked. At one end of the room was a grand old fireplace that looked as if it hadn't been lit in decades, filled with ancient ash. Beyond the windows he glimpsed a large walled garden with ornate but overgrown paths, and a dried-up, sad fountain.

The women made him sit down at the long table placed in the centre of the room. It had a padded, leather-covered top which was cracked like an old man's skin. Not the sort of table you would eat off, though he'd seen similar in a hospital before.

These were not simple peasants, he realised.

"*Alors…*" said Selene, as she reached around and unbuttoned the jacket of his jump suit. He twitched when her hand almost touched his crotch undoing the lower buttons, but she never flinched. He put his machine gun on the table and the two women both removed the jacket with enormous care and hung it over another large, high-backed chair.

They wrinkled their noses and laughed, making little waving gestures. He must stink, he realised, sniffing at his own armpits. Though he winced when he moved his arm too high. Astrid began unbuttoning his shirt this time, tut-tutting at the sight of the blood where the fragments of shrapnel had raked his bicep.

"Aw hey, come on now…" he muttered, but not

wholeheartedly. And then "Ah ah ow!" as the heavy cotton was peeled off, leaving the gruesome sight of his scarred arms.

"*Eh, voila!*" said the *grand-mère* triumphantly. "*Fer dans le sang. Je te l'ai dit.*"[1]

"*Tu es un prophétesse!*"[2]

"*Ils sont comme des étoiles*," she marvelled, plucking out some more metal from his skin.

Like stars, my ass, he thought, though he said nothing, keeping his blank expression. In fact, he had the odd feeling that he was being examined like a young bronco before a rodeo. Still, they knew what they were doing with his wounds, starting with his right arm, so he figured they must have been nurses before the war. Stripped to the waist, he sat down with his arm placed on the table, the leather top cool beneath his skin.

Selene unlocked and opened the largest cupboard, which took up most of the end wall. It was filled with boxes, tins and dozens of bottles of all sizes and shape. All of them labelled and many of them containing coloured liquids. The sun reflected off them and turned the far wall into Chartres.

"*Notre médecines*," explained Astrid, seeing his curious expression.

"*Médecines secret*," added the other, shaking one of the bottles and squeezing out the cork.

Sure it was secret. He guessed that the Germans would have occupied even that little chemical corner of France if they'd known it existed.

Selene produced a little blue bottle and measured an amount into a test-tube again. This was the stuff that had made him feel so good when they sewed up his leg. Before they gave it to him, they took a sip each, smiling, showing perfect white teeth, like naughty schoolgirls. Seeing them like this, up close, these two sure weren't as old as he had first thought. The *grand-mère* couldn't have been more than thirty-five. Perhaps forty at best. Maybe they had kids young in France!

"Okay...okay..." It flowed through him again, reaching into lost and forgotten parts, making him close his eyes and sigh. Was this morphine? Who cared! He could get used to this.

---

[1] There you go! Iron in the blood. I told you.
[2] You are a prophetess!

Selene shook another bottle and applied the contents to his cuts and scratches with a soft cloth. Carefully, lovingly. Whatever was in that drink numbed him up fine, allowing Selene to go to work with a pair of tweezers and a wicked-looking scalpel. Digging, cutting, or pulling the bits away from his flesh, she dropped each piece into an enamel bowl with a ping! giving a little flourish. Astrid looked at these fragments intently, shaking the bowl and making the metal tinkle. She studied them like the old Irish cook in Michael's school used to study her tea-leaves. There was some blood, but they dabbed the wounds clean and just left them to the air.

The sun poured through the windows in thick bars. To Michael it seemed as if the room itself gave a big sigh of relief, like coming into warmth after a long, cold journey. Or maybe it was the 'secret medicine' scorching through his veins.

Then the older woman did what would have seemed a very odd thing any other time, but by now felt quite normal in this most abnormal of worlds. She ran her open palms over his wounds, sort of peeping and muttering under her breath. Although she never actually touched him, it felt as if there was a small electrical current agitating his skin.

"Heeeeyyyy…" he said, but his words and thoughts tailed away under the goodness of the feeling.

Selene went out through the big door at the far end of the room and he could hear her opening more shutters, clattering over floorboards, and clanging what sounded like levers.

"*Est-il prêt?*" she asked, coming back into the room, and although he knew she'd just asked: *Is he ready?* he didn't worry about it.

Astrid, meanwhile, indicated that he should take his trousers off so she could check on his leg wound.

"Oh now c'mon! It's fine, I mean…"

She gave him a little slap on his bare shoulder as if he were a naughty boy and rolled her eyes with exasperation.

"Pah!" she snapped, and he got it straight that she really *was* a nurse, and this was France anyway. And everyone knew that French gals did things differently – though he never liked to think that way about his Mom. Besides, he just felt *sooo* good after that little drink.

He heard water gurgling and rattling somewhere through

pipes, sounding like an old Chevy, and more clanking of levers from next door. He removed the Hawkins anti-tank mine and put it and his .45 on the table. Then he removed his left boot easily enough, though he winced when he bent to undo his right, and so Selene did it for him. Then she did this weird thing: she brushed his bare feet with the tip of her single pony tail, and both women laughed, as if it meant something. Though he sure as hell couldn't figure out what.

So he sat there butt naked, covering his dick with his Tommy gun, trying not to get aroused. The silvery-haired women removed the endless dressing on his leg and made clucking noises of approval.

He looked down at the long, zig-zagging wound: as far as he could tell they'd done a damn good job. He must have lost a lot of blood somewhere amid the corn. No wonder he felt so weak.

Lighten up, Michael, he thought to himself again. *No need to feel guilty. Not with a wound like that.*

"*Vous avez un gros fusil,*" Astrid said with a straight face and he knew that *fusil* meant gun. Hell, he didn't care! His body was soaking up the warmth of the sun through the windows. When Selene came back in, and gestured for him to come on through, he just stood right up and limped after her, though he kept his guns. Old habits. Long training. Them being nurses, they didn't give two hoots about his body; their faces were masks, no shame there!

Yet behind his back: little girls' grins of delight, all twitching eyebrows and pursing lips, and little gestures of wicked joy.

A big, white, claw-foot bath stood in the centre of the next room. More like an old armchair than anything else, with its high back and low front. The floor around it was covered by thick white towels, steam rising gently to the ceiling. Selene had poured some green crystals into the water and was swirling it around with her hand, her sleeve rolled up beyond her elbow showing her milk-white skin.

"*Pour vous,*" said Selene, but did she mean *For you?* Or did she say *Poor you...?* Damn, that drink they'd given him was great!

"Hey, but I'm keeping my guns, ladies," he said, using both of them to cover his crotch.

They seemed to understand.

"*Votre jambe...*" Astrid said. "*Vous devez protéger votre jambe droite*," she insisted, indicating his stitched leg. She mimed with her hands and her own leg, that he must keep the damaged limb straight and out of the water. "*Sec...sec...*" she insisted. There was a little stool on the right side at the lower end, on which he could rest his foot, out of the water. They'd thought of everything.

"Oh yeah I get it...keep it dry and straight, keep it out of the bath. I knew that."

"*Nous vous laisserons tranquilles, m'sieur.*"

Their accent was different to his Moma's. Much thicker.

"Okay, I get it, you'll leave me alone, leave me tranquil, huh?" As he lay there butt naked he had a brief pang of worry: he might have revealed too much in other ways.

By this point, he wasn't real sure he wanted them to leave, but they wore their Nurse Faces, just as he still had on the smeared remnants of his War Face. Then they turned and left him. He hooked his Tommy gun over the big old faucets, put the .45 on the little rack that held square bars of green soap, stepped into the deep, inviting water and sprawled obscenely with his injured leg draped outside the low end of the cold enamel bath. He sighed, all guilt forgotten, the war on another planet, beyond the sky from which he had fallen.

In the next room, barefoot and silent, the two women did their strange little dance again, their faces shining.

20

Not too many kilometres but a wholly different world away, in Neuilly, Father Fournier had his bed-sheets and his underwear boiling in a big copper-bottomed pan. As it boiled and rattled downstairs, he scrubbed every centimetre of the windowless little cell that he used as a bedroom. Scrubbed until the tips of his fingers almost bled, as if it could drive away the guilt. He knew this was cleanliness being next to godliness: using the former to make up for failings in the latter. And also because he knew that when he came to confront The Thing – whatever it was – it would derive power from his own darkness, his own dirt. It fed on dirt. Sometimes, he had felt in the past, so did he.

Luc had gone, fading out into the world beyond as subtly and surprisingly as he had appeared within his life. The boy was kind but uncanny. In Gilles Fournier's present fragile state, he wondered if he was really an incubus sent to test him. In this eldritch rural backwater, the very air was rank with superstition. Superstition? Or was it all truth? Here in Neuilly such things were not quite as absurd as they might have seemed in Paris. In fact, it made his destined encounter with the Thing – *Le Noirceur* – almost logical.

There was a noise from downstairs, which made him jump. It sounded like someone clattering at the door. He stood still, holding his breath, every nervous muscle tensed. Not sure whether he was more scared of a visit from the Gestapo or his own Bishop. Then he relaxed, realising that the sound was the lid of the pan rattling as the washing boiled over.

"Calm down, Gilles…" he told himself.

Shaking his head at his own fears, he went downstairs to adjust the pan, watched his grey sins boiling and bubbling. He soaked up the warmth of the roaring fire and sat blinking out at the cold dawn. Through the arched window the steel sky was broken by flights of Messerschmidts and a single stooping hawk, regally impervious to machines.

He took a deep breath. He must try not to be afraid of every shadow now that the very incarnation of Shadow was so close.

Swallowing hard, breathing deeply to calm himself, he went

along the empty corridor, through the empty classroom, and on into the empty church. These days, the Stations of the Cross, the statues of the Virgin and St Ywi were mere incidents around the walls, rather than crucial items of faith. What scared him was what lay outside. Certainly, there was a demon beyond the walls, in the dark places, taking on disguises. Once, before the trouble had erupted in Paris, he'd tried to explain his fears to his Cardinal but had been brushed aside. The man had been too absorbed with worldly events, as if the opportunities available via the Third Reich were more valid than the Holy Trinity.

Although he wasn't sure he had the authority to apply it, he had been studying a battered copy of the *Exorcism of Satan and the Fallen Angels* from the 'Rituale Romanum'. He had not yet learned it off by heart. This was because, if he were to use it, he would have to confess his own sins to his superior. And the very thought of *that* made him shudder. But, turning the pages rapidly, he was able to take small comfort from the initial Prayer to St Michael, which he knelt and said now, before the altar:

"St. Michael the Archangel, illustrious leader of the heavenly army, defend me in the battle against principalities and powers, against the rulers of the world of darkness and the spirit of wickedness in high places. Come to the rescue of mankind, whom God has made in His own image and likeness, and purchased from Satan's tyranny at so great a price. Holy Church venerates you as her patron and guardian. The Lord has entrusted to you the task of leading the souls of the redeemed to heavenly blessedness. Carry my prayers up to God's throne, that the mercy of the Lord may quickly come and lay hold of the beast, the serpent of old, Satan and his demons, casting him in chains into the abyss, so that he can no longer seduce..."

He had modified it slightly for his own needs. He didn't think God would mind, though some of His mortal representatives within the Church might quibble.

The words helped him feel safe. He knew where he was with them and through them. Fournier got to his feet, crossed himself, lit a candle in memory of his mother and went to the door of his little church, creaking it open.

Outside, in the dank churchyard, crows made obscene noises. He shuddered and tried not to see the world in terms of good and bad omens, even though this seemed an eminently obvious approach to life these days. They were just crows, not emissaries of the Devil. They had always nested there. *Calm down Gilles, calm down...*

He couldn't have named the aircraft but in the sky above, zipping in and out of the clouds, twin-boomed P38 Lightnings from the USAF were locked in high-altitude combat with various aircraft from the Luftwaffe. As they dived nearer he could see the crosses and stars on their wings. There was – literally – a War in Heaven right above him. Yet he was preparing himself to fight something far more deadly, that involved souls and not machines, spirits and not flesh.

Two old women in clogs and headscarves hurried past, and nodded grimly. Then another two, one of them with an idiot grin on her toothless face, pushing an empty wheelbarrow. He had not seen any of them in church yet. Then again so few people came. Was it the war that kept them away? Had they heard about his misdeeds in Paris? Did he just look too deformed? Could they see the foul creature behind him that leered and kept him chained to its service?

The Cardinal had been studying the new-fangled ideas of the psychiatrist Emil Kraepelin, and lectured him about the dangers of becoming 'paranoid'.

"I am not mad!" Fournier had dared to thunder back at the older man.

"No, Gilles. But in paranoia you can have delusions without any deterioration in intellectual abilities."

What do Cardinals know! Truly, the people of Neuilly looked at him oddly. Could they see the demon to which he was bound? Plus he was so worried about the Paris scandal catching up with him that he had refused any offers of a parish secretary, or a parish sister to help visit the sick. He had even turned down the offer of a permanent deacon to help him with pastoral and administrative affairs. They all thought him very odd, and were waiting for him to prove himself, and fit in.

So he stuck to the seven sacraments – or tried to: Baptism, Confirmation, Holy Communion, Confession, Marriage, Holy Orders, and the Anointing of the Sick... Anything that involved water – holy water. His private looming devil, which seemed to have a noose around his neck, didn't seem to like water. He washed himself a lot, scrubbed, really scrubbed, forty times.

"You must *learn* to fit in," his bishop had said, months earlier, drawing deeply on the dark tobacco of his German cigarette and blowing out a perfect circle. "This parish you are going to is spiritually sick. Like most small places in Normandy and Brittany it's a place of paganism – witchcraft! They have old legends of *lupins*, wolf-like beings that talk at night in graveyards in an unknown language. And also *lutines*, wicked little sprites, which tangle horses' hair into elf-locks and cause havoc in the home. And then there are the dreaded *Dames Blanches*, who lurk in narrow places and lead travellers to their doom. I heard all this myself in Confession. Can you believe that? Some of *them* evidently do. I'm sure Neuilly has superstitions of its own, equally absurd. They are peasants, but not always noble ones. It is always wise to learn their superstitions."

Of course. Yet he, Father Fournier, was a good Catholic and had no room for juvenile customs. Or the sort of juvenile behaviour that named itself as 'witchcraft'. When you come close to the *real* demons, all else is play-acting.

A freckled young woman came thundering up on a very wobbly bicycle, with a crooked front wheel. Her hat was jammed down over her fly-away red hair, making it stick out wildly. Eyes wide with fear, she shook as she tried to stop the machine, but the brakes were gone. She had to put her feet on the ground and scrape to a standstill, almost going over the handlebars.

"Father…" she begged, trying to keep back the tears. "My name is Sophia Le Fourré. My aunt is ill. My cousin wants you to come. Come now, please. I think my aunt is dying."

Bless you, he thought. *Oh bless you.* Whatever mistakes he may have made with his own life, he at least understood death better than most.

"One minute, girl," he said, though she was probably older than he. "Let me get my things. I'll follow you…"

21

Hauptmann **Schimmel's grand office, with its windows from floor to high ceiling, had thick cobwebs in the corners containing dead or dying flies.** The panes were dirty outside and in. Neither the window-cleaner nor the domestic had turned up since news of the invasion had spread. Here, from his desk, with the unemptied waste-bin still stinking of vomit, he could look down upon the town square and remember that he was still – just – the most powerful man in this area.

The room shook as more heavy vehicles thundered past. The whole town was filled with the olive-green, grey and brown tones of their camouflage: a few old *Panzers*, the sound of their metal tracks against the cobbles screeching like a million mice; two of the multi-tube rocket-launching Nebelwerfers; what seemed like a cornfield of 88mm Flak guns, (most of them pulled by teams of the small *panje* horses that had been brought back from Russia). And then there were the heavy Büssing trucks grinding along, burning oil. And in between all these, ranks of white-faced, earnestly-marching men, all of them squeezing through the narrow crossroads at the centre of Neuilly.

Yohan Le Blanc and Henri Lueur, stood to attention before Schimmel. They felt somewhat comforted by the sight of the firepower heading toward the distant battlefields. Yohan because he was a chancer, and wanted to ride the winning horse for all it was worth; Henri because he believed in the union of the two nations, and wanted to save France from Jews, Roma, Communists. Not to mention some of the boys who had bullied him at school. They twitched their noses and tried to ignore the stink from the vomit.

"This is for you," said Schimmel in his flawless French, indicating a large metal box on the floor. "Give them out to the others." He fiddled with the crucifix tucked away behind the gorget, and made nervous little noises of metal against metal.

The Frenchmen opened the case with some trepidation, then whistled with admiration. Inside, gleaming black and brand new, were several dozen MP41 sub-machine guns.

The officer picked one up and demonstrated. His foul mood

was tangible, as was his hangover.

"This is a standard Schmeisser, but with this wooden stock added. This allows you to use it as a club in riot situations. See?"

With a loud snarl he made as if to club Le Blanc's brains out but stopped short, leaving the man cowering from the mock blow.

"They hold thirty-two rounds and are accurate to a hundred and fifty metres with a rate of fire of five hundred rounds per minute." He spoke as if the details would somehow help him through his agonies, and find salvation. "It is a blowback operated, selective-fire weapon, which fires from open bolt. See? You will not hesitate to use them. You will not hesitate!"

"*Jawohl, Herr Hauptmann!*" they said in unison.

Yohan made sure that he didn't say it too loud. He didn't want the officer to smell his breath.

"Don't go far. I will need you both later. I want you, Lueur, to look at some maps with me. And you…" glaring at Yohan: "If you drink again on duty, I'll have you shot. Do you understand?"

"*Zu Befehl, Herr Hauptmann!*" said Le Blanc, whose German was adequate.

Schimmel turned away and stared out at the forces of war moving below his feet. He hadn't wanted these weapons before, as he'd had no need for them. He was a Francophile after all, a man of culture and learning. Not like those secretive animals in the Geheime Feldpolizei, Gestapo thugs, most of them. The French people should love him, he told himself, clenching and unclenching his fists. He was like a lion-tamer, controlling the beast through firm and intuitive compassion. Yet now, having buried his son in a shallow grave on foreign soil, he would have no qualms about nailing the animal who'd done that to the biggest cross he could find.

He didn't care about the Second Front opening up; he wanted the cruellest revenge that any father could muster.

So Henri Lueur remained to look at the maps, which covered an entire wall of the office. There were eight in all, in a scale of 1:100000, unfolded, overlapped and pinned in place to show the whole area. They reproduced the world surrounding Neuilly-sur-Fronds in grey, two dimensional terms, showing every hill, every stream, and house.

"I'm sorry about your son, sir," Lueur offered as he stood waiting, holding his cap in his hands.

Schimmel nodded a brief thanks. *Duty... Duty...*

"Look at this, Lueur ..." he said. Using the heel of his hand, he pressed and smoothed the edges where each map connected, trying to do similar to the rough parts in his own head. He was sick inside; the brain was loose within his skull. He used all his officer's discipline not to show it.

Henri peered at the display. He was an *Oberschutze* – Private First Class. The only other Frenchman among them – Yohan Le Blanc –– was merely a Schutze – and he was outside cleaning cars. The rest of the troop had been recruited from towns along the Franco-German border, and spoke very good French; the two natives had never been fully accepted.

"I need your local knowledge to help me make sense of this."

"You will have it, sir."

Silence from the older man. He waved his hand vaguely at the lines, as if they might stand out and make sense of the realm outside.

"You were good friends with Dieter," said Schimmel sadly, after a long pause.

"Yes, yes I was, sir." *I thought him a piece of shit.*

"I thought I would save him from the Allied bombing by having him join us here."

"Don't blame yourself, sir, not at all." *He should have stayed in Germany.*

"That idiot out there," Schimmel added, pointing to Le Blanc in the square, "only joined to avoid being sent away like the others. Unlike you, he cares nothing for the cause."

Henri kept quiet. That was just as damning.

"The men respected my son. He was a good soldier."

"They're a fine bunch of men." *But your son was a coward.*

"He was a good son to his mother."

"All sons should be good to their mothers." *He thought she was a bitch.*

"His younger sisters – twins – Ilse and Eva, will miss him so very much."

"He often spoke of them, sir."

"Ach what fun they had playing! Their laughter!"

"They were very close." *They played sex games with him. He said they were nymphomaniacs.*

Schimmel sighed and straightened, ran his hands back through his thinning grey hair, smoothing his head as he had just smoothed the map. Now he had a mission in life that – for once – was nothing to do with the *Fuhrer* or the Fatherland. Somewhere on that yellowing map, within the maze of grey and black lines, were clues that would help him find his son's killer. He had to control himself now.

"This is where Dieter was murdered," he said, putting on his wire-rimmed glasses and placing a pin with a red top at the exact spot. "Look at these…" *These* were three cigarette butts. "This is a French cigarette, a Caporal, like that idiot down there is smoking when he should be working. This one is a Hannover, such as you all smoke. But this one is a Lucky Strike – see, see the last of the name here?"

"American."

"Unless there are deep infiltrators into Normandy, this has to be from a parachutist. So we will search outward from this point here. I want you to go down and get that moron, Yohan le Con, to study this area here. See if you can come up with likely places for the killer to hide. Between you, you will know who are likely to be the sympathisers with the Resistance."

"There are many kinds of *resistants*, sir. There are the *Francs-Tireurs et Partisans, Armee Juive, Bureau Central de Renseignements et d'Action, Maquis, Force Françaises de l'Interieur…*" Their names rolled off Lueur's tongue. "Not to mention what you call the *flintenweib* – the shotgun woman – who can shoot Germans as well as any man. Plus all those plain and simple French men and women who cannot see beyond their simple worlds."

"I'm impressed. Though not by the *Maquis*: two men and a few boys with sticks, playing games. What do you make of this?" Schimmel asked, pushing across a small pamphlet.

Henri wiped his hands on his trousers before turning it around to read the title: "'*33 Conseils à l'occupé*'[1] I have seen this. 'THEY ARE NOT TOURISTS. They are conquerors'!'" He laughed as he read it. "It advises polite aloofness. Oh, and I like where it says – here it is – 'On the outside pretend you do not care; on the inside, stoke up your anger…'"

---

[1] '33 Hints to the Occupied'

"Are you stoking up your anger, Lueur? Can we trust you?"

"Absolutely, sir. It is destiny. The idiots who wrote this imagine they are freedom fighters. They are fools." Spittle left his lips with his intensity.

"Good, good. We need your knowledge. We need to find the killer."

"There are a lot of farms to search in this area. Most of them are little more than one house, a wretched old woman with an old man, a field, and two cows."

"Then we will search them. Every one. You are still improving your German? Good. And you want to be part of the *Neuordnung Europas*[1], of course."

"I believe Frenchmen and Germans should always march side by side."

"You're also a Catholic, aren't you?"

The young man hesitated, not sure of his ground.

"Don't be half-hearted. I am a Protestant. An early member of the German Christian Movement. I was at the Marine Church in Wilhelmshaven, standing just behind Abbot Schachleitner and proud as the devil in my crisp, new brown-shirt uniform. When the *Fuhrer* acknowledged Ludwig Müller as the 'Bishop of the Reich', he looked at me – me! – and nodded."

Lueur widened his eyes to show he was impressed. Because he really was impressed.

"Listen boy, Nazism is *truly* Christian. Original Christianity bore no relation to the actual teachings of Jesus, or the sect that his disciples founded. The Roman Catholic Church, as it became, took the name and principles of the true Christians in order to enrich itself at the peoples' expense. That's why, in the Nazi Party, we've replaced so-called 'Christian' symbols with our own, because our brand of 'paganism' is actually *true* Christianity."

Despite his pounding headache, the speech rolled out. He had said it in his mind to imaginary audiences a hundred times and was word perfect.

There was noise outside, of men and their metal vehicles rattling and screeching through narrow places of stone. As a major in the *Feldgendarmerie* he should have been out there looking

---

[1] The New European Order.

for solutions to the increasing chaos. His thoughts were elsewhere.

"I wrote several essays about this, some years ago. Could never get Dieter or his mother to read them, though. But Jesus, you have to remember, was an Aryan – who was killed by the Jews."

He pointed to the portrtaits on the wall. The boy looked surprised.

"Yes, Aryan. Jesus, you see, was not born in Bethlehem in Judea but in a quite different Bethlehem within Galilee. There were any number of Aryan tribes present in Galilee. After the Assyrian conquest, Galilee was devoid of Jews. Jesus' parents were only Jews by 'confession', not by racial identity, and were in fact descendants of King Herod's Aryan cavalrymen..."

"I did not know this, sir."

"Now you do."

"I'd like to read your essays sir."

Schimmel stared at him. "You're not bullshitting me, are you?"

"*Nein! Niemals. Never. Jamais!*" *Well, not entirely...*

Der *Hauptmann* sighed. He was trying to be strong in a world in which half the people hated him, while the other half wanted something from him and probably hated him also. He often felt like Jesting Pilate: asking what Truth was. He saw the way the French looked at him: as if he lay somewhere between a meal-ticket and a piece of shit-on-shoe. If only they knew how much he had saved them from true evil – the Gestapo – they might see him differently. If his own men only knew how much he craved their love. He hoped they might call him the 'old man' or Papa as the ordinary Landsers[1] called their company commander. After all, he thought of them as his *kinder*. He peered at Lueur. "Good. I intend to recommend you for promotion when this is over. I see you as a high flyer."

Oberschutze Henri Lueur puffed out his little chest and glowed.

---

[1] Colloquial term for the ordinary German soldier.

22

While Lueur was puffing out his little chest, Astrid was offering Horsett a bath-robe, so that they could take his uniform away to wash. Well, it might smell, but so did the two brothers, he thought. Let him be as French as them in that respect. He needed that uniform. It told him who he was, and why he was here.

"*Merde!*" she said, but left him alone to get dressed again.

The others were waiting for him. They stared at the map as if he were going to unfold a plan there and then. Instead, after a quick glance, he folded it neatly and placed it securely in the large pocket on his thigh. After a long and expectant silence, he did no more than stare into his upturned helmet with the anti-tank mine cushioned inside. After the bath he felt pure again, strong, but with a hankering for some more of that medicine they had given him. There was a small glass of plucked flowers on the table. He pulled it over and sniffed, saying not a word, as if the scent was the most important thing in the world just then.

The old guy Jules gave one of his Gallic *bofs!* and went off to get some *real* fighters, as he said. Michael, who got the insult but gave nothing away, just wanted to buy himself time to think.

Astrid sat looking at him keenly, her legs folded under herself on the chair like a little girl. Her eyebrows rose. "*Allez à la classe. Enseignez-lui français,*" she ordered, then turned away with Selene, certain that she would be obeyed.

Michael remained expressionless, again gave no indication that he understood. Colette gestured, he hauled himself up on his staff and followed her and Luc. They took down another long corridor into yet another musty room. This was empty, but for a crate of books and two stuffed birds with long, curving beaks that were mounted on the wall at either side of the door.

"What is this place?" Michael asked.

"This was a, er, room for class." Said Colette. "Look – the high windows. Pupils cannot look out. They had to... er – what is the word?"

"Concentrate," offered Luc.

"Ah *oui*...concentrate."

"No I mean the whole goddamned building. It's huge!"

"It was a *l'hôpital*," Colette said. "Called St Martin's. And a school."

"For idiots," Luc added. "And lunatics."

"But no!" said Colette, shaking her head. "Well, perhaps. That was three years ago. They did the therapy electric. Exercise. Lights with colour. Music. Riding horses. It was a place, very happy."

"What happened?"

"The Gestapo came."

"I heard it was the *Milice Francais*," said Luc.

Colette glared.

Horsett didn't know what the *Milice Francais* was, but he was always gonna take Colette's side He countered: "Okay, the Gestapo came. And what? Shot everybody?"

"Astrid and Selene, they did hide me. I did not see. But the Gestapo put the children in trucks. Took our horses. They shot *Monsieur*."

"*Monsieur* who?"

"*Monsieur* Michelet. Le Cohen. He was our...our *proviseur*. What is the word...Master?"

"Headmaster," said Luc.

"*Nous avons tous aimé le maître*," Colette muttered sadly.

Even if Horsett hadn't known French the expression on her face told him that they had all loved the man.

As they'd been speaking, Luc had used long poles to open the internal shutters. No startling surge of sunbeams: heavy rain drummed against the glass by now. There was a blackened, wood-burning stove against the outer wall, and the crate of old books next to it.

"You saw all this? You saw the Jewish guy being shot?"

"He was not Jewish!" she corrected. "No. Astrid and Selene, we hid. They covered me. It was very quiet. Then. We have been left alone. Er, *depuis*."

"Since. Left alone since," added Luc.

"*Bien sûr!* And Astrid, *la grand-mère*, she make the place invisible – same word, yes?"

"Invisible. *Invisible?!*" from Horsett. "You believe that, don't you? Knock it off!"

"Narck it arf," she teased, though still sad with remembering.

"Sorry," he said. He shouldn't have teased. Not her.

Luc rolled his eyes in scorn, hoping to get the American to do the same.

Michael ignored him, and looked around. Putting his weight on the staff, and standing on tip-toe, he glimpsed a large garden outside. "Will I get to see the whole thing, or is it just one room at a time? Astrid wasn't gonna let you have the whole bunch of keys, was she?"

"Not all is safe. *Grand-mère* is very careful. We have no, er, assurance."

Horsett stumped across the room. The heavy staff thumped on the floorboards and made the dust spurt. Large spiders scurried into a corner. "So what's gonna happen here?" he asked, still aching, still bandaged, limping heavily. Still difficult guilty as hell that he wasn't out there fighting with his buddies – wherever they were.

"As *grand-mère* said, we are to find the dictionary. It is here somewhere. See these books? We teach you more of *Le Francais*. We speak the same."

Sounded like a plan. This would buy him time. He looked into the crate and then sat on the floor next to it, his wounded leg stretched out in front of him. "These are kids' books. My god they're old. Look at the pictures!"

"Children's' books are good to teach a new language," offered Luc. "Eh, *voila!* Here. A French-English/English-French dictionary. Perfect."

Colette snatched it from him. "We had books. A thousand. Many, er, furnitures! There were times, ver' difficult. We burnt a lot of things, things taken taken from us, *aussi*, and we sell – no - sold much, many things."

"And sold our souls to the Germans," muttered Luc. There was a story behind the silence that followed. Neither Michael nor Colette wanted to hear it.

"So how did you both learn English? Do they teach it in schools here?" Michael asked.

Grand-mère did a… I do not know the English…a *sortilege*. Do you know the English, Luc? No?"

Luc pulled the book from her, riffling through, dust coming from its pages. "Ah. Here. *Sortilege*. It says 'spell'. Her '*grand-mère*' is believed to see things. The future. Sometimes the very distant past. Ghosts." Again the rolling of the eyes.

"She did a *sortilege* for me," Colette said. "I must to learn. She said I am special. She paid for the lesson. For, er, with Miss Felkin, who worked here. For a little time. And also *Monsieur*, he spoke it often. Now, I able to see the *pourquoi*, the er, reason. I thought it to please our Master. But the reason was... you."

Although Horsett raised an eyebrow, for some reason he was not surprised. When in doubt, never show it. That's one lesson he learned without needing private tuition. "Why do you say '*grand-mère*' like that? Isn't she?"

Luc laughed.

Colette glared. "Another time," she said to the American; from her tone, that was one story he wanted to hear. In private.

"Where did *you* learn, Luc?"

"I lived with my mother in St Malo for many years. I er, I worked for many English men. Rich men."

Horsett wondered, from Luc's hesitation and blush, exactly what he had been doing with the rich men in St Malo.

Clearly awkward now, Luc made a great fuss of pulling a hefty, illustrated volume out of the crate. A large – very large – hairy spider scuttled out and over the edge. He squealed and jerked away. Colette crushed it instantly with her foot.

Luc blushed.

Colette laughed.

Horsett sneered inwardly at the boy for reasons that were nothing to do with the spider. "I was about to shoot it," he said, looking at the crushed insect, which gave them all a chance to laugh.

And all of them were plummeting as far and as fast into love as the American had fallen from his plane in the first place.

23

"Pas difficile," **Horsett said as he leaned back against the wall, cracking open his Lucky Strikes.** His leg was throbbing, his whole body ached. "Not hard at all." He lit up and never thought to offer one to Colette.

Luc had gone to get some wood and kindling for the stove. There were squalls outside. They might as well be warm in this bare place.

"You learn quickly," Colette said. *"Vous êtes très intelligent.* But I think you know that! You already know everything in your little book. Are there French speakers in your family?"

"No," he lied. He wasn't sure why he lied. "My pa died over a year ago. My ma is back home knitting me a scarf."

She frowned. Didn't fully understand.

"Ma Père...mort. Mon mère..." He got the *le* and *la* wrong deliberately, then mimed the knitting.

"Un fils d'une veuve..." she muttered to herself as if quoting something.

Son of a widow he heard in his head. He wondered why she seemed to find this notable.

Colette came over and sat next to him, their backs against the cracked plaster of the wall. Their every movement left snail-trails in the dust of the floor. There was a rumbling outside that might have been a storm or a flight of fighter-bombers. Neither wanted to stand up and look.

"If... your leg was not, er, *mal*...bad? What...er you will, er *would* be doing?" She gave a little gasp after she got the sentence out. Wrestling with English tenses was hard work.They didn't have such things in French.

Horsett sank his head back against the wall, closed his eyes as if to help him see. "I'd be on my mission. It was my job to illuminate a drop zone. I was given Drop Zone 'A'. Then when the other troopers arrived, I was to assist the battalion commanders in assembling their units. I was tasked with giving their respective commanders all the information I could gather about the enemy situation. Instead...here I am in school, miles from anywhere, feeling so damned stupid. *Stupide.*"

"You are very clever," she said, looking at him with delight, not understanding a quarter of what he said. "The pupil who is best. You learn the French very fast. Perhaps you live here in another life" she suggested nervously, with an *I'm-only-joking* giggle. Though the nerves came as much from the question as the hope that he might pounce on her.

"Sure I'm clever. Brightest kid in school. Past life? Nah..."

"You are Catholic?"

"No honey, Baptist. Don't mean a thing."

"Your teachers ... they very proud? Yes?"

"They hated me."

Her eyes widened.

"I would do things like this..." and he lifted one side of her long hair and produced a small, battered flower from her ear. The simplest of magic tricks that he had learned as kid from reading a book by Harry Blackstone. He put on a lot of shows for his Mom, with numerous little trick. Trying to bring laughter to her sad life. She was the perfect audience and was always suitably amazed.

Once though, his Dad had come in, seen them and sneered: "Couldn't you go out and play ball like a normal kid!"

"Sssh Joe," his Mom had answered, frowning "He is not-"

"Ah for Crissake..." his Dad had snarled, then stormed out.

They were simple tricks, though. All to do with misdirection, deception and getting folks to look where you want them to look. He had stolen two small flowers from a vase earlier, ready for the moment with Colette. It was easier with coins.

She gasped, felt around her ear. He showed her his empty hand, pretended to stare up her nose, said *"Excusez-moi..."* and produced another.

"When the teachers passed by me in class, and they bent over to see the work of the kid in front, I'd produce coins from their asses. They thought I was a cocky little devil. *Petit diable!*"

She only understood the last two words but she reached over and touched his hand. Both their hearts were pounding. Only one of them was scared.

"So where's *your* father? *Où est votre Père?*" he asked making an effort to change the drift. "Nazis ship him off to a camp?"

She gave a little frown and shrug, glanced away. He wasn't gonna press it.

In fact he was breathing heavily by this time as she leaned

nearer. He had never been in this situation before. Sure, he'd heard the other guys talk, and a gal had sat on his knee in England. But he was so damned drunk that he never did anything but gabble. And then he had passed out, coming to, hours later, under a poster that showed a couple necking. On it were the words: THEY TALKED... printed over them in big red letters; while on the bottom half it showed a German bomber dropping bombs with the words: THIS HAPPENED... printed over it in yellow. It did cross his mind that maybe this was why the plane had taken so much flak on the way over.

She was so very near him, and he was so very aware. He took a deep breath. It was like firing himself up to shoot the motorcyclist all over again, but even more scary. "Je veux vous embrasser" he blurted out, and he knew damn well this meant *I want to kiss you.*

She gave a little gasp, and pretended to study the picture book about *Leon et le Lion.* "But Michael, that is not in this book! It is not wise to embrasser such a wild creature as the lion. And also, aussi, mustLeon use the *'tu'* form? *Oui?*"

She was teasing, and he liked it. In return he took out a large handkerchief and with arch expressions to counter hers, folded it into a small mouse.

"What is it Michael?"

It is – *c'est* – *un sourire.*"

She frowned, scrabbled through the dictionary. "*Non,* I think you mean *une souris.* A Mouse! *Un sourire* is–"

"A smile." Then he made the mouse-smile run up his arm and then onto her lap, causing her to giggle.

"*Vous êtes drôle.* You are –"

"Funny. I'm a joker, sure I am. It's been a long time since I've..."

He leaned across to kiss her. But the door crashed open and Luc staggered in with his firewood, dropping bits and pieces, stooping to pick them, not noticing what had almost happened.

Colette sighed and smiled, reached over to Horsett's cigarettes and took one without asking. Luc was about to speak when the sky above them thundered with very low-flying aeroplanes. Grabbing his staff, and hauling himself up to the window, Horsett just caught a glimpse of the last ones.

"Luftwaffe..." His voice tailed off in disappointment.

"I've heard someone in town, who knows someone in the

Milice, that the battle goes not well for the Allies," said Luc, lying. He didn't know why he lied either. "The beaches between Sainte-Honorine and Vierville are thick with dead American soldiers. They are being driven back. The Atlantic Wall is impregnable. Jules knows someone who heard Rommel himself say that, and Rommel doesn't lie, even if he is a German."

Colette frowned but didn't challenge him.

Horsett frowned also, and leaned heavily on his staff, brow against the still vibrating window pane He still didn't know what to think or what to do.

"Come…" said Colette gently. "You see, we know not your plans, but you must to learn the French."

"And get your hair cut!" added Luc.

"Do *what*?"

"That Indian…er…"

"Mohican."

"Ah *oui!* Mohican. Whatever your plans here, for us, with us, you cannot be a warrior secret if you go out with this."

Luc ran his hand through Horsett's single ridge of hair, from front to back.

"Hey, quit!" Horsett pushed him away, reaching for his Colt. "Back off!"

The younger man was horrified, embarrassed. It was as if something had been opened that should have been left shut. Blushing, flustered, he left to get some more wood for the stove.

Colette laughed. She ran *her* hand through the trooper's Mohican cut and he didn't object at all.

"Do it again," he sighed, putting his head back and closing his eyes in mild bliss.

She shook her head. "You must forgive Luc. We call him, behind his back, *le garçonne*. See? I write it for you. Not *garçon*, but *garçonne*. Hear the end of the word: *garçonne*."

"Meaning what?"

"Er…how to describe… You know those young women, before, who wore skirts very short, and put their hair in er er… but I do not know the word." She shaped her hands to show what she meant.

"Bobs?" he ventured.

"Ah *oui! Oui!* Bobs. And dance to the jazz?" She did a little dance, all elbows and flinging legs.

"Flapper? You mean a flapper!?"

"Ah *oui!* A girl who is like a boy. But for us here, Luc is like... a *boy*, who tries... to be a girl, who... *Alors*, I do not know the words."

"A faggot, you mean." Horsett struck a mincing pose of his own to explain. "Light on his feet."

"Faggot? I guess what means that. I do not know if he is. I do not think he does. He has not tried to kiss me. Never."

Their eyes met. Horsett's heart was pounding as it had done before killing the German. He took her hand and pulled her gently toward him. But she surprised him by drawing back and making the handkerchief mouse's head shake from side to side. They both laughed.

"Not yet!" she said, but brightly, taking up the children's book again. "First, more French. I have my own mission, Michael..."

24

Two *kübelwagens* filled with men were strung out on the narrow lane, their engines grinding loudly and echoing between the hedgerows. *Hauptmann* Schimmel sat in the front one, watching and wincing, while his tame Frenchmen hammered on the door of the first house. He had given command of the rest of his men to Oberleutnant Hartmann, who assured him he could attend to things in and around Neuilly. He would use these ones to find Dieter's murderer.

At his feet, getting in the way and getting muddied, were the various placards they always carried, ready to hang around the necks of any victims, bearing the legends: *Traitor to the Reich; Deserter; Bolshevik; Coward* – or simply *Jew.*

He could hear the others laughing. Despite his efforts to build team spirit, the two Frenchmen had never fitted in. They were the *Olalas,*[1] and no-one trusted them. They didn't even trust each other.

"Open! Open now!" Henri shouted, in the high almost girlish voice of a young man who had not yet shaved. Rooks took flight. Hens squawked.

Yohan used the stock of the new weapon to make a satisfying noise on the wood, though he looked embarrassed by what he was doing.

The door remained closed.

"Ach Gott," Schimmel bristled. This was taking too long. Anyone could have fled out of the back and into the woods, minutes ago. "Holen Sie sich das Bomber" he ordered.

His driver turned, whistled and pointed to a man in the following car. This was Karl Schatten, whom they all called 'Der Bomber'. This was partly on account of his squat, almost barrel-like shape; mainly because of his raw physical power. The man got out of the vehicle with slight difficulty, as he had lost some of his toes to frostbite near Stalingrad. Plus his left leg wouldn't fully bend. He turned that fact into something of a motto: *It won't bend; neither will I.*

---

[1] From the French exclamation *Ooh la la*!

Henri looked ashamed when the German, limping, elbowed him aside. Yohan gave a weak grin and weaker shrug. Der Bomber measured a certain distance from the door, rubbed his flattened, broken nose with the back of his hand, took a deep breath, and then just smashed it open with his shoulder, almost losing his footing inside.

"*Kommen* in, *hosenscheisser*[1]," he said to Henri with a gracious bow and a wave of a hand.

Outside, Schimmel studied his map, ready to cross this one off. It was a typical Normandy hovel. No parachutist or *resistant* would have used this as a base. Still, it had to be eliminated from their enquiries and would give the two cuckoos in their midst a taste of real policing.

From inside, floating out to them on the spring air, they heard an old woman shouting "*Non Non Allez Allez*" – nothing unexpected.

Der Bomber emerged from the doorway and looked proud of himself. This was so much better than the Russian Front, where his task had been to shoot deserters and cowards when they couldn't find any Jews. His pals in the other cars applauded him, then stopped when Schimmel turned to glower.

Henri emerged blushing. "*Nichts! Rien!*" he said in the vague general direction of the convoy, unable to meet anyone's eyes.

Yohan made a token effort to fix the unseen occupant's simple lock: "*Pardon,*" he whispered back into the sobbing darkness. "*Vraiment, pardon…*"

When Henri Lueur, the trouser-shitter, bashed the stock of his gun against the forehead of a suspect – and they were all suspects – he noticed that the slight curvature of the very bottom of the stock would, with German ingenuity, match the curvature of their skulls. At that moment he was breaking down more doors, in more hovels, either egged on or ably assisted by Der Bomber.

Yohan le Blanc looked on, trying to appear supportive, trying not to look like a fool. The rest of the men who stayed in the cars, and were mainly as back-up, cheered and applauded. In fact, the more Lueur slapped, punched, shouted, swore and wrecked the pitiful contents of the homes, the more applause he got. Yohan

---

[1] Trouser shitter

knew that their compatriots were mocking, but this seemed to be lost on the younger Frenchman. Yohan himself had given up saying *"Sorry"* to the women and old men they had questioned after the tenth raid. He shook badly, though this was more to do with his need for a drink than conscience.

Crash! Another door kicked open by Der Bomber – quite unnecessarily. The occupant had seen them coming and was about to open it, but now had it smashed open, into her face, her hand cut open by the latch.

"Where is he?!" shouted Henri, in the falsetto voice of a teenager.

"Who? Who?" begged the terrified old woman, sprawled on the floor and trying to staunch the blood from her hand and cheek. The eye was already swelling and turning black.

Henri gave a satisfied nod. In his increasingly maddened state, this was the right answer. If anyone wavered and answered remotely in the region of "I don't know!" he would have taken them in for questioning. As it was, he slapped, kicked and punched them around their rooms, leaving it to the idiot Le Blanc to overturn things and look for clues.

Hauptmann Schimmel clutched the board on which the folded portion of his map was fastened. His knuckles were white as mountain ranges, thoughts as bleak. His head was pounding and he felt sick. There were other ways to deal with this, but his responsibilities as an officer rose through his grief – it might help them come together as a unit. Which was something he had failed to achieve so far.

Slumped in the seat of the car, he was haunted by the wraith of his son. And the fact they had never had a good relationship. Dieter had often acted as if he hated him. He, in turn, had never felt the surge of love fathers are supposed to feel. A good soldier, he substituted Duty instead. *When the war is over...*he had kept telling himself, *then we will come close.*

The air above their heads exploded. Everyone ducked. Even the policemen in the house dived to the floor. It was a Focke-Wulf, flying very low, either heading to attack or fleeing from something behind. Two of the men lost their caps from the downdraft, it had been so close. Schimmel's precious map was almost plucked from his hands.

They stood looking, turning on their heels, weapons ready in case an Allied fighter followed. The sky above them was deep blue, not a cloud in sight. The countryside was still. There was no war in this local little heaven, no matter what was happening on the beaches.

Henri turned back to the woman, who had shuffled over the floor and up against the corner, her heels tearing the edges of her grey, worn skirts. This time he was *really* angry, and would *really* show he meant business. He just wanted to belong!

"Henri..." Yohan muttered, grabbing the young man's arm; Henri was on another plane of existence.

"Look!" he snarled back, shrugging himself free, pointing to the Police Eagle on the left upper arm of his tunic: an Eagle-and-Swastika emblem surrounded by an oval oak-leaf wreath

To Yohan it might as well have been a duck, though he would never have said that.

But this meant something to Henri: the eagle was a symbol of renewal, power and strength, as all good Nazis knew. And he wanted so much to be a powerful, strong and good Nazi. To him, when he struck these wretches, it was not bullying. He was acting on behalf of something greater. Something they could never have understood.

He moved toward the woman, who shrivelled into a ball.

"Leave her," said Der Bomber, who was getting bored with this and now came and stood in front of her. No-one had any illusions about what would happen if Henri had tried to push past *him*, although they were eager to see him try.

Henri came out into the light, trying not to breathe too heavily. "Where next sir?" he asked, leaning into the car and turning back the corner of *Hauptmann* Schimmel's map to sneak a glimpse.

The officer glared, and slapped his hand away. "*Vorwärts!*" he snapped in an officer's voice, pointing. Engines revved and the convoy snaked its way between the hedgerows toward yet another anonymous dot on the map.

In truth, Der Bomber had had enough of this sport. This should all have been left to the GFP[1] in his opinion. He was tired of

---

[1] Geheime Feldpolizei

being Der Bomber and wanted to be Karl Schatten again. An ordinary man, and not a battering ram. He was sick of killing and wanted to learn to live, because he hadn't been able to die at Stalingrad. His shoulder was sore; his feet ached; his sinuses were playing up; he had a headache and he was hungry. More than that, he was tired of trying to humiliate Tulemong and Wulewuh[1] as they called the two pitiful Franzosen who had squeezed their way into their group.

"*Your turn, kleinen Jungen,*" he said, staying in the vehicle.

Henri squirmed at being called a little boy.

"Go on, enjoy your war," said another, languidly, leaning over the edge of the wagon's door and plucking some daisies. "The peace is going to be terrible!"

Although the place looked decrepit and unlived-in, white smoke was puffing from the chimney and a rusty black bicycle leaned under the windowsill. Silently, Henri lifted aside the broken gate and made straight for the lopsided wooden bench next to the door of the cottage. He hauled it up, steadied himself, and with three swings to and fro, used it as a battering ram against the cracked old door.

Or he would have done if the door hadn't opened at the same time. He staggered into the room under the impetus and fell awkwardly, full length, losing his helmet as he did so.

Father Fournier's face was red with fury, his body rocked, his rage was towering. To Henri, completely shocked on more than one level, it could have been Pope Pius XII himself who loomed above him, instead of this somewhat shrivelled French priest.

Oberschutze Henri Lueur rose to his knees and bowed his head. In the shock of his entry, 1900 years of Catholicism instantly over-rode the authority vested in him by the Third Reich. He suddenly felt a very little boy indeed.

"In God's Name have you no grace? Have you no heart?" the priest thundered. "I am giving Extreme Unction here! Could you not have knocked as human beings do?"

The priest seethed. It was almost healthy for him, having shut so much up within himself for so long. He had just got to the point

---

[1] Germanised nicknames derived from *tous le monde* and *voulez-vous*

in the Last Rites where, having administered the consecrated oil he must say: '… may the Lord pardon thee whatever sins or faults thou hast committed…' when he saw the German imbecile creeping down the garden path with a stupid look on his stupid face. In fact, those words were floating in the air of his mind like birds, sustained by long practice and frequent use, when the wretch was sprawling on the flagstones before him.

Henri looked into the darkened corner where two women cowered next to the sick-bed of a waxen-faced third. The room stank of death, and wet bed-linen. A large cheap, garish crucifix glowing with luminous paint, hung above the bed.

"Well?" the priest hissed, bending down and almost spitting in rage.

Oberschutze Henri Lueur rose to his feet and picked up the bench. He felt as if his ribs had been cracked in the fall. It hurt him to breathe. Aware of Le Blanc in the doorway and a plume of light behind him, he couldn't find the words or the attitude.

Even more enraged by the dumbness, the mad priest took off his biretta and beat Henri about the head with it, driving him out of the door and grunting like a beast.

"*Allez! Allez!*" the good father snarled, venting against his own demons as much as to the hapless Lueur, though no-one else on God's earth except his own bishop would have known that. The biretta split; the pom-pom rolled into the mud.

Outside, the men in the vehicles thought it one of the funniest things they had ever seen. "*Encore! Encore!*" they cried, until Schimmel turned and glowered, then got out of the car to deal with the situation himself.

Ooh…whispered Der Bomber, who wanted to see how an officer would handle this, especially as he was unbuttoning the Luger from his holster, while clutching at whatever lucky charm he wore beneath the moon-shaped gorget, the *ringkragen* that the man loved so much.

The barrel of the Luger aligned toward the centre of the priest's forehead as the officer strode to within two metres, taking first pressure on the trigger. His cold fury was on a collision course with Fournier's burning rage.

"Go back to the wagon," he told the two soldiers, never taking his eyes from the target, never blinking.

Yohan Le Blanc bent and picked up the pom-pom and offered it to the priest, but the man never saw it. Le Blanc threw it into the house instead, like a grenade.

"GO!" roared Schimmel to both, as the younger man dithered and started to speak.

Schimmel glanced beyond the priest, into the darkness of the room, at the cowering figures.

Fournier looked beyond the officer, toward the setting sun and the mass of aircraft approaching, like flies.

"Shoot me," said Fournier, dripping with scorn. "I will not hide or run any more. You come to me like I am a criminal. But what I do is right and holy! I will not let you judge me, I will not be judged!"

Schimmel blinked, was non-plussed. What was the idiot talking about?

The priest tried to peer deep into the eyes of the officer to see if the Thing, *Le Noirceur*, was possessing him, but the man turned to look at the approaching aircraft. Their engines throbbed upon the breeze and seemed to make the droning sound of *amennnn amen amennnn*... vibrating in the air around them and making the nape hairs prickle.

With his left hand, the German rubbed his thumb against the hidden crucifix, and the squirl of metal that represented the True and Aryan Christ. This priest before him was everything he despised: a crippled figure who walked a perverted path, worshipping a corrupted version of the Saviour. But... clearly he was not afraid.

"Bof," the priest grunted, as the villagers would grunt. He turned his back and went indoors.

Schimmel, glancing up at the American bombers for a second, took careful aim and shot into the house. The bullet shattered the large and tasteless crucifix bearing the 'wrong' Jesus that hung on the wall above the bed. The women screamed. Someone slammed shut the door. Schimmel walked back to the *Kübelwagen*. "Liberator bombers," he said, pointing the aircraft above.

American, in large numbers, and no good thing.

"You shot the priest, sir!" said Der Bomber with astonishment. The other men looked eagerly toward the door of the cottage, but it remained closed.

"Well done sir!" said Henri Leuer with admiration, still smarting from his own humiliation.

Schimmel shrugged. It would do him no harm to avoid the truth. "That was no priest," he sneered. "Now drive!" He snatched up the map again.

25

The old woman was dead. The shock of the exploding icon, with bits of Christ's plaster body bursting all over her like shrapnel, had been enough to send her on her way, Last Rites or not. The two young women helped Father Fournier remove the debris and one of them made efforts to repair his biretta, fastening the pom-pom back on with a safety-pin.

He was magnificent, whispered Elodie, the daughter, eyes glowing, sad but glad that her ailing mother had died at last.

"You were magnificent, Father," said Sophia, the niece, out loud.

Fournier looked away, tried to remember what he had said, whether he had said too much.

This is a real priest, said the whisperer.

"This is a real man…"

Just what they'd been waiting for. They'd follow a priest like this to Hell and back.

Sophia was brimming with excitement. For a few brief weeks she had worked with the mongol children before the Nazis arrived. Thus she was a nominal member of the small *covine* run by Astrid. There, they talked drunkenly about little else but politics, men, and what they could do with them. Although she would never blab anything that might betray the group, she couldn't wait to spread the word about the man *she* had found!

And later that day, that same *covine* gathered in their secret place. This was the old, green-mouldy, round tower that Michael had glimpsed, which was capped off by a slightly askew conical roof of red tiles. It was almost hidden in the woods that edged beyond the garden of St Martin's. Centuries before, it had been an oratory, dedicated to a now-forgotten female saint.

Despite the outer air of decay, it was entered only by a large and very solid wooden arched door, to either side of which had been placed – just for the occasion – rams' skulls mounted on red-and-black striped poles. In the keystone above the door was chiselled in block capitals: VITRIOLUM.

Inside, on the ground floor covered with rush carpets, sitting primly on old wooden school chairs, were Astrid and four local women. There used to be more, but the War had eaten the rest. There were two floors above them, reached by curving steps in the wall, but none of the visitors had been allowed up there. It had always been implied that, when they had proved themselves, access would be granted. Then they would have *such* fun, and see *many* wonders. Yet it was never quite clear what they had to do to prove themselves. Or exactly what form the fun would take.

They called the tower *La Maison D'Oiseaux*, but they sometimes also called it, giggling, the *House of the Cock*. The visitors had had heard rumours of the things that had gone on here. It remained their little secret. Even the Germans had missed the place when they had raided the house itself. The women felt good that they had something like this in their lives. Far safer than the secret communist cells in Neuilly that would make everyone equal when the Russians came. But which kept getting people shot in the meantime.

Each of the covine had drained little silver cups of a special brew given to them on arrival, which seemed to make their brains float and their aching bodies feel good for once.

There was:

Hélène, a 22-year-old married into unhappiness with a spineless stick of a man, who had managed to avoid the Compulsory Work Order. The Nazis needed so many soldiers for the Russian front that, with the help of the Vichy government, the *Service du Travail Obligatoire* had deported huge numbers of able-bodied French males to work in camps in Germany, to help the war effort. It was for everyone's good. To save the world from Communism. And Jews, Poles and other sub-humans. It would have helped Hélène if her man had been taken, but no such luck.

She had been a cleaner at the big house and worked more hours than she should. This was because the owner, the one they called Le Cohen, always spoke to her as if she was Someone, and not a mere cleaner. She had adored him and their occasional sex, which compensated for the low wages.

Hortense, a stout, gloomy woman in her late twenties. Her mood seemed to attract the darkness that rose from the base of the tower upward, as the sun went down. The darkness had grown worse of late, the more she missed the man who had appointed her to work in the schoolroom. There she had taught the little unteachables. Or sometime acted as a seamstress, fixing their clothes. He had called her 'tu' from the very start and she loved him for it, and the fact that he made her feel beautiful, not dumpy or dowdy.

Juliette, who agonized about being pregnant, now wondered if Uli had cared for her at all. She had taken her hat off, and ran her fingers around its brim, biting her lower lip and desperate for help from any of the six directions. The special drink didn't seem to affect her as it seemed to do with the others. She and the Cohen had had such fun together as she worked in the stables with the little ponies that the children rode upon. These had all been taken by the Germans when they raided. She saw them working the beasts occasionally, dragging small cannon that Uli said would destroy large tanks. He was an ordinary German was her Uli: she placed no blame upon him for the wrong-doing of the Gestapo.

Sophia, who left the space of a chair between herself and the others, her red hair exploding from the band she wore, apace with her thoughts. She had not been working at St Martin's long enough to have a clearly defined role. Yet she remembered *Monsieur* Michelet, Le Cohen, a man of great presence and winning smile who had whispered at her interview: *You are special, Sophie. You will have a great future here.* She also remembered how Astrid and Selene, at either side of him, had smiled on hearing that, and welcomed her with their eyes. Nothing came of it: the Germans raided soon after and shot him.

"Is Anna coming?" Astrid asked of Sophia.

"My aunt is dead."

"*Zut!* The cancer?"

"Yes. Elodie and I were with her at the last. And the new priest."

"Oh oh oh…" said Astrid, shaking her head as if she might have been able to cure her had she been called. Anna was slightly famous for having had her warts removed by Astrid with no more than a few touches and mutterings.

They all sat respectfully and expectantly in a half-circle around Astrid. She wore a prim blue dress fastened tightly to the neck with tiny little pearl buttons. Her hair was loose, flowing to her shoulders, with little kinks in it from where it was habitually bound. She looked over her very thin, silver reading glasses as she scanned own hand-written notes, and then took these off to rub her eyes.

"Now, everyone, stay awake while I speak of important things…"

They sat and listened dutifully to Astrid's lecture about the philosophy of Synarchy, and the Unknown Superiors who ruled the world, and communicated their ideas via special individuals. She left them in doubt that she was one of these, and so they must listen very carefully indeed. There was no room for democracy or social equality in her scheme. Be dutiful to those above, in the secret scheme of things. Be kind to those below.

The walls curved and soared around them, letting in the last half-hour's light of the day from the empty window-spaces. It was hard not to nod off during the address. They were all, in their own ways, rather afraid of Madame Riche. Especially the ones who owed her rent.

The compulsory lecture over, they waited for the next part. Astrid noted all that she dealt with in a large ledger-like book, that she now put on the floor next to her chair.

"Ah! I almost forgot," she said, delaying the moment. "Show me," she commanded, and they all raised their skirts enough to display the garters they wore, as secret badges. Astrid inspected them and nodded, satisfied.

This was the moment they wanted, and sat nervously as Astrid picked up a deep blue basin of water, put it on her lap and explained to Sophia, the newest one:

"This ancient bowl once belonged to Michel de Notre Dame. You have heard of him, Nostradamus. He predicted the end of the world. *My* Master, whom I called Ded'e – The Cohen – gave it to *me*. It attracts the spirits of the depths."

She breathed heavily, with eyes closed. Muttered some words upon the surface of the water, and whether it was just echoes from within the rim, or something otherworldly, the basin seemed to breathe, and utter sounds of its own. Astrid bent her head and listened carefully, smiling and nodding. In a thin voice she spoke into the bowl, and looked through it.

. "*Eh bien*…I see a name forming. And the name is…Hélène. Hélène first. What is your problem?"

"My cow is not giving milk, *grand-mère*," she complained, trying to peer across the circle and see into the waters herself. "She is agitated…"

This was not a small thing. In their world, under all the other deprivations and with a useless husband, this could be disastrous. Astrid screwed up her eyes and stared into the air behind the woman, as if seeing its cause on a cinema screen.

"Someone is sending you bad wishes, and affecting the beast. It is one of your neighbours, to the left of your field."

Hélène gasped and her face hardened. She might have known! "Can you stop her doing this?"

"I will send a good thought after it, a good and strong thought to bend the bad wish. It will go back upon her. Give it three days. Mind you, all the bombers flying above won't help."

"Thank you, *grand-mère*," said Hélène, and the others nodded to each other, sending her encouraging smiles.

Astrid closed her eyes and divined another name from the bowl, her eyes moving from one side to another as if unrolling a scroll of paper to read:

"Hortense…"

All heads turned. They all knew what she would ask.

"*Grand-mère*, my brother…"

Her brother had helped an airman, an RAF pilot shot down. The Gestapo found out and tortured his wife and young son before him, until he told them where the man had gone. Then they shot all three, on the spot.

It was tragic, it was appalling, but everyone knew about this. What they wanted, and the sort of power that kept the group together, was a clear demonstration of what they *didn't* know.

Astrid closed her eyes, smiled hugely and swayed slightly in her seat, as if to some inner tune. The other women looked on, while Hortense wrung her hands in her lap.

"I have your brother here. He is radiant. He is at peace. His wife and son are also with him. They wave to you."

The women wanted more than this.

Astrid's eyes opened, very wide, so you could see the whites all around the iris. They bored into Hortense this time. "He says that he always knew it was you who punctured the tyres of his new bicycle. He always knew it was you who stole that money from the little fob pocket of his jacket. But that he never stopped loving you, his little sister. He also gives you the words… 'red fork'? Yes, 'red fork'. He says you will understand."

If the solid bone and muscles and flesh of a human face could crumple like wet tissue, Hortense's did then. "Thank you, *grand-mère*. Thank you…"

Again, the mutual nods, and the regal air of beneficence from Astrid.

The others took deep breaths of admiration. This was the sort of thing they came for. Those nearest patted Hortense on shoulder and arm.

"And now," said Astrid with unholy pride, "the final choosing, for The Charm, in the last light of the day."

All sat upright. Each one tried to will her to 'see' their name within the unfathomable depths of the little bowl. They saw her face go through many expressions: searching, confusion, puzzlement and then revelation. She looked up, smiling, and then at each one in turn, tantalising, teasing. They were young chicks holding open their beaks for the worm.

"And the chosen one is… the chosen one is Sophia!"

Sighs, gasps, clucks of disappointment, especially from Juliette, who was in dire need of a miracle just then. But from Sophia:

"Oh thank you, *grand-mère*, a thousand thanks!"

"Here," said Astrid, handing '*Le Charme*', a small brown sealed envelope, to the lucky one. Sophia took it with delight. "Remember the rules: tell no-one, show no-one, and never *never* open it to see what it is inside. You will have luck for the next three months, and then you will throw it on the fire, exactly as it is."

Sophia, who was young enough and pretty enough to have high hopes and a wish list as long as the Cotentin peninsula, glowed with pleasure. These charms, these *petites cadeaux* of Astrid, were much prized. Most of the women around her could testify as to their effectiveness. Good things happened. Doors were opened.

"I wish I could do you all," Astrid sighed. "But I'm far too old for that now."

"You are not yet forty!" said Hortense.

"*Ta Gueule!* I lack the inner fires. I'm sorry."

A large key groaned in the lock. The door was pushed open with some difficulty, catching and scraping on the floor of the tower. Selene came carrying a lantern. They didn't realise how dark it had become. "Are you finished now?"

"I haven't told them yet."

"Told us what?" they asked at once.

Astrid and Selene stood together. The light was held as high as she could. Huge shadows leapt and swayed upon the curved walls.

"He is come."

"Gestapo?!" gasped Hortense.

"No. The Hawk Lord."

They looked at one another, mystified, then turned to Selene for confirmation. They regarded her as the more level-headed of the two. She nodded.

"What is a Hawk Lord?" asked Sophia, who was thoroughly enjoying all this, and clutching her *cadeau*.

Astrid rolled her eyes, as if she had been explaining this all along. "He is the one who will come from above to save us. Le Cohen prophesised this many years ago, did he not, Selene? Did he not read to us from his Book of the Law?"

Selene nodded, and quoted in a clear voice: "We will see the Hawk-Headed Lord of Silence and of Strength, the Hawk-headed mystical Lord! He will enjoin us to be goodly: to dress in fine apparel; to eat rich foods and drink sweet wines and wines that foam! Also, to take our fill and will of love as we will, when, where and with whom we will! He will bring us unimaginable joys on earth: certainty, not faith; peace unutterable, rest, ecstasy; nor will he demand anything in sacrifice."

Astrid nodded agreement, and added some quotes of her own: "Remember, all of us here, that existence is pure joy; that all the sorrows are but as shadows; they pass and are done; but there is that which remains. The Hawk Lord's servants will be few and secret: they shall rule the many and the known…"

"*Mon Dieu…*" said Juliette, who would have prayed to the Devil for a bit of help just then.

"**Notre Dieu**," corrected Astrid. "He is here."

"Where?" asked Sophia, who was completely enjoying this insanity.

Astrid tapped her nose.

"Where did he come from?"

Astrid and Selene, as if rehearsed, pointed upward in unison. They all looked up as if 'he' might be there now, on the floor above.

"Can we see him?" asked Hélène in some excitement, for she

could do with a real man to enter her life, and she'd heard rumours of the things that had gone on here before the Germans arrived.

"Not yet."

"But how do you know he is the one?" Hortense asked.

"He has all the signs, has he not, Selene?"

Selene nodded. They all knew Selene had her feet on the ground. Their big secret made their faces glow with pride, they could have snuffed out the lamp and no-one would have noticed.

"His name is Michael – after the Archangel of Fire. And his last name is Horsett. Hor. Sett."

Their faces were blank.

Astrid explained: "Hor is Horus, Lord of Light. Sett is Set, Lord of Darkness. That is no coincidence. He is a man of Fire and Air. He is the one. The One!"

"And this man - *our* man – he does have a big cock, eh?" added Selene with a wicked look.

Ooooooh, they all went, seeing pictures in their minds' eyes.

"Listen, my sisters," said Astrid, standing up straight and bold. "Remember what our Master foretold. Soon, we will meet properly, in power, with our robes and garters and we will weave the light. It will all happen as it was meant to happen…"

Aaaaah, they responded wonderingly – though Juliette's tailed off into a very quiet *Hmmmmm…*.

This was all so much better than joining the Resistance.

26

As the women in the tower finished their business, thrumming to the notion of their Hawk God, Michael and his new buddies in the classroom came to the end of their own day. The crate was empty of its books. Horsett was sitting on the floor, leaning back against the wall. His leg ached. The Tommy gun was propped by his side with its safety-catch on. Luc and Colette sat cross-legged in front of him, looking impressed. He was almost glad the kid was there to act as gooseberry, though he wouldn't have admitted that to any of his buddies in the Airborne – if any of them were still alive.

"Truly you speak well the French," said Luc,

"I sure do buddy. Always been a fast learner."

"You can use '*tu*' - You do not have to be formal with us!" said Colette, with eyes sparkling in a way that meant he didn't have to be formal with *her* especially.

"No, I kinda prefer the '*vous*'," he said, grabbing the staff to haul himself painfully upright. Not noticing the quick look of hurt that crossed her face, or the slight triumph that glowed on Luc's.

He stretched to look out of the high window at the shadowed garden, in the last light of the day.

"The garden is overgrown," he noted, seeing the long grass of what had been lawns, the huge weeds, overgrown bushes and hedges, and the dried-up fountain. "Don't you have anyone to look after it?"

"No," said Colette. "Not now. The war…"

"Those woods…are they yours too?"

"Mais, *oui*."

"What's that tower?"

"It is a – how you say – *ruine*? Ruin?"

"Look honey, put the dictionary down. Speak French from now. Keep it simple. I'll get the gist."

"*Alors*, the ruin is very dangerous."

"The war again, right?"

"Oh no! Some were built to look old. The ancestors did such things."

"They were mad," offered Luc, putting the books neatly back

in the box. "But the English milords did the same. They called them follies. They would wake in the morning and look out of their windows and see old castles. They thought it romantic. Very expensive to build."

"Hell, a Sherman tank could make anything look ruined for nothing." He took the map out of his pocket and unfolded it, spreading it across the sloping windowsill. "Is that thing marked on here?"

"No."

"So beyond those woods, that's a river, right?"

"Le Fronds."

"And a road," he mused, studying the unfamiliar style of the map, angling it into position.

"There are many roads. This is called by some *le val sans retour*. Strangers get lost." Colette had a sudden memory of Dieter, and the briefest of pangs.

"I want to go look."

Colette's face fell.

Luc's brightened. "The *grand-mère* and *maman* do not like people to go out there," Luc said. "They are very private."

For the first time Horsett looked at the Luc. "*You* been out there?"

"Never."

"Then I need to look. I'm going out."

"Michael," Colette said, "that is not a good idea."

"Too bad, honey…" He might be falling in love, but he also had survivors' guilt and needed to work out some kind of mission for himself.

So Horsett clanked his way down the maze of corridors, his wooden staff making righteous noises on the wooden floors. Luc and Colette followed: one excited at what might be revealed, the other anxious for the same reason. They came back into the room where they had first gathered, the two dogs in their baskets in the corner, Astrid and Selene clearly just having come in from seeing off the others.

"He wants to see the woods," said Colette hurriedly.

Astrid never faltered. "Of course. But it is getting dark, and you need to eat. I will show you tomorrow. I will show you myself!"

"Have some *sirop*. Our special *sirop*."

"Syrup. Syrup, sure." Horsett remembered how good that was. It wouldn't hurt none to wait a while longer. Besides, his leg was hurting badly, he needed to rest it.

The weird cat came into the room and sat next to him as the dogs swirled in their baskets and looked nervous. There was something very odd about that creature. It looked at him in an almost human way, as if it saw right through him and was somewhat scornful of what it could see. His 'father in heaven' as he mockingly thought of his Dad, had done the same.

"*Allez*," said Selene to Luc, and with the three women looking at him the way they did, he nodded to Horsett and left.

"Drink," said Astrid, handing the soldier a small silver vessel engraved with stars and suns.

It went down him like honeyed fire, and warmed him from within. The whole room glowed. "Wow..." he said. Suddenly, there was no pain, no worries, no war and no inhibitions. No 'me', no 'you': a holy nothingness, in which his whole body was being massaged. Outside, an owl went *ouh ouh...*, as his Mom used to sound them when she told him stories, and another answered. He'd only heard that noise before in the movies. This was a dream; this was how the world should be. He told himself that he would be nicer to them all from now – like the good kid he was before the Airborne swept him up.

"The garden..." he muttered, finding marvels in the mathematical centres of the cat's eyes. " That tower..."

"*Fay çe que voudras*," Astrid said softly, affectionately.

Colette ran her hand over the Mohican strip. He gasped. It felt so good. "I want to shave this," she said.

"Sure ma'am, sure. Whatever you say. *Fay çe que voudras*," he mumbled from the depths of his gentling bliss, reaching out to stroke the cat that was so much more than a cat.

"And then you will sleep," soothed Astrid. "Leave your smelly uniform at the door and we will clean it for you. There is a room ready. The time for mangers in stables is past."

27

An hour later Astrid and Selene had gone back to the tower, and climbed into the windowless middle floor. They sat at either side of a little octagonal table and listened by candle-light to the wheezing and whistling of an old radio.

There was a framed photograph on the table of their bearded Master, sitting on some kind of throne-like chair. He was wearing a formal suit and a garish sash, with a chain of office and various medal-like items pinned on his chest. Normally it hung on a nail on the northern panel, just below a lonely silver star. They had taken it down and looked at it now with fondness.

The room itself had been turned into a kind of eight-sided vault by the addition of wooden panels:

The pitch black panel of the Winter solstice in the north showed nothing more than a star set above head height.

The second panel, to the right of that, was a bleak 1 *Février* landscape of bare trees, heavy scudding clouds, and patches of snow.

To the right of that, the Spring, with the trees hesitantly coming into leaf, snowdrops and daffodils poking above a more hopeful ground.

The panel for 1 *Mai* showed rolling fields of deepest green, and fat grazing sheep, while the fifth panel to the south, the Summer solstice, was that of a huge blazing sun, and all the colours of light and fire rippling around it.

Then came 1 *Août* where the land was more burnt than verdant, and glowing.

The western panel, the Autumn equinox, showed the falling leaves and the fading colours of a land settling into rest.

And the eighth panel, for 1 *Novembre*, showed the failing of the light and what looked like spirits rising from the lonely darkening land.

Astrid and Selene's heads were almost touching as they listened. The radio was normally kept hidden under a floorboard. It was an offence for which they could be executed. Even Colette didn't know they had one. It was turned on low, waiting for the programme *Honor and Homeland*, that was broadcast by the BBC's

French Service from far-away England. They always laughed when the 'troubadour of the Resistance' Anna Marly whistled the first notes of '*Le Chant des Partisans*': her sharp, clear whistling was believed to pierce the static of Nazi jamming. And then her opening lines:

> *Ami, entends-tu le vol noir des corbeaux sur nos plaines?*
> *Ami, entends-tu les cris sourds du pays qu'on enchaîne?*[1]

They joined in with the song, softly. The words made them tearful, and proud. The radio could have been a baby. They turned the photo of their Master toward it, as though he were listening too.

Astrid did that strange thing with her hands, seeming to pull invisible things down from the air above, as if it might help the reception. Selene reached under her chair and produced a small bottle of thick, dark-blue glass, and two tiny goblets.

The news was good, the news was bad. Fierce fighting at the coast. The Hun was being driven back. The Allies were being crushed. The two women rolled their eyes. In those days, no-one put too much faith in what was said by either side, although they tended to trust the BBC. Selene shook the bottle and poured out two precise measures. They raised their cups to the sky, and then brought them down to land with a hiss.

"To the good folk," said Astrid.

"To the good green land," Selene replied.

They clinked and drank. They swallowed and gasped. They showed the whites of their eyes and swayed a little on their chairs.

"Bleugh!" said Astrid, reaching into a bag and bringing out a little silk pouch. "The hawk man's good red hair."

"Why did you want his hair shaved? Do you want to make a voodoo doll, or create a magical link with him?"

"No. It just looked stupid. We don't want our saviour to look like an ass or an ape."

She then took out a rolled parchment and spread it on the table with a quiet tra-la!

"I had almost forgotten this!" cried Selene. "It is the god Set-

---

[1] Friend, do you hear the black flight of ravens on the plains?
  Friend, do you hear the muffled cries of a country in chains

Horus!

"*Non*, Horus-Set."

"I drew it at our Master's suggestion. He told me how important it would become."

"Ah *oui*, he knew things did he not?"

"But look, his head is tilted. Remember how Michael's head ws tilted to the left when he appeared?"

"*Merde*, it was to the right."

"To the darkness of Set or the light of Horus?"

"We must release the darkness. We must straighten him toward the light."

"Do you mean to kill him?"

"Never kill. Free him. Remove the Set creature."

"But first."

They giggled.

Selene smiled, satisfied. "She is a good girl, Colette."

They dipped their fingers into the bag and felt the hair.

"He even had pictures of the Hawk on his uniform!" marvelled Astrid again, referring to the Screaming Eagle patch of the 101st Airborne.

"All things are coming into place, just as Our Master predicted and you foresaw."

"Me and the Book of Numbers: 'How art thou fallen from heaven, O Lucifer, son of the morning! How art thou cut down to the ground, which didst weaken the nations!'?"

"I thought it was Isaiah, the twelfth verse," mused Selene.

"Pah! It was Numbers. But our man *Michael* – he has fallen from heaven and come to weaken nations, to crush the Boche. As it was foretold."

She gave a great and satisfied *Aaaaaah*...as she peered in at the shorn hair again, and all that it represented.

"Such a pity he won't be with us for long, Gods never are," she said, fastening up the bag.

"*Bien sûr*..." sighed Selene but without remorse. "But we can have some fun with him until then..."

They stared at each other.

"Oh-*kay*!" they said in unison, and laughed.

28

Michael Horsett was trying to get to sleep between the crisp sheets in the large bed, in the room they had specially prepared. It had a huge stuffed hawk in a glass dome, on a high and narrow black table, right next to the window. He frowned: you can get too much taxidermy. *Couldn't these gals just do knitting!* Selene had pulled the shutters closed and Astrid drew the blackout curtains across. No light could escape and bring the Boche fluttering at their windows like moths.

He smiled at the irony. Out there in the barn he was a God of Light. Enough equipment to illuminate half of Normandy, but no reason for using it. Here, they were afraid of the merest pin-prick creeping out.

"You will be safe now," said Colette, watching from the doorway.

"Good night, sleep well," they all had said, making their exits, closing the door.

He undressed with difficulty, dropping his clothes on the floor then leaving them outside the room as they had asked. The single candle guttered in the draft; there was a shortage of these so he pinched it out. Although he didn't like such absolute darkness, he didn't have much choice.

His nights so far had been riven by pain and bad dreams. Now, he was on a soft mattress comforted by the cold metal of the Tommy gun propped up next to the bed, and the .45 under the pillow.

Then came the dreams, or the half-dreams, as he drifted in and out of sleep.

A door inside his head opened. His thoughts took him into a bleak land scattered with open coffins. Out of these popped memories of his sergeant, and the guys that should have been with him: *Al, Archie, Harry, Tommy, Troy, Daleth, Janko, Hoss.* And the frightened face of that German kid he had wasted when he could have shown him mercy. They loomed and leered around his mind. Were they judging him? He woke in a sweat each time, and wondered if the syrup that Astrid had given him was causing this. Or maybe it was just guilt at having survived, and not being where he should be. Not so much a SNAFU as a FUBAR.[1]

The shroud of darkness smoothed around him. Utter silence. Despite his various aches he tried to relax by imagining himself after the war, taking Colette back to meet his Mom. But then the faces kept coming back: *Al, Archie, Harry, Tommy Troy, Daleth, Janko and Hoss,* and they were frowning now. They didn't want to go away.

There came a rush of cold air and he knew that the door was opening oh-so silently. A figure came toward him, he could smell her warmth.

Please let it be her, he thought, though he knew it was. *Oh please let it be her!*

"Who's that?" he whispered, glad of the chance to sit up and meet this head-on. He wasn't a kid any more, living at home with his Mom. He was a Screaming Eagle. He was a paratrooper. He had come to save France yet somehow found himself hiding from the Nazis in a lunatic asylum!

Jesus...

His heart leapt and his dick stiffened as she slid in next to him. This was what his buddies had talked about, dreamed about, all the time. And it was happening to him, for real, as her cool bare flesh curved against his, careful of his wounds, her finger on his lips:

Sssssh...

Of course! Not a word. Not a sound. He framed the word *Merci.* This was like the first time he made a jump in training, from a tethered balloon. All the guys hated that balloon. Jumping from a, airplane was easier. But as he had paused at the gate of the basket, looking down, the feeling he'd experienced then echoed what was in him now. He so desperately wanted to plummet into scary love with this woman.

Strangely, she wouldn't kiss him, no, there was that finger on his lips. But she pushed him on his back – he didn't fight none – and she licked him, quickly, briefly, moving here and there on his body. Then she moved his hand to let him touch her, in all the secret places he had dreamed about. There, in the uttermost night, in this alien world, she came on top of him and made a man of him at last, and crept away as silently as she had come.

---

[1] Situation Normal, All Fucked Up. Fucked Up Beyond All Recognition.

And the damndest thing in that damned place was…he was sure he heard a cat purr, and the slightest change of weight as something left the bed just after she did.

Ah hell, who cared! He was a paratrooper, he was a Screaming Eagle. And even better than that, he was now a man. Wherever they were now – in heaven, hell, or just holding the roads out of the beachheads – his buddies sure would have been proud of him.

29

Private First Class Michael Horsett hauled back the heavy black curtains and pushed open the shutters. The light punched into his face. He blinked. What day was it? Thursday, it had to be. June 8. His leg was hurting like crazy. Still couldn't put much weight on it, but it was a whole lot better than it had a right to be.

Had he dreamed last night? If so it was the best dream he'd ever ha. There wasn't a mark on the sheets, and his skin still flowed with the memory of that lithe flesh agin his. He was a man. At last.

Outside there was bird-song and barking. The two dogs were running around and around, chasing their tails. Plus, Astrid and Selene were out there doing that strange dance again. Their wooden-soled shoes echoed on the cobbles as they called out: *Hor! Hor!* Luc was right – they were nut-cases.

As promised, his uniform had been left outside the room, washed and mended. Still slightly damp but smelling fresh. He got dressed and looked at his face in the gilt-framed mirror: no Mohican, no traces of war paint, a lot of thin scars from the fall. Plus a light behind his eyes from Colette. He still thrummed from that herbal medicine and the memories of first sex. Did he look different? Would anyone know he was no longer a virgin?

He holstered the .45, slung the Tommy gun over his shoulder. No way would he ever let them out of his reach: his sarge would have screamed: *Gimme fifty, you bellyachin' son of a bitch!* and he'd have done fifty push-ups and a whole lot more besides. Old habits.

It was difficult getting his right boot on because of his bandaged leg. Taking up the pole on which he'd come to depend, he let it take his whole weight, and stood for a while circling his bare right foot. The smell of coffee floated up and into the room. Grabbing his boot by the laces and getting a good grip of the staff, he limped downstairs.

Colette and Michael exchanged smiles but said nothing. She helped him get the boot on, and tucked the trouser leg into the top to make him look like a paratroop again, tut-tutting as he winced.

A cup of coffee steamed on the table, ready and waiting. They looked at each other shyly. The door to the yard was open; the other women could be heard chatting outside. He was about to whisper: *Vous êtes merveilleux*, when one of the dogs put its front paws on the edge of the table to get some scraps. Colette whacked it with such cold and unexpected power that Horsett raised his eyebrows. The dog, Nu, slunk off whimpering; the other, Geb, nuzzled around it in sympathy. The two older women came back into the room.

"Say, ah, what is this stuff?" he asked to cover his awkwardness, nodding down to his drink.

Selene shrugged: "It is *called* coffee; truly it is toasted barley mixed with chicory. Now translate this Colette. Don't sit there looking stupid..."

"He wants us to speak French from now. He has a good understanding. He learns fast. I think he is a master."

Selene raised her eyebrows. "Well then, Michael...This coffee is all we can get. Lots of things are rationed," Selene added, slowly, as if she meant much more than coffee. "Do you not like it?"

"No it's fine ma'am, *bon, delicieux*, mmm-hm yeah, oh yeah! Bingo!"

"*Menteur*," she said. He knew she had just called him a liar as she poured some more, and there wasn't much warmth in the word. Had she heard him with her daughter last night?

"Here..." he offered, thinking he'd better keep her sweet, reaching into his cargo pocket where he had a dozen white tin foil packets of instant coffee that had survived his fall. He took one out. "Try this. The real thing. *La réalité*."

She reached and took his offer, then turned sharply to look outside to the yard. The dogs were barking and leaping up at the main gate. Above their yapping, channelled by the narrow lane between the high hedgerows, they all heard the unmistakable churning of Jules' tractor.

The tractor wheezed and coughed itself to standstill, driven by Jules, with Luc next to him, towing an equally decrepit trailer. Perched on this was Armand, and another old man. It was met, as before, by the trinity of glowering women.

Looks were exchanged but mouths were zipped until the engine died, which it did unwillingly, with loud threats and much smoke.

"*Fou! Fils de put!*[1] You swore to tell no-one!" snarled Astrid at Jules, glaring.

Jules turned his head and looked in all directions with exaggerated caution. "But you know our friend Thibault! He and Armand were old *poilus*. You know he is to be trusted. Where is he? Where is the American? We want to speak to the American." There was an electricity in saying it, out there in the open, beneath the clear skies of France. The men climbed down to stand facing Astrid.

Astrid gave the newcomers a look like spit, as Thibault with his yellow, protuding buck teeth, and two dead hares hanging from his belt, calmed the dogs and made them sit. The two parties glared at each other.

"*Zut!* He is gone," said Astrid with a shrug. The other women gave synchronised nods.

"You are too late. He went last night," Selene added.

Colette caught Luc's eye and gave a wry, sad nod of her own.

Armand straightened, smiled and shook his head. He pulled his battered hat down over his head. Steadied himself.

"Actually, I think that he is in that outhouse. Standing in the darkness, back from the window so that we cannot see him. But with his seam-ripper of a gun sighted on my chest...here."

"*Bof?*" exclaimed Astrid, shivering with contempt. "If he were here – which he is not – he would aim at that stupid head of yours."

"But my sweet Astrid, Great Mother of All, if he aimed at my old, ugly head then the recoil of such a weapon might make it kick upward, and the bullet whizz harmlessly through my hat. So he will be aiming lower, at my heart, at this instant. Is that not so?"

The men beamed. Armand was their hero. He, along with his *ami*, Thibault, had been a *poilu* in the Great War of 1914-18, almost won his *croix de bois*[2] a dozen times without ever being awarded any of the medals they called contemptuously 'cookware'. And he really had waded chest deep in mud and

---

[1] Fool! Son of a whore!
[2] Winning the Wooden Cross was slang for being killed.

corpses.

"Pffft…" Astrid countered, blowing air out of the corner of her mouth and upwards into her hair, while raising her eyes to heaven. "I say again. He has gone. Get off my land."

"We should go," muttered Jules, keeping his eye on the internally raging woman.

They turned to leave but:

"*Arretez!*" came the American voice from exactly where Armand had guessed.

The American came out of shadows and into the daylight. The air almost exploded with the men's excitement as they eyed up this stranger from the skies.

"G'day, mate," said Thibault, who had briefly served next to Australians in the previous war, though he had never learned more than a few phrases.

"Okay okay…I wanna hear what you've got planned. Plus that kid there, Luc, got me this map. I need you all to look at it. I need some help here."

Luc translated. The men glowed. Luc shone. Michael felt good that he was taking command. Even if he was only eighteen he was a man now, after all.

"Here," said Horsett to Selene, reaching into his cargo pocket to fish out two more packets of coffee. "Why don't you make the guys a real drink?"

The women were nonplussed.

Thibault began to offer Astrid his hares but one look at her face told him to pick Selene instead. She nodded, said: "What use is this, heh?" but took them anyway, and ignored the wink he gave.

Astrid stood and blinked, and blinked hard. Anyone could see the tension along her narrow jaw.

Something about that damned blink troubled Horsett but he pushed it out of his mind. He wasn't gonna let a bunch of women control his life, even if they *had* saved it. These guys might be what his sarge once described as 'white bread troops' – old and toothless – but they were guys, willing to fight. And if he, Michael Horsett, a Screaming Eagle, didn't get to real fighting soon then he was just pissing in the wind.

His sphinx-like war face was somewhat spoiled by his open mouth at the sight of their old tractor as he passed. A useless hunk of junk. He'd never seen anything like this in Detroit. "Hey, this thing has got wooden wheels. And iron tyres! *Iron* tyres! Is that normal? Is *anything* in this world normal?"

There was dead stoat crushed flat around part of the rim. The engine blew out clouds of smoke. How could he use a heap like this to fight his war? It would all be down to luck.

Astrid blinked again. He looked away, didn't know why.

"Come on, buddies," he said, leading them on inside. "*We* need to talk..."

30

The *Feldgendarmes* had parked their vehicles under trees. Three of them played the card game *skat*, while the rest were eating the black dry bread they called *stalintorte*, swilling it down with their *kaffee-ersatz*. They all complained because the young Frenchman – Henri the Bubi – had forgotten to bring sugar.

It was safer under the trees: they had glimpsed more Allied aircraft than German, and the latrine gossip back at base told them that all was not going well for their own lads.

Schimmel sat in the first vehicle and stared intensely into his map. He tried to make sense of the lines and words but his mind flew all over the place. As he sucked in a deep breath, he tried to shut out the images that rose in his mind: memories of a son whom he had never really loved, but should have done. He felt cursed by his sense of duty.

Concentrate, concentrate...

In the *wagen* behind, Der Bomber was telling stories about his time in Russia, about the *rattenkrieg* – rat warfare – among the ruins of Stalingrad. How they'd had to eat *eisbrot* – frozen chunks of bread – and eventually their little horses. And all the while their ears were assaulted by the *ratsch-boom*[1] of the Russian high-velocity cannon. The rest of them made noises about being impressed, and were grateful that they were sprawled here in France drinking *Muckefuck*,[2] indulging in what he called the *Sitzkrieg* in contrast to the *Blitzkrieg*.

Fat Uli had raised a very tall aerial and tuned in the radio to the '*Promi*', the Propaganda Ministerium, with its latest broadcast from the Fatherland. The machine hissed and crackled as he fine-tuned the knobs, then:

"It's Jupkin!" he cried. "Come and listen. Come on..!"

Henri looked blank. Schimmel let himself surface into the real world, closing his eyes and taking a deep breath, leaning backward, face to the sun.

"They mean Goebbels," he explained to the two Frenchmen, then turning to Uli: "Turn it up!"

---

[1] Crash-bang
[2] Nickname for malt coffee

The quavering voice of the Minister of Propaganda and Public Enlightenment told the men what was *really* going on here in France:

> "The invasion is nothing more than an ingenious, strategic coup by Hitler. The Allies have been lured into France so they are no longer out of reach as they were when they were in England. Now that we have them within reach, our troops will destroy them with our V-2 bombs and the secret weapons to follow…"

His words floated off into the trees. The men looked at the speakers on the radio and at each other. They burst out laughing. Schimmel frowned.

"Hey hey hey," said Uli, conspiratorially, "I've heard that a man took his radio to confession in Aachen because it had been lying too much…"

Their laughter exploded among the trees again like a hand grenade.

The two Frenchmen didn't know how to react, even after Gunther explained it. Henri felt dismayed: he believed in the Nazi vision, and the hierarchy. Yohan, not for the first time, was thinking that choosing the German side in this war was probably a very bad career choice.

When the laughter died, it was Der Bomber who recognised the new sound that pushed its way through the canopy of leaves:

"*JABO!*" he shouted.

"Fighter bomber," snapped Schimmel, doing a double-take. "Get in the –"

The P47 Thunderbolt was only in their sight for a second. It roared past, metres above, giving them a glimpse of blue cowling and white stars, with a bright orange tail fin. The shock-wave of its passing scattered the men, hammered their ear-drums, broke small branches and sent down an autumn shower of bright spring leaves. Then it stopped as suddenly as it had begun.

"Well done," said Schimmel, who had never known combat, and who was trying to hide his shaking.

"We had those same air pirates against us in Italy," said Der Bomber calmly. "Noisy bastards. Knew their engine noises. But it was their *Gabelschwanz-Teufels*[1] we were scared of most. You could never hear them coming. They'd be shooting your arse off before you knew they were there."

They stood in silence. The woods came back to life. An old man cycled past with bread in a large funnel. No-one cared to check his papers. The birds started chirping again.

"Then it is not a raid," said Yohan, who knew he had to start thinking of a way out. "It's not a diversion. Truly, it is the invasion." He just hoped that Goebbels was telling the truth about those V weapons that would save them all.

"Better the Amis than the Ivans, that's all I say," snorted Der Bomber. The rest stared into distances, quietly worried about the future while examining their pasts.

They started up their engines and checked their weapons. Far better this vigilante action by their boss than having to enter the real war.

"Right, come on. We've got homes to search," said Schimmel.

"Don't forget your brides!" cried Der Bomber, referring to the new Schmeissers which – unlike real wives - would never leave their sides.

---

[1] Twin-forked Devils - the German name for the twin-tailed P38 Lightning

31

Father Fournier, at Mass, tried not to see faces in the shadows. Or think of those creatures that stuck on the other side of the glass like snot. All of them, harbingers of *Le Noirceur*. He sweated and shook. The Latin poured from his lips but failed to wrap itself around him like an old, warm coat as it once had done.

Over a dozen women of all ages, and three ancient men attended: the church had never been so full. A sparrow had flown in through an open window and was flapping around. Someone tried to trap it, but the creature bulleted into the red sanctuary candle, beside the locked box of the tabernacle, containing the Eucharist. Everyone was shocked. One of the other women came over and fumbled with matches to re-light it, spilling some in her anxiety.

The people looked at him oddly, he felt. He feared it was distrust, tinged with disgust, and was sure they had heard about the 'trouble' he'd had. Perhaps Dr. Kraepelin's book about this new mental illness called 'paranoia' might be worth reading after all. There was some talk of the Jew Freud who dealt with such things but the very thought of reading him was distasteful. Then there was the German analyst Jung who wrote about something called the anima, which could manifest outwardly as a kind of dark goddess or crone within. He was not sure he understood that either, and he left the book back in Paris anyway. On his good days he told himself that *Le Noirceur* was just a jumble of things in his head: guilt over his sexual appetite, his failings toward the Christ and his Cardinal, his difficulty in relating to people except through the routes and rituals of the Sacraments. Not least his belief that he, a priest, was not a good man. Luc, in his quiet ways had helped him with some of this. Yet at other times, like now, *Le Noirceur* emerged as a creature in its own right. A monster that seemed intent on wanting to torture him, without ever quite coming within reach.

In fact, the people had all heard how he had attacked the Germans single-handed, and were looking at him with admiration and curiosity: Priests like that, they could follow. Besides, with the War in such an uncertain phase, they needed the kind of free insurance policy that only God or one of His servants might offer.

He began the Oratio Ante Communionem: "...libera me per hoc sacrosanctum Corpus et Sanguinem tuum ab omnibus iniquitatibus meis et universis malis" - *deliver me by this, Thy most sacred Body and Blood, from all my sins and from every evil.*

He managed to squeeze out the words in the deep voice that some had said made him a natural priest. Words that enabled him, as priest, to change the simple white bread and rich red wine into the Body, Blood, Soul and Divinity of Jesus Christ Himself.

This he believed, as priest, with all his heart. That he couldn't also transmute certain sources of nourishment within himself into something purer, was nothing less than an agony.

As he intoned, he was sure that the church dedicated to the local Saint Ywi was increasingly occupied by more than merely human presences. There was even a legend that Ywi, who had died in 680, still lay uncorrupted in a shallow grave under the flagstones before the altar. When it had last been ripped open by treasure seekers during the Revolution, they had fled screaming and later lost their minds entirely. In Paris, he would have sneered at such lore. But here, now, trying avoid his sins, he felt that malignities – whatever they were – had flowed in when he blinked. They were everywhere. The simple folk had no idea of the foul creatures they shared pews with, blending with their own shadows. He hardly dared blink again in case he let in more darkness.

He looks as if he is going to faint, whispered Sophia to her friend.

He looks drunk. All that wine!

Sophia giggled. Father Fournier saw that giggle, and from her startled face – so familiar but he couldn't quite place it – he knew that he had *not* imagined it.

He seemed to be carried along by the ritual, like a cork on a river, rather than conducting it. There was cold sweat on his brow and sickness in his gut, but he found a tiny spark of comfort in the eyes of the frizzy-haired girl who had giggled: they were shining, they were innocent. And he knew innocence when he saw it.

"*Pater noster, qui es in cœlis*," came the familiar words from his lips. "*Sanctificatur nomen tuum...*"

All eyes were on him, human and demonic; he didn't know which was which any more.

Are they tattoos on his arms? whispered Sophia again, who liked unusual characters and was thoroughly enjoying this Mass.

Everyone heard her. They all leaned slightly to one side in their seats to peer. To Father Fournier it was as though a wind had blown them, like long grass.

"He is coming," he said out loud in French, as the Mass fell apart, and he didn't know if he'd said it out loud and he didn't care. "He is coming at last…"

Sophia sat bolt upright.

"That's what Astrid, the Great Mother said!" she marvelled, and she didn't care whether anyone heard her either.

Life was suddenly *very* interesting.

32

After Michael's snub of the women and his summons to the men, Colette went with Astrid and Selene as they stamped back into the house. Dust rose from every hard step. She followed them down the long dusty corridor, tracing her fingertips along the greasy handrails that ran its length, drying them on her pinafore. They went through a locked door, and then more locked doors, through the maze of shorter corridors into the room where Astrid customarily did her embalming.

In the 'old days' – only three years before – the locks had been to keep the mischievous little imbeciles from danger and harm. Now, Colette could see no need for them. But the two older women acted in mysterious ways and could be completely stubborn. Often for no reason that she could understand.

The shelves on the walls were filled with failed examples of Astrid's craft: misshapen ravens, broken-back stoats, red squirrels with drooping tails and sagging beer bellies, a fox with bizarre symmetries to its body, headless geese and owls... There were also framed 'thank you' letters from various appreciative institutions. Colette never looked twice at these and was more concerned with the atmosphere around the other two.

Why? she wondered.

"Shall we make a pie with one of them?" Selene asked, slapping the hares on the table. The mood came largely from her, and even a stranger would have sensed that hares and pies were the last things on her mind.

"*Non!*" snorted Astrid, who had put on her surgeon's gown and was preparing her equipment: a variety of scalpels, scissors, syringes, empty bottles. Plus other bottles filled with liquid and marked with the label 'Natron'. She snorted the word with such contempt that it was clearly the stupidest question that anyone had *ever* asked. "They are for the Work. Thibault knows...he knows about the Hare. But do you want to do this one? As practice?"

"*Non!*" came Selene, in fair parody.

The two older women stared at the hares, which lay on the operating table, head to tail with each other, like a yin-yang. They were seeing through them and beyond to places that Colette could not yet imagine.

"He has a mission. He needs his men."

Astrid's lips pursed, her jaw tautened. "*Merde!* He came from above – for *our* mission. We need our man. Our Master needs him. The land needs him."

Colette opened her mouth to ask a question, but they both pounced: *Shut up!* and *Not yet!* coming from them simultaneously. She, who was a Good Girl, kept quiet. This was all incredibly interesting, and she was on Michael's side no matter what.

Astrid cut open the chest of the first hare and slid it along the table to Selene, who removed the main organs, making sure that she left the heart.

"Do we leave them for the forty days and nights?" asked Selene.

"Not these. Not this time."

After that had been done, Astrid pushed a needle into the creature and, using a small hand-cranked pump, withdrew its blood, then injected the embalming fluid into the empty veins before passing it back to Selene. Who then began stuffing the empty parts with straw (*Not ideal – but this war...*)

Colette passed across some handfuls and watched intently as the small bodies were filled and pushed into shape.

"*You* will never need to learn this," said Astrid, in a tone that brooked no obvious question in return. She took up her needles as though they were weapons for battle, and sewed the creatures back together.

"The eyes?"

"This time I will sew them closed. Hares can see too much, and carry tales."

"So can men," said Selene gnomically.

As they started on the second hare Colette was given all the unwanted, slimy, rippling bits and pieces to drop into a polished steel bucket. She remembered Dieter and the brief flirtation at the gate. Later, she would throw these remains to the crows.

Astrid looked up sharply. "Remember...We are not doing this – any of it – for ourselves. We are doing it for the land. For the spirit within the land. This is bigger than the three of us. This is bigger than France itself."

Selene nodded.

Colette nodded too though she had no idea what Astrid meant. Nor did the other two attempt to explain. But that had always been the way. Astrid had such a powerful presence that people around her tended to see things her way, and agree accordingly.

There was an insistent chiming within the room, from high up in a corner. It came from the box on the wall, a left-over from an era when many servants used this as their base. A little disk swung back and forth, in time with the chimes. This showed that someone was at the side door that had once been the Tradesmen's Entrance.

The women looked at each other.

"I'll go," said Selene, knowing who the caller was and what she was likely to want.

33

While the three women fumed and schemed in their locked rooms, Private First Class Michael Horsett of the Screaming Eagles, was looking across the table at his *troupes du pain blanc.*

"Help me out here Luc... What's the verb for to trust: *confiance?"*

Horsett knew this, of course. His Mom had used it a lot, not trusting her husband at all during his weekends away on the sorts of 'business' she didn't trust at all. Trust, lack of trust, loss of trust, once trusted...he knew every aspect of this verb. He had listened quietly while she moaned to him about the demi-paradise she had left behind in Paris. She had only once returned, for her own mother's funeral; her father had been killed – like thousands of others – on the first day of Verdun. This funeral was in the year before Michael's birth. Everything told her that she should have stayed, and she often mused sadly about this while swearing her son to silence. He was just a child: he didn't know the questions to ask that might have made a wasteland flourish again.

"Faire confiance," Luc confirmed, impressed by the American's knowledge.

"Okay, then tell them I have to do the trust thing with them," he said, unfolding the precious map.

"Il n'a pas le choix," said Armand.

"Oh I got that! You're damned right buddy, I don't have a choice."

Armand raised his only mobile eyebrow. His forehead was a ploughed field of wrinkles. The guy had obviously learned French very quickly. Michael felt a twinge of guilt. He didn't normally speak to people like that: he was trying so hard to be a Warrior rather than a worrier.

"You are not a saboteur," Armand continued. "You have lights and coloured panels, but no bombs, no radio. Not much ammunition."

Horsett said nothing, just stared at him with his war face. He knew he needed to switch into the cold menace of the paratroop. Who was no longer a virgin.

"You were dropped in the wrong place, *m'sieur*. Your aeroplane was hit and you had to jump too early. I think you were supposed to guide the other soldiers to their targets behind the landing beaches. Because it *is* the landing, isn't it? It is not a raid, or a diversion."

"*Invasion* is the word," Horsett replied, giving it a French inflection.

"Not for us! 'Invasion' is when the Germans came in 1940. For us, you are part of The Landing."

He emphasised the last words: *Le Debarquement*. Luc showed Michael the word in the dictionary. That was a new one, not something his Mom had ever used. But he realised that the old guy wasn't hostile, or accusing. He was telling it like it was, clearing things up. Real men did that.

"So what are you suggesting, *Armand?*" he countered, still conscious of security, still making sure he hadn't said Yes and hadn't said No, and emphasising the name as if it was the most stupid name in the world. His captain used to do that.

Armand pressed the map against the table, smoothing the creases as though it might smooth out the war upon the land. "I think that you should lead us against the Boche."

"Would you follow me?"

"You were sent to us from above, for a reason. If you cannot join your *frères d'armes* at the beaches, I think you should use your skills. Here. I think you want to kill the Boche."

"That's what I do."

"Have you known combat?"

"Sure..." he said, stone-faced, and he wasn't gonna say more. How could he admit that his only combat involved machine-gunning some kid on a motorbike from behind? How could he say that the whole 101st Airborne, until D-Day, had no history, only a destiny – as the officers kept saying.

Horsett leaned across the table and said earnestly: "Hey buddy lemme ask you this: have *you* seen combat? Do you know what you're asking?"

Armand nodded. "In the last war I fought at Verdun. So did Thibault."

Horsett shrugged. Truth is, he'd never heard of Verdun. His knowledge of the last war was hazy: his Dad got angry when he tried to ask.

Jules, eyes glowing with brotherly pride, added: "He was a sniper. He has medals. He has killed many!" He mimed all this with his hands.

"Sure..."

They heard the gate creak and the dogs bark. The men left the table and huddled back into the room, far from the window. From the safety of the net curtains, they watched as a young woman came nervously into the yard. The weight of a world upon her shoulders. Michael recognised her at once as the one who had had sex in the grass with the fat German.

The woman – Juliette – took off her hat and swiped at the dogs with it. Pausing for a moment to look at the famously decrepit tractor, she almost turned to leave, then disappeared around the far corner of the building.

"What does *she* want?" muttered Michael. "It's like Grand Central Station here." The lone American felt unsafe: if that woman had been with Germans, what would she do if she knew about him? "Who was that?" he asked

The Frenchmen looked at each other. Luc picked up on his emphasis and wondered if he knew her, somehow. "One of the *covine*, I think."

"The what?"

"A group," said Jules. "Stupid women. They talk politics. They knit. They get drunk and fix the world."

"Why's *she* here now?"

Jules shrugged, tapped his nose, raised his eyes, put his palm on his belly and then moved it forward to indicate expansion.

"What?" asked Horsett, who increasingly found this sort of thing irritating. He looked at Luc for an explanation.

"Probably, she is pregnant," Luc said.

Horsett still looked blank.

"The women here...I told you they are mad," Luc continued. "They do *l'avortement*. Erm... erm...abortion. Yes, that is the word."

Inwardly, because he was just a young hick, Michael cried *What!!?* Outwardly, because he was supposed to be a killing machine, he kept his face stone.

Luc spoke in English: "They really are mad, Michael. Even Colette. I know you like her, but perhaps because of the language problem you don't realise that she is...how do I say it... very simple. She is like a puppy to the other two."

Luc swallowed after he said that. Wondered if he had said too much. None of the other men would refute him even if they had understood his words.

But Horsett glared like one of the menacing gargoyles on St Ywi's church. "Look, meathead..." he said.

"Soldier!" said Armand, leaning across and gripping the American's arm. The old Frenchman had no idea what had been said, but he felt the ice. "We need to talk, not fight. Come, all of us, sit down again..."

Horsett took a deep breath and nodded. Last night had been the most wonderful experience of his life. If this little ass-hole ever insulted Colette again then, war or not, he would blow the creep's head off.

"Let's talk about this goddamned map..." he growled, smoothing it out yet again as if by getting rid of the creases it would remove his problems. "We need some ideas. Because here is what I've got: one Tommy gun with four sticks of ammo. One Colt .45. One small mine for blowing the track off one tank. All the lights and coloured panels you can shake a stick at, a jump knife and, er... that's it. So, ah, what do we do then? Surround them?"

Luc translated. The others laughed.

Armand turned the map and traced along it with his gnarled finger. "Look, here is the river. Here is the *réservoir*. You understand. Same word, *oui*? Reservoir? And here, here are the... gates, locks. Do you understand?"

"Er, well, sluice gates, I reckon," Horsett said. "To control the flow."

"Ah, *bon!* They are small gates. It is not a big river."

"Okay, Armand, so what is your plan? *Briser les portes? Noyer l'armée allemande?* Break the gates and drown the whole German Army?"

"Drown them!" snorted Jules. "It would not even wet their ankles. It would do no more than wet the fields and return them to marsh."

Armand took a deep breath and glowered. "Exactement," he said softly.

"Listen buddy, I don't get it."

"Look! Look at this map! These roads, all with high hedges.

The tanks will struggle to get through. Look at the way everything comes toward here – *here* – the crossroads in the centre of Neuilly…"

"So?"

"*Dieu!* Can you not see? If these fields *here* and *here* and *here* become marsh again, the heavy guns and especially the heavy tanks will get stuck."

"I thought tanks could cross anything," said Jules.

"*Non!*" said Armand, who had seen German tanks floundering in the mud in the previous war, and two modern *Panzers* struggling on exercises to the west of Neuilly, thwarted by just such hedges and marshland as he had described.

"Hell, no," agreed Horsett slowly, musing. He had seen a couple of Shermans having real problems with soft ground during training. They'd also had trouble with the much smaller hedges back in the lanes of Devonshire, in England

"And also," enthused Armand, encouraged by this comment, "there will be huge *embouteillages*…you know the word? *Embouteillages?*"

"Traffic jams," helped out Luc.

"Ah *oui*, 'traffic jams' as you say, toward and within the town."

"Like rats in a trap."

"*OUI!*"

Horsett was impressed again. "Okay okay… that's one plan. Any others?"

Thibault put his hand up, shyly, like a boy in a classroom. "There are the railway tracks. There is a large convergence of lines near the town. I have often seen them carrying large numbers of tanks and men to the south. If we blow them up it will be hard to bring reinforcements back *from* the south."

Horsett, while still impressed, was somewhat envious. These two guys had been fighting the Germans in their heads at least, long before he arrived. "Good idea buddy. Railroad. That would slow the bastards. Any more ideas?"

Jules rubbed his hands together as if he'd dirtied them somewhere. "*Essence,*" he said, tapping the side of his nose. "Gasoline. There is a large area where they fill up their vehicles en route to more important places than Neuilly. One little spark and…BOOM! One little spark is all you would need."

"Hey that's a good one too. Damned good."

"But I will search the woods for more weapons," offered Thibault. "There were others dropped near you. Perhaps some of their equipment can be found."

"Not a bad idea, buddy."

Inwardly, Armand bristled at this. They were all so stupid! How could they prefer the plan of the idiot Jules to that of himself? "*Merde!* If we breach the dam that is when you call down help from above – from your bombers and fighters."

They all went silent.

"These bombers and fighters," mused Thibault. "How do we summon them? Have you a radio, *Monsieur*?"

"No."

"But he has flares and the coloured smoke!" added Luc, caught up in them. Plus he liked the dam idea. It sounded less dangerous.

"What can they do?" scorned Armand.

"If the fliers see, they will surely come. Then if they see the Boche tanks trapped in the mud they will attack, and call on more bombers. If we can get them stuck in the centre of the town they will stand no chance."

They all went silent, staring at the black lines on the large sheet as if it had become a cinema screen showing trailers for the future.

"Jules…can you really contact the Resistance?" asked Horsett.

"*Certainement!*" said Jules, though no Frenchman in the room believed him. "They regard me as a Prince among men. Tell me what to say, and what you want them to do, and Jules will contact them."

Eyebrows were raised. Snorting noises were made.

"Okay," said Horsett. "It seems we got the start of something, huh?" He felt that it was worth a shot; he had nothing better to offer other than holing up and waiting for the Allies to find him. Tempting though that was, now that he had found Colette, there was still a Screaming Eagle inside himself raging to take flight. He owed it to his buddies. To his country. The world and his Mom, even. "So which do we choose? The dam, the railway tracks, or the gasoline dump? Or if you can find some more explosive, Thib', all three?" He lit a cigarette without offering one to the others. "One little spark…" Then he inhaled deeply and sat back in the chair to blow a perfect smoke ring. They watched it rise and disintegrate.

"*Il est fou, aussi*," muttered Armand.

"Sure buddy, I sure am crazy. I'm in the right place, huh, Luc? Whaddya think – which place is more vulnerable? Which is impregnable?"

Armand: "No-one guards the little dam."

Luc: "It is easy to get onto the railway junction. I often use it as a shortcut. Neuilly is a – how do you say – a *coin perdu*, a backwater."

Thibault: "I can get you under the fence into the compound where they keep the gasoline. For me, very easy."

Horsett saw that no-one doubted the guy Thibault, even if he did look like something from a cartoon. They all stared at the American, waiting for his decision.

"They're all good ideas guys. Let me think it through. Thibault – go looking for some more stuff. Jules, see if you really can contact the Resistance – but don't bring 'em here! Armand and Luc…we've got a lot of work to do, a war to fight, huh?"

Armand nodded, looked pleased. "Now Thibault and I must start the war in our way. We must stop shaving."

"What?"

Jules explained, somewhat scornfully. "The old soldiers called themselves *biffins*, after rag-pickers, or more often *poilus* – hairy ones."

"Oh I get it. Dirty and scruffy. Life in the trenches, huh?" Horsett himself hadn't started shaving yet. Maybe he'd just stop washing to hide the fact.

Jules nodded. He was often annoyed that age and circumstance had denied him his own history on the battlefield. "But I, Jules, have only one request," he insisted. "If I am to attempt such a dangerous task, and bring us to the Resistance, I want to spend the last five minutes of my worthless life nuzzling Colette's titties."

He was definitely serious about that.

"You're joking, right?" asked Horsett, laughing.

"Jules, he never jokes – though no-one ever believes him!"

Now that he had a plan, Horsett felt himself beginning to lighten up, and allowed himself a smile. "Listen buddy, if you can get a message to the guys 'up there', you can nuzzle my titties as well…"

Luc gasped, but bent down over the map again.

34

Juliette reeled, drugged, as the three women helped her around the corner and across the yard, into view of the men again. The flowers on her hat seemed to droop in sympathy as she slowly wrapped the green scarf around herself, and sank further into her large, old coat.

The women – one at either side and another behind – pushed her while she half-hauled herself up onto the passenger seat of the tractor. She looked as if she was about to collapse.

The men watched from within the kitchen. Jules made a sharp, vertical pulling gesture with his index finger, at waist height, evoking a clear picture in the air of something being hooked down and out, and thrown away.

Whore, whispered one of the men behind Horsett; he didn't know who. He heard other sentiments too as he stood there, face close to the glass, not sure what to think or feel:

She killed her baby.

One less Hun in the world

Only did it because of the Landing. She would have kept it and married her Boche otherwise.

Murderer. Whore...

The glass steamed up from his breath. His leg had started aching again. As he watched the hunched, young woman with the clouds of despair around her shoulders, he felt sorry for her. In some way, down a chain of cause and effect, his arrival had played no small part in that small tragedy.

Astrid came straight across the yard toward their room, aware they were all watching. The map was folded and given back to Horsett, who tucked it into his cargo pocket. Around him there was an air of strong men bracing themselves.

She opened the door without knocking. It was her house. Horsett guessed had had enough of little men and their small schemes. "You will take the girl home, on your tractor. One of you will have to walk."

"*Non,*" said Armand.

Astrid's eyes widened; her long pale eyelashes seemed like rays. Someone sucked in their breath.

"Armand..." said Selene, in a more pleading tone.

"*Non*," he said again.

The tension between them was almost physical. Horsett found himself fascinated by those eyelashes for some reason, and the way they flickered. Were they false? He'd heard of such things. Is that why he was taken by them?

Then Astrid did a strange thing. She stood on her right leg, made a fist of her left hand then extended the index and little finger, pointing at Armand's heart like two horns. She was breathing heavily and hard, as if sending evil out through those fingers into the target, muttering under her breath.

The old man, who until recently had been wading through the corpses of Verdun, reeled. Horsett put out a hand to steady him, amazed and fascinated. What was going on here? And there was Selene looking almost sorry for the guy, and Colette excited by the whole thing.

It was Luc who stepped in, broke the moment. "Come, uncle. I will sit in the back. We are guests here We must do as Astrid asks. We must fight the Germans, not each other."

Armand, pale of face, took a deep breath and straightened. He was a good Catholic; he was not afraid of their stupid sorcery. Silently, he led them all out. They started up their noisy machine and drove off, Luc walking behind to shut the gate after them.

When the yard returned to silence, and sun began to fizzle somewhere toward the real battles, Astrid resumed a normal posture and beamed at Horsett like a little girl saying *See what I can do?* And blinking: one, twice, thrice.

Then it was his turn to reel.

Those eyelashes. Last night, when he had lain naked in the pitch black of his room, Colette had done things to his body with her eyelashes that were exquisite, unexpected, unimagined and sublime. She had done things with her sharp pointed little breasts that had touched his soul.

But looking at the three women now, Colette had very short eyelashes. So did Selene. And neither of those two, looking at them now through their clothes, had that shape of breast. So it was not young Colette who had made love to him, nor Selene.

"Selene and I have much to do, Michael," said Astrid, perhaps reading his mind, and seeing his shock. She gave him a huge slow wink with her left eye, so the long lashes lay upon her cheek like sunrays. "You two go and play…"

35

Colette looked at Michael with shining eyes and those too-short eye-lashes. Did she know about last night? Dare he say: *Honey, your grand-mère fucked me?* No, say nothing, misdirect, wear the other mask, war-face, thousand-yard stare. Anything. It had been wonderful.

"Come with me," she said, tugging his hand, a sparkle in her face as if she might take him straight to bed. Or was he being hopeful? She carried the dictionary under her arm as he carried his machine-gun.

"Where?"

She put her finger to her lips and giggled.

Astrid had touched his lips last night. Was she teasing him? *Did* she know?

He could still smell Thibault's flame-thrower bad breath, which had scorched out from his splayed teeth. His good leg still echoed with the 'accidental' pressures from Luc's thigh under the table; his bad leg ached like hell; and his whole body thrummed with the memory of last night's sex with Colette, who had not been Colette at all.

In the distance, airplanes were droning. That was where he should be. Yet his head was full of the plans that had been agreed with his new 'troops': these had to be made real. He had come down into this world knowing he might end up sacrificed. He had to get the wheels of his destiny moving. As a Screaming Eagle of the elite 101st Airborne, he had to be bad, truly bad to rid this country of evil; but as young Mikey he just wanted to do simple, good things involving love.

His mind was splitting in two. This is all crazy, he thought, in a place that had once held lunatics.

"Come," said Colette again, and she took him through another series of passageways and finally outside to the back of the house, into a large walled area.

"This was, er, the *cour de recreation* the er..."

"Playground," he added, to save her having to riffle through the words. She liked that book. She liked speaking English. Was probably preparing for when he took her home to Detroit.

The high walls were more suited to the exercise yard of a prison than any school. Moss and tall weeds pushed up between the uneven paving stones. On them was the residue of old painted crosses that marked out old and forgotten schoolyard games.

"*La porte du jardin,*" she nodded to the far wall. There, wedged between two very high and square posts that once held lamps in the top of each, was a large, ornate, wrought-iron gate of flaking green paint. Before it, was an ankle-deep pool of stagnant water caused by a faulty drain somewhere. A dead creature floated white and rotting just below the surface. Colette stood by the pool, beckoning with her eyes, but clutching the phrase book.

Suddenly the two dogs appeared from nowhere and started yapping and chasing each other around the yard.

"Nu! Geb! *Allez! Allez! Vous bêtes stupides. Stupides!*" She kicked them, full on and hard and wacked one with the book. They yelped back inside.

The contrast between her apparent gentility and her contempt for the animals took Horsett by surprise. *Tough little gal!* he thought. She had two sides to her as well.

Colette stepped around the scummy pool and indicated the big and rusting padlock that kept the gate firmly shut. She turned to Horsett, grinning, showing him him a secret. "I am strong," she said wickedly. "And I am clever!"

The padlock stayed where it was. She lifted the gate from its fishhook-like hinges and pushed it inward, creating enough space to squeeze through.

Aah! he winced as his leg caught the metal. No sympathy though.

"*Viens,*" she enticed, with widened eyes. "*Où peut-etre,* perhaps, *Venez* as you prefer, *hein*? Come…"

The maze of paths between hugely overgrown hedges showed the neglect of years. Storm-fallen branches that had never been cleared, lay rotting. A dove-cote that had once perched on a long pole now lay sprawled in the long grass. Its white paint was now yellowed and peeling, the wood cracked. Every growing thing gone to seed; the whole garden echoed with long sadness and shadows.

They came to another ornate iron gate, only waist height. Its swinging edge was buried into the gravel floor. Michael and Colette had to lift and push this one together.

"You sure like your gates, doors and locks in this place," he muttered.

"But it was a hospital. For er…what is the word?"

"Lunatics, Luc said."

"Luc? Pah! Do not listen at what he said."

"So he lied?"

"Yes – ah, *Non*. They were *imbeciles* and er, babies-not-wanted."

The gate screeched against some stone. Horsett looked around.

Colette smiled. "No-one for to hear. No-one for to see. Truly! Come…"

Shucks, why was he worried? He was a paratrooper, trained to bust down the Gates of Hell!

He found himself in the heart of garden he had glimpsed the previous day. Had it been tended, it might have been beautiful. There were yew trees and willows, pathways between once-low, once-ornamental hedges that had grown out of their topiary into bizarre, sinister shapes. Perhaps remembering the unloved and neglected humans that had been shepherded here.

"So where are they now, these *imbeciles*?"

She shrugged. "The Nazis took them. The old priest we had then, Father Romilly, showed them where to come. And also the Jews. We had a few Jews among the staff. They took them all away."

"Where?"

"Madagascar, I think. A camp. Astrid was *tres tres furieux*. She did a spell against that devil Romilly. He died of cancer last Christmas."

"A spell, huh?"

"You don't believe? Soon, she will make you believe."

"I can't wait," he said, squeezing the handle and shaft of the machine-gun again. It helped remind him of who he was, what he was.

Horsett looked across to the house, with all its shuttered windows and broken, red roof-tiles, and its blanked-out expression of security and hopelessness.

She stood behind, leaning against him. He could feel her tit against his arm. As he turned to try and kiss her, she pulled away, kept him at arm's length with both hands.

"Are all you American soldiers so strong?" she teased, looking him up and down with admiration.

"Hell, no. You just had to be sane, a little over five feet, weigh more'n a hundred and five pounds, have more'n twelve of your own teeth and no flat feet. Nearly half of the guys in the room with me failed to get enlisted."

Clearly, she didn't know what feet or pounds were and didn't care. She skipped away from his obvious desire. "Michael, look. The *fontaine*... is that the same word?"

"Fountain."

"Ah yes. Come. Look."

The fountain was a large saucer-like bowl some twenty feet across, with a thin central cone topped by a large, eight-pointed star. There were little thin dishes of increasing size all way down the cone, from which water would once have tumbled. Horsett, who didn't know any more about fountains than he did about dovecotes, thought it looked more like a radio receiver. The base of the bowl was filled with stagnant water , floating leaves, what might have been dead fish, a few pages of an old newspaper, plus the soggy remains of a children's story book about a camel with three humps.

Colette took off her shoes, raised her skirt and stepped up into the bowl, one foot in the shallows, one at right angles along the rim, bending to scoop up water with each palm. Letting it drip from her pale fingers. Watching as the sun turned the droplets into jewels.

Horsett sat himself on the brim of the bowl to ease up his leg and rubbed the bristles of his head with one hand. He enjoyed the feel, remembering by a process of tactile rhyming the rasp of Colette's bush that hadn't been Colette's at all.

"Michael, for me, is it possible to...?"

"Fix it."

"Ah *oui*. Fix it. Fix. For me?"

He was about to say *Sure* but the air above them exploded, two bursts in succession that almost blasted them off their feet as the two fighters scorched across the garden and over the low hill. German? Allied? Neither of them saw: the two machines were already gone.

"Did they see you?" she asked.

"Hey hey, at that height, at three hundred miles an hour, no, honey, they didn't see me."

She came close and sank against him. He couldn't help but note that this body was so different to that which he had held last night: less angular, softer, different smell. He liked this one too, just as much! "You scared the Krauts are gonna come and get me?"

"I am scared that the 'Krauts' *and* the Americans will come and take you."

He lightened up – and he melted. In God's holy name, this was a lot better than being a killing machine! The Screaming Eagle was becoming a dove. Was there any guy in the 101st who wouldn't swap with him now, or blame him?

"Listen Colette –"

"But they will not find you! No-one will find you. We are in *le val sans retour*."

"The valley of no return, huh?"

He pulled her to him, the machine-gun slung on his back, all the weight on his good leg. Tried to kiss her, use his tongue. Put his hand on her tit, which sure felt different to the last one he had felt. But she pushed him away, so that he almost overbalanced. He might have fallen backward into the curve of the fountain if he hadn't checked himself..

"Not yet, Michael. I am not ready." She said it smilingly. It was like the sun and the Morning Star shining at him.

"Colette, I –"

Shutters on the house groaned open. *Goddam but that place needed some lubricant!* They looked over to the upper level of the windows. Selene poked her head out and saw them, called them both to eat, like two children at play. She was annoyed about something. Again.

"Not *yet*, Michael," Colette said again, almost solemnly, as if the impending sex act between them was somehow arranged for a special time, for a sacred reason. "We must go in now."

Michael nodded and sighed. He'd been trained to kill and destroy; he hadn't been trained to love. Careful, careful, he didn't want to break anything. "Okay. Oh-*kaaaay*…"

36

Schimmel was also wincing at the sound of old, groaning metal. Only this was not caused by youngsters scraping open gates into a sylvan realm, but by a single old tank grinding slowly below his office, its gun facing to the rear. An almost obsolete *Panzerkampfwagen* I. The creature's engine retched as if it might break down at any moment. The walls of his office vibrated; the stuffed black dog that for some reason was the late Mayor's pride and joy, seemed to shiver into life. He stared down at the olive and brown steel monster, his palms flat against the window, his peaked cap rattling against the pane like a small woodpecker.

His mood had plunged into chasms he had not known existed. Somehow he had to climb back up again, using the footholds of Duty and Vengeance. And also with the help of the little Pervitin tablets he had been taking, that combat soldiers – real soldiers – used to keep awake. He unscrewed the cap from the little metal tube, removed the wad of cotton wool and took another two. '*Vorsicht!*'[1] it said on its label.

He looked down from his office window to the mess of roads converging on Neuilly's centre. The southbound road, as it entered the town square, was actually called the Street of the Bottle. It was wide enough for two cars, for much of its length, then narrowed considerably before it entered the *Place de Soleil*. It was just wide enough at that point for one tank, no larger than a *Panzerkampfwagen* II, to scrape itself through into the square while ripping up the walls of the buildings at either side.

There, where old men used to play *boules*, or gossip on wide benches, were scenes of bubbling chaos: every square centimetre seemed filled with belching, armoured vehicles. None of the men were sure if the Normandy beaches were just a diversion, with the real invasion being pitched at the *Pas de Calais*.

Should the approaching *panzer* divisions go north-north west? – or full throttle for the north-east? Either way, large numbers of soldiers and machines just had to go through his domain of Neuilly-sur-Fronds, while small numbers of higher ranked officers

---

[1] Caution!

were unable to decide which way.

Some of his own men were down there, directing the increasingly dense military traffic. The town was in danger of becoming clogged in the four converging streets. If any of the Allied fighter-bombers were to overfly this now…

Schimmel grimaced. He thought of how the regular army dared to call his men, the *Feldgendarmes*, the *feldmäuse* – fieldmice! Well these fieldmice were quietly, without any fuss, making sure that the *Wehrmacht* was not going to get harvested before their time.

He opened one of the windows and shouted down to the street: "Make them swing!"

His two Frenchmen were standing in front of the three corpses swinging from the lamp-posts, clearly marked with the signs: DESERTER, TRAITOR, DESERTER. They looked up, but pretended not to hear. He made allowance for the dreadful noises made by the vehicles and the frightened teams of horses behind, pulling cannon. The town was full of horses; the *Wehrmacht* couldn't function without them, even if their propaganda films, the weekly *Wochenschau* newsreels, made it seem as if everything was mechanised.

"Swing them!" he shouted again, and mimed the effect he wanted.

Young Lueur took the feet of the First Deserter and swung it against the Traitor, whose arc made the Second Deserter bounce, like a macabre Newton's Cradle. The young man was excited by his first taste of killing. He would go far. In sharp contrast Le Blanc helped, but half-heartedly. Schimmel would have to discipline him soon. Or just shoot him.

They still hadn't found the monster who had murdered his son. He shook when he thought of Dieter, with the sort of trembling that was not far removed from First Love. He felt sick with guilt and tried once more to summon up just a few warm, loving memories of them together. But this paternal failure steamed up his thoughts like his breath on the window.

"*Ils se balancent!*"[1] cried the young man below with delight, pushing the body from the side, avoiding the shit, building up the momentum.

---

[1] They are swinging!

Schimmel bestowed him a sort of *Continue* gesture with his hand, which came across like a spastic Hitler salute. He allowed his gaze to travel upwards: from the shit at the bottom of the lamp-posts, over and across the roof tops of the old and rickety houses and their chimneys. Beyond, he could see the dark clouds toward the distant coast and wondered what might be coming at him from that direction. In truth, although he had always affected regret that he had been posted to this backwater with his second-rate men, inwardly he had thanked his Aryan God.

It had been Der Bomber who did the dirty work usually, while he, Schimmel, looked on impassively. Outwardly he showed an officer's respect and indulgence for Der Bomber. Inside, he was afraid of the squat wretch, felt inferior as a fighting man, and horrified by his tales of the Russian Front. Sometimes, when Schimmel gave them his orders, the little man looked at him oddly. He was sure that Der Bomber could see right into him, and knew there wasn't much inside. Yet he wanted nothing more than to become an 'old hare' like him – a veteran sprightly enough to stay alive.

In the narrows below, one of the horses went berserk. It couldn't escape anywhere because of the monstrous machines roaring before and behind, but crashed back and forth between the cold iron of the vehicles, gashing itself open so that blood poured over its flanks and over the two young soldiers trying to restrain it, flinging them against the walls.

Schimmel took his *Schmeisser*, opened the window wide, leaned out, and called down to the *landsers* to step aside. The horse wedged itself into an angle between the cannon and the house opposite, and bobbed up and down as if on a wave. He fired a short burst into its head and watched it collapse. One of the two soldiers, who had an affection for the beast, clearly mouthed *Etappenschweine!*[1] up at Schimmel but he let that pass.

He loved horses! He used to take his children riding. And when he had joined the *Feldgendarmerie* he had been assigned to duty with them. He was ordered to determine the logistics of how four thousand horses and their handlers could be shipped across the Channel for one infantry division alone. A very important task, he was told, because they could not get the equipment up the

---

[1] Rear swine. A term of scorn for rear service troops.

beaches without them.

As it was, the Invasion of England known as *Unternehmen Seelöwe[1]*, had been called off – to his immense relief – and so he was sent back to his normal duties of controlling humans and their traffic.

He closed the window without looking out at the result of his action. The black dog still shook from the vibrations of the traffic. He removed the glass case, grabbed the beast, and threw it out of the window under the tracks of any tank that might squeeze by. Then, clutching the crucifix under his gorget, he went back to the big map...

---

[1] Operation Sea Lion

37

Hours later the square was still full of dark shapes. Men, machines and horses, all surging in one direction in the last rays before sunset. Guided by the evening-shift of *Feldgendarmes* who used flashlights with narrow slits. The muttering of the common soldiers was a babbling river: rippling peaks of excitement, troughs of great worry, whirlpools of confusion. Still they flowed through.

In the high buildings around the square, uniformed men drew curtains and closed shutters like good little *hausfrau*, ready for the complete blackout. Now that Allied fighter-bombers had been seen in the vicinity, everyone was determined that *their* light would not call down the fires from above.

No-one challenged the naturally dark shape of Father Fournier as he put the short ladder against the lamp-posts. Then, with the help of Luc, cut down the stinking corpses one by one. Each made a sort of hollow sound on the paving like dumped rolls of carpet. The passing soldiery, or those creaking past in their vehicles, had more obvious things to worry about.

They heaved the three corpses unceremoniously into a narrow handcart. The bodies were too heavy, and the two men were not strong enough to be decorous. Later, away from this cauldron and in the peace of his church, Fournier would do what was spiritually necessary for them. Meanwhile he tore into shreds the placards they had worn and flung the pieces into the road. Over the years, he had had invisible but highly readable placards of a different sort fastened around his own neck. He hated to see these wretches labelled, as much as he hated to see them murdered.

Across the square, a few elderly citizens of Neuilly, hurrying home before the 8pm curfew, pulled up sharp at the sight of Father Fournier: they had heard he had been shot. Wondering whether they were witnessing a ghost, a small and local resurrection, or just the result of bad gossip, they crossed themselves and melted off down narrow alleys.

As the pair grabbed the long handles of the cart and turned it on its axis to head off down a tight passageway to the church, Luc felt someone grab his shoulder from behind. Fingers dug in like a claw and turned him around. He froze. Thought he was about to be rounded up in a *rafle*, which was when the Gestapo would appear, arrest any young man on any pretext and send them to work as forced labour in Germany.

"Who gave you permission to do this!" snarled *Oberschutze* Henri Lueur.

Luc might have spoken. He might have gone into the deferential mode that was necessary when your identity papers were not exactly accurate. But Fournier pushed him aside as forcefully as the young policeman had done.

Lueur was startled. He too had thought that *Hauptmann* Schimmel had shot the man, yet here he was. Also, he had been brought up as a good Catholic by pious and stuffy parents, and had all those added elements of guilt in being a Frenchman wearing a German uniform in Occupied France.

"Do you have permission from up there?" he asked, rather than demanded, somewhat unsettled by the mad way the man was staring at him. He nodded up to the high window where Schimmel had his headquarters.

Father Fournier followed his gaze and gave a sour smile. "I take *my* permissions from a higher source than that. Now go back and fight your stupid war."

The priest took up the shafts again and headed on his way without a backward glance.

Luc stood there, rooted to the spot, marvelling at the man's nerve but not having authority within himself to match it. He was embarrassed by the shit on his hands and clothing.

"I am sorry officer," he said. "Father Fournier...he is...well, forgive him."

Lueur, who looked unsteady without his *troop* around him, shone his torch into Luc's face. *"Schwichtl..."* he muttered, wrinkling his nose in disgust as he strode away, as if on great and urgent business.

Luc had never heard that actual word before, but he had been called many things in the past in just that scornful tone, and so he just knew that it meant faggot. *"Merci, Monsieur. Merci beaucoup,"* he whispered to the disappearing shape.

38

Selene handed Michael a glass of dark liquid: "Take. Drink. The pain will go…" she said, standing behind him as he sat at the table There was an emptied plate of food before him, placed just in front of his Tommy gun. The candles around the room flickered, bringing spasms of life to the many stuffed creatures.

He had been well fed. No austerity here. The dogs were in their baskets by the door. The old clock ticked and tutted. Colette and Astrid stood side by side, arms linked affectionately, watching and approving everything he did or said. But his leg ached and raged. Tried not to show it. The guys on the beachheads would be knowing worse than this.

The drink – whatever it was – started to take effect. Damn fine herbs in that garden! Selene dragged her fingers over the stubble on his head, massaging. It felt so good; and the drink was making him so woozy, there must have been liquor in it. He'd ask them later. What day was this? "*Quel jour il est?*" he asked with deliberately bad French.

They smiled. Shrugged.

"*Vendredi? Samedi?*" he persisted.

They beamed, as if it were a silly question. As if he had been here for months, and had just come out of a deep coma. Maybe he had!

"God…" he sighed.

"*Detendez-vous, n'ayez pas peur,*" Selene soothed, a warm voice at the back of his head, a clever touch on his scalp. Her hands smelled of something antiseptic, maybe from all the taxidermy. Or maybe just from the herbs they seemed to use on their food.

Despite the unfamiliar accent, so different to the pure tones of his *maman* back home, he knew she had told him to relax. Not to be afraid. His Mom had also whispered that to him when Pa came home drunk and started a fight, and left them quivering. It was their secret language, the *langue* of their *love*, his Mom had said, stroking his hair, shushing him. *Ne pleure pas.* She always smiled, always told him there was nothing to worry about. All would come well – even though he knew she was crying inside. From the age of five, he had always wanted to kill his Pa. When they did bayonet practice in training he always visualized *Père* Horsett. His fierce War Face wasn't entirely an act.

But just now he was feeling good, and he shut those memories out. Here he was with these women and they weren't hurting him none. Hell, it was just like one of those Parisian cathouses that the guys would josh about. He felt normal in that respect. For a brief moment, when he thought of those fabled establishments and remembered that his Mom had come from Paris, he had a surge of horror.

"Ssh…" whispered Selene, stroking his brow as if she had seen the thought. A door in his brain closed, he was safe again.

This is weird, he thought, not fighting it. Hell, all three of them were weird. Even Colette.

Astrid came over and touched his shoulder. *"Tournez,"* she said, so he spun to one side on his chair to face her, and she used her knees to force his own knees apart so she could stand nearer. He winced from the sudden contact on his wounded leg. She gave that contemptuous *bof!* sound again and put the first and second fingers of each hand on his temples, while Selene continued with the stroking.

Horsett swallowed hard. He was close to the woman's fine, hard body, remembering being even closer, in the darkness, in the silent rapture. He closed his eyes, knowing that Colette was watching; he didn't want to know if she knew. Just then his whole mind was woozy, his whole body relaxing, the pain simply ebbing away.

This was insane. This was excellent.

"Your 'men' are coming tomorrow, for their silly little war games."

He frowned, but Selene's fingers smoothed it away. *War games, sure they were. Weren't they all just playing?*

"Vous les enverrez loin."

"I will what to them?" – though he knew exactly what she had said.

"Tell them for to go," added Colette. "Er, send them away."

"Huh!?" His eyes opened. Selene closed them, gently, while Astrid's touch upon his temples continued, her fingers agitating gently, drawing little soothing spirals that seemed to go clear down into his head.

"You will send them away. We have important things to do."

Impor…impor.. .imp..? He kept his eyes closed and allowed his words to fade away. He relaxed in the chair, and seemed to be floating above himself, into a cloud. So much like those clouds he had so often plummeted through in his training. Yet it felt as if he was falling upward, into a dazzling darkness. Everything became distant, and nothing related to him, Screaming Eagle who had broken wings.

"*Que voyez-vous?*" asked Colette eagerly, and Horsett was vaguely aware and dozily wondering why she used the '*vous*' form toward Astrid.

"*Crotte!*[1] I see…I see…" It was Astrid's turn to frown. "I see closed doors! But I cannot open them."

"Then he belongs here, surely, among our own closed doors," muttered Selene.

Astrid tried again, while Michael's head just lolled back and he sighed with pleasure.

Colette removed his boots. He didn't object. When she stroked his feet with her hair, he smiled and sighed, and couldn't understand why the two older women gave little claps as if she'd done something clever.

"*Allez au lit maintenant,*" Selene whispered, into the crown of his head, her lips slightly brushing against the stubble of his hair.

Sure, sure…Go to bed. Now. Sure he would. He was just so damned relaxed it was almost a sin…

---

[1] Turd!

39

In the priest's house, in the small priest's bed with the priest himself, Luc asked: "Why did you look at me so fiercely?" As he asked, he smoothed his hand over what he knew was the frazzled skin of the lightning-flash, and felt the other man tense and then relax, before finally accepting the touch. With a sort of gasping noise, like a death-rattle.

"When?" asked the priest.

"Before you kissed me. Before you extinguished the candle. You glared, as if you hated me."

"I hate myself," said Gilles Fournier, looking into the darkness, sighing at the delightful touch of another human being on what was surely his own personal Mark of Cain.

"What we do is not wrong," answered Luc sadly, turning onto his back to share the other man's stare into the Stygian night. He spoke to the world beyond as much to the person next to him.

"It *is* wrong. And it is wrong for me. I have an obligation to observe perfect and perpetual continence for the sake of the Kingdom of Heaven."

"What is the point?"

In the darkness, the older man's breaths sounded like the turning pages of an inner rule book. Luc could almost see his lover's mind dipping into his memory, finding the words by which he tried to live.

"Celibacy is a special gift of God, by which sacred ministers can more easily remain close to Christ with an undivided heart, and can dedicate themselves more freely to the service of God and their neighbour."

"You have learned that by heart. You don't believe it."

"I must!"

They lay side by side, in the night, listening to what might have been distant rolling thunder in previous weeks, but was really the huge voice of The Landing, creeping ever closer, ready to change all things for all time.

Luc's hand sought out that of Gilles – he refused to think of him as just 'the priest'. For a moment the fingers of the older man flicked away, but then they crept back, like a spider, and he sighed.

"Tell me what you did today," Luc encouraged, drawing him out like a parent would a child.

"I cleaned my shoes, and shaved. I said the Divine Office. I celebrated Mass. I anointed a sick woman who will soon die. I proclaimed the Gospel to a German, and visited four housebound women. I mended the puncture on my bicycle. I ate a simple meal. I prayed."

"What did you pray for?"

"For you. And me. But mainly for me to be a good man, and brought to a god end."

"Do you mean for us?"

"There can be no 'us'. You know that."

Luc sighed. He had taken enough money from English gentry, and seen enough of their increasing bravery when it came to their desires, to hope that a change would come to the world. And that the love, which they all said 'dare not speak its name' would one day shout it loudly.

Large aircraft flew over. He knew from their engines they were not German. The old red tiles on the roof shook and tinkled.

"They are suffering in Caen," he mused, not having any idea of what it would be like to be bombarded.

Then he thought of Michael Horsett, left with those madwomen in the old asylum, and Astrid's frequent use of that odd phrase from Rabelais: "*Fay çe que voudras.*" Which, as far as she was concerned, explained or justified everything. She would be doing with the big tough paratrooper what *she* wanted – her and the *covine*. He was infatuated with the outwardly beautiful Michael, but then they all were in their differing ways. Yet he *truly* loved the inner beauty and lion heart of this man next to him.

"What are you thinking?" asked Gilles Fournier, who was good at sensing other peoples' moods even if he couldn't regulate his own.

"Nothing."

"Liar. Would you hold me again?"

Luc jiggled in the bed and put his arm around the other, who sighed and curled up under the embrace like a little boy. Fournier would, he knew, punish himself and probably Luc also tomorrow, when the guilt rose with the dawn. In the meantime ... "Are you afraid of the nightmare?"

There was a long silence.

"I am afraid of the Thing itself. The nightmare is merely a portent..."

"*La Chose*...is it a woman?"

"No – Or perhaps yes! It is not male, or female."

"Tell me what this Thing is." Luc could feel the priest tense when he asked this, as if the memory brought things nearer.

"It is evil. It is a devil – perhaps *the* devil. When I was a child of three, sleeping in my mother's bed, I was aware of it in the darkness beyond. It had no shape or form, but it made me shake with fear."

"Did it have a face?"

"*Non*. But I know it can appear as male, female, both, or neither. It can appear as a black snake, fox, crow or jackal."

"Then the thing you fear so much can appear as almost anything!"

The priest withdrew slightly. There was a hint – a tincture of disbelief – in the way Luc said that.

"Does it have a name, Gilles?" said Luc, sensing this, and drawing the other man to him until he relaxed.

"I named it *Le Noirceur*. A silly name, meaning nothing very much, perhaps, but I felt if I could name it I might be able to control it. I think exorcists do this. Yet I felt that *It* looked at me, as if this great fetid cloud beyond the window knew me. I could never sleep unless all the doors and the windows were closed, no matter how hot it was. That is why I like the blackout now."

"Did it speak, somehow?"

"Not in words. But it seemed to say: *I am coming nearer, with every bad thing you do. One day we will meet...*"

"Is that day soon?"

"Yes. Absolutely. It is my destiny, given by God."

The older man's voice was so despairing that Luc cuddled him firmly and wrapped the blankets tightly, sealing all the gaps.

"Don't be afraid," said Luc, who had little belief in the otherworld, but much hatred for the present. Especially the Germans who'd killed his mother, and all the devils in hell that seemed to be fighting for the very soul of distant Caen.. "Sleep, and wake up pure. You *are* a good man."

40

The drink that Selene had given Michael before bed was taking effect now, in the darkness. He could feel the pain in his leg ebbing away, and the slow, wicked bliss which filled every part of his body. He sighed. That was good hooch. Who said war was hell? In his case, here among the women, that was pure baloney. *His* war was goddamned good! The Big Guy in the Sky, that some of his buddies talked about, had made him land in just the right place. Those flyguys in the Air Corps were ace!

Beyond the horizon, toward the sea, carried on the wind like sprites, came the grunting and groaning sounds of German artillery. Especially the thin eerie shrieking of the six-barrelled rocket-launchers that the guys called Screaming Meemies. He'd seen them on newsreels, in a different world to this. Here, they were thin and distant banshees. While outside among the trees, wholly unconcerned by a world at war, two owls called back and forth: *ouh ouh...*

He lay there atop the bed listening, fully clothed. Too goofed to undress himself. For the first time he didn't give a damn that he wasn't out there with his buddies. At that moment he was not a Screaming Eagle: he was a small parakeet, quiet in its cage, trying to put his head under his own wing and go to sleep.

Despite the overlay of noise, he still would not have heard the latch of the door open. It was done so cannily. There was no light within the house, yet he felt the difference in the air again. And he was certain that something small and light leapt up on the bed and didn't move. Hell, if that stupid cat wanted to watch, what did he care?

Then the human weight as someone came into the room and sat on his bed. The finger on his lips once more enjoining him to silence, utter silence, as his visitor undressed him with slow movements, putting his clothes silently down on the floor after folding them. He knew that from the air currents too. He tried to touch her, but she brushed his hand away, until she was ready.

And boy was he ready! The main thing the guys in his troop had hoped for was at least a couple of wall jobs with some willing whores, but this – this was heaven. This healed all sorts of agonies and doubts. He was a cocksman, damn sure.

She stood next to him and undressed herself as silently. He could feel the little flicks of air as her clothes were removed and put aside, oh so carefully.

As the bare, cool body curled against his, careful to avoid his injured leg, he knew right off that it wasn't Astrid. It wasn't because of the slightly fuller flesh, and the meatier limbs. Or the different size of her breasts, the broader nipples and texture of the hair. Nor was it the differing use of her tongue... It was the smell of her hands, the strange medicines and chemicals she utilised during the day. This was certainly Selene.

Jesus he thought, but he let her take him anyway. Then when she was astride him she didn't move, not a twitch. Just stayed there as if she was soaking up the pleasure. As if she hadn't had a whole lot of that for a long while and wanted the moment to last. And when she did move it was slowly, squeezing him, pressing hard against him as if she thought their flesh could melt into each other. She wasn't as skillful as Astrid, but she was more intense, and if he could have seen her face he knew it would have looked frantic.

Mon dieu, he heard her whisper, in the tiniest and tinniest of voices, lips so close to his ear.

Sure honey, whatever you say, he thought, taking the deepest of breaths and reaching up to cup her breasts. Knowing that he had the damnedest smile that no-one but himself could ever know about.

41

While all these sexual encounters, battles and skirmishes were going on in St Martin's, and the priest's bedroom in Neuilly, Horsett's 'white bread troops' were out in the darkness sliding the bodies of two German soldiers into the river. They had made sure that everything useful had been plundered from the corpses, starting with their excellent boots and ending with their Mauser rifles. They had to prod one of them with a branch to make it break free of the shallows and float off down toward the town.

Thibault fancied himself as a joker. He had once marched behind his column along the the *Voie Sacrée* – 'The Sacred Way' - that connected Bar-le-Duc to the vast killing fields of Verdun, going *Bêê Bêê – we're sheep to the slaughter*. Now, he put a lighted candle in each of the helmets and floated them off while the other two were manhandling the corpses.

"*Stupide*," said Armand, breathing heavily, as the little metal coracles bobbed in the water after their owners; but the deed was done and they needed to get away.

Too exhausted to speak, they went silently along wooded trails, using the flashlights they had plundered when they knew that no-one was likely to see. Besides, judging from the distant sounds of a truly serious and unending battle, two dead soldiers and their candled helmets were hardly likely to be priorities for the *Wehrmacht*.

They came to the back of Jules' home: a battered old former bakery with a leaking roof, many mice and two dead bread ovens. He secured the doors and made sure everything was blacked-out. Then he lit an oil lamp, as they grabbed chairs and crashed down around the table. They looked at each other, and their blood-stained clothes, with their booty before them.

As one, they roared with laughter. They thumped the table and stamped on the floor and made nonsense noises with their lips. They were teenagers again; they acted as if they had just had sex with their headmaster's daughters.

"Ah that was good!"

"They squealed like kittens, hey, like kittens!"

"Pieces of shit."

"Dirty little Fritz-whores."

"We did it! We are not too old. Like *this…!*" from Thibault as he mimed the stabbing with a clenched empty hand, that was like masturbating.

Shaking from excitement, Jules poured them wine into cracked cups. Despite what he often implied to outsiders, he had not served in *La Grande Guerre* as had the others; the killing he had helped do tonight had made a man of him at last. And they had been German soldiers, armed, so he never thought of it as murder, and the other two had done the messy bits anyway. "Very easy, very easy…"

"*Mon Dieu,* but it was easy," agreed Armand, raising a glass. "And that bitch Astrid…her curse didn't work on me, hey!" He flexed his bicep like a little boy, showing off his strength.

"Was it too easy?" cautioned Thibault. But they heard the distant cannon and the droning bombers and they allowed themselves to be swept along on the current of victory. "But it was *good…* I had forgotten how delicious it was to kill the Boche."

Armand almost crooned: "Superb. Not having the Germans shelling us with their cowardly *surpalite.*[1] To be in the woods, above the ground, and not half-buried in the shit of the trenches."

The two old soldiers started singing, softly, their old favourite: *Il y a loin à Tipperary.* Followed by a *Ba-ba-ba-BOM!* in laughing unison.

"Hey hey, I heard a great joke," said Jules feeling excluded again. "Two people whispering: 'Do you know what happened near Neuilly at 9.20 pm? A Jew killed a German soldier, cut out his heart and ate it,' said one. Then the other one replied: 'Impossible, for three reasons: A German has no heart. A Jew eats no pork. And at 9.20 everyone is listening to the BBC'." He laughed loudly, repeated the final line again, but they were scarcely listening, reliving their triumph.

"Armand, we must tell the *Ami,*" said Jules again, touching his brother's arm to bring him back down from his clouds of glory.

"Do you think he will care?"

Armand and Thibault shared looks: there were clearly some things that they had discussed together.

---

[1] Diphosgene gas shells.

"Is there something I should know?"

"Perhaps he is not what he seems," ventured Thibault, speaking into the depths of his cup.

"What are you saying? He is a spy?"

Jules' voice shook with horror. Pictures stormed across his brow: all the things he had said to the *Ami*; all the things that could happen because of it.

"No, not a spy..."

"A traitor?"

"*Non, non...*"

"Then what? What?!"

"Perhaps he is not the man we hoped for," suggested Thibault, mildly.

"I agree," said Armand, inspecting the captured Mauser's bolt action with an expert's eye, and comparing it unfavourably with his beloved sniper rifle from the trenches. "He came to us like one of those priest-kings that old Father Romilly bored us about. Yet I begin to think he is just a child. He has never heard the drumfire, the endless noise of countless cannon. *Il n'a jamais fait Verdun*, as we say. He doesn't even shave, and is younger than Luc. He is a little 'green.'"

"He is *very* green," added Thibault reaching for the bottle, wiping his nose on his sleeve.

"A green man."

"I don't know what you mean," said Jules, who had never fought in a real war and was exasperated and suddenly afraid.

"Perhaps," said Thibault, with a gleam in his eye, "we're going to get covered in shit."

"*Eh, bien*," said Armand the Hero, "he might be the saving of us all, or the death of us all..."

42

Dawn. The Germans made the two Frenchmen in their troop wade through the marsh and into the shallows of the river. Ducks fled with loud wing-beats, making noises eerily similar to laughing, as the men plunged to where the corpse lay face down in the water. The Germans sat on the bank and watched, amused by the way the outsiders tried to hide their humiliation at being given the dirty jobs again.

"He's got a mouth like an arse," said Gunther, looking at Le Blanc's pinched face.

"And the *bubi* is wondering that maybe he chose the wrong side after all," said Der Bomber, who had seen the Russian Nazi-sympathisers do the same at Stalingrad.

Henri the *bubi* and Yohan the drunk looked at each other, took deep breaths and waded deeper. They pushed aside some floating rubbish to reach the white hand of the body and pulled it toward the bank, where Schimmel waited impatiently.

It was Henri who did the hard work, seeking to earn points. He gritted his teeth against the feel of cold, dead, wet flesh and heaved it toward solid ground. The water in the puffed-out uniform made glupping noises. It was Yohan who grabbed the floating helmet that had stuck in reeds, and tried to control his shaking hand while offering it up to Schimmel with the observation: "There is a candle in it. It is burning…"

As Henri tried to turn the corpse on its back. he overbalanced and fell backward into the shallows. The men started laughing.

Schimmel was in no mood for this. "Get in there!" he ordered Gunther and Albert. "Help him. Get the body out."

So they did. When they turned the bloated, sodden lump over it was obvious from the cut throat and stab wounds that it was the victim of simple murder rather than honest war.

Schimmel looked upstream. The dark, black-green River Fronds flowed north and snaked slightly west, eventually reaching the sea and the beaches where all the fighting was taking place. When the sky was clear you could see the distant dots of aircraft above that horizon, like shifting midges in a summer haze. If this body had floated down then it meant there was a killer – perhaps his son's killer – loose *behind* their lines: or else the local *maquis* had found their balls at last.

"*JABO!*" cried Der Bomber, for the second time that morning. The branches of the trees were blasted by the downdraft, creating a shrapnel of leaves. It was over them and past before they could even react. They saw the black crosses on the wing and smiled.

These low-flying planes seemed to arrive with no warning, just exploding into their immediate sky and disappearing again. Despite the shock, they were encouraged by this. Nothing, surely, would get through the Atlantic defences that Rommel himself had approved. The Allies were being crushed on the anvil at Caen. The *Panzer* divisions were on their way. The *Feldgendarme*s would guide them.

Schimmel never moved. The burning candle inside the helmet had been snuffed out by the fighter-bomber's turbulence. He looked deeply into the metal bowl, as if seeing the future and the past. When the men dragged the body to his feet, the officer gave no more than a cursory glance; he was totally lost to the world and its war. With the edge of a small clasp knife he removed the candle and its base of molten wax and put it carefully on the hood of the vehicle. His face so intense that he was clearly on the brink of a revelation. Almost frantically, he unfolded his large map and prepared to work something through.

"Lueur...measure fifty metres upstream from this point, and when I tell you float the helmet down. I want to time it."

The rest of them smirked and stood under the nearby trees, smoking, as the soaked young *bubi* squelched his way to the required spot and did as he was told. As a good soldier must.

"Now!" cried Schimmel, looking at the second hand of his watch.

The helmet floated slowly, rocking slightly, bumping into branches, but made a stately sort of progress down to where it had been retrieved. Schimmel looked at his watch and made notes in a small notepad.

"Right," he said, "I need to do some research with this candle."

Der Bomber frowned. His presence was such that even his commanding officer felt obliged to explain.

"By determining how long this candle was when it was first lit – presumably at the same time and place this wretch was murdered – then I can work out how long it has burned and by the speed of the flow, how far up the river this occurred."

They all frowned even more, but he was oblivious. He measured the remaining candle, estimated its original size from the melted wax that had been at its base, then relit it and timed its rate of burn.

Schimmel watched the flame as if it were an echo of those fires that had consumed his son. Meanwhile his men moved further back under the cover of the trees and enjoyed their day.

"Clever man," said Yohan, dully, who could think of nothing beyond his need for alcohol.

"Dumm…" said Der Bomber. "Why does he need his stupid maps?"

"To find out where the killer is!" offered Henri, soaked and unhappy, with as much of an edge as he dared.

"In a minute he will make us march upriver. All that shit with the candle…Look at him: he looks like a *wahrsagerin.*"

Henri and Yohan looked blank.

"Someone who tells fortunes," helped out Fat Uli, who had been a librarian until the excitement of bombing Poland inspired him to join up.

"All that shit with the map and candle," Der Bomber persisted. "He thinks he's a detective instead of a traffic policeman. In five minutes he'll decide that the murder happened a kilometre up that way."

"He's not calculating things, he is brooding," said Alfred Dunkel, who had lost two brothers in North Africa, and recognised the absorption.

"At least we aren't doing traffic duty in Neuilly," said Gunther, squeezing the water from his trouser legs. "It was mad there yesterday." He had been a garage mechanic before the war, and had a wife and two small girls that he dreamed about. As he looked sadly at the white, bloated, cold-as-a-dead-fish countryman, he noticed something odd about the helmet. He took it toward the corpse and measured it for size without touching the body.

The field radio in the wagon crackled into life. They all knew it was the *Generalleutnant* himself trying to contact *Hauptmann* Schimmel. Demanding to know where he was.

"Ignore it," said Uli, leaning over into the vehicle to inspect the device. "That was Schimmel's orders to me. 'Our mission comes before traffic duty'. That's what he said." Uli did things with dials that would make the person at the other end believe there was no signal in that area.

Henri looked at Gunther and the way he was gingerly putting the helmet to the corpse's head.

"Have you noticed," said Gunther, "that this helmet is far too small for him? That means…"

Henri leapt up and hurried over to Schimmel, interrupting his calculations. "Sir… the helmet is too small for the corpse. That could mean–"

"Another body, sir!" cried Uli, stealing Henri's thunder, who saw the second corpse floating slowly toward them.

This one came conveniently toward the solid part of the bank and presented itself for inspection.

"Same as the other," said Schimmel, almost happily. He had now found a double justification for ignoring all attempts to use his whole troop for traffic duties, in and around the congested lanes of Neuilly-sur-Fronds. "Now…we will follow the banks and look out for anything suspicious. I calculate that they must have been murdered a kilometre and perhaps a little more in that direction. Look out for anything that might suggest a parachutist."

As Schimmel forged ahead, Der Bomber gave the rest of them his *I-told-you-so* look, and helped pull the second corpse onto dry ground. They left the bodies face down, not wanting to see omens of their own future in the dead and staring eyes.

"Arse-licker…" whispered Gunther to Henri.

"*We* know what you are," added Fat Uli.

Henri Lueur shouldered his Schmeisser and squelched ahead to be with the *Hauptmann*, leaving watery footprints as he went.

"He is not *my* friend," said Yohan to the others, shivering from a need that had nothing to do with his sodden uniform.

43

Michael was in the walled garden again, next to the broken fountain, soaking up the sun. His leg was still aching; he needed the staff even more. He figured he must have cracked a couple of ribs too and wanted another shot of that stuff that Astrid had given him. Colette was wearing a thin green dress and twirling two sticks with long ribbons on the end, making strange patterns in the air. He had never seen anything like that, the way she stepped in and out of spirals, laughing, flashing her bare legs, light as a breeze.

There was something childlike about her at that moment. He didn't know whether to use his charmed or scornful face – though he sure did wonder what she looked like naked. Michael, who had had two women and was confident of getting, the third and best, felt pretty damned 'old' just then. His Pa, he was sure, had never had this success during his own time in France. He hoped the guy was up there looking down, jealous as hell.

"You are sad. What are you thinking?" Colette asked, pausing from her twirling, slightly breathless and red-faced.

He was wondering if what Luc had said about her being a bit mad was true. Seeing her dancing around the overgrown garden like this made him wonder. "Not sad, confused."

"Why?"

He had to stop himself thinking of that syrup. Then: "I don't know where I am," he countered after a long pause. It sounded lame, even to himself.

"But the map! We show you the map!"

"It's not that!" he snapped. "Listen, honey, I put my career on hold to join up and save the world. I spent a year training for this invasion, this 'landing' as you call it. It was in my head all the time, me and the guys, fighting the krauts, doing our job. The planning, the training, the night drops over England. We had to crawl through ditches filled with the innards of dead animals to get used to what we might have to do. We had the day drops. The night drops. The combat training, fitness training… And yet here I am in a garden where everything is overgrown, where nothing works, with three…women – and that darned cat – watching me while I do nothing. Nothing!"

That was largely true. There was another side of it, though, which he himself didn't fully understand: that all this was meant to be. Somehow. As if he himself was just a small part of some drama being controlled by an unseen director. Colette clearly didn't understand all his words, but got the gist of his tone and smiled. That irritated him more.

The Matagot appeared and sat on the path, watching him. He limped over and stroked it. The beast closed its eyes and purred. When Colette approached and tried to do the same it hissed and disappeared into the bushes.

"Ugliest cat I ever saw," Horsett muttered.

"But you see!" said Colette. "The Matagot knows you. You belong here." She turned the back of her head to him and took up the ribbons again and started skipping between their arcs, as if all things had been resolved.

"Will you come back to the States with me?"

She laughed, and carried on dancing. "I do not want to spend my life with a soldier."

"Honey, I'm only doing this for the war. I'm not a paratroop all the time!"

She paused. Looked surprised.

Horsett was annoyed. She just didn't get it. Maybe Luc was right. "Look, my buddies in the airborne all got regular jobs; plumbers, pool hall attendants, mechanics, electricians."

"And you?"

"I'm a student. I want to be a great teacher."

She looked at him as if he was teasing. He conjured a red rose from behind her left ear and white from behind her right. He had plucked them earlier and concealed them. A simple conjure. She squealed with delight. "Seriously Colette, this paratrooper *uniform*, ain't skin. When the fighting is done we all take our uniforms off and become human again."

"What do you say to me, Michael? That I must take your uniform off?"

He put the machine-gun down and sighed. He would never have dared do that during his training, or in the days before The Fall. Then, it had been a part of him. Now, he felt a little stupid carrying it. He placed it next to the much-thumbed English-French dictionary that went everywhere with them. The damned book was almost like a chaperone. When he tried to grab her tit, or just have a kiss, she'd find a reason to flick through the pages for another word. He wondered what the French for 'cock teaser' was. It was not the sort of term he could have learned from his Mom. Maybe his old pa had thought the same about his Mom when — as he told it — he'd rescued her from the back-streets of Paris?

"Colette," Horsett said, beckoning her over, determined to get a kiss and maybe fool around at first base.

"We are being watched," she hissed from the corner of her mouth, but laughing, as if she could read his mind.

He turned and looked back at the house.

Astrid and Selene were peering out from separate upstairs windows. They each gave him little discreet waves, with their hands scarcely higher than their waists, neither aware of the other.

Pain shot through his leg. It made him think again of that syrup. It had to be morphine? He wanted more. "Colette…that drink that Astrid gives me. What is it?"

"Ah. It is the *herbe d'or*.

"Golden herb, yeah I got that. What sort of herb?"

She shrugged. "When Astrid gathers it, she does so wearing a white dress, and with bare feet washed clean, without using a knife, her right hand wrapped in silk, after offering bread and wine to all those present."

"What?"

"It is a remedy against all evil," she offered, shrugging, acting out the postures Astrid used for gathering the herb.

There was an old green-metal bench almost engulfed by the shrubbery on three sides, its frame patterned with serpents that writhed and locked to form the back and arms. He sat down and stretched his leg, glad that he was now out of sight. "I don't get it with you women. Are you supposed to be witches or something? Luc says you're all crazy."

Her face fell, then brightened again. "And Luc, he says that you are a very bad man. Is that true also?"

His face fell, and remained in a glower. How did he know? *What* did the little faggot know?

Colette took up the twirling ribbons again. "Toutes les gens — all the people, yes? — they are all *oooold*." when she said 'All' she twirled the ribbons in a great swathe, as if taking in the whole of that world. "All old. They think the young are mad. Because we will wear not the dark clothes and *sabots* and hats which are – what is the word? – sensible? Because we are not like them, they call us mad. They call me mad. But they are the ones fighting; they are the ones at the war. Who else is young here? There are no young men."

"*I'm* a young man," he said softly, seeing the sense in her words, not wanting to have hurt her.

"Do you think I'm mad?" she said, coming closer, sitting on the bench and putting a light hand on his wounded leg.

"No, honey," he said. "*Pas du tout.*"

"Not at all! You are very good. The French, the English we are speaking. We are a... match. That is good, yes?"

His brain was racing apace with his lust. If he hadn't bagged her mother and grandmother, he would have asked her to marry him right there and then.

"Colette, would you –"

As he moved toward her, a surge of pain shot up his leg; he gripped the arm of the bench, gritting his teeth. It looked as if he were throttling a snake. "I reckon I need some more of your grandma's special drink. Your grandmother she –"

"But she is not my mother's mother!" cried Colette, laughing, realising something at once. She sat down next to him, the crumbling slab base of the seat crunched as it rocked.

Horsett frowned. Had he got the French wrong? *Grand mère?* Grandmother surely!

"*Non non non…* it is a..." She got out the dictionary from a deep pocket. "It is a 'title' *Grand mère*. Great Mother. She is '*grand mère*' to the women in her *covine.*"

He was in too much pain to chase the words too deeply. He even lost his hard-on. "So now you're gonna tell me that Selene, your mother, isn't your mother either, right?

"*Mais non!* I am an orphan. I call Selene '*maman*' because of respect. My true parents – I do not know who they were – left me here. I cannot remember my father at all, but I think my mother was very beautiful. I was three, I think. I *think.*"

Well that made him feel a whole lot better about having had them both! They weren't her mother or grandmother at all, so that made it pure again. Weird but pure.

"Did Astrid really make you learn English because she knew I would appear?"

"Yes. *Oui.* Yes yes…" She answered as she skipped and twirled again.

This was all too crazy. When he was still in England, waiting for it all to start, he and his buddies had had a few hours in the little town of Swindon, where they'd got drunk and acted stupid, and old women and older guys had said, scornfully: "Don't you know there's a war on?" That's what he wanted to say to this dancing doll woman now: *Don't you know there's a war on?* But if there was, he sure as hell couldn't get there, could he?

"Miiiichael!" came a voice from a high window in the main house. It was Astrid, perhaps wondering what they were up to. Sure as hell, sure as hell. Christ, but his leg was hurting and his ribs ached…

"Michael… come and eat. Take your medicine. Come in now!"

"It was the 'medicine' he wanted. Even more than he wanted Colette. "Sure, Ma," he muttered, not loud enough for Astrid to hear. "We're on our way, ain't we, babe?" As he turned to limp indoors he caught a glimpse of the tower – the Cock House – poking above the trees. "Hey Colette, what *is* that place?" The side of him that was still a paratrooper knew it would be perfect for a sniper.

"Another day. We will go there another day."

She danced on ahead, stepping in and out of the huge spirals of ribbon, singing.

44

Although Thibaut couldn't dance and skip because of cartilage trouble, he moved through the woods in a sprightly enough way, flicking his leg out over the rough ground, whistling *La Marseillaise* through his protruding teeth. He was pleased that he had caught another two hares in his traps, which dangled from his belt as he made his way back home, bashing against his thigh:

Aux armes, citoyens,
Formez vos bataillons,
Marchons, marchons!
Qu'un sang impur
Abreuve nos sillons!

Thus went the old, grand words in his head, riding on the uncertain sonics of his tongue. Did the American know this, he wondered? They summed up the last few marvellous days since June 6th: *To arms, citizens, Form your battalions, Let's march, let's march! Let impure blood water our furrows!* He felt something again for that image of the beautiful woman with the perfect tits - '*La Belle France*' - that he had not known for a long time.

He felt something for the hares too. Two hefty old ones, with rounded and rough claws, the teeth long, yellow and irregular, like his own, with white hairs in their muzzles and traces of grey in their wavy coats. After he had hung them for a week there would be enough meat for a family.

Aux armes, citoyens! he whistled again, being rather hazy about the whole anthem.

Before the American had arrived, Thibault had started to feel his years. He creaked, he moaned, he bitched. Now, as he remembered and relived the moment they had killed the two stupid Boche, he felt like a young man again and oddly hopeful. As he strolled through the ancient woodland, at the start of June, summer was approaching in more ways than one.

And as he thought of how his victim had gasped *Nein Nein* in the last seconds of his life, in the darkness, a gate opened to

Thibault's memories of the previous war: the trenches filled with dead young men; the mustard gas they'd dreaded more than the shelling; walking over ground that contained more human meat than soil; the hatred of the enemy and the unresolved need for revenge. Those dirty Fritzes deserved what they got. And he was going to bring them a lot more of the same now that the *parachutiste* had come among them.

The woods had the almost spicy scent of wild garlic, of rotten bark and fox turds. The rain had brought the normal smells out and made them more intense: flowing mixtures of damp earth and fern, wood and wild flowers assailed him at every step. The mosses on the north side of the trees clung like old coats. Thibault, whose worn clothes were the faded colours of the forest itself, stepped among the mushrooms and toadstools, making a mental note where they were. He could come back later and gather some.

With them and some onions, some garlic herbs and red wine, he would eventually braise the hares until the meat was tender, yet deeply flavored. Accompanying the meat with fresh mushrooms, he would cap it all with a perfect, silky sauce and he would eat like a king.

Thibault was happy. Here amid the chaos of trees, within the great abbeys of light created by the sun punching down between the canopy, he could find the sort of peace that no priest of any god could ever give him.

And then he stopped. He knew something was badly wrong.

Approaching the cottage very slowly, he could smell the wood smoke from the fire, and also a little whiff of vehicle exhaust, which sort of popped at his flared nostrils and told him to be careful. There was nothing to be seen yet, but he could hear voices.

He saw the two German cars parked outside the door and his heart sank. With their sharp grey lines and fierce angles at odds with the curving, bending, bowing shapes of the trees, they were so out of place they looked obscene.

There was no-one in the second car, but its engine was still running, pulsing out stink into his forest. The Boche were all indoors; he heard Armand cry out in pain.

He crept nearer. No Apache warrior could have moved as silently through the trees as Thibault.

His first glance was at the hen-hut behind and up against the house. There were the rifles and other items they had taken from the murdered soldiers under a false floor. Plus a couple of arms they had kept from *La Guerre des Guerres* and used for hunting before the Germans invaded. That cache was untouched, the hens clucking serenely as Armand screamed from behind the adjoining wall.

Thibault's first plan was to creep across and get one of the rifles then burst in and shoot the Boche.

Bad plan. A slow, bolt-action Mauser would get him killed before he could fire a second shot.

He crept nearer still, mastering his breathing, using all the heavy, twisted foliage to conceal himself. His bad knee caused him no trouble now!

His second plan was to leap into the empty car and drive off. When the Germans rushed out to follow him, Armand would surely escape.

Stupid plan. He had never driven more than tractors. He would soon be caught and they would both be shot.

Two of the German policemen dragged Armand out. He had a noose around his neck and his hands tied behind his back. Blood poured down his face. The officer took the end of the rope and tried to throw the end over a nearby branch. It took him three goes before he managed. Armand said not a word. The other soldiers looked bored.

"Tell me," said the officer, pulling on the end of the rope so that Armand was hauled onto his toes, almost pirouetting as he choked. "You are hiding something. Tell me and I will see you get a fair trial."

He released the rope enough for Armand to come back onto the soles of his feet again, and struggle for breath, his face turning purple.

"Tell me. *Dites-moi*," the officer said, softly, almost as if he cared, then pulled on the rope once more.

Which left only one plan that Thibault could possibly try now.

"G'day cobbers!" he cried, coming into the clearing, smiling hugely, total innocence and amity.

The Germans spun around, all their weapons pointed right at his heart, the officer loosing the rope in surprise.

"Bonzer day. Fair dinkum?"

Their faces were blank. None of them spoke the Australian

slang he had learned in the previous war. None of them knew what he was saying. Then again, Thibault hadn't expected them to. *"Mais bonjour!"* he continued brightly, as if there hadn't been a man on the end of a rope, gasping heavily, about to be killed. *"Ça va?"*

The whole troop looked at him and then at each other, and then at Schimmel, who pushed his officers cap up from his brow. "Who are you?"

"But I am Thibault!" he said with boldness, striking his chest. "Do you not know me? Thibault of the Woods. Thibault who brings the Sun, who charms hares into his traps. Would you like one? Both? They came to me when I called. Here, take them for your wife..." He offered the hares to Schimmel.

The officer recoiled.

"Ein Wahnsinniger,"[1] muttered the tough-lookng one.

"Do you know this man?" demanded the officer.

Thibault grinned hugely, displaying all of his very bad teeth, and hugged Armand, as if he often found him with his hands bound and a rope around his neck, and blood pouring down his face shirt like puke. *"Bien sûr!* My great friend. What has he been doing now? Poaching again? I told you, Armand – Don't. Poach. Did I, Thibault, not tell you?"

"This man is hiding something," said their leader, somewhat thrown off-track by this newcomer who sprayed as he spoke.

Thibault's idiot grin faded. "Armand..." he said with a voice of infinite sadness, stooping slightly to peer into the swollen, blackening eyes of his friend. "They have come for you at last. I am sorry, but no more lies, no more secrets. *Monsieur* General, Thibault will show you what he is hiding. There will be no secrets in *my* forest."

He took one of the hares and lifted its face and put it next to his own, looking to the left and to the right. Made it seem as if he and the hare were sniffing out secrets.

"With me. Come. Do not be afraid..." he said to the officer.

Thibault guessed right. The Germans found his tone so unexpected, his words so bizarre, and perhaps their own hearts were so weary, they all lowered their weapons. The officer let Armand sink to the ground and followed on into the house.

---

[1] Lunatic

The rooms were wrecked. Thibault hated mess but he maintained his hideous grin. "Beneath that bench *m'sieur*, there is a large square stone in the floor," he said to the youngest. "It is in there."

"What is it?"

"That which he hides."

The young French policeman threw the bench backward and revealed that there was indeed a flooring stone that looked as if it could be removed. The soldiers huddled around. The officer pushed his way forward as the junior used the edge of his knife to prise up the stone and heft it backward, revealing a narrow square hole almost a metre deep, containing an old, long and narrow leather bag.

"Stop!" cried the officer, no doubt thinking this might be a booby-trap left by the parachutist. "Le Blanc...you take it out and open it."

Le Blanc, whom Thibault had seen around the town for many years, looked desperate for a drink. The whole of Neuilly knew of his problem. It was obvious how important he was within the troop. That is, not at all.

The others stood back. Thibault glanced out of the door and saw poor Armand kneeling on the ground as if in prayer, both eyes almost completely closed, coughing badly. He maintained his air of righteous disapproval toward his friend.

Le Blanc took out the long bag and laid it on the floor. He frowned. There was no telling what it might contain. He undid the fasteners one by one, trying not to let them see his hands shaking but they all did. As he pulled it open, slowly, he peered in. Then opened his eyes wide with surprise and then offered the contents to the men.

"*Pornographie...*" he whispered, showing them a stash of dirty magazines and even dirtier postcards, black and white images of all those parts that many had never seen. Thin women, fat women, standing or bending, smiling or beckoning. Big tits, small tits, long legs, hirsute or shaven. Something for everyone. "*Dégoûtant,*"[1] Le Blanc added with feeling, but he also used the bag to hide the American cigarette butt he had seen in the corner of the room.

---

[1] Disgusting.

"This is how he makes his living," said Thibault with disgust. "Will you hang him now?"

The men laughed, the mood had changed utterly. For a few precious seconds, they were naughty schoolboys as they grabbed what they could, before their *Hauptmann* snatched it back and threw it on the fire. There was so many the flames went out.

"Leave this filth," the officer snarled, striding out to the car. And to Thibault: "Idiot."

Behind his back, the German members of his troop were stuffing postcards in their pockets. As far as they were concerned, they had got what *they* wanted from the raid.

The radio crackled into life. One of them hurried to answer but looked at his superior first.

"Leave it," came the command. "There is no reception here in the forest."

Thibault, who knew the way of men and their lies in wartime, guessed that someone, a superior, was trying to contact them.

The officer stared at his battered map. He looked drugged. "Leave that pervert," he ordered. "Get in, all of you. We have other places to search. *Mach schnell, mach schnell!*"

Le Blanc removed the rope from Armand's neck. "I am sorry, *m'sieur*," he whispered, then got into the *wagen*.

The vehicles revved up and trundled off along the rutted tracks that served as a road. Thibault waved them off with his dead hare, made sure they had gone, and helped Armand to his feet.

"Bonzer," he said softly, though he never knew what that meant.

"I...said...nothing," Armand gasped, spitting blood,

"Good on yer, mate," said his friend, though he wasn't grinning now, or looking haughty. "My father taught me that when suspected of something bad, always plead guilty to a lesser crime."

"Idiot..." muttered Armand through broken teeth, using a word that meant the same the world over.

45

The Good Father forced his way along the streets of the town. His mind was so focused that the soldiers around him were no more than blurs: grey and green, brown and olive shapes that possessed pale blobs where calmer observers would see faces. He surged through them, his cloth acting like a knife to those members of the *Wehrmacht* who still believed.

A chunky *Obersturmbahnfuhrer* elbowed him into the road and almost under a half-track that was grinding over the cobbles. Gilles Fournier was unmoved. This was nothing to the chaos he had been involved in two years before, when he had helped the *gendarmes* in Paris seek out the pockets of Jews:

"By what authority do you do this?" an old rabbi had whined as he was being marched away.

"Your own!" Father Gilles had responded, "As stated in Matthew 27, verses 24 to 26, when the Jews cry out: 'His blood be on us and on our children'!"

So he had watched until the French police did their great round-up and pushed them all – thousands of them – into the *Vél d'Hiv*[1], cleansing the city at last. One day, the Germans might learn to show him gratitude for his own small part.

Today, however, he was almost panting as he scurried. One hour before he had prayed, really prayed, with a soaring intensity he had not known for a long time, but to the *Dei Genetrix* this time: *O holy Mother of God; despise not our petitions in our necessities, but deliver us always from all dangers, O glorious and blessed Virgin...*

He asked Her for some clue as to where he should look next, how best to find the demon that had tormented him for too many years. Had She uttered names and addresses within his head he would have been delighted, but he knew that She did not work like that any more than did the Son. Instead, Fournier rose from his prayers, wiped his lips and the front of his *soutane* with his handkerchief, and flung open the side door of his church.

There, driving swiftly past, but perfectly framed for that one half second, was the pale, haunted face of the German officer

---

[1] Vélodrome d'Hiver

who had so recently conducted that wretched funeral. The one who had had the temerity to shoot the icon of Christ.

This, surely, was Fournier's answer. Was that his nemesis? He had to find out. He had to look into the depths of the man's eyes again, and thus into his soul – if he had one.

He moved quickly. A side of him was pleased that, in extremis, the old fears had left him and he was heading to battle with almost a light heart. He would have made a good soldier.

Schimmel, in his office, unaware of the priest, had to rest. He felt like shit – worse than shit – and had not slept since Dieter had been murdered. The Pervitin tablets helped; so did his guilt.

Outside, in the distant blue skies, were swarms of planes like the tiny silverfish in his aquarium back home. What was Der Bomber's joke? If they're silver, they're American; if they're khaki they're British; if they're invisible, they're Luftwaffe.

He took the framed photograph of his family and put it to his brow, as if he could soak the images into his mind during these mindless times.

Although he knew that you must never take Pervitin with alcohol, he poured a large glass of *Jaegerbranntwein*[1] and downed it in three gulps. Then he put his head on the desk, next to the photo, waiting for it to take effect. The thick wooden top vibrated gently from the heavy traffic outside. It was vaguely comforting, and he rolled his brow from side to side across the cool, dusty surface.

He was getting nowhere in finding the man who'd killed his son. And he was also getting dangerously close to disobeying orders from his superiors: his Major, his *Oberstleutenant*, the *Oberst*, *Generalmajor* and even up to the *Generalleutnant* himself – who was only a few steps below God and Hitler. So far he had managed to hide behind the chaos of the invasion, but there were only so many ruses he could use to keep on avoiding them.

Peace, peace, he wanted peace. For him, that could only come from revenge.

Through the vibrations on the floorboards outside, which ran up the table and onto his forehead, he could feel someone coming up the stairs. It would be that little arse licker Lueur again. The

---

[1] Quality cognac

door burst open and almost before Schimmel straightened up, focused his tired eyes and put his cap back on, there was the bent little priest quivering before him.

"*Gott!*" he cried in surprise, and reached for his Luger.

"I am looking for something," said the priest, completely unmoved by the shaky muzzle of the pistol.

Schimmel breathed heavily. It would be so easy to kill this man. Although he had ordered hangings, firing squads and plain-and-simple bullets in the back of the neck for miscreants of all kinds, he himself had never killed anyone. He put the gun on the desk, though kept his hand near it and the barrel pointing toward the madman. "You have come into my office without permission. I could shoot you."

"You came into my churchyard without asking. I could have…"

"What? *What* could you have done?" scorned Schimmel, the alcohol and the Pervitin making his brain open up.

Fournier paused, not because he was uncertain of what dread he could have inflicted on spiritual levels, but because he saw the crucifix hanging out from the man's metal gorget. He had to be careful. Even demons could use holy symbols for their own ends. He was holding his rosary in his good hand, for protection, and had a vial of Holy Water in his pocket as a weapon. But he had to have another look at this man's eyes, although they were fixated on his own fused fingers and the marks on his skin.

"You are a cripple," the German said.

Fournier rolled up his sleeve to show more of the lightning-patterns, and let him have a good look at his damaged hand and arm. He did this sometimes, in a rage, when people stared. *This, this is what God can do!* he would think at them. "You must be the officer who took away all the defective children from the asylum."

The accused blinked hard, shaking his head. "No. No that was not me. That was my predecessor. But I would have done the same."

"You would have innocents sent away for murder?"

"It would have been a Christian act."

"*Christian?*" Fournier was keenly attentive now: the devil might reveal itself through what he would say.

"Of course. Those pitiful wretches…would they go to Heaven or Hell? – both of which I believe in, incidentally."

"Heaven. Of course," said the priest, warily.

"And there they would be made perfect, free from pain, normal at last, loved and wanted?"

Fournier said nothing. He saw the trap. He wanted to catch a glimpse of the man's eyes more than he needed to refute his absurd argument.

"Then, my little crippled priest, it was surely an act of Christian compassion to send them to Heaven as soon as possible rather than to have them suffer here?"

He gave no answer.

Schimmel took a deep breath and sat up. He started to feel a bit better. He should have just shot the man but he wanted to spar, to prove to himself he was still human.

"You see, *Monsieur Le Curé*, when I was a boy and knew no better, I was brought up by my ignorant parents to be a good Catholic like yourself. Then when I was able to see and think for myself, I converted to Christianity."

"Your Christianity is offensive to me," was Fournier's response.

"Then forgive me, Father, for I have sinned."

Monsieur Le Curé was unnerved: not by the gun, but the words. He took the Schimmel's photograph and looked at it.

"That is my lovely wife, my beautiful daughters, and my brave son," said the officer. "My wife and daughters are in Germany, safe in the countryside. My son is safe in your graveyard."

"Your son…?" Fournier saw deep into the officer's eyes at that moment, and could have drowned in the great pool of sadness – entirely human sadness. It was a pool so deep that he could almost see his own reflection in it. Taking a step back he sighed and said simply: "*Je suis désolé*," and handed back the photograph.

On another occasion, as someone who prided himself in his insight into psychology, Schimmel might have allowed himself to be intrigued by the complete change of mood, but he was too tired. He took the frame and re-positioned it, angling it so he could look at his family and this odd specimen at the same time.

"I made inquiries about you."

The curé stiffened.

"When in Paris, you helped the authorities round up some troublesome Jews."

Fournier relaxed. "I did. I have no qualms about that. Jews murdered Our Lord did they not?"

Schimmel nodded, matter-of-factly. No argument there. "That was a good piece of work."

"Thank you."

There was silence between them.

Fournier, who knew about the way people would hide things, was confident that there was nothing else lurking behind this man's words – nothing about the scandal.

Schimmel, in turn, almost felt the cold kinship that soldiers on opposing armies can feel. "But what is it you want from me? Why did you come up here?"

"I am looking for a demon."

The German blinked. Was the man being ironic? "A demon? And you thought *I* was that creature?"

"I had to be sure."

"Is that why you clutched your rosary? To protect yourself from *me*?"

"Is that why you have your Luger? I know which is more powerful."

"What will you do when you find this creature?"

"Send it back where it belongs."

Schimmel removed his cap again and slumped back in his chair, laughing. Looking out of the windows made increasingly dirty by the traffic, he saw even more aircraft glinting in the distant skies. The world was coming to an end and this man was chasing demons! He really did feel himself to be in a nightmare.

The priest turned to go.

"Wait!" said Schimmel, though his voice was soft, tired, almost friendly toward this odd character, who had balls if nothing else.

Fournier turned, warily.

"That asylum you mentioned. Where is it, exactly?"

"I have never been. I imagine it is a ruin. I think it was somewhere between here and Forguet."

The windows shook. They both looked out at a flight of Messerschmitts screaming urgently toward the coast. In the square below, Yohan le Blanc was riffling through the dirty magazine he had looted from the peasant. The priest tutted.

Are you and I looking for the same thing? Schimmel wondered, looking at the scorched side of priest's face.

The Frenchman turned and stared at him, unblinkingly, showing both sides at once.

"I know what you're thinking," said the priest.

Schimmel looked away, feeling vaguely embarrassed, not sure what he meant. "I'm thinking that..." But his visitor limped awkwardly down the steep stairs without waiting for his reply.

46

Ici Londres! Les Français parlent aux Français...

The voice was tinny but Astrid and Selene were enthralled, huddled as they were in the octagonal room, in the tower, listening to the BBC's French Service again. They were tuned into *Radio Londres* as broadcast by the Free French Forces, though Astrid had to fiddle with the aerial to get a good signal. They could be shot for this. The thrill was delicious.

The Matagot was sprawled along one of the walls, under the scenes of Spring, licking its paws. The two women were smiling, and had been for some time. Both of them leant forward, over the table, as if being close to the altar of the little box would make the messages more comprehensible.

Before we begin, please listen to some personal messages.

They smiled even more at that. Everyone knew that the absurd sentences which would follow were seeded with coded messages to the Resistance. It was a game to guess what was which:

Jack has a brown moustache.
There is mould on my aunt's hat
The long sobs of the violins of autumn.
The mayor has eaten a small cat.
The dice have been thrown.
It is hot in Suez.

"The dice!" hissed Selene with excitement. "'The dice have been thrown': that means something. I can feel it. You could hear it in his voice. He almost laughed when he spoke of the mayor and his cat, but then his words were pure and clear about the dice, because he knew they were important!"

She slapped the table in delight.

Astrid nodded. She got tired of being the sybil all the time. Let Selene have her fun.

"Soon," Selene continued excitedly, "we must go into town and draw V signs on walls. *Victoire!* That will make the Boches tremble. *Victoire! Victoire!*"

"Pah! No need for that. Remember how our Master would stand in the garden waiting for the sunrise?

"It was the Morning Star, surely?"

"*Zut!* It was the sun!"

"And it was the evening."

"*Crotte!* It was the dawn."

Selene shrugged. It was never wise to argue with Astrid. "Then remember how he used to visit our little cretins and imbeciles every morning in their beds, saying so tenderly: *Réveil, petites fées?*"[1]

"Yes," Astrid said softly. "He was so gentle, and so very strong." Sighing, she switched off the radio, stood and put her arms above her head into a V shape. Selene mirrored her. "And remember also how we would salute Ra, the sun-god who is also Horus? I feel that a new sun is rising over a new France. *Un, deux, trois.*"

They came very close as they said the words, which were more than words, touching their palms as they raised their arms in the V above their heads.

The Matagot yowled; they turned to look, and gave little nods.

"Our Master wants us," Astrid said.

"Shall I let him speak through me?"

"Not yet, Selene. We will put you in the full trance for the next meeting of the *covine*. Not all of them have seen this, or been spoken to directly. Now, let us look at the cards…"

She put a pack of tarot cards on the table, held her hands over them with closed eyes, whispering. Then she isolated the twenty-two cards of the Major Arcana and shuffled them. "What is our man now do you think? Is he The Magician? The Hierophant? Is he stuck in The Chariot or an echo of Death? He cannot be The Hermit – not with us! You choose."

Selene cut the pack and slid out: "The Fool. He is still the Fool."

"*Bof.* That will change. I know it. Am I ever wrong?"

"*Fréquemment.*"

"*Merde.* This time…But even the biggest fool will still be able to give Colette the child. And us."

"You are too old, but it might be me!" Selene said wistfully.

"*Merde.* I know it will happen. I have the body of a young woman."

Selene looked thoughtful. "You *are* too old – it might be a

---

[1] Wake up, my little fairies

mongol."

"I hope it is. Did we not love our little fees?"

"We did! Then St. Martin's will rise again with them."

"All thanks to our Master."

The cat rose and scratched at the floorboards.

"Shall we go down and pay homage?" asked Selene of the creature. "It has been a while."

"There is no time in the underworld, in *La Douât*,"[1] corrected the other.

The Matagot scratched more firmly, dust rose under its claws.

"*Le Maître* would be pleased," Selene said.

"Yes, yes. Let us go to *La Douât*. The Matagot leads us. The Master must be within him."

They lifted a board and hid the radio in the space between the levels. Astrid extinguished the candles and they climbed down to the ground floor. Making sure that the door was firmly locked, they rolled back the heavy carpet almost to the centre, uncovering a trap-door in the floor. Taking hold of the little inset handles they lifted it and propped it carefully at right angles. On the underside of the door was a red arrow pointing downwards into the pitch blackness and the legend: *Voici La Douât. Voici le monde souterrain. Voici est la Lumière.*[2]

Cold air rose, and the cat purred, then shot down the stairs with the two women following.

---

[1] English: Duat, or Tuat, from the Egyptian for underworld.
[2] Here is the Duat. Here is the Underworld. Here is the Light.

47

As the two women descended into darkness, Armand in the forest was emerging from a dark place of his own, having lost consciousness for a while.

"I told them nothing," he muttered through swollen lips, his left eye black and almost closed from the beating. The remaining hair on his head was matted with blood. He wheezed every time he took a deep breath. His throat bore the rope-burn of the noose like a turquoise and ruby necklace. "Nothing!" he said again, spitting blood on the stone floor, and he was proud.

Jules and Luc had turned up after the Germans had gone. Their first response was relief: it meant *they* were safe. Their second: they were enormously impressed. This was a real warrior who was coughing before them.

"What were they looking for?" asked Luc, who knew nothing of the dead soldiers from the night before.

Armand paused to rinse his mouth with water. Spat it into the bucket that Luc brought next to him. Prodded gingerly at his teeth. "A parachutist, they said. I think they said. But they were vague. I do not think they know."

"Can someone have betrayed our man?" asked Thibault, covering his own prominent teeth, and shuddering at the thought of anyone smashing them.

No-one answered. Betrayal was a constant fear, whether it involved harbouring parachutists, stealing hens, murdering soldiers, or breaking the curfew.

"They do not know who or what they are looking for. The officer spoke as if he were drunk. The others seemed bored. I do not think they were close to their quarry." Armand curled up in pain, and groaned, holding his ribs, spitting more blood into the bucket.

"We must delay our plan," said Jules. "You need to recover."

"Let us take you to the women," said Luc. "They still have medicines."

"No!" hissed Armand. "I had worse than this – much worse – in Verdun."

"True," mused Thibault, who had been there with him. "But

that was caused by Boche gas and bayonets, and not a beating by their military police. Or that witch Astrid's curse."

For Armand, Verdun was his own *Noirceur*: he measured everything by the darkness, despair and pain he had known then.

Thibault, who sometimes lived in more worlds than one in the depths of the forest, shrugged. "*Eh bien*, she may have been responsible for them finding you."

"That is even bigger shit," added Jules, who had no doubt where the womens' loyalties lay. "They would never have told."

"But I am not saying that they told! Perhaps, in other ways…" Thibault's words petered out. He found it difficult to explain the workings of the folk magic he believed in, and the strange ways that curses can work. In truth, he quite liked the mad women, who never judged him by his looks and who seemed to understand his own curious links with the wildwood.

"But we need you to lead us," Thibault continued. "The American is lame – and I am not sure of his spirit. We are on the *Voie Sacrée*.[1] We cannot turn back now."

"And also," added Luc, "I heard that the landing has failed. I heard that the beaches are filled with burning tanks and dead soldiers."

The men looked disconsolately at one another, not daring to believe this. It was easy to be *resistants* when the Allies were next door.

Armand, sensing the others' fears, knew he needed to rally them again. "Give me another day – two days. I will get strong again. The American will get stronger. Then we will triumph."

"Have you spoken to your friend in the Resistance yet?" Luc asked of Jules. "I think that we will need all the help we can get."

"*If* he has one," muttered Thibault.

"Not yet! But yes, I will. Soon. Caution, caution my friends."

"Don't tap your nose, Uncle Jules."

---

[1] The 'Sacred Way' – a WW1 soldier's term for the route to and from the front.

48

While the men in the forest talked themselves through what had happened, and what they had avoided, and decided what to do next, Sophia in the heart of Neuilly was briefly paralysed with fear.

It was caused by the insistent knocking on her door: three lots of three raps. Taking a deep breath through an open mouth, she gave a little cry of shock when she opened it, to find Father Fournier there. Every bad deed she had committed in the past few years surged into her thoughts, riding onto her freckled face on top of the blush. The garter she wore on her leg as a token of commitment to *covine* felt as if it was burning. She wondered if the lucky brown envelope of the *petite cadeau* that Astrid had given her was out on display, although it hadn't brought any luck yet.

"I need to talk to you," the priest said, softly. That and the fact that he said *need* rather than *want* took away a tiny fragment of her fear. "I need your help." Did she imagine it, or had he put the tiniest of emphases on the word *your*?

She brushed her hands up and down her clothing as if she could tidy herself. The priests of Neuilly-sur-Fronds tended to visit on matters of death, reproach, or donations. This was unusual.

"Come in Father. Come in..." She looked outside, up and down the narrow street before she closed the door after him. No-one was out there.

The priest settled himself rather awkwardly on a stool. She noticed that he positioned himself so that his damaged hand was concealed under the table, and the damaged side of the face away from her. There was an exhausted air about him, like a sparrow in winter.

"I have coffee," she offered, reaching for the jar and her best cups.

"Thank you," he said. "Black, *s'il vous plait*."

"I have some bread and cheese," she offered; he looked as if he needed a good meal. He was uncertain, oddly vulnerable. "I insist!" she said brightly, and he nodded, with a tiny smile on one side of his mouth.

She used the time in her tiny kitchen to run a brush through her frizzy red hair as she scanned her conscience, prepared him the drink and food and tried to conceal her anxiety. Nothing had happened between her and any German, although she had been tempted as every woman had been. She hadn't stolen anything, or sold anything she shouldn't. She didn't owe money. This had to be about the *covine*.

Well, if excommunication was the worst he could do, then she had little to fear. She had done nothing wrong with that lot either, despite all the hints of forthcoming wickedness the older women made. Besides, the secret communists at the other side of town had a lot more to offer in that respect. And made a lot more sense.

She brought in a tray and handed him the cup, black and steaming, covertly looking around her own room to see if there was anything he might find damning. The old cuckoo clock made its quarter-hourly squawk. She wouldn't have noticed it if the priest hadn't looked up and smiled. He had the 'good' side of his face to her as he stared up at the device and its dusty pendulum and chain. He looked quite beautiful.

"My mother had one like that," he said, with almost a sigh. "She had red hair like yours, too." For a moment, he was a little boy again, perhaps back with his *maman*. "I did something to the cuckoo's beak, with glue. When it came out, instead of *Cuck-oo!*, it went *Currrrgk. Maman* blamed the poor Austrian workmanship."

Sophia wanted to chuckle but wasn't sure if that was appropriate. She gave him a warm smile instead. He almost returned it.

When he had finished eating she washed the plate, knife and fork and blew on them to dry them. The priest smiled.

"Our home was like this," he said. "Very small, very pretty. Warm."

"This is rented by my cousin. I have to leave it soon."

"Still…" he sighed. "It is so warm. Welcoming."

He said that last as if he had not known any welcome anywhere for a long time. As he sat there in a kitchen that Sophia sensed was – at some level – the kitchen of his childhood, his cares seemed to lessen. He held the cup with both hands, shielding the deformed one, and kept peeking up at the clock as he drank coffee and memories. Sophia, who had many motherly qualities and only lacked a man in her life, might have given him a young-motherly hug if he hadn't been a priest.

Poor, poor man she thought. He needed looking after.

"What can I do for you Father?"

He looked at her earnestly. The fierceness she had seen in Mass, coming out of him like flames, was now something like a glow, as if he had allowed himself to relax for once. She had heard he suffered from epilepsy, too – the whole town spoke of it – but so had her late brother and it didn't trouble her. Unlike them, she knew it was not a disease.

"I have been told, Sophia, that you know everyone and everything. About Neuilly-sur-Fronds, that is."

She laughed out loud. "Me? I can imagine who has been spreading such nonsense!"

"You are highly regarded. You worked for Father Romilly and also as a teaching assistant. You worked in the library, bakery and the butcher's. You helped run the little cinema they used to have here, before the Occupation. And you did voluntary work with the old people."

She shrugged, and wrestled with her hair, trying to fasten it in a single strand behind her head. "Someone *has* been talking! I have had many more jobs than that, Father. I'm a good worker. Yes, I know everyone in town."

He drained the cup, and looked into the dregs. Wolfed down the cheese and bread, then wiped the crumbs from his mouth and clothes.

"Some more? *Non?* I have a drop of brandy. Father Romilly liked his brandy!"

Fournier shook his head. He really did have a lovely smile when he was relaxed, as he seemed to be now, in the light from the little window.

"Heh! Temperance in all things. That's my curse. I have to juggle what I love with what I need. No, this is sufficient, thank you."

What was this about? she wondered. Having always had a taste for the unexpected and absurd, she was marvelling at this new turn of events.

"I expect you are wondering what this is about, Sophia?" He paused, and looked beyond the walls of the little room, pondering. "I am looking for someone," he told her.

She moved to the edge of her seat, eyebrows raised for more detail.

"I am not sure who – or perhaps *what*."

"Very difficult father! It sounds very mysterious," she said brightly, and he smiled again.

"I feel that I must become a detective. Sifting clues spiritual and material."

"I don't understand."

"What was my predecessor like? Father Romilly."

She gave a little laugh, as if he had been much loved but odd. "He had a problem with his neck, so that his head faced always to the ground. It was difficult to talk to him, except in Confession, when that did not matter. He was a good man, but he became…"

"What?!" he pounced, slightly sharper than he meant to, so that she sat back and looked anxious. "Listen, you will not get into any trouble. But you must tell me the truth, without fear."

She paused, considered. She noticed that he curled his deformed hand into himself, and leaned forward slightly, as if anxious about what she might say. She was certain that somehow this was connected with the *covine*. And what Astrid had said about the mysterious stranger who had appeared. "He became troubled. No, that is not the true word. Perhaps he was…"

"Possessed?" the priest interposed.

She looked at him. That was not quite the word she was looking for, but it was clearly important to him. "Possessed. Yes, a little. But I think cursed, also."

Aircraft thundered very low above the house. The windows shook, the pots and pans rattled on their shelves.

"Cursed." It was not a question. "Tell me."

Sophia knew what he wanted. He was a little boy, fishing. Should she tell him that old Romilly felt cursed by his curved spine, and the pains in his neck and head? That he seemed utterly wearied of his Church? That he had money problems? That he felt everything was going wrong for him? "I don't know Father. I know that he had bad dreams. He told me so. But he could never remember them. I was his housekeeper for a time, until he died. I was told you had no need of one, so I came here."

The priest's face shone.

"I did not know that. Sophia. But I would like you to be my housekeeper too. You will have your own rooms as before. You will be paid. Would you consider this?"

Her face shone, as she nodded, marvelling that Astrid's pagan *petite cadeau* had swayed this priest to make this offer. "I will say yes, Father. And I thank all the powers above that you have asked me."

He smiled, paternally. She could have hugged him. In fact, she was now enjoying juggling her secret knowledge of Astrid's *covine*, and this confidential quest of the priest's. A move back to her old rooms would solve many problems.

"We will talk about this soon, *ma'mselle*, but now I must ask you some strange questions. No, don't blush, nothing personal. My bishop, who is a very wise man, told me that when I came here, I should learn about the local superstitions. He had heard many strange things, but I never took him seriously at the time."

Sophia smiled inwardly. She had had a similar discussion with Father Romilly when he had chided her cousin for being '*superstitieux*' – dragging out the word scornfully – because she had faith in her St. Christophe medallion. *But Father Romilly, what is the* **opposite** *of superstitious?* she had asked, in all seriousness. He had looked at her sharply – or as sharply as anyone could with neck and spine problems. How could he, who had to believe in Jesus walking on water, raising people from the dead, and changing water into wine, lay claim to being a rationalist? *You are clever, Sophia, but you are not wise,* he had chided, before limping away.

"Well?" asked Father Fournier, making her snap back to the present. "You seem to find this amusing. Is it?"

"Forgive me, Father. When people come to our little town from the big cities, they look upon us like pygmies, with amusing customs and strange attitudes."

"Oh but I am sorry, Sophia! I do not mean to patronise. I have a reason for asking these very important questions, which I will try to explain. Tell me, please, of any local beliefs, or strangeness, no matter how small. I beg you…"

She sat back in her chair and clasped her hands on her lap. This was all very interesting! Should she tell him about Astrid and Selene and *Le Charme* that burned away in her pocket? No, not yet. The little envelope that she had 'won' in the Cock House would only work if it was never opened. She believed that. Some things must always be kept sealed, even if it felt as though there was nothing in it but some small stones, or nuts, wrapped in a material that crinkled to the touch through the paper. Besides, before the war everyone in and around Neuilly belonged to a group of some sort: communists, royalists, anarchists, free-loving flower-arrangers, truffle-maniacs, anti-vivisectionists and train-spotters... Astrid – and by extension her *covine* – was hated or simply scorned by just about everyone because she had money. Many who had never met her paid her rent through an agent. They never quite knew what used to go on at St Martin's before the War. Everyone had or needed their secrets. Sophia would keep hers for a little while longer.

"Well?" Fournier asked, leaning forward eagerly.

"Ah well, Father...then shall I you about *Les Rongeurs d'Os*[1] - huge black dogs that will hunt you down on lonely roads? Or the wrensthat bring fires from heaven? Or the cursed families around Neuilly who bleed from the navels on Good Friday? Or the *lutins* who wear red hats with two feathers, which makes them invisible, and by which they can fly, or go through the ground without dying, or plunge into the depths of the sea without drowning? Oh yes, and who can attack you anywhere, even though all the windows and the doors are closed? Or about the *vouivre*, a flying snake, with a carbuncle for an eye, that has caused much trouble to many people I know? Perhaps I should explain about the *lupeux* – gnarly creatures you can often see sitting on twisted tree trunks. Or about the race of hornèd men who steal young girls because there are no longer any hornèd women. Or shall I tell you about *Les Dames Blanches*, spirit women who challenge and tempt and sometimes drive people to madness? Or shall I start first and tell you about the magical cats known as *matagots*?"

She felt smug. In her own small life, she knew exactly where to find a true *matagot*, at least two *Dames Blanches* (she wasn't sure if the girl was one yet) and was quite confident that at least one hornèd man would appear soon.

Fournier sighed. Sophia guessed he felt sure that – at last – he was getting close to his quarry, whatever that was, and believed these tales would help him get the scent.

"I want you to tell me everything," he said.

---

[1] Gnawers of Bones

49

As Sophia told her tales to the priest, a creature who was every bit as weird as those she yarned about was in the garden of St Martin's. He was gently stretching and bending his leg, trying to put more weight on it, trying to do more than hobble. Horsett was determined to get fit. Determined to fight. Inside, he was a coward trying hard to be brave; a weak man wanting to be strong. That's another reason he never wanted promotion: he would be found out too quickly. His own father knew that. And that ugly cat looked at him as if he knew it too. The staff had been cast aside. He rested under a tree, leaning back against it. It was raining, cold and grey, with strong winds that knocked the leaves down, so that it could have been Fall. If it had been like this a few days earlier, the Invasion would never have happened.

He clutched at his two oval dog tags. Before D-Day, these had been taped together so they wouldn't make a noise. Now, having cut them open with his combat knife, he could feel on the markings his name and serial number, Blood Group A. Baptist Other, and confirm to himself that he and the War really did exist.

He gripped his knife, turned and stabbed it savagely into the tree trunk, as if making up for all the Krauts he should have been wasting. He was as much fighting against himself as against the enemy. The two sides of him were at war. Their conflicts were starting to emerge in the thin light of day, in this garden gone to seed, at the far edge of a battle for the sake of the world.

So here he was, Michael Horsett, Screaming Eagle, who felt more like a giant turd that had dropped from God's asshole. His sarge once said that all a trooper needed to keep his morale in the field was dry socks and hot chow. Well, he had all that and more, here, but his morale was in a pit. Sorry sarge but that was hogwash. His leg was aching but they had stitched it up well, better than any Army medic. Credit the gals for that. They fed him better than back home. And that medicine they gave him regularly...he sure was getting a craving for that. Most of his buddies, who were probably rotting in ditches or shallow graves by now, would have chewed him out for feeling the way he did.

For Chrissake buddy! Lighten up! they'd have said.

"This whole thing's just a game to you," the Lieutenant had said back at Fort Benning. "I'd like to know your history."

Michael had snapped to attention, with exaggerated style.

"I have no history sir – only a destiny. Colonel Frederick told us that. Sir!"

"You know everything, don't you, you little shit."

"If you say so. Sir!"

"How long is a string?"

"Twice as long as half its length. Sir!"

"Drop and gimme fifty…"

You'll be sorry, he'd whispered as the red-faced officer walked away.

Now he set himself a route between two trees, along the gravel path. His aim was to get from tree A to tree B, faster and faster, no matter the pain. By the time he led the old guys – his Whitebread Troops – into action, he wanted to be able to run double-time again. Jeez, it was hard. He almost felt the stitches bursting. But the pain helped him blot out the shame of missing out on the War, and the confusion of delight he felt here, among the women.

Astrid had come to him again last night. She had crept in as before, had sex with him and left. It was uncannily like all the times he had trained: when he would sneak up on guys in the dark, with a phoney knife, practising for the time when he might do it for real and leave some schmuck with a slit throat for a grin. She was that careful, that ruthless. Terrific, no denying it.

Would it be Selene tonight? And *then* Colette? Oh it was all *Merveilleux!*

He sure had come a long way. In fact he'd fallen into a kind of paradise. So why did he feel so bad? A sense of duty? A feeling that he wasn't being what he could or should be? Shit, he sure needed a slug of that medicine. Instead he took his combat knife again and stabbed so furiously into the trunk that shrapnels of bark splintered up around his face. Then he sheathed it, started on his hobbling run again. The pain helped. Was he going mad? As mad as Luc said these women were?

An old, grey-whiskered and weary-looking fox ran across his path, some distance away. It paused and looked at him. He paused and looked right on back. He had never seen a real one before.

They weren't too common in Detroit.

Stay there, buddy, he whispered, taking the Tommy gun off his shoulder and slowly raising it, lining up the rear and front sights on the creature's face. He had no intention of loosing off any rounds, but he put first pressure on the trigger anyway, just to remind himself who and what he was.

"Shoot," came Colette's soft voice from behind his shoulder. Her arms snaked around him.

He hadn't heard her sneak up. He felt her warm breath against the back of his neck.

"Honey," he smiled, pleased with her attention. "*C'est difficile a ce moment. Je suis er, je suis dur...*"[1]

It felt pretty good saying it like that. Bold. A real swordsman.

She reached around his waist, her small hands almost touching where he most wanted to be touched. Her gentle laugh rippled down his spine like a pure stream.

Slinging the gun back over his shoulder he turned, awkwardly, as the pain shot through his leg. He might have stumbled but she held him. "Kiss me," he said softly, his hands on her thin shoulders.

So she did, very demurely, her face shining as she pulled away again. "Not yet, Michael."

He smiled. With all the covert sex he was getting from the other women he had no need to complain. This gentle teasing suited him just fine. "Oh I get it...you want me to respect you, huh?"

"Huh? Huh?" she teased again, mocking his Americanism, dancing to one side out of reach, but not explaining either.

The two dogs Nu and Geb came bounding out of nowhere. Barking, leaping, they almost knocked Horsett over. It was Colette who took a stick up from the ground and whacked the one called Nu with unbelievable and cold force, causing it to whimper and limp back into the trees, followed by the other.

Jesus, thought Horsett, who was again surprised again by the sudden transformation. Yet here she was, sweet and gentle, skipping away from him, a teasing grin on her perfect face. His own *maman* had always been sweet and gentle, but these rural French were something else. He didn't quite 'get' them. It

---

[1] I'm hard.

sometimes felt as though he were putting the like poles of two magnets together: something invisible – cultural, electrical, spiritual – pushed him away. Maybe he could spin himself around, somehow, then the unlike poles would draw him in.

He hobbled after her, clenching his teeth against the pain. She saw his hurt and stopped, looked genuinely upset.

"Okay okay…not yet."

He stooped to run his hand down the seam of his wound, as if to rub away the pain. His *maman* used to do that when his Dad wasn't looking. Else the old guy would snort: *For Crissake*…and storm away. When he straightened, he saw the top of the tower through a gap in the trees. He had forgotten about that. Making out with Colette could wait: it wasn't as if he was sex-starved. And here in France he had to keep telling himself – because none of his buddies were around to remind him – that he was a soldier first, a cocksman second – sure he was!

Colette turned to see what he was looking at. "Ah, *La Maison D'Oiseaux*. I told you, no man is ever allowed there. And also, only women who have eighteen years."

"Listen, baby, *I'm* allowed there," he muttered, almost pushing her to one side and heading in that direction.

Colette looked worried. "Michael!" she hissed.

He stopped for a moment. He had never heard her make that noise before. "Hell, it must be important," he said, and carried on down the path that curved through the overhanging trees, his jump boots crunching on the gravel and fallen twigs.

He might have gone further, but the damned cat they called The Matagot was sitting on the path, just looking at him.

"Michael stop, please. *Arretez, s'il vous plait!*"

She sounded worried. But was it because of his intention to visit that tower, or because that damned creature was blocking his way? It sure didn't look as if it was about to move as he limped toward it.

This was crazy. He, Michael Horsett, pathfinder for the 101st Airborne, was having a showdown. Not with some battled-hardened soldiers of the Wehrmacht, or the famed Waffen SS. He wasn't staring down the barrel of an 88 or about to be mown down under the tracks of a Tiger tank No, he was being eyeballed and challenged by that ugly, old, flat-faced cat. Well he had an answer for that!

"Michael no…" said Colette softly.

He unslung the machine-gun, undid the safety catch and decided that he really did need to fire a single round into its stupid head. Nobody would hear. Not in the middle of this place, in the middle of a war.

"Michael, the cat is a *matagot*. It is magic. It protects our home. We give it the first mouthful of food and drink at every meal, and so we stay er, *hors de danger*, er.."

"Safe, you mean," he said, lining it nicely in his sights, watching how it licked its paw without taking its eye off him. It seemed to know he was never gonna shoot. In truth, he wanted to take out his own insecurities on something, anything. The cat was an easy option. Was there such a thing as a scapecat? "It didn't help you when the Nazis came and took your imbeciles away."

"Then, we did not have The Matagot."

"Well you sure ain't having it for much longer," he said, taking first pressure on the trigger.

"Michael! *Non!*" she cried, although she stood rooted to the spot.

Horsett felt he could have plugged the creature, sure he could, to make up for what he should have being doing in the war. But at that very moment someone from the depths of the trees and shrubs called out:

"G'day mate! Fair dinkum!"

"Thibault!" said Horsett, almost pleased that he had an excuse not to fire. "Thibault, you asshole, I couldha shot you," he hissed.

The Frenchman emerged into the light, his eyes wide with incomprehension. He was draped with Tommy guns, grenade belts, and more Hawkins anti-tank mines.

Colette put her hand on Michael's arm and gently lowered his aim.

Horsett sighed. The damned cat had disappeared anyway. This was more important.

"*Vos amis sont tous morts,*" Thibault explained. He tried to make his mouth and face look sad, but that was difficult with his protruding teeth.

"All dead. Sure, I figured that."

"*Mais … j'ai pris ces armes,*" he said brightly, holding out the Tommy guns on their slings, as if they were dead pheasants.

Michael took the stuff from him, piece by piece and placed it all the long grass. Five machine guns, three Colt .45s, five Hawkins mines, twelve grenades.

"*Suffisant pour une armée, non?*" said Thibault brightly, his arms still sticking out at either side even though all the weaponry had been removed.

Colette frowned, crossed her arms in distaste.

Horsett gave a huge grin – "What's wrong, honey?" he asked, seeing the dark cloud across her face.

She snorted, and stomped off toward the house.

"*Now* it begins," he said, though he winced sharply as he bent to pick up the mines.

50

While Michael Horsett was in the middle of that lost garden preparing himself for battle, the *Feldgendarmes* stood at a crossroads not too far from there. In the crux of the roads, someone had painted a large red V on the remains of an old, rotting, empty chicken shed that leaned into the ground.

"As if that would frighten us," sneered Der Bomber, making a V sign with his fingers, frowning and pretending to smoke a cigar like Churchill.

"Well, what about this?" noted Alfred, pointing to the cut telephone wires dangling from their poles. "The work of the Resistance," he said, twirling the loose ends.

"All two of them," said Der Bomber.

"I could join them up again," mused Alfred.

"Waste of time," said Der Bomber. "They will be cut further along, too. It was like this in Stalingrad."

"Look," said Lueur. He pointed to a thin line of a few dozen civilians coming inland, carrying their scant possessions on barrows, donkeys, handcarts, in cheap suitcases or strung over bicycles. Hollow-eyed and gaunt, children wailing, babies in small buggies with tiny wheels and thick solid tyres. Old grey folk trying to keep up with the column, egged along by a battered-looking, bare-headed, unshaven priest who was straight as an umbrella. All of them glancing warily at the sky. When Lueur watched this he felt that the bright, shiny future of Nazism might be clouding over.

It was Günter, the family man, who took it upon himself to redirect them away from the main road that the *Wehrmacht* convoys might need. If and when they ever decided where, exactly, the Invasion was actually happening. He stood there at the crossroads with his feet together and his arms poised outward like a *balletomane*. "*Vous devez aller dans cette direction. Vous serez en sécurité*,"[1] he assured, nodding as they passed, the very soul of kindness, the Good German.

The meadow was wreathed in thin mist. There was a smell of

---

[1] You have to go in that direction. You will be safe.

crushed grass beneath the wheels of their vehicles. It was almost idyllic. The rest of the troop, standing idly and waiting for orders, watched the wretches go past. The policemen all had *Why?* etched on their faces.

"Most of those French bastards don't even speak French," said Uli, who had tried to sire a few in his time. "Hey, Le Blanc, you know their *patois*, go and ask them where they are going? *Why* they are going? Do they want to be on *our* side now? Shouldn't they be throwing garlands around their 'liberators' and having sex on their Shermans?"

Le Blanc rubbed his hands on his trousers in that nervous gesture he had, and went off to question the one most likely to have some alcohol.

Der Bomber spat on the ground, close to Lueur's boots. They watched it glob and fizzle, and then sink into the earth. The younger Frenchman knew the man was about to tell them yet again that he had seen all this before, in Russia. If he were to say once more: *Ich habe das alles schon gesehen, in Russland* then he, Lueur, might have to go somewhere to scream.

"*Ich habe das alles schon gesehen, in Russland*," said Der Bomber on cue, as he sprawled back into the car to rest his sore feet.

Lueur clenched his teeth instead of screaming. He took comfort from the fact that Uli and Gunther both raised their eyebrows and gave minute shakes of their heads as they sat on the verge, smoking. He also noticed that further down the side road his fellow Frenchman, Yohan Le Blanc, was going from one dishevelled refugee to the next, before getting into deep converse with what must have been their local priest. Lueur had come to loathe these Norman priests and their obsession with the poor, buzzing around them like flies to the shit. As for Le Blanc, he was just a turd in his own right, a complete embarrassment.

Hauptmann Schimmel sat alone in the second car some way up the road, studying his map as usual. Or seeming to. They could see from the tilting of his head that he was actually trying not to crash out with exhaustion. He was fixed into the rear of the car, the map spread out on the adjoining seat, staring at it as if it were a crystal ball. It was torn and much creased now, covered in thick pencil crosses and question marks, arrows, plus many more cryptic symbols that only he understood. It showed, to him at least, where they had been, where they might go next. The more he stared, the less sense it seemed to make. He needed sleep. He needed some more Pervitin.

The radio made loud crackling noises. He had tuned it so that he could not answer, and could – yet again – blame it on a fault. Or the Allies jamming. The men all feared that the plain-clothed *Geheime Feldpolizei*, the army's security and intelligence police, might try to find out exactly what was going on. But he didn't care how high up the demands were coming from: in his lucid moments he knew that he was *so* close to that which he sought down here.

The rest of the men heard the commotion, and wondered how long they could get away with this sham war of their own. They wandered up to their officer's car.

"What are you looking for now. Sir?" asked Der Bomber.

Schimmel tried to look alert and normal, scanning every millimetre on the paper. "An asylum, a hospital," he muttered.

The men looked at each other, faces expressionless.

"Asylum, *Herr Hauptman*? You are trying to find an asylum? He wants an asylum, lads."

The insult would have been obvious to Schimmel only days before. Now, under the influence of exhaustion, grief, guilt and the drug, he only nodded.

"You really need an asylum," Bomber added, without any inflection.

It was all getting too grave for the rest of them to snigger. Even though the Invasion had not directly touched their lives yet, its very presence, growling and roaring beyond the low hills on the horizon, was making them anxious. If they stood on high ground and looked toward the coast, they could see a low tidal wall of smoke beyond their horizon, caused by the explosions.

"The priest in Neuilly told me."

"A priest told you that you needed an asylum?" quizzed Bomber

"Yes! Are you stupid?"

"Where did he say it was, *Herr Hauptmann*," asked Lueur, in a mollifying tone.

"He thought it was between Neuilly and Forguet. It was also a hospital. Where would an injured parachutist go but to a hospital, jah? where, where, where..." Schimmel frantically unfolded the map to its full extent. Then, on an inspiration, he fumbled into a pouch and took out the burnt remains of the map that his son had used.

Le Blanc rejoined the group. He told them what he had learned, though no-one was interested. "Those people... They are from a small village, ten kilometres from the coast. Yet the Allied bombers and battleships are destroying everything before them...French, German... They just blow everything up. This lot want to come as far inland, and away from the fighting as they can. At least the Germans never bombed their villages, they said. They are all saying it," he said, eagerly.

"Arse licker," whispered Der Bomber.

Uli, standing behind him, mimed taking a drink.

Hauptmann Schimmel was oblivious and indifferent to everyone and everything but the map. "Get in your vehicles!" he shouted.

The two Frenchmen and Der Bomber climbed in with Schimmel. The rest took their places in the second car.

"Where are we going now, sir?" Le Blanc asked, made hopeful by the liquor he had bullied from the refugees, careful not to breathe on his commanding officer as he sat next to him, helping to straighten the map.

"We are trying to find a hospital asylum," Schimmel snapped, as though it were obvious. "It's near here somewhere."

"St Martin's? where they had mongol children?"

"You *know* it?" asked Schimmel, startled. "*You* know it?!"

"Of course, *Herr Hauptmann*. Why didn't you ask me before, sir?"

Yohan Le Blanc felt better and better. Der Bomber, in the driving seat, glowered. Young Lueur pulled a face.

"Show me," said the officer, leaning over and offering the much-marked and infinitely precious map.

Le Blanc savoured the moment. He was seeing what none of them had been allowed to see: a simple local map that was almost defaced by his superior's unintelligible, mad symbols.

"Here, between these marks, sir. I did some work there many years ago. It was always extremely difficult to find. Perhaps deliberately so. If we..."

"JABO!" screamed Der Bomber, as the sky cracked open and a twin-tailed plane with black-and-white stripes on its wing scorched overhead. Its airstream struck them in hundreds of continuing punches, before it curved upward into the clear sky, turning, twisting, rolling as if it had all the time in the world. The downdraft blew the map out of Schimmel's hands.

"*Der Gabelschwanzteufel,*" said Der Bomber. "Into the trees! It will come back!" cried the man who had always seen this sort of thing before.

"No!" cried Schimmel, even louder, when he saw the aircraft dawdle away and be lost to sight over the tree-covered hill ridge. "It has gone. Why would it be out here? It is lost." He got out and retrieved the map, brushed it with the side of his hand, saw the anxious faces of the men in the other car. "Stay in your vehicle and follow us!" he shouted back to them. "We are going to…"

But the Lightning had only been circling for the right angle of approach. Now it appeared again, literally out of the blue, and was coming straight down the road at head height. And before anyone could blink there were lights flashing from its nose, as its cannon blasted away, ripping the second car and its occupants to shreds, blasting it on its side.

"*Schnell! Schnell!*" cried Der Bomber though largely to himself, as Schimmel leapt back into the vehicle. Bomber spun the wheel of the wagon, put his foot down hard and crashed through the ruined fence next to the old shed. The car fish-tailed across a meadow toward the line of homeless who – afraid of *all* the armies and their air forces by now – were bent and huddling into themselves.

Behind them, there were explosions and screams: grenades going off, a fuel tank igniting. Hot metal, exploding bullets and shrapnel fragments zinged past them. The other three were flung around in Bomber's car like dolls. A large portion of the fence he had smashed still clung to car, sticking out like a scythe. Wheels spun in mud.

"Shit! Shit!" grunted Der Bomber who gunned the car out of the mud and sent it careering across the field, aware out the corner of his eye that his friends were being consumed in a fireball, vaguely human shapes within the flames.

Ahead was the priest trying to shepherd two small, sobbing children out of the way. Der Bomber's eyes were glazed with terror, he didn't see them. They looked at him as if he were the Angel of Death. It was Lueur in the passenger seat who grabbed the wheel with both hands. *"Dummkopf!"* he yelled, and pushed it around so they missed the innocent trio by centimetres, and hurtled toward the protection of the trees at the other side of the field, bouncing in and out of the dips and furrows.

They stopped. No way through, but they had gained some shelter from the enemy above. Pigeons flitted from branch to branch, cooing peacefully. Sun filtered down through the leaves like a cooling shower. The sky was empty and pure.

The four of them sat there, white faced, breathing heavily, shaken and bruised. Eardrums still echoing from the explosions. Behind them, on the road edging the field, were the remains of the other vehicle. The front wheels were missing, its body had been driven down into the earth like a deformed chariot. One side was blackened, the other almost white with the heat of burning metal. Bizarrely, one of its headlights still shone like a single reproachful eye before winking out. At either side of the the pyre of twisted, burning metal were molten black and white lumps that must have been their former companions.

"Uli, Alfred, Gunther…" whispered Le Blanc to himself, as if the naming might somehow maintain their existence. "Uli, Alfred Gunther…" His shaking this time had nothing to do with alcohol.

"There's Uli. Above you," said Der Bomber, pointing to the severed head still wearing its helmet, wedged between branches, an oddly startled look on its face. As if he had just recognised someone and was about to speak.

Lueur got out of the *wagen* and vomited. The *Hauptmann* could smell his own piss. He could also see, taking shape within the poisonous smoke, the outline of his son. Dieter seemed to be wagging his finger reproachfully.

A tall column of acrid-smelling, black smoke, shot through at the base with gold sparkles, rose toward the empty and crystal-clear sky. At least no-one was screaming: they must have been killed instantly. The only sounds came from the popping of the ammunition as the fires took hold.

The refugees hurried on without looking. They had seen too much of this already since being liberated. Their priest shepherded them through a gap in the tall hedge and gave the survivors of the troop a last, baleful glare before disappearing himself.

"What now?" asked Lueur, who didn't need an answer. He

looked scornfully at Der Bomber and wondered if he had really been at Stalingrad. Then the three of them looked to *Herr Hauptmann* for leadership.

"God..." he muttered, who had never been fired at before. "God, god, god..." he said, fingering the little cross under the gorget, wondering where Dieter's ghost had gone.

Not far from this carnage, Jules the Shadow was hidden in the long grass and patches of corn, behind shrubs at the edge of a wood. He had watched as the twin-engined Yankee plane had scorched overhead then turned to attack the German vehicles. Then he had felt a certain pleasure watching the smoke from the blasted car rising to the heavens in rapid spurts, like dead souls.

Beyond that, the blood-red sun was going down on the Normandy beaches. He knew that what sounded like the very distant rolling of surf had to be continual high explosives. He ran a hand up his long, balding forehead, sluicing off the sweat, and scratched what remained of his hair. Someone in that world was getting a pounding, though no-one knew for sure which side.

Possibly one person knew, and Jules had been following him, determined to show the world – especially brother Armand – that he too had substance, that he too had balls.

L'Étincelle, whom Jules knew was connected with the Resistance, was busy placing across the road a series of little wooden blocks. These had nails inserted so that one would always point upright. Then he draped grasses and twigs around each to make them seem like the normal, natural debris of a country road. He was moving quickly, nervously, like a rat; looking in all directions and ready to flee. Yet there was a deliberation in his placement; he was determined that this pattern would puncture at least one tyre from a passing German car.

"Is this a new version of Boules or Petanque, my old friend?" called Jules boldly, from behind the bush.

L'Étincelle froze as he put the last device in place, in the centre of the road. He answered without turning, knowing the voice so well. "Jules Allumage...Go now, or I will kill you."

"*Crotte!* When we were young, Emile, I used to beat you up after school."

"*Merde!* That is not how I remember it."

"*Zut!* Did you not call me Jules Le Marteau?"[1]

"Never! I think that everyone called you Jules the Big Mouth."

"Hmmmm…perhaps they did. But with my big ears I can hear a car coming."

L'Étincelle turned and leaped across the ditch, crashing through the bushes and heading past Jules, deeper into the woods, out of sight. When he thought it was safe, he stopped, crouched behind a huge fallen tree and tried to control his panting so he could listen.

"You see," whispered Jules, coming down next to him. "I am not out of breath. We are the same age yet –"

He couldn't finish. L'Étincelle put his right palm over Jules' mouth and his left on the back of Jules' head, shushing him. Together, they listened.

Through the trees, over the noise of a breeze in the branches, birdsong, and the very distant barking of dogs, they heard a vehicle coming along the road, changing down a gear as it approached the sharp bend. And then…two sharp bangs as the tyres burst, then a skidding and squealing of metal against road, and loud German voices shouting as the unseen vehicle went into the ditch.

Making sure the great trunk kept him from any possibility of being seen, L'Étincelle half-rose, and indicated to Jules that they should head deeper into the woods. At first they almost tip-toed, yet bent double. Further in, they ran as fast their middle-age would allow.

"Did we kill anyone?" asked Jules, when it seemed that they were safely distant, and beyond any likelihood of pursuit. He washed the mud from his old boots in the small stream.

"What do you mean 'we'? That was *my* doing. You're just a windbag." L'Étincelle was trembling, breathless.

Jules leaned back against a tree. He saw the broken branches above, and the tangled remains of what had to be a parachute harness, dangling.

"Emile, my old friend this is all 'little' stuff. These spikes…pah! If you want to be a real Resistant, not just in your head, then your old pal Jules the Marvellous will show you something big. Very big," he said with shining eyes, and tapping

---

[1] The Hammer

the side of his nose.

"Shit. As always. And your nose will fall off if you keep doing that."

Jules reached up and pulled the length of harness, so the branch bent like a bow. "Do you know what this is?"

L'Étincelle said nothing. It looked like strands of a parachute harness, without its canopy. "So tell me," he said, in a bored tone.

"This," said Jules, "is part of something that will help us win the war..."

51

Horsett lay in the bed, in the complete darkness, naked and alone. The throbbing in his leg, and smaller wounds were easing off. The medicine that Astrid had given him, *"Pour prévenir l'infection,"* flowed slowly through his veins. Outside the windows, the closed shutters rattled.

With what was left of his rational mind he knew it was the wind, carrying the distant violence of battle. But the drugged and guilty side made him wonder if it was the ghosts of his buddies. What were their names again? Oh yeah – *Harry, Tommy, Troy, Daleth, Janko, Hoss and Sarge.* He said them again, in a whisper: *Harry, Tommy, Troy, Daleth, Janko, Hoss and Sarge.* Had he forgotten anyone? As he said their names, he saw their faces, white and almost luminous.

> *Lighten up Mike*
> *What you doing here, buddy?*
> *You left us*
> *We need you*
> *We're dyin', you know that?*
> *For Chrissake…*

He wanted to light a candle, but there were none at hand. Besides, the two older women were all pretty freaky about keeping the place blacked-out. He didn't know if they were more afraid of Allied bombers or Germans soldiers. Or whether they mainly wanted to keep what was happening a secret from Colette.

His buddies marched past him again. Christ did he feel guilty! But then someone else appeared, this spirit brighter than the rest, almost solid in comparison. This was an older man, cheerful.

Hello, my son, he seemed to say, and it was almost like a blessing, and he sure needed one of those just then. *Be what thou wilt within thee.*

"Huh?"

The moment he spoke, the vision ended. He sat up in bed and thought of Colette. Usually when he did that he sort of sang, inwardly, but today when they came indoors she was cold and distant. Angry. The fog around her was so dense he could have put his helmet atop and it would have stayed there. If he could have found the helmet, that is. He touched her arm, gently, and tried to say *What's wrong?* But she shrugged it off and stomped away.

The two older gave him *I-told-you-so* looks, though they had never told him anything of the kind.

One moment she is up! said Astrid, her voice pitched accordingly.

And then she is down added Selene, likewise.

Okay okay, he got the picture. His Mom had been like that too but he put that down to her being in the wrong place with the wrong man.

Another ghost appeared. He knew this one.

Get your gun, son. Come out here with us. You're goin' crazy – All these women.

"Sarge... is that you?" he whispered to the darkness.

Get the hell outta there, son!

"Sarge…"

Nothing. Silence. Darkness.

Then he felt the draught as the door opened, as he knew it would. Noiseless as before. He turned on his side, ready to touch whoever it was. If her tits were small and pointy it would be Astrid; if they were rounder, then Selene.

You got it made, buddy! That voice was so clear.

"Hoss... Hoss is that you?" Horsett whispered. Hoss was a big Texan, he would have approved, sure he would.

But a cool finger touched his lips, as a slim body crept into bed next to him. He was about to explore it when, to his astonishment, another body snuck in from the other side, and he knew right off that was Selene behind him, and Astrid in front.

Allongez-vous, someone murmured. Or was it *Lie back.* Did he hear it with his ears, or in his head?

"Jesus…" he gasped, as the touching began.

"*Non, pas lui,*" said Astrid, real clear. "*Il y a des choses que vous seul pouvez nous donner.*"

"Things that only I can give?" he said out loud, but still very softly, shivering as Astrid's eyelashes stroked upon him. They could have what they wanted. The spirits of his buddies should be cheering him.

"*Tu es notre Dieu,*" answered Selene, giving a little gasp as he began to touch her.

His head swam. Was it the women? Or the medicine? Or the ghosts?

"*Mais je n'aime pas le 'tu'*," he insisted, before giving in to them, like the warrior he was.

52

As Horsett had lain in bed, receiving his own kind of
liberation, Luc was sitting in the darkness of the church in
Neuilly, wringing his hands. The crude stained-glass windows
kept flaring with the lights of the distant battle. In them pulsed
the gaunt, greeny-grey figure of the patron, St Ywi, who could
cure eye problems with his spittle. The bigger the explosion, the
brighter the blast, the longer the saint glowed. He seemed to lean
toward Luc. He seemed to be sneering.

Luc had arrived at the priest's house just after the curfew. All
the shutters were closed. Not a chink of light escaped from it or
any house around, though there were still two hours of daylight
left.

He tapped on the back door, his secret code: *Tap. Tap-tap-tap.*
And again. The door opened slowly, he thought his friend might
be teasing him. His oft-admired, winning smile froze into a rictus
grin when he saw Sophia.

"Come in!" she said brightly. "Be careful of the light, Luc.
Through this curtain. Come in. We are about to eat."

"Father ..." said Luc, as the priest came up and shook his
hand. A cool and formal handshake. Business-like. There was a
gleam in his eyes. Luc wasn't sure if it was of smugness or
treachery.

"My new housekeeper. You know Sophia of course. Sophia
knows everyone."

Sophia beamed and gave a little open-handed wave. Luc
nodded. Yes, he knew her.

The room was full of freshly-cut flowers, lushly displayed in
every variety of vase, jug and bottle. The feminine touch! He was
annoyed how the woman, wrapped in a voluminous and entirely
respectable white dressing-gown that trailed to the floor, sat at the
table like an empress. She even flicked up her open hands in a
brief gesture as if to say *Yes, she was astonished by all this too.*

He was irritated how Gilles angled himself to keep his burnt
side away from her gaze. They offered food, but he declined.

"Father Gilles said you were interested in the priesthood,
Luc," said Sophia to cover the awkward silence.

He looked at her. He looked at Gilles. The priest looked at

him. Between the three views there was an unholy triangle of knowledge.

"Yes," he had said. "I have a lot on my mind. I just came to ask if I could sit in the church, and pray."

"Of course, Luc. May you find understanding and peace in there," said the priest, handing him the keys.

So he sat in the church and he waited. He adopted all the outer visible signs of inward spiritual grace and kept his ears pricked for when Gilles would sneak out and see him. It would not be the first time they had had intimate moments here.

He waited.

He waited.

Empowered by the distant fires, St Ywi leered.

Back in the little kitchen, Father Gilles felt safe. Sophia made him feel safe. It was like the years of his childhood, sitting next to the fire with his *maman*, listening to her stories. Sophia now was probably about the age his *maman* had been then. And the same dimples in her elbows. Even the same way she licked her fingertips before turning each page of the old *'Je suis partout'* magazines he had brought from Paris, with their important observations about Jews.

Luc, and all the temptations that Luc brought, was pushed behind thick walls and two closed doors. That side of his life must never be released again. It was almost as if he wanted 'Luc' – or what the boy represented – to rot and disappear into the good earth in a way that St Ywi never did.

Protected from his lusts by this woman, who had entered his world, he could now concentrate on the forthcoming battle with his demon. She would help him find it, he was sure.

The mirror shook on the wall. The windows rattled behind the shutters.

"What was that?" gasped Sophia, who knew exactly what it was: the great door slamming as Luc had got fed up waiting and stormed out.

"Nothing," said the priest. "A troubled soul, perhaps."

He hoped that he would sleep well tonight. He needed the oblivion. The demon was close, he knew that. It would take a clear mind and all his strength if he were to defeat it.

53

For the remainder of that night, the four surviving *Feldgendarmes* – Le Blanc, Henri, Bomber and Schimmel – had been awake, patching themselves up, clearing up the mess in their lives caused by the 'twin-forked devil'. Three of them were close to collapse, as if the dark war-beast was pulling bits off and casting them away in random directions. They were held together by frayed sinews of duty, obedience, various kinds of guilt, and their increasingly mad *Hauptmann*. Now, just before dawn, they were out on the road once more.

"Where? *Where!?*" barked the officer, half-turning to Le Blanc in the rear of the wagon, who was trying to give directions to St Martin's, where Schimmel was certain his prey was hiding. "*Where!*"

Le Blanc was confused. There was only a faint glimmer of the pre-dawn, and pulsing, growling radiance from the battle in the north-west. *Think, Think* he told himself, nervously. The hedgerows and the lanes leading to the old hospital were, he remembered, confusing. Deliberately. He knew of the natural screens used to hide the access gaps in the high hedgerows. Everyone said that finding the place was bewildering: locals, tradespeople, officials. Once, on a weekend, he had ridden there with his horse and cart, delivered some timber and done some carpentry – and had had a brief encounter. Even though he had directions, he had had the devil's own job in finding the little lane that twisted and turned its way to the entrance.

"Where?" said Schimmel, softly this time, drawing his Luger and turning full on to point it in the man's face. It wavered.

"*Herr Hauptmann…*" said Bomber, fighting against Stalingrad's legacy of battle fatigue, which he tried to shut out by talking about it all the time. He pushed the officer's shaking gun down and to the side. "Let him think. Give him the map."

Le Blanc unbuttoned the square, flat flashlight from his tunic, took off the red filter, bent low in the back of the vehicle, cursed at the weak beam from the fading batteries, and tried to save his own life. He kept the map spread taut against his thighs to hide his alcoholic tremor.

"Look," said Henri Lueur, leaning over from the driving seat. "We are here. This is the way we came. Now remember...Remember." To Le Blanc's ears the young man said it as if the future of France and its liberator Germany was hanging on this.

Yohan knew that his life was on the brink. He had been bashing at the gates of remembrance without response. And now, as he was about to plunge into his own complete darkness, a woman's face appeared on the cinema screen before his brow. A woman's face and two black puppies!

"What is it?" asked Lueur, seeing his face brighten.

"I saw a a woman with silver hair, gorgeous she was, with knowing eyes, pushing back the overhanging branches of...a willow tree. Two black dogs yapping at her feet. The tree had two huge roots that looked like the crossed legs of a woman."

"Are you dreaming this?" snapped the officer.

"I am remembering, sir. Yes, she pushed back the screen of branches and showed me a rough track behind."

Everyone gets lost coming here, she had said with a sparkle in in her eye, as if he might get something. *Come through.* Then she had climbed aboard, and smiled, and his heart had leapt – or was it his cock? *Turn right.* She'd pointed.

Are you sure, he had asked, as in all honesty it seemed as if that could not lead anywhere, whereas left or straight ahead seemed more likely.

But she had smiled, and he'd smiled, and right it had been, and she had pressed against him on the narrow seat of the cart.

He must have looked confused as he'd nudged the old broken-backed horse along, the dogs running ahead.

Only people who are destined to come here can find us, she had said.

He'd felt honoured. He'd felt important. He'd been tempted to try for a bit of tit.

"Well?" asked Schimmel, and Le Blanc was out of the warm, hopeful otherworld and back in the war-zone.

"There was a willow tree, a stream. A fold in the land and lanes. Tree roots like a woman's crossed legs."

The other three looked at each other.

"Back that way," said Der Bomber.

54

As the four exhausted Germans closed in on the former hospital, Sophia was woken by the sound of screaming in the priest's house.

An intruder? She'd pulled her overcoat over her nightdress, grabbed a fire-iron, and hurtled into the corridor to confront whoever might be there. The door of the priest's cell (she could hardly think of that windowless cube as a room!) was still shut, and there was whimpering from within.

"Father? Father Fournier!"

No answer, although the whimpering was suppressed into a snuffling, and the snuffling gave way to little coughs.

She opened the door. He was curled up on the bed, a compacted foetus, darker than the rest of the room. She could smell his sweat, feel his fear.

"The evil one is coming," he said. "*Le Noirceur.*"

Her little brother, who had died after a severe epileptic seizure many years ago, had had such terrors too. They'd had a doctor, Dr. Encausse, a big powerful man with a long forked beard who stank of tobacco. He had laughed when the old people in the village still referred to it as *Le mal de Saint Jean*[1]. He'd explained about the 'aura', the presentiment that a fit was on its way, and the different ways this could express itself: voices in the head, distortions of vision, nausea, strange lights, panic attacks. And then afterwards, the memory loss, the confusion and sometimes the calmness or incontinence.

She'd used to cuddle her brother. She couldn't do this to the priest, or even presume to tell him what she knew. Though God knows he could have done with both of that.

"It's the war," she said, making her voice as soothing as if she had wrapped her arms around him. "You can feel it in the ground. When the cannons go, and the bombs drop, even the ground vibrates. Nothing is coming to get you. No evil spirit. It's only the war."

The priest looked up. The woman's frizzy hair flowed to her

---

[1] The evil of St John the Baptist

225

shoulders, glinting by the candle she had just lit. He breathed deeply and felt comforted by her in a way that Luc could never achieve. She had come into his room like his mother had once done, and with as much concern. Thank heaven for her!

"Come downstairs Father," she said. "I will make breakfast. You will feel better in the light, I promise."

Sometimes, with her brother, she'd been able to deflect its onset. Sometimes it had come and gone quickly, almost without him realising. She suspected the priest's seizure had already been and gone in the darkness.

So he dressed and came downstairs, exhausted and fearful as he always did after such inner encounters. She put her hand on his shoulder, pushed the wooden kitchen chair behind his knees, and forced him to sit. There were sausages frying, the coffee steaming from the mug.

"You spoil me," he said, humbly.

"Somebody must."

The unearthly wailing of distant rocket-artillery pierced through the walls. They both looked through the icon of the Madonna that hung above the fireplace, toward the huge battle for Caen, above which floated the thick black smoke of burning oil depots.

"I knew an Irish priest once," Fournier said. "He believed most earnestly in a spirit called a *banshee* as I recall. He said they would appear when someone was about to die, and hover around the house, shrieking. Perhaps they are banshees we hear."

"It's only the war, Father. Trust me. Now eat up, like a good boy."

"Thank you Sophia. Truly, thank you…"

55

A few kilometres away, as the crow might fly, they found the willow, the two huge roots crossed like a woman's legs. The nearby stream gurgled over rocks.

"Look at that, look where the clump of moss is, just like a woman's –"

Lueur's observation was drowned out by loud, shrill, howling noises. The men stayed motionless in their vehicle, in the country lane. The branches of the tree draped over the hood of the wagon.

"*Nebelwerfers*," said Der Bomber, who had seen and heard the multi rocket launchers in action often enough. "Ours. The Amis called them 'Moaning Minnies'. The Ivans had their own, called *Katushyas*, though we called them Stalin's Organs."

"Dawn attack," opined Henri, rolling his eyes as the others used to do when Bomber started on about Stalingrad. As he sat there in that battered car, in the dark, down a narrow lane amid high hedges, he wished he had joined the Waffen SS instead of this lot.

"Then the invasion really is Normandy. It's not a diversion," muttered Le Blanc.

"Silence, all of you!" hissed Schimmel. "Now you stay here," he said to Henri Lueur. If there'd been enough light he would have seen the young man grimace. "Do *not* answer the radio. Remember, as we go in, we are not policemen now – we are soldiers. The rules of war apply, and there will be no fair trials."

"Are you certain, sir, that what we are looking for is in in there? It was just an asylum when I knew it. They were all mad."

"Just lead the way, Private Le Blanc." Schimmel was hallucinating but he knew it: he saw his son standing in the road, smiling. He saw his son turned into a burnt log. He wanted to end this and his own madness, now.

All three got out of the *wagen* with difficulty. All four had minor shrapnel wounds from the fighter-bomber. They creaked and groaned, and tried to maintain a soldierly silence. Their Schmeissers were ready, safety catches off. Le Blanc found the screen that was used to conceal the lane and pushed it to one side. He led the men in single file along the twisting and curling lane, following tracks that were surely caused by an old tractor. Buildings loomed into sight at the faint glow of dawn, at the sound of distant cock-crow and cannon fire,.

"There," whispered Le Blanc triumphantly, stepping back to let his leader lead.

Schimmel had withdrawn his Luger, and held it against his chest at shoulder-height, the barrel pointing upward. His face was green wax, his hands shook as much as Le Blanc's. There was a tic in his eye that Morse-coded his exhaustion.

The three of them heaved open the rickety gate, having to lift one end completely off the ground and swing it open. Le Blanc looked around. The memories entered his senses again, like morsels of chocolate lost behind the teeth.

"There...the stables. They had little ponies for the imbeciles. And there, the main house of dormitories behind this little block..."

Other than watching people being hanged as traitors, malingerers, or *resistants,* and always finding an excuse to avoid being directly involved, this was his greatest moment as a *Feldgendarme.*

56

As the thin shroud of dawn finally wrapped itself around St Martin's, Horsett saw it as a faint greyness through tiny cracks at the side of the blackout curtains. His head felt as if he had a hangover. He had to stop taking that syrup! The two naked women were curled around him and each other like two fishes. Every time they moved, they would rasp against his scars, or his aching leg. He wasn't complaining.

They woke, disturbingly, almost at the same moment and looked up at him with little girls' eyes.

"*Malgré ce qui se passe, nous vous aimons,*"[1] Selene said into his chest, in a sad voice. Astrid nodded. He knew exactly what they said but still frowned as if he didn't. They loved him? Well that was just fine. He could handle that. Yet what did they mean by the first part?

"Colette?" he said softly.

"*Colette vous adore...*"

"*Et Luc vous adore aussi!*"

They giggled at that one.

"Luc's a faggot," he growled. "Homosexual."

He could feel their bony shoulders give gallic shrugs.

"*Qui s'en soucie? Ce n'est pas grave.*"[2]

"*Vraiment: Il n'ya pas de grâce, il n'ya pas de culpabilité. Telle est la loi: Fais ce que voudras.*[3]

"Our Master used to say that. He judged no-one, loved all."

Horsett looked down at the women. Their heads were still only dark shadows against his body but they were utterly sincere.

This is crazy, he thought – again. But he also felt good. They really didn't seem to care about ordinary things. He would never invite his *maman* to meet them! They would never judge or scorn him like his pa had done even when he had turned up in his paratrooper uniform, satanically proud and hoping for due praise at the last. In fact his Dad's last words to him, squeezed out through the ravaged muscles of his face, had been: *When I was your*

---

[1] Despite what happens, we love you

[2] Who cares? it does not matter

[3] There is no grace, there is no guilt. This is the law: do what thou wilt

age, I could have torn you apart and scattered your useless pieces everywhere…

Anyhow, these two women holding his cock, who had done things to him and each other other in the night that he had never imagined, gave him the best praise in the world.

Something soft brushed his feet.

"That stupid cat is here," he said. "Have you always had it? Get rid of it."

"Pah. In our tradition, you must not keep a *matagot* all your life long: if the owner is dying, he will not suffer a long agony – as long as he does not free the *matagot*. It will go soon."

"I don't get it."

"Our Master sees through The Matagot's eyes."

"Your Master? Oh yeah, the Cohen guy."

Astrid tutted and tapped him on the wrist, like a naughty boy. "Our Master, he was a prophet. He saw the world turning and changing. He saw the Hawk God's coming, and the destiny of France to lead the world. In the beginning there was the Great Mother, Isis. I am her priestess. And there was her consort, Osiris, who was torn to pieces by the dark god Set and scattered over the land to give it life."

"You don't say. *Vous ne dites pas!*"

Selene tutted and tapped this time. She followed on with the story: "Isis gave birth to a son Hor or Heru or Horus. He could soar, he could plummet. He could fight. He had to fight the darkness of Set and win. You are Hor and also Set."

"What a crock of shit," he scorned. Yet his nape hairs prickled: this was too much like what his pa had said that time. "*C'est un pot de Merde.*"

"But you are part of this. Our prophet is with us still. He lives in a realm that intermingles with ours. He sees through The Matagot. He guides us daily," Astrid insisted.

"What, from the next farm?"

The women were both silent. Horsett felt their speeches had been said before. Yet he didn't want to be a smart-ass after their kindness.

Something light and soft fell onto his face and chest. He peered. "Feathers. Three feathers. Where did they come from?"

"They are apports," whispered Selene. "From Amenti, the realm in which our Master abides. It is a sign he is pleased with you."

"Knock it off! Harry Houdini spent half his life proving all that to be horse-shit."

More fell.

"Are they white? Are you saying I'm some kinda coward?"

"*Non!*" from Astrid. "They are golden. They are the feathers of the Hawk."

He sat up and looked around, lit a candle. Another handful of feathers emerged from the darkness at the ceiling. He picked some up and studied them, then ran them along the women's nipples. "That's some trick, gals."

"It is not a trick Michael," whispered Selene. "Truly, it is a Sign."

More petals fell. He felt oddly distressed. The cat seemed to be smiling at him.

Selene touched him gently on the cheek. "Your father could not have torn you apart, Michael."

"Jesus! Can you read my mind?"

Astrid snuggled against him and started playing with his cock. "We can do many things, *m'sieur.*"

He was deeply troubled now. What else could these gals see inside him?

They grabbed hold of him again, he lay back. They stroked him, sushed him; it was perfect, took all fears away. He relaxed. Live for the moment, the plunge. "So gals… what do you want from me?"

"We need to make babies," said Astrid.

"They are vessels, vehicles," said Selene.

"Do *what?!*" He sat up sharply this time, disentangling himself from them. He would have asked more if it hadn't been for the gunshots outside.

Then the door burst open and Colette stood there quivering. Even for the brief second before she spoke, Horsett knew she wasn't surprised to see them like this. "The Germans are coming," she said.

And hell exploded into their world.

57

Outside in the yard, two dogs hurtled out of the shadows, snarling, straight for Schimmel.

"Shit!", he hissed, as he shot them both, though not before one of them had raked his left arm with its teeth. The one called Nu curved upward on its paws, gave two long gasps and went silent. Geb whined on its side, and twitched into silence. *Herr Hauptmann* stood up straight and pointed his Luger back up at the stars again.

"There. In the house. No need for silence now. Bomber – break that door open!"

Bomber looked at the large door. If they had rammed it with the *Kübelwagen* it would probably have held. He limped over and rattled the large brass door-knocker instead, thinking *"So shoot me"*. He rocked on his heels and presented his broad and utterly weary back to *Herr Hauptmann*.

Upstairs, Astrid and Selene poured into their nightdresses, flinging Horsett's clothes at him. He hopped into his pants and would have made for the door, but Selene opened up a panel in the wall revealing a small, dark, cupboard-sized space he hadn't known existed. Then and – unbalanced as he was – she pushed him in without his weapons.

"Stay in there," hissed Astrid, closing the portal, as the two women slid a small dressing table in front of it. "Now Selene... sick old woman with fever," she commanded, and slapped the other's face, hard, several times. They saw the Tommy gun and the Colt. Astrid grabbed them and put them under Selene's legs, under the covers. "If necessary, use them. Now Colette...play the young frightened idiot – with me! Pretend! Pretend! Act 'as if'! Look everywhere but *there!*"

Hammering on the door. Then a harder noise – the butts of their guns. Astrid had heard this before when they last came.

She and Colette lit a lamp each as they hurried. Down the narrow stairs, along dark corridors. More hammering, loud German voices.

"*Nous arrivons! Attendez, attendez!*"[1]

She undid the locks. The darkness of the little hallway flowed out to enshroud the soldiers with their flashlights: black shapes against the greying sky.

"Pah! The Three Wise Men!" said Astrid as they pushed her aside. "Did you find nothing in the stables?"

They pushed through into the little kitchen, started overturning chairs and small furniture, crashing everything loudly.

"What do you want?" she asked, her arms protectively around Colette. "What are you looking for?" She didn't expect an answer. She was also keenly aware that the men were exhausted, and almost going through the motions of a raid. She pulled back the curtains and threw open all the shutters. "Now you can see. Go on, look everywhere. But all the little imbeciles and Jews have already gone."

Schimmel stared at her, swaying. Although she knew nothing about Pervitin, Astrid could see that he was under the influence of some drug. "Ah, *Monsieur* Frankincense. Whatever star brought you here, you will be disappointed. Colette, here are the keys. Let them into every room."

Colette dropped the heavy bunch in her nervousness. Der Bomber picked them and gave her a curt nod. Astrid sensed he was tired of frightening people to order, and this was just a pretty young girl. On another day she might have asked, gently and teasingly: *What sort of man have you become?* and he would have been clay in her hands.

As they lined up and waited for her to unlock the first door Astrid looked closely at him. He rocked back and forth from his good foot to his bad. She touched the side of his head, as near his temple as the helmet would allow. "You have come from a very distant, cold place," she said quietly, as the officer and the girl rattled at the first lock. "You have been brave, and have many wounds. If we were friends, I would treat you with myrrh to clean them and prevent infection. It would stop the spread of gangrene that worries you so much. I would help you like this if I could…"

Der Bomber closed his eyes. He closed them hard, perhaps trying to drive away the memories of the frozen steppes. When he looked at her, it was with the eyes of a frightened young man.

---

[1] We are coming! Wait, wait!

"*Danke,*" he mouthed.

The door creaked open.

"What is up there?" asked Schimmel, pointing up the narrow staircase.

"Three small bedrooms. My sister is in bed with a fever. We think it is diptheria. It may be contagious. But go up there, please," Astrid pleaded, with a mad little chuckle. "Go up and catch the fever! Please please!"

"Le Blanc," said Schimmel, "You go. Search every centimetre. If the woman causes any trouble, shoot her. Just once, in the back of the head. We are not barbarians."

He pushed Colette along the corridor, toward the first door at the end, and left the Frenchman to get on with his search.

If Yohan le Blanc had thought he'd won some measure of approval or acceptance, it faded with this command. He took a handkerchief and made to cover his mouth and nose, to keep out the germs, and turned to go up the stairs.

But Astrid took his hand and looked intently at him. "But I know you..." she said.

He pushed his helmet back and shone the light in his own face. "I did some work here, madame, up those very stairs, before the war. You met me under the tree. Later, we..."

Her face shone. "*Monsieur d'Or*,"[1] she said, touching his heart with the palm of her left hand. "I remember you *very* well. I never forget a handsome face, even though you've changed so much." She looked his uniform up and down, with a *pah!* behind her eyes.

And – Astrid knew – Yohan le Blanc's memories flooded out, five years ago, before the Fall of France, before his own fall from grace.

He had worked upstairs repairing some floorboards first, and then added some new pannelling to the walls of a bedroom.

She had sat on the bed, which had been covered in a large dust sheet and watched him, kicking her heels and singing to herself. Yohan, who'd had little experience of women, had the mad sense she was attracted to him. The way she'd perched and sometimes sprawled on the edge of the bed, and flung little compliments, had

---

[1] Mister Gold

made his hands shake for reasons that had nothing to do with alcohol. Not in those days.

Once, twice, a strange but impressive elderly man whom she had introduced as *Monsieur* Michelet, Le Cohen – whatever that was – floated in and inspected his work. The man had worn what he at first thought was a floor-length red nightshirt, but realised was more of a robe. Both times he had winked before he left.

Then when Yohan had finished his work, the remaining scraps of wood neatly bundled and his tools in his leather bag: "*Approchez*," she had commanded. Her eyes had sparkled, she'd still been sitting on the edge of the bed. "Here," she'd said, handing him an envelope containing his money. "It is correct and as agreed."

He'd put it in his shirt pocket, quivering inwardly, yearning just to reach and touch her, those perfect little breasts.

"But you also get *this*, as a bonus…" she'd added, and had slowly unbuttoned him, all the while keeping eye contact. Then she had taken him in her mouth and done things he had scarcely believed possible with her tongue and long eyelashes.

"Thank you," he had said, when it was over – all too soon. "But what about you?" he'd asked gallantly, though he wouldn't have known exactly how to return a favour of that kind.

Her eyes had clouded over for a second. She had bitten her lip, and seemed to look at something inside her head. "One day…one day you will do me a favour."

"That I promise!" he'd said. He might have said more, he might have asked to see her again, but he'd beenstartled by a huge laugh from behind. There in the doorway was the *Monsieur*, with his arm around another woman. They must have been watching all the time!

"*Encore, encore!*" the man had said, clapping, coming forward as if to shake Yohan's hand. "Was that not magical Selene?"

Astrid had skipped off the bed and had stood beside the other two, linking with the man's free arm.

"Will he join us, do you think? Did you *see?*" the man had asked her, using his flared sleeve to wipe the corner of her lips.

"I saw something, but I am not sure. Not yet. But one day…one day I know that he will help us."

"Bravo!" the Master had said, giving Yohan a powerful pat on his shoulder. "Would you stay for a while? Would you eat with us?

Selene here is very impressed by your work. We need a carpenter here, don't we?"

Yohan had blushed. He'd beenso embarrassed that he'd taken up his gear and fled, down the stairs, along the corridor, through the kitchen, across the yard where the little slant-eyed children had been playing.

And now here was Yohan once more, looking up that same dark staircase toward the rooms that he had often revisited in his lonely sexual fantasies. Over the years, he'd relived again and again what had happened between him and Astrid. He had often moved the memory on, tumbling into what *could* have happened with him and Selene also. And then yet further with him *and* Selene *and* Astrid! *Mon dieu…* If he had had courage; if he had not gone down those stairs five years ago, what might have happened in his sad life?

The flashlight buttoned onto his tunic next to his heart flickered. He had to lean back to send its light to the top of the stairs. A cat sat there, on the landing, its eyes glinting back. Because of *la précarité* – the threat of an uncertain future – everything he had done had been like this: a light shining along a dark path. It was the one question that agonised everyone in France: where did the future lie? By 1940, he'd thought it lay within the bright glow of the Third Reich. But as the drumfire reached even here, in 1944, he had huge doubts.

He should never have fled down those stairs in '39, like the foolish virgin he'd been. Then he might not have spent the following years drinking too much, and thinking *if only, if only…*

Here in the present, the batteries of his light finally died. Astrid handed him her lamp.

"*Merci*," he whispered, though it meant he now had to hold his machine-gun with one hand.

Off to one side, along the first corridor, Schimmel shouted at Colette, who dropped the keys in fear, seemingly not sure which was the right one for the next door.

"I must go with your boss along that corridor," whispered Astrid to Yohan. "You must go upstairs. Now remember who you are, remember what you are – and it is not *this*." she said, scornfully stroking the German uniform.

Outside, the radio in the *wagen* crackled into life. Young Henri Lueur had been ordered not to answer it, and he was trained to obey orders. But there he was in a dark and narrow lane, between high hedges, feeling trapped. He didn't like being left alone like this, just as Der Bomber didn't like enclosed places. No shame in that. Besides, Schimmel was cracking up. Der Bomber was on the edge. Le Blanc was just an idiot. All the rest – his mockers – were deservedly dead and there were approaching fires in the distance that told him the world was changing.

Loyal to a concept (the Third Reich) rather than an individual (*Herr Hauptmann*), he flicked the switched and tuned the dial that connected him with those higher powers he most certainly yearned for.

"*Wo zum Teufel bist du?*"[1] crackled the voice of the *Oberstleutnant.*

Lueur looked up and saw a line of flares at the horizon, like bursting flowers, and felt dark shapes thrumming across the sky. Like his fellow countryman Yohan, and almost at the same moment, he asked himself the eternal question: *Where does my future lie?* To most French people *La Précarité* had become as tangible and terrifying as the priest's demon.

"I must speak to you, sir," he said, his voice a salute, tuning the dial more precisely for a true connection.

---

[1] Where the devil are you?

58

"God in heaven, what is this?" slurred Schimmel when he entered the room full of stuffed animals.

"It is my hobby," said Astrid mildly, taking Colette's place. She gave a final glance back toward Le Blanc before he made his way up the stairs. "And I sell them to schools throughout Brittany and Normandy. You see I make things last forever. Can you make things last forever? You have one of my creations in your offices, I think."

"That stupid black dog?"

"Black dogs are never stupid. They can lead us to things, they open ways."

He stared around at the assorted creatures: owls, hawks, several hares, a red squirrel and a grey squirrel, two foxes and various unidentifiable birds. They seemed to flicker with life as he shone his flashlight from one to the next. Was that in his mind, or was it the slight tremor in his hand that caused that illusion?

Astrid opened her own ways within the large house, freely and – apparently – cheerfully. Going from room to room, with a sort of *tra-la!* as she opened each new door. She showed him the old school room, the old infirmary, the bathroom, the various empty side dormitories and the toilets (with the miniature seats for short legs), and the hand-basins so close to the floor.

Schimmel blinked hard. He remember his son's first school, and the small hand in his own, and he wondered why this mad woman was looking at him so intently. As if it was *he* who had something to hide.

"And finally," she said, opening the blinds and shutters in the last room to let the pale yellow June light ooze into the darkness. In the distance, swarms of bombers in formation. She opened the window to let in the pure morning air and the tiny bee-like droning of the aircraft engines. "Listen, I know what you want. I know what you're looking for. I am tired of this so I will give it to you. Do what you want with me, hang me, but leave the rest of them alone. Here…" she said, leading the two Germans to a metal-doored, padlocked cupboard built into the wall.

Taking a small silver key from the bunch, she undid the lock and the door creaked open...

Colette showed Yohan up the stairs. He clutched the Schmeisser, which he had not yet fired in anger. It still smelled of gun-oil and polish, and its grip was greasy from the sweat on his palm. He struggled to hold that in one hand and also shine the lamp steadily with the other. He couldn't trust the girl to help him.

The landing outside the bedrooms was familiar. It was beyond that first door that things had happened and choices had been made. A fragment of himself was still in there. He was sweating, shaking. The lamp quivered, and so did its light. He was not sure if he could even fire the gun with one hand. Yet he dared not put it down.

"Open," he whispered to Colette, his left shoulder forward, his weight on his front foot. Call him a drunkard, but no-one could say that Yohan Le Blanc was ever *jaune*.

She shrugged, pushed the door open and stood aside, letting him enter. He felt that the young girl was ready to leap on him from behind and stab him with scissors – anything to protect whoever or whatever was in there.

There, sitting up in bed, in the bed was Selene. Yohan almost smiled when he recognised her. He could have had her too, if he had had the nerve, those years before. Colette came over and showed him the woman's slapped face by candlelight. She made no effort to open the blackout curtains. No doubt she had her scissors ready and would go for his eyes.

"See," she said. "How red and fevered!"

In the silvered half-light, Yohan thought she was wide-eyed, vulnerable and beautiful. He had always preferred her to Astrid. Selene coughed pitifully then she frowned. He saw in her face that she recognised him too.

He remembered the work he had done right here:

The sense of something about to happen.

The smell of sawdust, paint and glue.

The sex.

The sense that something awesome had indeed happened.

And then, in the present, he also saw the thin trail of what was surely blood leading from the side of the bed toward the wall. A few drops of blood at the edge of the bed. A thicker trail that ended at the wall, under the dressing table.

When he had been here last, there had been a strange and useless space that might have been a priest-hole. When all the other work had been done, they asked him to use thin, vertical wooden planks and some plasterboard to cover it, and create a hidden door that was flush with the rest of the wall. He'd never asked why. He had been entranced by the two women who'd floated in and out as he worked, flirting, and the *bonhomie* of the man they called, almost teasingly, Master.

Now, he could sense the agony of the woman in the bed pretending to have a fever. And the young woman next to him was almost shaking. Had she been here last time? No, he hadn't seen her then. She had probably been outside playing with the young imbeciles. He had heard the Gestapo later cleared them all out, but that had happened when he'd gone for his training in the *Feldgendarmes*.

His foot banged against something on the floor. As he bent and shone the light down there, he saw an upturned helmet. Colette stifled a gasp. Selene sat up in terror, no doubt guessing what he had seen.

Calmly, with the edge of his boot, he pushed the helmet under the bed. "Sorry about your *vase de nuit*[1] *mesdames*," he said. "There is clearly nothing here. But listen, please. Sometimes, we have to make strange choices in life. Please remember that I, Yohan Le Blanc, am, in my heart, a *Frenchman*. I bid you *adieu*…"

He clicked his heels in the Germanic way and clattered through the other bedrooms in a token search, then back down the stairs.

"*Zut! This* is how I foretell things," said Astrid to the two Germans, showing them the radio set. "I am not a sybil, as you may have heard from the idiots in the town. I listen to the BBC."

Der Bomber was not interested. He had to lean against a wall. The balls of his feet were giving him great pain. The sight of those real bombers, and the constant rumbling of high explosives in the distance, threatened to take him back to a bad, cold and murderous place. A place which was approaching by the minute and – though he could not know it – every bit as terrifying as the broken priest's nightmares.

---

[1] Chamber pot

Hauptmann Schimmel blinked hard. He felt as if he might faint. He was shaking. The stuffed creatures all around seemed to be completely alive. Their eyes glowed. They looked as if they hated him and might pounce. His brain wasn't working properly. A small portion of it knew it was the Pervitin causing this, as well as his grief for Dieter, and the loss of his men only hours before. He couldn't really take in what the woman was saying. Sun was pouring into the room now. He felt like shit. Yet he was an officer in the Third Reich and he had to function like one.

Le Blanc clattered downstairs and came along the corridors. "There is no-one, *Herr Hauptmann*. I searched everywhere. Under the beds, in the cupboards. Nothing. Just a very fevered old woman. It does look like diptheria."

"I told you," said Astrid. And although she didn't look at Le Blanc he felt as if some part of her reached out to hug him, as if – left alone – something wondrous might happen between them yet again.

Schimmel toyed with the radio. It was old, the wires worn. "I could have you jailed for six months."

"*Bof!* Do so!" said Astrid in a sprightly tone. "The Allies will be here in days." She could see the man was exhausted and close to collapse. Both the Germans were.

"What did the *B.B.C.* say?" he asked, and Astrid heard the scorn in every letter.

"That American parachutists have landed around St Mère Eglise and their armies are on the beaches of Normandy. That the English and Canadians have come ashore around Caen. That the Landing has begun."

Schimmel, who had studied human psychology in the police academy, was startled to hear her use the actual word 'parachutist'. If she really was hiding one, she would never have dared mention that word. He took out his Luger and brought the butt down on the radio, smashing hard three times, as if to shake himself alert again. Glass from one of the valves made his hand bleed. "Propaganda! If the thing happens, it will be near Calais. Our *Fuhrer* believes so. Whatever is happening over there" – he nodded out of the window – "is a diversion."

He said it dully, to himself. Had he actually *been* himself, he would never have said that to this wretch. If it really was simply a large diversion, he could justify his own personal crusade to find Dieter's murderer.

He raised his left finger, as if to utter a reproach, when the cry of a cockerel floated into the room, threading its way between the warp and woof of the war sounds.

"*Cocorico, cocorico,*" said Astrid. The cock crows twice."

Schimmel frowned. What was she talking about? She was mad, surely. But... "What is outside? I want to see outside," he said.

59

Upstairs, in the pitch darkness of the psuedo priest-hole, Michael also heard the cock-a-doodle do, and the very faintest whisper from Colette on the other side of the door:

"Stay there. Stay there."

So he stood in the dark place, half-naked, clothes in his hand, defenceless. Trying to make sense of what was happening. The girls must have hidden his Tommy gun and Colt, surely? After what seemed like an hour of sheer terror, but was probably only a few minutes, someone had come into the room, and sniffed around between the bed and his hiding place. What lay behind that door now? Waffen SS? Gestapo?

He reached down and felt how wet his leg was. Had he pissed himself? Or was it blood? He reached down and sniffed, tasted. It was blood. That was better than piss.

Dear god, dear god above, when he got out of this closet he was gonna be a man again, and a Screaming Eagle!

Downstairs, Der Bomber creaked opened the double doors that now gave them a glimpse of the overgrown and neglected garden. Crows, startled by the noise, rose *en masse* and flew off. Fresh air surged into his lungs. To the north, above Caen, the Allied bombers still swarmed like flies, lifting suddenly as if on the breeze, after they dropped their bombs beyond and below the horizon.

Breathe, breathe, he thought. He had hated searching those dark, narrow rooms with the stupid, stuffed animals. Throughout, he had been fighting off the flashbacks: of the cellar in Stalingrad, where he had been trapped like a cockroach, next to broken sewers and shattered bodies, where they had eaten rodents to stay alive.

But the open doors, the light of the day and the clear sky to the south saved him. Here it was pure, clean. For a moment, he could almost fancy he was back in the big overgrown garden of his own home, and his parents, grinning widely, were about to appear with arms full of windfall apples. There they would spoil him like the little boy he really wanted to be again.

He leaned further back against the door frame, his feet *really* hurting him now.

After Stalingrad, after getting the *heimatschuss*[1] that had released him from that hell, and then being transferred by lucky routes to this peaceful heart of Normandy, he had felt safe. Now he was considering his future. After all, he had been told the Atlantic Wall was impregnable. The *Wehrmacht* was all-conquering. There were V weapons that would blast the English cities. New aircraft that could travel at enormous speed without propellers; deadly new submarines that never needed to surface. All of which guaranteed final victory.

But, from all he had heard – even from this mad woman with the radio – the Wall had been breached, and the Allies were coming.

"Schatten, stand up straight," said the *Hauptmann*, wearily.

Karl 'Der Bomber' Schatten leaned back more heavily and closed his eyes.

"Obergefreiter Schatten, I order you to stand up straight."

Der Bomber opened his eyes. He looked out upon the garden again and breathed in the clean air. A large black cat sat on the gravel path and looked at him.

"But the poor man…his feet are in agony!" said Astrid, giving the most sympathetic of looks.

"Schatten!"

Shoot him, said a voice in Der Bomber's head. *You don't have to do his murdering for him. Take over this place. Remember the young man you once were.*

He might have done. He really might have done, but at that moment all heads turned toward the noise at the front gate. As they went to look, the noisy and shrapnel-spattered *Kübelwagen* turned into view, bumping over the bodies of the dead dogs and making the broken springs shriek.

Hauptmann Schimmel turned his attention from the tower he glimpsed above the trees and looked at Henri Lueur with eyes widened and made more wrinkled by rage.

"I am sorry *Herr Hauptmann*," the young man said, shouting over the divide. "I must tell you that *Oberstleutnant* Funke wants to

---

[1] Literally 'Home Shot' - a 'lucky' wound which enabled combatants to escape the horrors of the front line.

to see you, and wants to see you *now.*"

"What…? How?"

"He is angry, sir. Very, very angry."

All eyes were on Schimmel.

Der Bomber was relieved that he didn't have to disobey orders. At least not yet. The little shit Luerur looked smug. He had probably said all manner of things to the *Oberstleutnant.* Was probably, even now, under a higher protection.

The *Hauptmann* snarled and made his way back through the rooms. No doubt he would ask the treacherous little *Franzosen* about the 'how' later. The other one, the drunkard Le Blanc, was waiting for them at the door.

"For your journey," said Astrid, offering two glasses of dark red wine. Schimmel took his and threw it into the empty fireplace. Schatten, when the officer's back was turned, snatched his and glugged it in one. That was something else had learned in Stalingrad.

As the car left their grounds, with Lueur driving, Astrid stood once more on one leg, making the horned devil's sign with her left hand, pouring hatred and death into the back of the departing visitors. "*Zazas, Zazas, Nasatanada Zazas…*"

The yard was silent again. Selene emerged once she was certain she would not be seen. The Matagot sat for a while before it slunk off into the bushes.

"What did you give him?" Selene asked.

"*L'Herbe de Mort Juste.*"

"You have perfected it?"

"It is similar to the one I made for our Master, but much stronger. Very very *very* strong. Michael's draft is much weaker. It will help him perform for us all. But that cripple will be dead before they get to Neuilly. He will die in ecstacy, with a stiff cock!"

They giggled. Little girl giggles.

The *wagen* rattled and gasped along the dirt tracks back toward Neuilly. *Hauptmann* Schimmel had no need to question Lueur as to what had happened. He knew exactly what the little *schweinhund* had done and why. He also knew how ruthless *Oberstleutnant* Funke, an overbearing Prussian, could be. Breathe deep, breathe deep. No more Pervitin. The war was coming – the war was here! He must push his thoughts of Dieter into some hidden place. Then at the first opportunity he would shoot Lueur in the back of his head. After all, it was he whom he should have sent back behind the lines. It was Lueur's fault his son had been murdered.

He was about to speak when Der Bomber, sprawling obscenely on the rear seat next to him, started gasping.

"*Was ist falsch?*"[1]

Le Blanc turned to look.

The soldier was arched against the seat, his head tilted back so far that his helmet was pushed down over his brow. His trousers bulged with an erection and his groin kept thrusting into the air in an obscene involuntary rhythm.

"*Eklig! Eklig!*"[2]

Der Bomber, who had seemed immortal, was now gasping his last as his breathing became more orgasmic, his tongue stuck out like a penis; he had been poisoned by the wine he had gulped.

Yohan Le Blanc thought he'd never seen the man so happy. He also understood why Astrid had not offered him a glass. It was quite simple. She was clearly in love with him.

When this was over...

---

[1] What is wrong?
[2] Disgusting

60

As the *Kübelwagen* rattled and gasped back toward Neuilly and faded from hearing, the three women hurried to Michael's hiding place, thrilled, scared and relieved all at the same time.

Selene rolled aside the little table and pried open the flimsy door with her fingernail. *"Ils sont partis. C'est sûr,"*[1] she said, though she still whispered.

"They are gone. It is safe," added Colette, just to make certain he understood.

For a moment he just stood there like a soldier in a sentry box, clutching his clothes around his groin. He looked beyond them to the guns that peeked out from under the sheets.

"Votre jambe est le saignement,"[2] said Astrid, pointing to the blood with more interest than concern.

"My leg is okay. *Ma jambe va bien.* Now get me that sulpha powder from my kit."

Astrid and Selene looked to Colette. She translated:

"Il a besoin de la poudre pour sa jambe."[3]

"L'herbe d'or?" asked Colette.

"NOT THAT CRAP!" Horsett yelled.

They were all blasted onto their back feet by his rage. And confused. Had they not saved him?

"Beat it. All of you. GET OUT! *ALLEZ! ALLEZ!*"

Their grins disappeared. They looked at one another. They went. Colette, leaving the room last, turned to give him a sympathetic smile.

"Damned idiots," he muttered, coming out of the closet and getting dressed.

Never never never again, never again! he told himself. He was a paratroop. He was a Screaming Eagle. He'd come to save the world, not let himself get locked in a closet.

---

[1] They left. It is safe

[2] Your leg is bleeding

[3] He needs powder for his leg

61

Luc was in torment as he cycled out to St Martin's. He was sweating, tired, and felt betrayed. He had been kind to the priest, helped him deal with his torments, guilts and desires. Now it seemed as if he had been cast aside by this flabby Sophia, who looked at him as if he was a piece of shit – although the Lord and the whole of Neuilly knew there was nothing pure about her!

Espèce de Merde, he muttered *Espèce de Merde…* again and again, louder and louder. He meant Fournier, the whore in the kitchen, and probably his own shitty self. Maybe his destiny, his happiness, lay somehow with Michael Horsett, who had come down from a purer realm?

He heard the noisy engine first. Then he was almost knocked over by the German wagon driven erratically down the narrow maze of lanes. It could only have come from the old hospital. From the determined look on the young driver's face Luc knew that he would have to give way. He pulled the bicycle to the side, mounted the steep grass verge, and created enough room for them to jolt past. The rear and side of the vehicle looked as if it had been shot at from above. He recognised Le Blanc and the driver from that time last week, when he had helped take the hanged corpses down. A man on the back seat looked as if he were already dead, his body arched back and rigid. The other three looked like corpses themselves.

"Bastards," he said when they had gone, and pedalled frantically onward, afraid of what he might find.

The screen of branches that hid the road to the hospital had been thrown aside. The big old gate into the rear of St Martin's was open and ripped off its hinges. The two dogs lay dead in the yard.

"Oh *mon dieu, mon dieu…*" Luc whispered. He put the bicycle against a wall, and tiptoed to the door. As he touched the latch, determined to sneak in, silent as a mouse, he heard a bold:

"*Entrez!*" – this from Horsett, who had seen him coming.

What Luc saw within the kitchen quite staggered him. Not corpses, not bulletholes, nor signs of any immense struggle. He found Horsett and the three women sitting there, silent amid a terrible atmosphere. The table had an almost sumptuous spread on it: there was, *pain de campagne*, butter, *rillettes* and a *saucisson*; a bottle of very good Champigny, goats' cheese, *crème au chocolat*, chicken. Madame Riche had spent at last!

"The Last Supper?" he asked, smiling nervously.. It looked as if someone had thrown one of Astrid's potions against the wall; the little cup was rolling back and forth on the table top.

The mood between them all was icy. Luc took it all in with his first glance and first intake of breath: poor Colette was bewildered, and sat apart from the rest, frowning. Was she descending into one of her little depressions? Astrid and Selene had the sort of tight expressions and tense shoulders that children show when they don't get their own way. Horsett... he was among the women and burning.

"Luc...you were right about me, buddy. All along."

Luc frowned, and started to glow. *What!?* Did he mean... *that!?* The love which the French sneeringly called the English Disease?

"You want me to lead you all, Luc. To resist. We're gonna do that from here on in. I been sitting on my butt long enough. Tell the guys I want them here. We're gonna go to war."

"Your leg is bleeding, Michael," Luc said.

"It's my leg. And here, when you get back you can have this..." Horsett reached under the table to bring out one of the Tommy guns that Thibault had scavenged.

Luc's eyes went as wide as the womens' were narrowed. His mouth opened as theirs were pinched. "But..." he muttered, meaning to mention about Armand's beating.

"It's okay, don't worry, I'll teach you. I'll teach you all how to use it. Oh, and get Jules to contact the Resistance guy – if it's not a load of bullshit."

Luc stood there for a moment. He wanted to ask what had just happened here, with the Germans having just left. And what had happened between Michael and the women. And what was happening between Michael and himself – if anything.

"Go quickly, Luc. Do what it is you have to do," said Michael, opening the door and almost pushing him out.

So with a rising heart, and thoughts of Gilles' betrayal suddenly forgotten, Luc took up his bicycle and went.

Astrid and Selene sat alone in their tower, in the eight-sided room.

The Matagot sat watching, head slightly cocked to one side, listening.

"Shall I go into trance?" asked Selene. " Shall I go to the Far Land and find the Master and ask him to speak to you?"

"No, he would say: 'Do What Thou Wilt' and leave us to choose."

"Then what must we choose?"

"I had hoped to keep Michael for a little longer – until the solstice of course. But now we must act sooner."

"But is that possible?"

"*Crotte!* Of course! The sun, the moon, the stars and their courses are all in here," Astrid almost hissed, tapping her head and heart. "Not out *there*," she added, pointing beyond the walls to where they heard the distant bombers and their bombings.

"I know that. I meant…"

"*Crotte!* I will contact the *covine*," Astrid ordered, looking into her own futures. "I will get them myself."

62

Colette was learning to strip a sub-machine gun. One of the half dozen that Thibault had scavenged. They were upstairs in the barn and Michael was talking with a new fervour, as if he'd got religion.

"Now Colette, honey, field stripping the M1A1 Thompson submachine gun is simple. You don't need any tools. See ...it all just slides and locks together. See if you can do it in under a minute."

He obviously enjoyed talking like a soldier again; it made her glow. She tried. She fumbled. She almost did it first time. Second and third attempts.

"Preddy dam good," she drawled, taking the mickey.

He blinked, then smiled. Winced at the pain in his leg but smiled again. She really felt he was looking at her in a different light, a good light. It made the *cafard* – her depression – fly away; she never wanted to feel it descend again.

As he started to do the same with one of the other weapons, he said, almost out the corner of his mouth and without looking at her: "So, er, you musta.. You musta got a shock to see the three of us together. In bed I mean..."

The Matagot appeared then and just sat there, in the corner, watching.

Colette smiled. She touched his shoulder. "You were having fun. It means nothing."

The Matagot yawned. Michael sighed. She could see he didn't understand, but there were more important things happening in the world. And important things happening between her and Michael, she felt.

"Okaaay... okay. Now this has got a rate of fire of six hundred rounds per minute. What do I mean by rounds? Bullets. These. It can fire six hundred of these in a minute. That's ten a second. They fit in this here box. Thirty of 'em. See how they fit in?"

She came very close to look. Although she didn't understand all that he was saying, she liked him like this. He might be going to battle, but he was big and strong again, rather than Astrid and Selene's puppet. Now she would fight by his side and have a purpose beyond all the years of mysterious hints from the two older women. "When you are older…" they would always say, but the journey toward that future point seemed endless, and very narrow.

"Now you hold it. Don't be scared, the safety catch is on."

She took it as if it were a delicate baby. "*C'est lourd.* Er er… it is heavy."

"Just over ten pounds unloaded. I dunno know what that is in your kilos."

"*Moi non plus!*"

"When the guys come, you can have this, and I'll show y'all how to use them."

"I am a gangster," she said, pretending to spray the walls of the barn with bullets.

"Yeah, well gangsters use 'em, but with the big round drum magazines. It doesn't have much range — maybe a hundred yards at very best — `but is very effective in close combat."

"What is 'close combat'?"

"Ah, lemme think now. That would be *'le combat rapproché'.* Fighting when you are very close to the enemy."

"Very close?" she asked, leaning against him. "This close?" she asked again, angling her face for a kiss. It had seemed like years since they had flirted like this, though it was only days.

He smiled but moved away, putting on the webbing belt that Thibault had retrieved, which had half a dozen loaded magazines. "No more games. Not yet."

"Games, Michael?"

"Hell, yeah. That's all I've done since I've been here. Playing weird games."

"Now it is time for war."

"It sure is. So will you and the guys fight with me? Become real Resistants? We heard that French women make pretty tough freedom fighters."

"I would do anything for you, Michael."

"Would you kill for me?"

"Do you love me a little? *Un peu?*"

"I might if I knew I could trust you with my back."

"Your back? *Votre dos?*" she asked, remembering not to use the 'tu'.

"If I was attacked from behind, would you kill to save me?"

"*Bien sûr?*"

"Thank you," he whispered, reaching behind her ear to produce a small bunch of daisies.

Of course she understood the trick now. Saw it coming. It was charming. And she meant it – *absoluetement* – she would kill to save him. She had been ready to stab that stupid policeman in the neck with her scissors if necessary. It felt so good! Then, when the Germans had all gone and Michael had emerged from the hidden space, so angry, lighting up the room with his rage, her heart had gone out to him anew. This was her man. He was certainly her own Shining One, driving away the shadows of her past: of the Master, who had been a father to her, and all the little, lovely imbeciles; the vague memories of her parents and the cloud of unknowing that enshrouded them; the *cafard* which made her feel as though there was something wrong about her, something unlovable.

"When this is all done would you come to the States with me?"

"Yes. *Oui.* Yes yes yes…*oui oui oui!*"

"I'll take you everywhere. My Mom will love you."

She bowed her head as if receiving a benediction. "But Michael, I have no skills, and do not have the magic like *mère* and *grand mère.*"

"Babe, that is all horse-shit. *Merde de Cheval.* You don't need skills. I'll get rich and earn enough for both of us. But there's one thing I'm gonna ask you to do, as proof of your love."

"*N'importe quoi.*"

"Anything? *Vraiment?*"

"*Oui.*"

"Then shoot that damned cat."

Colette gasped.

"Anything. You said. *Vous avez dit.* I will even use the 'tu' if you do."

She took a deep breath and looked hard at the cat, which just sat there in the corner with what she imagined was a scornful look.

Michael put his hands on her shoulders from behind. Reached around and took off the safety catch. "Okay," he whispered. "*Tu as dit. Tu Tu Tu…*"

That was what she wanted to hear. His long arms helped her

take the weight of the gun as she put the cat between the sights and squeezed the trigger…

63

Selene was frantically mixing potions in the kitchen, pounding away with her old stone pestle and mortar. She looked out across the yard to the two dead dogs, fuming at the atmosphere left by the Germans. It hung around in her nostrils and reminded her of that dreadful day three years ago when they had last raided, and torn her world apart.

"Sale sale sale…[1]" she muttered, remembering and hating as she mixed, echoing Astrid as she did far too often these days.

She glanced through the windows that were still half-covered by the blackout curtains, toward the barn, where she heard Colette's burst of laughter. She was annoyed that the girl could find anything amusing at such a dire time. But then, that had always been her way: laughing at the wrong time, crying at the wrong time. Never quite in tune with the real world. If only she knew what her true destiny was!

Selene hoped that Astrid would be able to gather the women quickly. They needed to act. She knew that instantly, on seeing Michael Horsett's rage when he had emerged from the hidden cupboard. They had never used this before, but Le Cohen, The Master – in his ineffable wisdom – had insisted upon it, and it proved its worth this morning. But now this man from the skies was no longer *un homme passif.* He might not easily fit into their plans for him in this state. They had to get him back under control until the *covine* got here.

I call you! Selene heard the voice of Le Cohen inside her head as she added more ingredients to the potion.

Merde! she hissed when she heard the short burst of gunfire from the barn. Her body jerked at each of the three rapid shots, as if she herself had been hit. This was not the Germans returning: she knew exactly what it meant, and felt it in her gut, as if she might throw up. *Salaud!*

Her knees almost gave way. She had to grab the kitchen table to steady herself. Astrid had already left, so she would have to deal with this herself, without her certain and powerful support. "Master, I'm coming!" she cried.

---

[1] Dirty dirty dirty…

64

At the same moment that Selene worked frantically on her potions, Father Gilles Fournier, standing before his altar at Prime, was allowing himself a simple anger. A *healthy*, simple anger. Somehow the arrival of Sophia and the departure of Luc had made his twisted life straightforward again. He had slept well since Sophia had arrived. In that brief spell he felt something of his old confidence start to return. Sophia, who had risen earlier than himself and prepared breakfast. Sophia, who was so much like his dear, late *maman*, and who treated him like a *normal* healthy human being. Sophia, who was at least a good Catholic, unlike Luc.

The anger he felt now was uncomplicated. It was not tied up with his guilt, or his deformity, or his perceived failings: It was all to do with the chaos of the world outside his church.

Beyond the thick doors and thin, cracked windows, the German war-machine creaked, groaned and moaned: all caused by the equipment that was being hauled or pushed along the narrow echoing streets. He couldn't have named all the things he saw, but the roads were thick with carts and trucks, each filled with soldiers who spoke in thin voices. Nervous horses pulled large cannon; they whinnied and shat, their hooves sending up sparks on the cobbles. Nervous officers shouted commands that tailed off into falsettos. Tyres squealed and brakes shrieked.

Inside the church, overlooked by the pallid glass image of Saint Ywi, the droning sound of the distant bombers filtered down to Fournier. It came down through the bell-tower in little pulses of sound. And the acrid stink of exhaust fumes and gun oil, of electrical, pneumatic, hydraulic things hissing and panting, smouldering rubber and men's fear - all crept under the doors and licked around his boots.

There really is a demon loose, he thought, but quite calmly, as he tried to offer his prayers at Prime, as the sun tried to rise. Somehow, he knew that today he would find and confront it. He remembered the words Goethe wrote in *Faust*: 'As long as people are so stupid, There is no need for the devil to be clever.' He had once used that as something of motto. Now, somewhere beyond the church doors, amid the masses of stupid people, he would find that even stupider creature – *Le Noirceur* – which had caused him such grief over the years. Find it and destroy it. Now, at the last, he was ready for the battle.

A tap on his shoulder. He wasn't startled, as he might have been in the past. He knew it was Sophia. One of the things left to him after the the lightning strike was a heightened sense of smell. She came to him on a cloud of baked bread, burnt toast, newly-ironed clothes and the slight aroma of carbolic soap. The brief contact of her single finger on his shoulder – offensive from anyone else – linked him to the simple things long gone from his life, and fortified him accordingly.

"Father, I must go to help one of my friends," she said, nodding toward the front door.

"Of course!" he beamed. This was typical of her: kindness, warmth, neighbourliness. "Anything I can do?"

She gave the merest hint of a wry smile and shook her head, as if to say quite charmingly – *if only you knew!* Women's problems, clearly, thought the priest wearing his new soutane of kindness.

He walked her to the door. There were two women waiting, holding their hats against the blast of the traffic and their noses against the exhaust-fumes. One of them, he recalled, had asked for his help last week, and he had failed her. The other, an older silver-haired woman, was a stranger. He fancied that they both looked at him with scorn.

He was about to say something priestly and kind, when the older woman suddenly bent double, as if something had stabbed her in the bowels.

"Astrid...?" said Sophia, going to her aid.

Astrid took a deep breath and straightened. She too had heard the same voice as Selene, the *I call you!* And at the same moment that Selene heard the gunfire from the barn, she too had felt it, in her guts, on the streets of the town.

Fournier, knowing that something very deep had just happened, stepped aside slightly and tried to look into the older woman's eyes; she concealed them by turning her back. Had that been the start of a seizure – or something else?

"Come with me," Astrid told the two younger women, straightening herself. She put an arm behind their waists and pushed them onward; they walked three abreast.

Fournier let them get a little distance ahead and then started to follow. There was something not right about this trinity, and he was worried about Sophia. The war had brought all sorts of lesser darkness to the daily lives of his flock: hunger, the need to collaborate and the inevitable blackmail, the demands and pressures of the black market... Was she being coerced? There was something odd about that silver-haired woman, he started to persuade himself, but he was being troubled by another annunciation: dark blobs on his vision; a band of pain across the living side of his face; nausea. He fought it, he always fought it.

To his left, at the junction of roads, a bedraggled German policeman was making pitiful attempts to control the traffic. He waved his *Winkerkelle*: a traffic wand with red and white roundels on the end, like a large lollipop. He blew the whistle that was attached to a lanyard around his neck. He looked grotesque. He seemed to grow big and then small. Horses were whinnying. A dog was howling. From somewhere the smell of mown grass. Crows fought aerial battles and a fat rabbit – presumably someone's escaped lunch – lolloped across the road.

Fight, fight. Fournier took deep breaths. Directly above him, in the large office, he glimpsed the *Hauptmann* staring bleakly down, his even gaunter face more suited to the Flying Dutchman than a backstreet in Neuilly sur Fronds. Fournier had the brief and mad idea that this man might help, might even be an ally.

The near-sunny jauntiness that Father Fournier had felt only moments earlier was gone. There were too many omens. Darkness descended like an eyelid. Where, finally today, was *Le Noirceur*?

An armoured vehicle, with wheels and tracks, almost brushed his shoulder as it screeched past, ushered on by the weary traffic policeman. The slipstream caused the white dresses of the women ahead to flicker up, momentarily revealing glimpses of thighs, and the red garters that all three wore.

The priest stopped dead. Wanting to vomit, he put one hand on a lamp post to steady himself and stare. One, two maybe, but *three*? That was not chance.

Mon Dieu, he thought. Could these be *Les Dames Blanches* that Sophia had told him about? The spirit women who challenge, tempt and drive good men insane? Was Sophia one such? And had she come to him, not out of heaven-sent goodness, but to keep watch?

He should have realised. *Le Noirceur* could appear as male, female, both, or neither. It could appear as a black snake, fox, jackal or crow to his certain knowledge. Could it appear as three women? Or were they its disciples? He looked up at the officer and wondered how much he saw – was he part of all this?

A dark electricity coursed up the priest's spine and into his brain. He went into a grand mal, on the cobbled streets, before the indifferent gaze of the soldiery.

65

Hauptmann **Schimmel stood with his brow pressed against the cool but grimy window.** There was that idiot below, Yohan le Blanc, knowing he was being watched, waving the *Winkerkelle* and blowing his whistle as if he cared about what he was doing and which vehicle should come through next. Schimmel pressed his brow harder against the glass, smoothing out the wrinkles, trying to smooth his thoughts, trying to work from the outside in.

He had to stop taking the Pervitin, which he knew was making his mind unbalanced. He had to stop thinking about his son Dieter and hallucinating him back to life. Plus he had to stop feeling guilty about the men he had just lost to the American fighter-bomber: Uli, Alfred and Gunther, who had all got their 'permanent leave passes'. Not to mention the bizarre death of Karl Schatten, of whom he had always been afraid. It could only have been a heart attack brought on by the torments and strains of the Eastern Front. In truth, he was glad to be rid of him. In due course, he would arrange appropriate funerals for all four.

Meanwhile, there were *Panzers* coming, iron angels that would save them all. It was his task to guide them to the fight. *Oberstleutnant* Funke had made that very clear.

In fact *Oberstleutnant* Funke had all but crucified him when he got back to camp. He ranted about dereliction of duty, threatened him with the *HängeKommando* who would give him a flying court martial and then execute him for deserting his post. Funke only modified his rage when he learned about Dieter, who had been friends with his own son now serving in Russia. So he then took Schimmel down from the cross and lectured him in gentler tones, pointing out that he, Schimmel, was an officer in the *Wehrmacht*, a good Christian who had taken an oath to serve both Christ and the Third Reich – the Holy Reich. – and that duty came before all things.

"You are not a detective," Funke had said, gently, as if trying to release torments from Schimmel's mind. "As of now, you are merely a traffic policeman. Your duty is to control the chaotic traffic within the narrow streets of the miserable little town to make sure the Panthers and Tigers go around. They are too wide for those streets. You know the route they need to take. Schimmel, I have finally had confirmation that the invasion is definitely at Normandy: the *Das Reich* Division is biding its time at Archeuille and will soon come directly toward Neuilly, bypass it then head toward Caen."

Funke had said that in a soft voice, as if announcing the Second Coming; as if the power that comes from knowledge was lighting him from within. Schimmel had nodded, closing his eyes and bowing his head to receive the blessing.

Now here he was back in his office, alone. The vibrations of the traffic had cracked the glass. It was a cattle market down there; all the beasts knew they were on their way to slaughter. The pictures of Jesus and the *Fuhrer* were both askew but he had no will to straighten them.

He stood at the window looking down at that drunkard Frenchman as he tried to herd the the dirty olive-green *Schützenpanzerwagen* half-tracks known as *Hanomags* into the town square where his other men, at crucial junctions, would send them on. It was a simple but important task: if the smaller *Panzers* I-IV could barely scrape below his office, it was absolutely crucial that the much bigger Panthers and Tigers took the larger if longer road, that curved at the south of the town.

The vehicles below were filled with nervous *spunds*, as they were called: young soldiers or new recruits. A couple of them were swallowing their *energietropfen*[1] ahead of time. When they had first arrived in this backwater in 1940, the soldiers had been exultant, Masters of the World and all its futures. They thought of themselves then as Old Hares, combat veterans, and lots of the French had welcomed them. Now, with Ivans pouring in from the East, and the Amis from the West, and the German cities in-between being flattened by the RAF, there were no shining faces any more. All futures were on hold.

Schimmel could see Le Blanc peering into the vehicles, smelling the liquor probably, aching to beg for a gulp but aware of his chief's gaze. Schimmel was about to open the window and shout down a warning when he saw three women almost marching along the pavement. He recognised the the one in the middle instantly: he had just raided her house not long before! She

---

[1] Energy drops. Alcohol issued just before an attack.

must have had an urgent reason to come into Neuilly so quickly. Indeed, she was almost pushing the two younger women at either side along. Why?

Then he noticed two other things: first, Yohan le Blanc gave the older woman – what was her name, Astrid? – a discreet, two-fingered V gesture that was almost a salute, which she acknowledged with a brisk nod. Second, further back along the pavement, moving when they moved, stopping when they stopped, was that black priest with a thunderous look on his deformed and ugly face.

"Schimmel…" he muttered to himself stepping back from the window: "*In Gotte's Namen, wach auf.*"[1]

Somehow, he knew that that unholy trinity of women and the shadowy sub-human following them were connected with that which he sought. He didn't care what the *Oberstleutnant* or even the *Generalfeldmarschall* would threaten. He didn't care that the *HängeKommando* would brand him as *Ein Feigling vor dem Feind* – a coward in the face of the enemy. It was time to stop being a man in charge of *feldmäuse*, grow balls and find his son's murderer.

No matter what.

---

[1] In God's Name, wake up.

66

Colette looked with dismay at the three holes in the wall of the barn. Three fingers of light poked through and stabbed at Michael's head, heart and belly. She hadn't expected how loud the gunshots would be; there was ringing in her ear. And he had a strange look on his face, as if the noise had reminded him of his previous life.

"You missed the cat, Colette. You moved your aim. Did you mean to miss it?"

He used the *vous* again. His mood had changed, as if she'd failed a test. She had loved it when he used the term 'honey', in the softest voice, and she had turned to honey herself, sweet and glowing. Now, suddenly, he seemed angry.

"It was the… er, what is the word…?" she mimed the gun pushing her shoulder back, the barrel jerking into the air. Her right shoulder hurt.

"Recoil."

"*Oui, recul.* Truly."

She was nervous. She didn't know whether to speak French or English. He had told her once, only days ago, that she made him 'all hot and horny'; it took her some time to understand the slang, but then she was charmed, and she wanted him to speak like that all the time, and use *tu.* Now he was cold, and very calm. His mood had changed as quickly as her own mood could.

"Michael, we will fight the Germans," she emphasised, touching his arm. "Do not be angry with *me.*"

She could see his jaw muscles tighten then relax.

"I'm sorry…" he sighed. "I'm angry with myself. I've become a dead battery here. I'm sick of being in this cathouse."

"But The Matagot is alive! We can find The Matagot, Michael. I will not miss again."

"Damn The Matagot," he said, not looking at her. "That's not what I meant!"

She watched him as he assembled the weapons that Thibault had collected, laying them out on the old table, then opening the container with the lights in, that he had been dropped with. He was intent on the process, as if they were sacraments. She felt invisible.

Selene appeared at the door. She looked at them both with a tight-lipped expression. Michael ignored her.

"Colette…come with me," she ordered. "There are things we have to do, and things we must explain…"

She looked at Michael. He seemed enrapt by the shape and function of what he told her was an anti-tank mine, holding it up to the light, turning and twisting it. Her own form had no interest or even existence for him.

"I'm coming, *maman*," Colette said, feeling defeated before the battle had even begun.

67

The *covine* gathered at the tower. They stood outside the locked door. None of them had dared argue with Astrid when she'd appeared out of nowhere and demanded their attendance. She was a whirlwind, almost unaware of the frantic Germans blowing past at every side. They were excited, like schoolchildren before a party, and kept playing with the brims of their hats or the ends of their scarves; they made polite noises about the grey skies and the impending storm and the burning aeroplanes when really, they were aching to know what was going on.

Mainly, they were aching to see The Man whose coming had been foretold.

Hélène, who was desperate for the sort of excitement that her broken husband could never provide, shifted her weight from one wooden clog to the next, her eyes shining.

Hortense's gloom seemed to have lifted for once and her mind raced over the times she had had here in the past, and hoped to have again.

Juliette, still in pain after the abortion, leaned against the wall and thought about Uli, wondering why she had never heard from him. But at least glad to have something to take her mind off her torments.

And Sophia – Sophia almost glowed as she held the packet containing the charm with all the reverence that some had shown for the Host. All those tales she had spun to the priest, of the otherworld and its inhabitants! Now she too was part of the magic and mystery.

The door opened, slowly. Astrid and Selene stood there in the arch, their expressions serious. They wore long dresses of indigo and blue, respectively, that had clearly – from the creases – been brought out hurriedly before they could be ironed.

"It begins now," said Astrid, beckoning. "We have gowns for you all, your colours. Come, get changed. You will now learn how to live forever..."

68

Michael had been cold toward Colette. Truth is, his leg was in agony and he had a real craving for that 'medicine' the old gals kept giving him. He'd seen guys from the Anzio landings so fired by the bennies[1] they took to keep on keeping on, that it had to be something of that sort.

He would stop taking it.

He would have one more slug.

The guys from the 101st would be here soon.

He wanted them; he dreaded them.

He needed to fight; he wanted to run.

It was all going back and forward in his head. It was like there was a conjuror in his own mind, misdirecting his every thought in order to achieve a phony miracle and raise the old Michael from the dead.

He picked up the M-227 Signal Lamp that looked so much like a bazooka. Its familiarity was a comfort. This device to summon death from the skies. Now, its only use was for lighting up a barn. He hefted it to his shoulder, swung it around the room, as if its light could punch more holes in the walls. The door rasped opened and Astrid stood there. Was she wearing her nightdress? He pointed the muzzle right at her face. Put his finger on the trigger.

"Bang," he said softly as he blasted her with the beam.

She didn't flinch. Didn't blink. She had balls. "Colette needs you." She said it with an air of gravitas and concern.

Whatever dilemmas he might have as to who he was or why, or where he was or should be, then he had to go. He put on his helmet and shouldered his gun.

"You do not need those, Michael," she said.

"Perhaps not," he said in perfect French this time. "But I'm wearing it. I'm a soldier. From the U.S. of A. Not from wherever it is *you* think I'm from."

She paused, rocked on the balls of her feet for a moment in surprise and shrugged acceptance. "*Bof!* Come... no, not the

---

[1] Benzedrine

house."

"What's wrong?"

"*Zut!* This is the most important moment in her life. And yours. She needs you. Would you rather play with your toys?"

He found himself sinking into the wackiness of the place again. It was like he was part of a whole magic show they had orchestrated, building up tensions, creating illusions through misdirection.

Something sure was up. He'd deal with this first, then he'd start the war when the guys arrived. Maybe he'd tap Astrisd for some of that medicine. Just a small gulp. Instead he followed her around the house and into the garden, and saw that they were heading toward the tower.

Michael was startled to see some women lined up outside the arched wooden door and the horned skulls wobbling on the striped poles. The women were dressed in every colour of the rainbow – literally. They were carrying looped crosses, like crucifixes. He clutched the shoulder strap of the Tommy gun more firmly and pulled the weapon against his back. What the hell was going on?! Was he expected to have all of them? Their eyes widened in various degrees of delight, wonder and fear.

Astrid introduced him. "This is he, the avatar of Horus, the one whose coming was foretold."

"Honey, I'm not –"

Selene put her finger on his lips

"He is Ra Horakhte. Horus of the Sun,"

He pushed her hand away. "Selene, I'm here for Colette. Where is Colette? I want her. Now."

"Now is the time!" explained Astrid with an expression on her face that made it seem obvious to anyone.

He looked at the women as he was introduced. They looked at him as if he were from another world. And he was.

"They are rays of light, Michael:

Rouge - Sophie

Orange - Juliette

Jaune - Hortense

Vert – Hélène

Bleu – Selene

Moi – Indigo…"

Three of them curtsied as if he were some kind of royalty. The one in orange, the one whom he'd seen coming for an abortion, looked as if she might burst into tears.

"Astrid...I've had enough of this. Tell me where Colette is. Now."

"She is the final arch of the rainbow. She is Violet. She awaits you. On the highest level. But first you must leave your gun behind."

"Listen 'grand Mom', this to me means whatever those crazy crosses mean to you."

"*Crotte!* At least take off your helmet. *Vous devez faire preuve de respect.*"

"Respect? OK, I get that. I'll show some respect" He took off his helmet and held it upturned, on his left forearm. Entered the lower room and saw the steps leading to the next level. "Colette!" he shouted upwards, peering. He heard the faintest of replies. "I'm coming, honey."

"Michael," said Selene softly, "She is in no danger. Trust me."

Oddly enough, he did. Of the two, Selene seemed the more human. Better at sex too.

"Now drink this," she offered. "You like this, you need this. It takes away all pain. Your leg is hurting. It is hurting badly. You know it is hurting, you want the pain to go," she almost droned.

He looked: it wasn't the stuff he craved. Maybe it was better. It *was* hurting badly, sure. She offered him the drink in a narrow silver vessel, almost like a wine glass. The rest of the women were holding similar, ready to drink.

"Cheers!" he said, remembering what they said in English pubs. "Down in one. Watch out for that cat!"

They turned to see The Matagot on the upper stair, calmly watching the proceedings. Michael tilted his head back, downed it in one, then licked the rim.

The women looked at him with adoration, except maybe for the one in red, with red hair: she was giggling. She looked like fun. The horny guys in the 101st would have been right behind him at this moment, and given their right testicles to be in his position. *Forward as One!* they'd have yelled. Or what was it Armand and his troops said? – *On les aura!* Let's have them!

"Now go up there Michael. *There* is your destiny..."

He turned and looked at the stairs.

What had he got to lose?

69

What is this place? **he thought, as he entered the next level. He saw the painted scenes of of the seasons and the painting of a guy wearing lots of medals, hanging below a bright silver star.** There was a big octagonal table in the middle of the floor, of the sort he'd seen old ladies in Detroit use with their Ouija boards when they tried to contact their dead sons.

The Matagot scurried up the next flight of stairs where Horsett could see Colette crouching, looking down through the opening in the floor. He left his helmet on the table: his little way of showing love. He was trying, he really was.

As he rose to meet her she gestured to him with forefingers like fish-hooks, trying to keep him barbed and caught.

She was wearing what looked like a violet wedding dress, with a headdress bearing a crescent moon, and a look on her face like a priestess about to commit heresy. All around her were high walls covered with more silver stars, and windows in the conical roof that would only let in light from the heavens. As she pulled him further into the room, he noticed the large mattress on the floor, covered by a sheet that was patterned with strange fruit. The boards to one side of the mattress were white, the other side black. Her normal clothes dumped, as if hurriedly, into a pile.

She looked fine – if worried.

She whispered: "Michael, did you drink?"

"Why'd you ask?"

"Because it is a strong herb, which will cause great erections and sexual madness."

"Bull. What a crock of shit!"

"*C'est vrai!* I heard that Le Cohen used it all the time..."

"Baloney. So they also want me to 'love' all those gals out there?"

"Did you drink it!?"

"I misdirected them into looking at the cat, poured it in my helmet. Easy-peasy. Remember, I can make things appear..." and he produced a bullet from her ear "...and I can make things disappear. Like that drink. I just licked the rim. I could tell by the colour it wasn't the usual stuff. I ain't stupid."

The Matagot seemed to glower, if cats could do such a thing. It ran off down the stairs and Michael shut the trap door after it.

"Colette honey, is that my *parachute* you're wearing?"

"Made by Hortense, who used to be a seamstress here. It is a strange silk."

"Not silk. They call it nylon."

She clung to him. It felt good, even if the parachute's material felt like he was stroking a fish.

"Michael I do not want to be a nun any more. Please…"

"And then they kill me, right?"

"I do not know. They worship you. How can they? They want you to live forever. For me – they have saved me for this moment, all my life. But explained nothing."

"Okay then, I'll tell you what we're gonna do…"

70

**Sophie was enjoying all this hugely. It was like being part of
la comédie – what the English called a pantomime – with
incredible characters, people who are never what they seem,
magic and dismay, follies and fun and tricks.** Apart from the
snivelling Juliette, there was an air of sexual tension among them
all. These women, who were short of men and the possibilities,
were in heat. It was quite clear that – if they wanted – they would
now have their own way with the man who had fallen from the
sky. Well, she mused with delight, 'man' was not a term she would
have used. With his silly hat, his too-large uniform and smooth
face, he was still just a boy, dressing up, playing at soldiers. This
was all so much fun! Plus Astrid assured them that because of the
special potion he had downed, he would manage them all.
Incroyable!

The trap door to the middle floor opened. All eyes looked
upward. This young girl, whom they had hurriedly dressed for a
wedding, now descended from above, grinning stupidly. Yet – it
had been so quick! Have gods – or Americans – no staying
power? Astrid and Selene frowned. Had she simply been ravaged
with great haste and supernormal passion? And behind her,
helmeted and armed, hawk-like and knowing, came the soldier,
with an expression that Satan might have copied.

"We are leaving," Colette said shyly in English, as if to make a
statement. As if in those three words she was telling a tale about
leaving France and going for a new life in Detroit.

Michael patted her shoulder with an *attagirl* approval. "*Nous
quittons*, folks. It's been swell!"

Astrid stood fast before them. "*Monsieur* Horsett. You may
leave with our blessings. But first, you must meet our Master. Le
Cohen. You must speak with him. Then you will go. If you want.
Will you do that for us, who saved you?"

Sophia thought he looked a bit woozy, as if the drug was
taking effect. "Respect Michael, respect," that is all we ask, came
Selene's plea. She spoke in a very soft, precise voice, touching his
arm as she did so. Was she trying to hypnotise the man? She had
heard the Master often did this to cure people of their fears,

though she had not been there long enough to witness this.

"Come," invited Astrid, who rolled back the carpet and revealed another trap-door leading to a lower level. "Descend into the Duat, and find Amenti…"

The other women gave little gasps. The young girl Colette made to speak but Horsett shushed her. Sophie was certain that she – and she alone – noticed the very slightest of winks that he gave her.

This was getting so interesting!

71

Astrid was pleased that the basement known as the Duat, the Underworld of the Ancient Egyptians they aspired toward, was as bright and clean as the Master, Le Cohen, demanded. In moments this room would prove to be a highway toward paradise.

The others descended after her and looked around in astonishment. It was filled with shelves ablaze with burning candles, each one with a mirror behind it magnifying the light, each one placed behind a sealed earthen jar. The floor was of pure black basalt, darker than the night. The walls were painted with murals of Egyptian gods and goddesses, including one of the Earth God, Geb, lying on his back, arching upward with his huge erection toward the figure of Nu, the Sky Goddess, curving over him: eternally waiting to receive his seed and give birth to stars. Astrid had painted all these herself. She had also, through her knowledge of herbal alchemy, fashioned the drug that would make any man become Geb, and any woman want to have him. It all depended on potencies. Michael was given a much lesser dose than the German. It would give him stamina. And it would take effect soon. After that...

There was a large curtain of spindly, five-pointed stars at the end of the room before which, head-on, was the hand-carved bench they had half-jokingly called the Ark of the Covenant. At the head of it, acting almost like a back-rest, was the outline of the god Shu. At the foot of it was a matching outline of Tefnut. The faces of the two deities would look down upon whoever stretched full-length upon the cushioned seat.

"Selene, Nepthys-in-Waiting, take your place."

"*Grand Mère.*"

Selene sat astride, hitching her robes and showing pale legs and the red vein of the garter. She leaned back against the shape of the male deity as if he held her in his arms. This left enough space for Michael to lie down with his head in her lap and be overlooked by the female Tefnut at the base. The women would then mount him. They would get pregnant. Through the child of one – almost certainly by Colette – Le Cohen would re-enter the world. No longer would he need The Matagot.

The other women were all staring at Michael. Except for the fool Juliette who seemed unduly interested in the earthen jars on the ledges. Astrid went and took her by the arm and almost dragged her back to the group.

"Michael... lie down. You must lie down. Michael? *Michael!*"

Astrid frowned. He was not as *distrait* as he should have been. He was a soldier. Perhaps she should have made the drink stronger?

"Erm... sorry ma'am, but *actuallement* – no. *Non. Jamais.*"

Wide eyes from everyone. What was going on, or what was going wrong? She glared. Words of Power surged toward her lips. She controlled herself. When he spoke he was very calm, not at all drugged.

"Listen Astrid, Selene, it's been swell. Fun. You saved my life, sure. Now before I go, tell me what this is all about. And what's behind that curtain."

Astrid glared at the stupid girl. What had they arranged? The American walked toward the curtain, winking at Selene as he passed. He gripped the edge, paused and looked back at the rest of them, a showman. She had never seen this side of him before.

Making a stupid trumpet noise he pulled the curtain aside and:

"Jesus Christ!" he said, bringing up the machine-gun to fire before lowering it again, with astonishment.

72

While Michael was coming toward his revelation in the tower, Luc and his uncle Armand were in the woods, beneath grey storm clouds, far from the road and along secret trails, busy killing a German.

It was Thibault who had seen the *Hauptmann* first, who was trying clumsily to follow the three women as they had hurried from Neuilly. Thibault became the German's shadow, elegant, silent. *Step to one side* he willed to the man and the wretch did.

Scheisse! came the whisper, as he became entangled in one of the hare traps that Thibault had set the previous night. Hares would have had more sense than this idiot. Silently, elegantly, Thibault crept up behind and clubbed the German unconscious with the butt of his gun. Then he removed the excellent German boots and put them on himself, standing and trying them out as if in a chic *magasin de chaussures*. And finally he used a small skinning-knife with a wickedly curved blade to cut the bastard's Achilles tendons. Then he went to see Armand.

"G'day cobbers!" he announced with a flourish, on entering the house. "*J'ai un lièvre…*" he had said to the much-battered uncle and his always-troubled nephew. He offered up the words in the same way as he had recently offered a hare to the mad women. From the way he said it, they knew exactly what sort of hare it was. "Follow me," he added, and they did.

This capture would be balm to Armand's wounds. Better than any medicine.

"Go and get the American," Armand croaked. "Take one of those anti-tank mines and blow a hole in that witch's tower for me," he added as an afterthought. "I can't let her think her curse worked on *me*."

"Bonzer," said Thibault, who melted into the trees.

So Armand strung up the *Hauptmann* as he had been strung up himself. The chance of justice made him strong. He gave Luc the end of the rope to tug on, as though it were in the bell tower of St Ywi's. The blood from both of the German's ankles drew runes on the hard black earth.

"*Vous êtes un morceau de Merde*," said Armand through swollen lips. It was clear he had no intention of giving *Herr Hauptmann* a quick death.

Luc had never seen a man being killed before – though he had often imagined doing so. He thought of the men who had been hanged in the town square. He thought of Père Gilles, whom he had helped to cut them down and his own heart gave a brief pound. *Pull, pull. Kick. Swing to and fro.* If he did not enjoy the slow torture neither did he look away. Perhaps he had become *Le Vengeur.* Doling out righteous vengeance .

"*Tirez!*" cried Armand who launched more kicks. So Luc pulled on the bell-rope but there were no great resonant clangs. Just a gurgling and a grunting and sound of breaking bones under his uncle's onslaught.

It was messy. It was unclean. Impure. He felt as the priest must have felt toward the personal demon he called *Le Noirceur.* With one antic swing the German was spun around to face Luc. His eyes in the scarlet face widened.

"*De terre?*" he seemed to croak.

Luc frowned and shook his head. He was not 'earthen', whatever that meant. He pulled even harder and kicked, so that the wretch faced Armand again to get more kicks and punches.

73

Back in the tower, as Michael made that stupid trumpet noise and used a flourish to pull aside the veil of the women's temple, it died on lips. He was shocked by what was revealed. Horrified. Astonished. Amazed. *Le Cohen!* he heard a couple of the gals whisper, so he figured this was the guy who had once run this place – now standing dressed like a Pharaoh, arms crossed on his chest, eyes closed, and obviously mummified.

Colette clutched his arm, breathing heavily. Terrified. *It's okay, okay,* he whispered. To the other women too. He'd seen this kinda thing in the travelling Freak Shows that would come to Detroit once a year, but never with a full human. There were all sorts of things he wanted to ask, but Selene, whose head was sunk on her chest, started to talk to him. In a very deep voice. A man's voice.

"Michael... It is I, Le Cohen, speaking to you through my medium."

"Selene honey, *ce n'est pas neccessaire de...*"

"I have waited for you, Michael. You have come from the skies. Your coming was foreseen. It was invoked."

"Baloney."

He saw Selene frown. She didn't understand the word. What a fake!

"Michael. Hor. Sett. Archangel of Fire. Gods of Light and Darkness. We called you and you came. From the skies."

"That's what paratroopers do!" he countered. In English this time.

The other women looked bewildered. They must have thought he was trading Abracadabras.

"Michael," Selene continued in her deep voice, "I have had enough of guiding everyone from Amenti, looking out through The Matagot. I will be reborn through your child, as will be carried by Colette. We want to make you live forever."

"How? By taking your place, huh? *Comment? En prenant votre place, hein?*"

Astrid gave him a look, which he could only describe as shifty. "Not for a long time," she blurted, "and only when you are already dying of cancer and your sons are ready to take up the fight against the Fourth Reich!"

"What? What?! You're crazy, all of you."

"Am I ever wrong, Selene?" Astrid asked.

"No…." said Selene after a long, cautious pause. "Never."

Colette shrank. Hugged against Horsett.

"But what makes you think me and Colette did anything?" Horsett asked in English, but he held in his mind's eye the unruffled bed, their whispered plan, and he looked right at Astrid. He saw the woman stiffen. Either she could read his mind or read his face, but he felt her blast of cold rage. She was insane. Sure was.

"Okay gals I've had enough of this. Selene, excuse me while I squeeze past…*Excusez-moi mesdames! Accrocher sur vos chapeaux.*"

He stood right next to the poor, mummified bastard and stared back at the women. The red-haired one was beaming, enjoying every moment. The other two looked cheated. The one who had fucked the German was standing behind everyone, prying into one of the jars. Somehow, he knew what she was going to find.

He took his helmet off, then put it on the corpse's head at a jaunty angle. He heard women behind him hissing, and one of them giggling. Then he tugged Le Cohen's beard. The stiff lips moved open a tiny fraction. Enough for him to ventriloquise. He used all his French now, no more pretence:

"*Mesdames…* He has his own mission. He came from above to save us all. He really has to go now. Be kind to the old ladies here. And if Astrid or Selene attempt to stab him and gut him when his back is turned, he will blow their little heads off with his big gun!"

Astrid stood on one leg. Made her fists into horns. She was breathing heavily, gathering up her rage to fling her most explosive curse when Selene wrapped her arms around her.

"*Remember the babies,*" she whispered. "*Remember them. They will happen! Do not curse!*"

"*I am not cursing Michael – I am cursing the ghosts of his soldier friends who are calling him to battle. Can you not see them?*"

"*Nique ta mere! Brûle en enfer!*"[1] she cried to them.

The candles flickered and almost went out. These were words Horsett had never heard his own mother utter, so he guessed they

---

[1] Fuck your mother! Burn in Hell!

were pretty bad, and thought they were directed at him. The atmosphere, he had to admit, was malign. What an act, what an act!

Come on, Mikey, You're a Screaming Eagle! No more, never again to be a piece of shit like Pa once said. He took the colt from his holster. "Colette, go get your clothes and out of this dress. And ladies, hey hey hey... howsabout I turn *my* power onto that piece of dead meat you call Le Cohen?" He pointed the gun.

Time stood still, as it used to do before the green jump-light on board the plane.

That was when Juliette screamed, when she saw the foetus of an aborted baby in the jar and thought it was hers. She ran up the stairs and out of the door. No-one tried to stop her.

In the hiatus that followed, when all eyes turned to him, he put first pressure on the trigger but no more. Because part of the tower behind the mummy exploded and ripped Le Cohen in half, showering them all in brick, plaster, splinters, dust, bandages and mummy-innards. The air was sucked from his lungs. His eardrums felt as if they had been poked with needles. The mummy had taken the main force of the blast and protected both him and Colette, though he was smashed to the floor, on top of her at last. The severed head of the Master, still wearing the helmet, faced them serenely, one of his eyes slightly opened.

A torpedo of light rammed in from outside, filled with specks of floating debris that stuck in his throat and made him cough. He couldn't see anyone else for the clouds of junk and dust. He only wanted to see Colette, and she seemed okay, although she was blinking hard.

An air strike? No, most of the explosive force must have been on the outside at ground level. A grenade?

Smoke and dust rose like spirits. Everyone was gasping. The whole tower assumed an angle of 30° and would surely fall. The women were on their knees around him, blinded, deafened, but still screechingly alive. Somewhere above them a radio had switched itself on and was belting out the BBC anthem of dot dot dot dash, of V for Victory.

A gargoyle face appeared in the hole, the sun behind its head, looking down into the basement.

"G'day mate! Fair dinkum!" said Thibault, grinning disgustingly. "Armand asked me to give Astrid a surprise. He loves her really. This is just his way. And now, Michael, are you coming to be a soldier now?"

The tower resembled a huge penis with clouds of dust at its base. They had all survived the explosion and came – coughing – into the day.

"Come," said Thibault.

Michael started to follow, but Colette let go of his hand. "Honey?"

She balanced exactly between him and Astrid.

"Stay," said the latter to Michael, trying her best to say it softly. "Stay and be our god. You are not a soldier. You are a being of Light – or will be when we teach you."

Michael frowned.

"Come," said Thibault. "You are a warrior, not a god. Or you will be with the men around you."

He hated this dilemma. Any dilemma. He'd never have made an officer. It was Colette who decided it. She walked toward him, away from the women.

"Show us the way, Thibault…"

74

Herr Hauptmann **Schimmel knew, with his last sliver of consciousness, that he would not escape this.** His hands were fastened behind his back, a rope around his neck. He was being hauled up and down like puppet on a string. The blood drained slowly from his severed tendons, though the Pervitin numbed the worst of the pain. The tiny crucifix made a light ticking noise on the metal gorget.

He never wholly left the earth, never fully sank back onto it. Yet they never quite let him lose consciousness. *Tick tick tick...* The man in front, gloating, was one he had visited, one he had done just this to.

Armand stood there, pushing him, kicking him, gloating. Inflicting on the officer the same injuries he had suffered. *Piece of shit, piece of shit,* he kept intoning to the spinning victim.

Schimmel squinted at the dark-haired boy beside him, pulling on the rope. With the blurring vision of his twisting body he gasped, croaked, tried to get air in his throat and called out:

"Dieter?" Or tried to.

The boy shook his head. *"De terre?"* He frowned.

Schimmel's ears were ringing, his thinking was crazy. He heard the boy confirm, as clear as day: *Dieter...*

Was? Was? Hilf mir... Hi-[1]

That was when he saw his nemesis approaching, limping through the trees. Through the collonades of light. American. Paratrooper. Angry. Followed by the girl. His very shape waxed and waned with Schimmel's blurring consciousness. He knew that he was now facing his Angel of Death.

He felt the rope being released so he dropped on the ground in a kneeling position. His gaze level with the tall soldier's groin, from which came the reek of incense and cordite.

"Howdy, bud. You been lookin' for me?"

Schimmel spoke no English. The rope on his neck had relaxed. The object of his mad hunt was there before him but *Herr Hauptmann* only swallowed and said "Dieter..."

---

[1] What? What? Help me...

The girl gave a little gasp. A recognition of the name. Schimmel lifted his face toward her, but the dark haired boy he thought was his son put a bullet through his head with his own Luger.

"Good shot," said Thibault.

"I was aiming for the heart. The recoil…"

Colette vomited.

At the same moment there was the rolling noise of large waves breaking on rocks, as the tower collapsed in the world they had just left. They all looked back for a moment. Horsett used his sleeve to wipe the spew from Colette's mouth.

"Justice," said Armand, who felt his strength returning. "Now get us back to my place, Thibault, and we will start our war…"

"Courage!" said Thibault, and on cue he and Armand chanted *"On les aura!"*

To which Horsett added lamely, coughing from the dust, "Forward as One!"

75

Thibault led them through the woods. Despite his bad knee and the need to flick his leg to one side as he walked, he moved smoothly: a fish twisting through green water, eyes that seemed to look to both sides at once. The rest of them limped and lurched, following with difficulty, carrying the extra weapons that they had retrieved, plus the long bazooka-like Signal Lamp. The big American carried that piece. He seemed to think it was important.

Thibault's old friend Armand had a battered rapture on his bloodied face; the nephew, Luc, was thrumming with the mixed emotions of his first kill; Colette, still in shock, stuck to her man like a shadow. From the way the couple kept shaking their heads Thibault knew they still had ringing in their ears from the explosion. He paused for a moment, saw their discomfort and smiled.

"You should have put your thumbs in your ears and opened your mouth. Then you would not hear the church bells!"

"I know that buddy!" said the paratrooper, although he didn't.

In fact the paratrooper was also thinking: *Who the hell is in charge here? What about bursting the dam, firing the railway yards?* His leg was hurting too much for him to forge on ahead and take the initiative. He limped badly. Not so much a stony war face now but one of grim determination. He kept having flashes of his moment in the tower: the adoring women; the insane mummy of the old guy they worshipped; his own smart words that had opened the heavens with a thunderclap; the idiot face staring down to them from the explosive light above.

Both Michael and Colette kept coughing from the sick dust they had inhaled and which was in their throats and nostrils. They were covered in crud. Colette stopped suddenly and squeezed his hand. There was ash in her hair and marks on her face. She was stooped from the shock. She looked old – older than her '*mère*' and '*grand-mère*'.

"Michael... Look..."

Up above the small clearing, in a sky that was blue and gold and clear, was a small circling Piper Cub. A spotter plane. It was against the sun. He could see the U.S. stars on its wings. The good guys couldn't be too far away.

God, god... he muttered, dropping everything else and getting the signal lamp ready. *Don't go, don't go,* he whispered as he put the device to his shoulder and flashed:

Dot-dot-dash; dot-dot-dot; dot-dash. Dot-dot-dash; dot-dot-dot; dot-dash. U.S.A. U.S.A. U.S.A.

Did the sun wipe out his own light? The plane did another tight circle and then flew to the east. Did it waggle its wings in acknowledgement?

"*At-il nous voir?*"

"Sure it saw us," he said, in a tone which implied that *everything* was going to plan. Turning, he ordered: "Keep up, Luc!"

Luc had no plan. He followed along in a stumbling stupor. It was all a twisted dream and he was among twisted people, although they were the best he knew just then. He had often killed Germans in his nightly slumbers to avenge his mother, or shot dead in fantasy people who had slighted him during the daylight hours. In those internal moments of slaughter, he was always cool and righteous. Now, he felt a complete mess. He kept seeing the way the bullet had gone into the soldier's brow: a neat hole followed by a red explosion at the back of the head, like the saintly aureoles in church paintings. If the German dangling from the rope had only maintained eye-contact for another second he would not have shot him. He would have reached into the muddy waters of that deep well of compassion and forgiveness that he had often talked about with Gilles.

Perhaps.

Because Gilles had betrayed him. With that woman. That was a bullet to his own heart.

Armand and Thibault would certainly have tortured the German. So maybe his single shot was actually an act of kindness?

Perhaps.

So maybe Gilles had been kind in his own priestly way?

He hoped. Yet...

I am a mess, he thought, taking in a deep breath. *What I did to that German was not wrong. Yet I am ashamed.*

Stop this.

"Don't fall, Colette," he urged, pushing her along. Midges of dust rose from her hair as she brushed through the overhanging leaves. It made him cough too.

Colette couldn't fall. She held onto Michael's belt. She had to, or else the image of Le Cohen's severed head rolling on the floor might have made her scream. This was the nearest she had ever known to a father. He was dead, then he spoke through Selene, then appeared behind the curtain. Then he was torn apart. She was on the edge of the sort of screaming fit she used to have as a young child, until the caring hand of Le Cohen would drive her terrors away as he stroked her brow .

Her world had been destroyed. In an instant by that gargoyle Thibault. She was no longer playing games of love and indulging in the *coup de foudre* – the lightning bolt that would grow into lifelong love. She just felt a painful ringing in her ears, and her mouth and lungs were full of the dust of an Age that was now dead. She clung to Astrid's prediction for her man, clung to the futures unmanifest. Now she had to stay with him, her husband in all but name.

She looked up at her man. He was in pain. He kept looking skyward as if that tiny aeroplane – little better than a gnat – were about to come back to him.

Yet for the first time – just a tiny, broken, dust-sized fragment of a moment which she killed – he no longer looked like a god.

Armand, back in his own little house, did feel a bit like a god at that moment. Because he had his little goddess with him. This was a woman whom he had slept with innumerable hours, who never strayed far from his touch, who never betrayed or failed him. He had cleaned her, washed her, kept her warm and smoothed her hidden places with precious oils. In return she had saved his life, and those of his fellow *poilus*, many times. She, and she alone, had made Young Armand more than a man and something of a hero. Her name was *L'étoile*, and he had named her thus himself in 1916, baptising her with the blood of many Germans.

Although he was aching from the beating he felt a curious peace come upon him as he caressed her now, her long, sleek shape, and polished her single glass eye which could see as mortal women never could.

This was the APX Mle Lebel rifle, with its beautiful, adjustable telescopic sight. With standard ammunition he could kill at three hundred metres.And feel nothing.

There was a sound outside, the strange *Cocorico cocorico cocorico!* that Thibault sometimes used to herald his approach. Armand stood back from his open window, in the shadows, and looked at the approaching gang by putting his good eye to the sight. The woodsman looked right at Armand, knowing exactly where he was and what his old *poilu* friend was doing.

The girl looked like one of Nosferatu's servants, such as he had seen in the cinema, almost white with dust. She staggered, red-eyed, wild-eyed, uncomprehending. Her American lover – for he assumed they were such, and if not what was wrong with the guy? – was not much better. Now that he was holding his Lebel, and remembering himself, he saw clearly that 'Michael' was little better than a toy soldier. Then there was his nephew Luc...well, he never knew what to make of him: sometimes like a virgin, sometimes sinister. And he had *always* known the relationship between him and the mad priest. Now the boy was just acting as if he was a big man. He must have done something bold. And then he saw the Matagot, following on behind.

Of course, he had always heard the stories of Matagots, but never quite accepted the rumours of Astrid's powers. Or believed that this creature was anything more than an ordinary cat. Yet he lined the flat ugly face in his sights.

"*Non!*" cried Thibault, limping forward and pushing the barrel aside. "There will be a terrible storm if you harm that beast. Truly."

Armand took a deep breath and nodded, yet fired anyway.

Horsett dropped to the ground and pulled Colette with him.

Colette cried out in pain as the signal light jabbed her and blinded her in one eye; then cried "*NON NON NON!*" And then "MICHAEL!"as she tried to get his weight off her.

Luc hissed, but stood there paralysed. He surprised himself: he had never made such a noise before.

The Matagot swerved and disappeared into the woods.

"Bravo, cobber! But you missed."

"*Jamais!* If I wanted to kill it, it would be dead. Now it has a new stripe along its fat body."

Thibault, totally unmoved, had spent years in the trenches learning exactly when a bullet or shell was dangerous, what sort of weapon fired it, was pleased to see his oldest friend getting back to normal.

"Come," said Armand, standing in his doorway and beckoning. "Now the war begins. But get rid of that useless piece of metal you are carrying, Colette."

Colette picked up the signal lamp and threw it into the woods like a javelin.

Michael said nothing.

Colette looked around at wrecked rooms in Allumage's house. Everything had been upended, broken, trashed, thrown. Her gaze was blurry, her eye-socket sore where it had been bashed by the stupid lamp. She was getting a black eye to go with her stupid wedding dress.

"I am sorry about the mess," Armand apologised, slurring through his swollen lips. "Germans came. I said nothing!" He ran his hand over the scars on his head, glowing with pride.

"He said nothing," Thibault echoed, smiling over his protruding teeth in that obscene way of his. "And Luc killed the officer who did this to *Chez Allumage*... Pffft!."

Armand nodded proudly at his nephew, giving credit where it was due. He picked up from the floor the framed photograph of his sister – Luc's mother – dusted it off with his sleeve and made a point of hanging it straight on the wall again.

Luc righted the bed and simple furniture in his own small room. The novels back on shelves; his work clothes and Sunday best back on their hangers. As he put each piece in place to get the little world back to normal, he had to press hard to keep his hands from shaking.Out of the cracked bedroom window he saw Jules emerging cautiously from the trees.

And someone else with him, lurking almost out of sight...

Thibault got to the front door before him. Thibault seemed to know everything that was happening in his forest. And no-one doubted that it really was *his* forest, even though there were no earthly deeds or documents to show his ownership.

"*Bienvenue* Jules! Welcome, Jules the Invisible One, the Finder of Paths!" He was always amused by the younger man's ego. "Who is that with you? Hiding behind the oak?"

"Hello Thib... Well, you see, I knew there was a lunatic loose in the woods. I followed him with my great skills. Then I heard a shot. And then I saw him looking at the dead German with a big grin on his face. He dropped his gun when he saw me. Now I ask you all – don't shoot..."

He waited until they had all nodded then turned and gestured to the hidden figure.

Slowly, shaking, with raised hands, Le Blanc of the *Feldgendarmes* emerged into the open. Horsett raised his machine-gun but Colette slapped it down.

"*NON!*" she cried. "This is the man who saved you, Michael. When you were hiding in the secret room."

"He's a Kraut, and I wasn't hiding."

"I am a Frenchman *m'sieur.* I made wrong choices. Bad choices. I want to atone."

All eyes were on the man. Huge, invisible things floated around them all in the silence: they had all made bad choices, they all wanted some form of redemption or atonement.

"And how can you do that?" muttered Armand.

"I can win your war for you. With this magic wand." He held up the *Winkerkelle*, the traffic wand that looked so much like a large lollipop.

"Hear his plan," insisted Jules. "Which was really *my* plan all along..."

76

Michael Horsett found himself having to admit something difficult and almost painful. It loomed large within his awareness and he was almost afraid to face it. The fact is, the 'whitebread troops' that he had so recently sneered at were actually pretty damned good. He had written them off as a bunch of douche bags and goons, but he was starting to feel a real warmth for them. Hell, why shouldn't he? He was half-French after all. His *maman* would be proud – even more proud! This Gallic side was another thing he had kept hidden from the world at large, and his old buddies in particular. For reasons of shame, or fear, he couldn't rightly say.

So they did it like this:

Thibault had got them through the forest and to the edge of the town. The guy had a bad knee but he moved slickly and silently, and it was all the rest could do to keep up. He made no allowance for Michael's increasingly agonising limp.

Jules, despite his bluster, really did know the back gates and inner passageways of Neuilly. They entered peoples' homes, him making brief apologies to various startled crones for bringing the death-encased soldier and his insane wife with him. They must have looked as if they had risen from the ashes of the fires of Hell, because some of them made signs of the cross and turned their faces to the wall. In one house, Jules put his finger to a frightened woman's lips and whispered – though loud enough for everyone to hear: "Madame L'Etincelle... tell your son the moment has arrived. He needs to bring us some fire – unless he is all piss and wind! I, Jules the General, tell him that." And the sight of the Tommy guns and the German policeman played no small part in preventing anyone objecting.

Yohan Le Blanc, meanwhile, marched them along a couple of short empty streets as if they were his prisoners. Helmetless, covered in crud that disguised the U.S. uniform, no-one looked twice. If they had, they would have thought this was a deserter, from some obscure German unit, being marched toward his hanging.

This was not what Horsett had planned. But at least he was on the front line where he was meant to be. It might be suicidal, but that was the paratroopers' way. The thought came to him that he had found himself. At last. He tried not to think about the apparent paradise he could have chosen, but if Astrid's prediction was correct then he was gonna get through this next bit anyway.

The whitebread troops and their erstwhile creator entered the rear door of the building from a small alleyway. There was no-one in. All out on duty. This was the real thing. The legendary and omnipotent *Das Reich* division was due to arrive any time now.

"Up there," Le Blanc had said. "That is what I told you about. From there, you will be able to stop an army."

"And you?"

"I will go and divert that army for you. Give me twenty minutes to get into place. *Au 'voir mes amis!*"

None of them replied. They locked the doors of the building behind them and headed up the awkward staircase. Horsett could feel the last of the stitches give way. Christ but his wounds were aching. He craved just one more glug of that potion the old gals had given him.

The office stank of vomit and dead air. The windows were dirty and sealed. There was a large map unfolded on the desk top, covered in small crosses, stained with coffee – or blood? There was a plate of stale sandwiches, untouched. Brown bread and cheese. Thibault, the old soldier, who knew that you must always eat when you can and sleep when you can, took one of these and turned his back to bite into it. Embarrassed by the eating motions he must use. He, Horsett and Jules went to the windows and peered outside.

Luc went to the pictures of Hitler and Jesus and took them down, turning their faces to the wall. He also studied the small photograph on the desk that showed a youth and twin girls in traditional German costume. He showed it to Michael, whose eyes narrowed. That, surely, was the dispatch rider he had wasted.

"You are bleeding Michael," said Luc.

He looked down at the lightning flash pattern where the stitches had come loose. The dust of mummies was gonna mingle with his wounds and give him something a whole lot worse than the gonorrhoea they were lectured about in England. He used his combat knife to cut a long strip from Colette's dress then tied it around his leg as a dressing.

Colette was too numb to say anything, to make any judgments or assessments. She stayed with Michael out of duty, but in truth she just wanted to go home, to the days before this 'hawk god' had appeared. It had been better under Hitler. She also looked down at the narrow street, too numb to say anything or even react. Her ears were still ringing, the others opened their mouths but she heard nothing. They were fish. This was not the sort of destiny that her elders had always brought her toward.

Something had been damaged in the last few days, since Michael had arrived. Perhaps she should have jumped into that side-car with Dieter and ridden away. She was sure he had wanted that too. Not all Germans were bad. And she was still in her stupid wedding dress, feeling like the idiot that so many always thought she was. An hour before, the only person she had thought of as Papa, and who she believed was in that heaven world they called Amenti, had risen from the dead from behind the curtain. Larger than life yet possessing not a shred of it. Her heart had almost stopped on its way to soaring. And then BOUM, he had died again as he'd been blown to bits And she'd found herself on the floor, amid separated limbs, the stink of old dust, straw and exotically scented stuffing and natron. And the blobs of foetuses everywhere.

She looked down, and for some reason she remembered an exquisite morning ten years before, looking into the still depths of the garden pond with The Master and some of his little *fees*, as he called them. They had small nets on garden canes, and were fishing for the tadpoles, which would one day become newts. Those figures down there now, black round helmets with frantic limbs attached, were cruel parodies. Then, in 1940, she had been in Amenti. Heaven. Though no-one knew it.

She moved to the back of the room and stood beneath the stuffed owl that she had helped Selene make in the pure world before 1940. Michael seemed to mouth the words '*Ne vous inquiétez pas*', and from the way he pouted his lips he still wouldn't, even now, *tutoyer*.[1] What did she care, standing there as she was in her

---

[1] The use of the intimate 'tu' form

torn, dirty and stupid wedding dress with its odd texture, looking and feeling like a zombie?

Luc, with a sympathy that was unintentionally cruel, took the photo over to Colette. Her eyes widened. Dieter!

"Michael shot him," he whispered. "Just before he came to you. I saw him. Shot the boy in the back. He burned to death when his motorbike exploded. This must have been his father's office."

He said it as praise of Michael.

77

Yohan le Blanc felt good about himself for the first time in years. He stood in the centre of the cross of roads that led into or around Neuilly and knew he was protected on many levels.

On the way, he had come across that infuriating priest, curled up on the pavement and probably drunk. The kinship was instant. Plus he saw a chance to insure himself against the future at another level. He dragged the wretch back into his church and whispered: *I am French. I serve France.*

Most *Feldgendarmes* defended themselves from the insults of the landsers by pointing out (in their own minds at least) that it took courage, real guts, to stand in open spaces, amid heavy fire and aerial attacks, and conduct the war with just a stick.

Most Frenchmen aligned with the Germans also told themselves that collaboration was a positive thing for their country: they could ensure justice would be done for both nations.

Yet one French *Feldgendarme* in particular knew that he had backed the wrong side and wanted – not just to save his skin – but to make amends. So he, Yohan, knew that a massive fate was heading directly toward him in the form a *Panzer* division: a monstrous python that he could re-direct. The brandy that Thibault had given him also helped.

Thibault – good old Thib – had given him a small bottle to steady his nerves. As he drank it, it felt like a communion. He was suddenly reborn. Pure again. As he had done when he pushed the American's helmet under the bed and made his clever comment, and the women had approved.

He also knew, some time before it arrived, that the little shit Henri Lueur, (newly promoted on the basis of arse-licking), would be approaching him from the side.

And Yohan also felt good that he could almost feel the heavy armour approaching: probably the *Das Reich* division, with its monstrous Panthers and Tiger tanks. And yes! Here he came – the little shit himself, Henri, red-faced and furious, reaching for his Luger.

But Yohan had no fear. Not this time.

He was protected.

The being who offered him protection was wedged firmly up a sycamore tree less than a hundred metres away, looking down toward the crossroads where Yohan had stationed himself. He was still aching from the beating. Yet he had said nothing, betrayed no-one. He would no longer feel *la précarité*, which had blighted his whole nation. How could he, when his beautiful Lebel sniper rifle was balanced firmly in branches, aiming directly toward Le Blanc as part of their agreement?

If the latter failed to do what he promised, he would get a bullet in his face. If anyone tried to stop him doing his duty, they would be cut down. The distant horizon was ragged with battle. The land was filled with a frantic army.

No-one would notice his little bullets.

Henri Lueur, who was glowing from the feeling of promotion and the sense that higher powers now acknowledged his worth, knew nothing of the *Hauptmann*'s death, only of his disappearance. He would now be fully justified in having the office hanged as a deserter when next they met. Before then, however, he fully intended to do the same to the idiot Le Blanc, who was standing in the wrong place with a drunken expression on his stupid face.

"What are you doing? Why are you here?" he raged as he drew his pistol.

The idiot smiled. The idiot, whose breath stank of alcohol, said, "*Bonjour, petit garçon*," and with his fingers made a pistol, that pointed right at his countryman's face.

Then Yohan smiled even more hugely when a small hole appeared in the smooth brow, as if by magic, while a huge mass erupted from the back of the head. Lueur sank down vertically to his haunches and remained there. Anyone watching would think Le Blanc was having his boots polished.

The ground beneath trembled. Le Blanc smiled again, lifted the traffic wand so that all could see, and turned his full attention to the approaching convoy, with its outriders and following of heavy *Panzers* and assault guns. He had not felt this good since that wonderful moment with the mad women at St Martin's, years before. When this was over....

"*Gehen. Dieser Weg. Schnell!*" he shouted, using the invader's language for the last time. "*Allez! Allez! Tout droit!*" he cried, becoming a true Frenchman again, watching with delight as the huge python turned at his bidding and headed toward the impossibly narrow confines of Neuilly.

Armand watched all this. *What a good shot I am!* he thought when he saw the young traitor crumple. The tanks and troop carriers full of *panzer* grenadiers were inexorably moving where Le Blanc had promised to send them. Armand watched as they inserted themselves deeply into the narrowing streets.

Was that idiot with his wand daring to give the thumbs up? Daring to imagine that he had atoned?

He put the cross-hairs of his scope on the man's heart, breathed out slowly and, using the second phalange of his middle finger (so as not to jerk the aim to one side), shot him.

Traitor, he muttered.

The whitebread troops stood looking down upon the flow. The town square was full of soldiers. Many of them were very young boys and very old men of the *Volksturm:* virgin soldiers and old men who could only just remember their own innocence, and the pure years before Hitler came to save them. They had been called up in desperation, to fill in the gaps by those thousands of regulars who would never return from the Eastern Front. Many of them didn't even seem to be carrying any weapons. Never mind – the real fighters were coming: The *Das Reich* division. Veterans. Warriors. They would save the Fatherland, here on French soil.

The small group who hoped to slow them looked down upon the narrow grey street leading into La Place. There were the remains of a dead horse, broken and slimed into the dark cobbles by some heavy vehicle; and a black dog with splayed legs that had been crushed as flat as a cartoon character.

They opened the windows. Fresh air blew in. They breathed deeply. The stink of burning oil and diesel fumes quickly followed.

"Okay guys, remember what I taught you about these grenades," Horsett tried to command, although he wasn't sure if he'd ever taught them anything and would have given anything for some of that *Herbe d'Or.* Or was it just straight out morphine? "When you pull *this* pin, and release *this* lever, you've got five seconds before it explodes. You understand, Jules? Luc?"

They nodded.

Thibault knew this already. Had he not thrown many grenades before, of all kinds? He touched Horsett gently on the arm: "When the time is right, cobber, give the order. And no matter what happens, thank you. Thank you very much."

Horsett frowned. Now was not the time to ask what he meant. But he felt a surge of gratitude anyway. Those words, from this odd man, made him feel as if he'd just got a medal.

Below, some thirty feet below, two open-backed troop carriers full of *panzer-grenadiers* paused at the end of the narrowing street, revving their motors, waiting for the congestion in the square to ease. Where were the men with the traffic wands?

Michael bent out of the window and peered further down the street, to the wider part. He saw the monstrous shapes that all the Allied soldiers had been warned about. Squat, angular, filled with absolute menace and obscenely long snouts.

"Panthers – or maybe Tigers," he said. "Not sure from this angle."

"Does it matter?"

"*Non, pas de tout.* Our traitor did as he said."

Below, a *Feldwebel* looked at the space on either side of the vehicle, and then back at the following tanks. He shook his head. Then he hefted himself onto the side of the truck to get a better look, judging widths and possibilities.

"Will that Le Blanc guy join us when he's finished re-directing?"

"*Non,*" said Thibault brightly. "Not unless he can rise from the dead. When he has fulfilled his promise, and done his duty for France, Armand will kill him."

"Why?"

"We did not watch thousands of our friends die at Verdun so that a young bastard like him could try to ride two horses at once."

"No forgiveness, then?"

"To forgive is to condone." Thibault spat, running his tongue awkwardly over his lips.

"Will Armand join us?"

"We will not see him again. The fires of Hell will get him. I know that."

Les feux de l'enfer? Was this guy as crazy as everyone else?

Jules felt good on hearing Le Blanc was doomed. For the rest of his life – however long that might be – he would claim full credit for this plan. He would feel like De Gaulle. Women would adore him – though he had lost all carnal interest in the corpse-like Colette, who was standing under the owl at the back of the room, as if she too were stuffed

"*Je te dis Merde!*" said Jules, tapping his nose.

Horsett frowned.

"It means, good luck," said Luc.

Horsett's Mom had never used vulgar idioms. She was pure.

Armand, wedged into his tree, felt a purity of his own. Even more so when he swore – *Fils de pute,*[1] – under his breath after each shot. With his smokeless cartridges, and the general chaos around the long, stalled convoy, he had already picked off ten Boche. The men of the Master Race fell like rag dolls. He felt immortal, invisible, choosing who might live and who might not. In this war, the Germans were not hiding in their deep trenches and sending over gas like the cowards they were. They were lining up for him, almost begging for it. Today, he was happy. This was a good kind of revenge. If he had been deeply ashamed of his country's surrender in 1940, at the Fall, this was his own means of redemption.

Now, taking care not make a noise, sliding like a serpent down through the branches, he decided to find another spot to resume firing, as all snipers must. As he put his feet together, ignoring the pain in his ribs and limbs, he turned to drop the last few feet to grass.

The last words he heard, coming from nowhere, were: *Du Hurensohn!*[2]

The intense yellow spikes and orange and red waves of *panzergrenadier's flammenwerfer* were the last light he saw, as he and his tree were immolated.

---

[1] Son of a bitch
[2] You son of a Bitch

At roughly the same moment that Armand was being obliterated by the flamethrower, the *covine* sat breathing deeply, in varying degrees of shock.

The Cock Tower had collapsed and lay in a broken line like a flaccid penis. They had all emerged in time, though it had been a close thing

Sophie had been stunned, but she was strong. Everyone knew that. She would always survive. No-one knew that. She sat on a lump of broken stone, in the red dress she had been given for the orgy, and was not sure whether to thank God for her salvation or curse Him for spoiling what would have been a lot of fun with that beautiful 'hawk god' – whatever the wild women meant by that. Sitting still for a moment, she made sure she still had the *petite cadeau*. It had saved her, surely. Then she removed the garter and skimmed it across the battered hedge.

Astrid and Selene saw this. They looked at each other and nodded. The older woman spoke:

"Go and find them, Sophie. You are strong. You have the wisdom. Bring them back here."

"Where?"

Selene pointed. There was The Matagot, waiting patiently, a line along his side that looked like a burn.

So she followed the creature, across fields, through wood.. At one point she saw a strange device that stood up from a bush like a spear. It was not a weapon, but some sort of flashlight. She pointed it into the shadows of the trees: *Dot Dot Dot Dash* – V for Victory.

That would do for a start.

Sounds of aircraft above. Many landsers calling out *Jabo! Jabo!* The *Feldwebel* below, a tough looking bastard who was everything Michael had once wanted to be, decided to glance up. He saw the aircraft – Thunderbolts – and then he saw Michael.

Their eyes met. Their eyes widened. Their mouths opened to utter their own words.

"Now! *Maintenant!* Throw! 5, 4, 3, 2, 1..."

The last time he had counted like that he had zapped that dispatch rider.

The grenades seemed to fall in slow motion. Then exploded. Blood and various body parts spurted as high as the office windows. The driver in the first truck was startled but uninjured. The driver in the second was slumped and bleeding badly. The *Felbwebel* urged '*Vorwärts!*' and others rushed to get the trucks over the bodies and into the square, then turned and fired upstairs with every gun they had

The air of the room was filled with glittering diamonds of glass and a maelstrom of lead. The bullets gouged across the ceiling in neat curves and brought down ancient plaster and lighting fittings, exposing the roof beams.

Thibault returned fire with calm, single shots of his weapon, shaking his head in disgust at its inaccuracy, then picking his targets better. Horsett loosed short bursts until he had to reload. Jules, his face scarred and bloodied by light shrapnel emptied his magazine in one sweep.

There might have been screaming from many dead, but the angle was too steep to see much below. The air was filled with the noise of fighter-bombers, and you couldn't hear much above that. The men below were more troubled by the murderous cannon of the aircraft than the pea-shooters above.

"Uncle Jules," said Luc, who was using a hand gun. "You missed everything. Your bullets went up the wall. Adjust for the recoil." Luc had killed. He knew everything as only boys do.

The heavy duty machine gun from the first tank bit through solid brick. Its shells sliced open part of their room at an acute angle, one of them slicing a neat line across Jules' midriff. His clothes started burning but he patted the flames out with his bare hand. Then went back to the window to fire some more.

Outside, the two burning troop carriers had been cleared from the street, leaving room for the the tanks to press forward. The leading Tiger had closed all its hatches. No chance of any grenades being dropped inside. As if it had been a living beast, it seemed to pause and think, studying the width of the egress. It raised its monstrous gun toward the office but was too close to fire. Besides, it was just as likely to kill its own men beyond.

Horsett could feel engines revving. It was like a bull pawing the ground before its charge. It only needed to chip a few inches off the brickwork at either side and it would roar out into the square.

"It's gonna try and smash through."

It started to do exactly that.

"Guys go – get out the back. Luc, take Colette somewhere safe. Go. When the tank jams I'll get down there and blow off a track. GO!"

But Jules was on his knees, white-faced and trying to push his guts back inside. "Luc, shoot me, pl…"

Thibault fired a quick shot into his temple, the brains splashing all over Michael's crotch like a pizza.

Colette screamed. Luc almost did, but he took her by the shoulders and forced her back down the stairs.

"Thib…" Luc gasped. Horsett was weakening. More bleeding from where a bullet had sliced through the eagle on his arm, and a piece of shrapnel that had damaged his neck. He waved the Hawkins mine, pointed to himself, and then downstairs.

"*Tu comprends?*" he gasped, giving Thibault that which Colette never achieved.

"*Certainement.* Bonzer. G'day Cobber…*Allez, allez…*"

He half fell, half slid down the staircase made slippery by his own blood.

The whole place shuddered, as the tank rammed the corner walls at either side. Plaster fell from the ceiling, internal windows shattered. Walls bent and buckled. The door to the street bust open. A yard away, going slowly backward, the tank was dragging itself free of the stonework for another ram.

That huge slab of steel was only two feet away. Horsett peered both ways down the street. He primed his Hawkins anti-tank mine and stepped out. A soldier saw him and raised his rifle, but Thibault dropped the guy like a stone. As he fixed the device between the cogged wheel and the track he saw the shell of a hand-launched *panzerfaust* blow Thibault into pieces.

"Michael…come!" shouted Luc. "Hurry."

Limping badly, bleeding badly, Horsett joined the other two at the rear of the building, their arms cocooning the girl as the mine exploded. It wouldn't damage the body of the tank itself, but it sure as hell wouldn't be able to move for quite some time. After that it would be up to the Thunderbolts.

"Come," said Luc, although he was not sure if anyone could hear him. "I know where to go…"

78

Luc, who felt as stupid now in his schoolboy's clothes as Colette did in her cut-up wedding dress, no longer enjoyed this game. Killing the Nazi had not brought him the peace of which he had always dreamed. Then the sight of his uncle being eviscerated... He was trying to blank that out of his mind by blinking and keeping the lids pressed hard for long seconds, even as he walked. The American, Michael, who at first had seemed the bright shining arrival, who would save them all, (with help from a million others), was a hollow man. He'd been beautiful at first – but not now.

Yet Michael was failing, and they had to move quickly. It would be up to him, Luc, to support him. Father Gilles would help.

That was what he liked about his priest-lover: despite his guilt, his outbursts, his crippling torments and fears of something inexplicable, Luc had often seen him take a deep breath, close his eyes and find some switch within that could turn on his courage and kindness.

Of course, Luc still felt betrayed by the priest, taking that cow Sophie as his housekeeper, but that was only practical. He, Luc, had already forgiven him.

"Come," he said. He dragged the dumb Colette with one hand and supported the American with the other, guiding them along routes that he and his kind often used: where they were not likely to be seen. Where they would be safe. Side alleys. The ends of lonely gardens. Squeezing between fences and houses.

The skies above Luc were turning into deepening shades of grey and charcoal, laced with indigo. Something burned across it from east to west that was red-gold like a cannon ball. Aircraft of every nationality – bearing crosses, stars and roundels – wove tortured patterns and spat lines of fire. One of them exploded and spiralled down into the distant woods where he lived. Was his home now destroyed? Shell cases rained down around them and singed the grass or hissed into ponds. The rolling thunder, which had previously only come from the direction of Caen, now surrounded them.

Was this the doing of L'Etincelle? Was all of France rising?

He would take them through this final field into the back of the church, which to him was a source of sanctuary and temptation. They would wait until it was safe.

"Be brave, Michael. Be strong. We are almost there. Father Gilles will help. He is a good man..."

Four horses erupted from a side street, screaming, their manes on fire. They galloped past with rolling eyes and lips drawn back from their teeth.

Father Gilles awoke from his seizure. There was cold stone under his face, and the palm of his right hand, where he was curled in the aisle. His crotch was wet and smelled of urine. He lay in shadows. There was vomit in his hair. His body felt so heavy and his head felt cold inside.

He knew that he had had a seizure, although the knowing didn't come in such logical terms. This was his experience. This was his routine, his life. He would remember the smallest details about his childhood, but his short-term memory would be gone.

First there was the waking. Then the intense headache and pains all along his spine. A metallic taste in his mouth and a swollen tongue where he must have bitten it. And the constant smacking of his lips.

Who was he? *Dj Dj Dj...* He heard a soft voice, a mother's voice saying *Gilles...Gilles...Gilles...* so he was a little boy?

He struggled onto all fours. When he moved his head, it felt as if his brain rattled in his skull.

He looked up. Where was he?

There was a cross on an altar. A stained glass window. He knew these things. And, and...a bowl of water. Yes, holy water. Other things floated in, slowly, crinkled leaves on a small stream.

Mass. He knew that word. Con..con...Confession?

They were words in his head. No more than sounds. Meanings would follow.

Was his *maman* taking him to Mass? To Confession?

He remembered a cuckoo clock. Soup. Clothes being washed. It was like walking on ice: he went backward when trying to go forward. A fear of falling.

Above him, somewhere, there were blasts of thunder. And

lightning? He looked at his hand, his fused fingers.

He crawled toward the altar, toward the light. Shaking his head from side to side. The stone floor was hard on his knees, cold on his hands. Something was dangling from his neck as he moved: a crucifix.

Gilles. That was his name. He heard the cuckoo from his childhood again. He heard it go *Currrrgk* because of the glue. That was a bad act. Not evil, but bad. That helped him remember.

I am a man not a boy. I am a priest. This is a church. My church.

He crouched there remembering and recovering. Panting. Exhausted. A man without grace but without guilt either. Behind him, the great door creaked open. A noise of thunder came in with a blast of cold air. He heard footsteps.

Colette had never been in the church before. In any church. Le Cohen always smiled when he mentioned such places. *That is not my path,* he would whisper. *Not my way.*

She made no judgment about the place. One of her eyes was swollen, the other was filled with dirt, which she couldn't scoop out. The *cafard* completely enveloped her. She stood, numb, looking out through the obscene eyes of the cockroach. She had seen the disgusting insects fly once – a whirr of wings and mad flight. She had no such wings – just a hard, dirty carapace. The soul of Le Cohen must have felt like this in the mummy, before he found comfort in The Matagot.

She held onto Luc's left hand. Where was Michael? Attached to Luc's other hand. She wondered if she still cared, still loved. He had brought them nothing but thunder and lightning, death and insanity, destruction of home and foster parents and women's dreams.

There was a large picture window with a man in it. He seemed to leer. At the end of the aisle, in front of the thing with the cross on it, was a large black dog, rolling its head from side to side, smelling of piss.

"Père Gilles..." said Luc.

Collette was startled. This black creature was not an animal. It was the priest she had heard about.

Michael Horsett felt his life draining away. His arm and his neck hurt as much as his leg. One side of his face was riddled with tiny shards of glass. His uniform was ripped, covered in blood, dirt, and pulverised matter. He no longer looked like a Pathfinder, a proud Screaming Eagle of the 101st Airborne – more like an old ass. Where was Colette? Why wasn't she helping him? Oh, yeah, there she was – standing back, looking dreadful. He'd never take her back to see his Mom now.

Who was this guy Luc had brought them to?

God, he was tired. He'd take any help he could get at this moment.

Père Gilles breathed deeply. Rose from all fours to his knees, grabbed at his crucifix and stood upright. He swayed, damaged by the seizure as much as Horsett was from firepower.

There was...Luc? Yes, Luc. He remembered the face, the *faux*-schoolboy clothes. Why did he wear those? Why was he looking so hopefully, as if they were old friends? What was his connection?

And the woman – who was she? What was she? One closed black eye of the sort many women got from their husbands, and one half-opened, reddened eye. Why did she wear that dirty, torn wedding dress? Was he supposed to marry them now?

"Bonjour, Père Gilles," said this Luc, this boy-man, nodding to the third figure. "This is…"

A revelation hit the priest that was every bit as powerful as the thunderbolt: "*Le Noirceur!*" he replied, with a terror that clutched at his heart and held its rising beat in cold talons.

"*Mais non. Non non non…*" Then the boy frowned, the wrinkles on his brow giving him his true age. And Gilles remembered telling him about *Le Noirceur* in the darkness of his bed.. Their eyes met in different revelations.

"Gilles, his name is…"

"His name is Legion. His name is Night. His name is Death, War, Famine and Conquest."

Fournier felt the strength of the End Days come upon him. No more running, no more hiding. *Le Noirceur* was here, in his church, an obscene presence in his sanctuary.

"Pater noster, qui *es* in cœlis; sanctificatur nomen tuum..."

Michael felt himself fading. He had to kneel down. He knew those words. His Mom had been a Catholic of sorts, though never allowed to express it. She'd taught him the French version instead. He muttered it now, as if it might take him back to a safe place:

"Que ton règne vienne, Que ta volonté soit faite sur la terre comme au ciel..."

Père Gilles smacked his lips. He could feel the aura of another seizure. His body was bathed in a prickly sweat. He must hold fast. The Latin would help: "Adveniat regnum tuum; fiat voluntas tua, sicut in cœlo, et in terra..."

His hand, his 'good' hand clutched at his crucifix. He held it toward this creature, with the side of his face scarred by what looked like diamonds, and felt this was the Unholy Trinity he was dealing with, *Le Noirceur* mocking his own deformity.

He was scared, *very* scared, and there was a taste in his mouth like an old franc, as he flushed and sweated. But he knew that he was also on the verge of a great victory, a true liberation. The creature, the demon, was kneeling down before his righteousness. His minions were trying to support him, but were too weak.

Michael stared at the priest. He was too tired to wonder. He was a little boy again saying his secret prayers in his secret language with his *maman*:

"Donne-nous aujourd'hui notre pain de ce jour. Pardonne-nous nos offences comme nous pardonnons aussi à ceux qui nous ont offensés."

Père Gilles was on the edge of an abyss. The Latin was leaving him: "Panem nostrum cotidianum....er,er, de... da nobis..." He found himself making the bizarre noises that were very bad signs indeed.

Michael was unaware of anyone now. He was missing a couple of lines of prayer. He hadn't said them for many years. So he let the rest trip out, muttering softly, suddenly warm and wanting to sleep, so very much wanting to sleep. He couldn't understand why Luc was shaking him. Where was Colette?

"Et ne nous soumets pas à la tentation, mais délivre-nous du mal..."

The priest knew he was being mocked. As he had been mocked all his life. And now here was Lucifer, asking not to be led into temptation, and to deliver him from evil. His reply would not come.

"Currrrgk Currrrgk Currrrgk!" he cried and with his good hand he raised the big brass candleholder above his head to smash the creature's brains out.

And then came the light. Of a kind he had never seen before. It was searing, cold and impossibly bright. He dropped the brass weapon. Put his bad hand to his eyes.

Another lightning bolt?

"Père Gilles!" came the reproachful voice – a woman's voice – from where the force had been unleashed.

Was this God?

The last thing he saw, before he went into his grand mal, was Sophia wielding the signal lamp that Michael had hoped would summon forces from above

Michael Horsett, who had once flapped around as a Screaming Eagle, without ever quite managing to soar, now found himself hovering next to the old rafters of the church. The tops of the beams were white with pigeon droppings. Below him were Luc and Colette. They had stretched his own body out on the floor and were trying to staunch his wounds.

It was weird to look down at himself but he wasn't startled. As if he had been through this before. Somewhere. Somehow. Everything glowed – even the many shadows. Intense colours.

And there was the priest a few feet away, with no light around him whatsoever, curled up like one of the foetuses that had burst from the jars in that tower. Was that recent? He had no feeling of time.

He saw a fine line, a shimmering silver cord stretching from his gut down to his body, like the static line he had used when jumping.

You are still alive, Michel, said a guy who appeared next to him, laughing.

Who are you? an angel?

I am Le Cohen. The Master, as they called me, often to my embarrassment. Your friend Thibault blew my stuffed head off. Your friend Armand shot at The Matagot.

Sorry 'bout that.

No you're not.

No I'm not.

It is strange to be yourself like this for the first time.
It sure was. Almost as if it was nothing to do with him.
What about Astrid and Selene and the other girls?
Well and happy. They wait for you.
You say that.
I do.
Horsett floated down and then up again. It was easy. It was
like his first jump at parachute training. Only this was gentle,
warm, filled with a silver-pearl radiance. He tugged at the silver
cord, and the body at the other end twitched slightly. Outside, the
battle was either ending or moving away, like rolling thunder. He
could hear birdsong again.
Is that priest dead?
*Yes. His heart was not strong enough for that last grand mal. Sophia
could have saved him, perhaps, but to what purpose? Besides, he is more alive
now than he has ever been. He is whole again, and pure, and marvelling at
everything. He was never a bad man. He could have joined us at St Martin's
if I could have got to him earlier.*
Will they save me?
*I think so. The darling Sophia, the red-headed one, always has a plan.
She has gone to get a nearby doctor. She knows one who owes her many
favours. But do you want to be saved?*
What's the choice?
You can decide to go there...
A short tunnel opened to Michael's right. Through he could
see a white realm: white hills, white grass, pure silver streams,
white houses under a perfect sky. No shadows.
That's pretty.
Do you want 'pretty'?
He shrugged.
*You have a destiny, Michel. I knew your mother for a while in Paris.
Did you not guess that?*
Bullshit.
*Which is a wonderful fertiliser. We used it on the vegetable gardens at St
Martin's.*
Baloney
Le Cohen laughed. It was like church bells. Michael floated, free of
concern, free of pain. The white world pulled at him.
*Really, Michel, you have a destiny. Your mother knew that. You know
that. You could be a great teacher – down there.*

Crap.

The red-haired woman burst in with an old doctor, who wore a bowler hat and carried a large black bag. Michael floated down. He wanted to see this. Luc was grey, Colette was covered in ash. A pretty battered bride. He moved closer. There were tears coming from her good eye.

"*Vivre,*" she urged. "*S'il vous plaît, vivre. Ne meurent pas.*"

He was touched: he could allow such sentiment now. She used the '*vous*', even now, because he had asked her not to '*tu*' him. She really wanted him to live.

Sophia was brisk. Powerful. As the doctor tended to his battered other self, she ran off to the priest's rooms and came back with three pairs of trousers and two broom sticks.

"We will make a stretcher. We will put him in the doctor's pony and cart and take him back to St Martin's."

Luc and Colette looked at her.

"The others are all waiting," Sophia said. "I saw them. We can start again there, with Michael. We will be safe."

Michael looked keenly at the young woman whom he had – technically – sort of married. Almost. He saw a light come around her, emerging from within. A large cockroach scuttled over her foot and she stepped back as Luc crushed it.

"Yes," was all she said, but it was a rifle-shot of a Yes.

It is a good plan of Sophia's. She grabs the moment and uses it, always.
Do I get mummified like you? Why're you laughing?

No, that was for another aeon. That has passed now. Now choose: go that way to the White World of endless peace. Or down there into – whatever you want to make of it.

Michael looked. There was no choice. He hadn't been much good as a Screaming Eagle. Maybe he'd trying being a Hawk God after all. He would tug the cord and haul downward, into himself again.

Forward as One, Michel?
You taking the mickey?
No Michel. But watch this…

However he did it – and Michael sure wanted to find out soon – Le Cohen apported a single rose onto Colette's lap, as she bent over the battered body. She looked up, as if she knew he was still around.

Geronimo! Michael cried in the astral realm, as he fell downdown into that length of flesh.

It felt heavy back in his body. Like when he had been loaded with all his kit and weaponry, scarcely able to shuffle toward the plane that would take him to France. It hurt, Jesus it hurt. The price to pay. There were things he had to resolve, to face up to. There was the smell of shit from somewhere. That priest? Himself?

He opened his eyes. A film of blood made everything red. There were three figures bending over him. Three heads bobbed and nodded, whispering. The red-haired one shushed them. There was ringing in his ears. Did someone describe that as church bells once? Okay, okay... It was Luc and Colette. The other one? That one seemed to be in charge, seemed to know what to do.

He wanted peace, needed peace. That's why he came bringing war. Sure.

Luc was at the top of his head. Colette next to his right shoulder. The other woman at his left. He opened his eyes stared upward, into the geometric centre of that trinity.

He opened both eyes, and looked into that neutral centre. He had to say it, at last:

"*Je t'aime...*"

Colette gave a grunt.

Luc smiled.

"Begin," said the stranger.

Finding the Lights Within

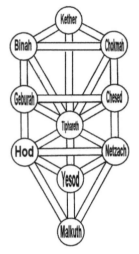

There is a game within the text, although the book can be read without any awareness of it. The entire twenty-two cards of the Major Arcana of the Tarot are described within the tale, starting with the *Hanged Man*, which represents Michael Horsett dangling from the tree.

The challenge is to find all the tarot images and determine how they fit upon the kabbalistic Tree of Life. No knowledge of the kabbalah is needed. You might want to google up the images of the tarot, preferably the Waite-Rider pack.

The Tree of Life is a symbolic representation of the universe and the human psyche. Although the original is defined by Hebrew terminology, it can be adapted by anyone of any religion; it can be used by atheists and agnostics. It works as a kind of psychological filing system.

The Tree consists of ten spheres, connected by twenty-two paths. One of the major aspects of the modern, magical kabbalah is determining how the tarot cards fit onto the Tree. One spiritual system can be used to energise and elucidate the other. The traditional Hebrew letters associated with each of the twenty-two 'paths' on the Tree are given as follows:

Path	Letter	Name	Meaning	Tarot
Kether - Chokmah	א	Aleph	Ox	
Kether - Binah	ב	Bet	House	
Kether - Tiphareth	ג	Gimel	Camel	
Chokmah - Binah	ד	Dalet	Door	
Chokmah - Tiphareth	ה	He	Window	
Chokmah - Chesed	ו	Vav	Nail	
Binah - Tiphareth	ז	Zayin	Spear	Hanged Man
Binah - Geburah	ח	Khet	Fence	
Chesed - Geburah	ט	Tet	Snake	
Chesed - Tiphareth	י	Yod	Fist	
Chesed - Netzach	כ	Kaf	Open hand	
Geburah – Tiphareth	ל	Lamed	Ox-goad	
Geburah - Hod	מ	Mem	Water	
Tiphareth - Netzach	נ	Nun	Fish	
Tiphareth - Yesod	ס	Sameh	Prop	
Tiphareth - Hod	ע	Ayin	Eye	
Netzach - Hod	פ	Pe	Mouth	
Netzach - Yesod	צ	Tzadi	Fish-hook	
Netzach - Malkuth	ק	Qoph	Back of head	
Hod - Yesod	ר	Resh	Head	
Hod - Malkuth	ש	Shin	Teeth	
Yesod - Malkuth	ת	Tau	Cross	

The basic arrangements of the Tree of Life are likewise given below:

—   +

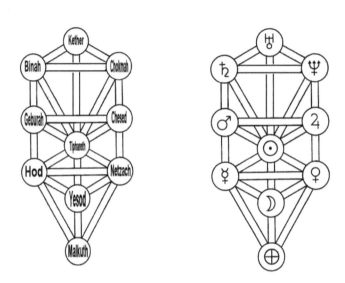

The task is to find the clues within the prose, as to where each card would fit, and see what patterns might emerge, in terms of positive and negative, anabolic and katabolic energies.

Once completed, the result will be a radical system of Correspondences leading to a complete system of tarot analysis.

The First and Only Clue:

In the traditional kabbalah each of the Paths on the Tree of Life is designated by a Hebrew letter. Each letter has both a numerical value and a meaning. Thus the path between Binah, the third sphere, and Tiphareth, the sixth sphere, is allocated the letter ז [Zayin] means 'Spear'. In *The Lightbearer* the character Michael Horsett is described as hanging upside-down on the tree, speared by a branch.

The tarot card known as *The Hanged Man* would therefore be

placed on the path between Binah and Tiphareth. Given that these are also associated with the astrological qualities of Saturn and the Sun respectively, this hints at something of the qualities found within that tarot card – and thus your own soul.

You might also want to ask why he is called Horsett. What are the meanings of Astrid/Selene/Colette? And the other characters? For example, why are the brothers called Allumage? What does 'Lucifer' mean? What titles apply to the planet Venus? Why are there seventy-eight chapters? What other cards from the Minor Arcana can be found?

And more…much more.

But mainly…who do *you* think the true Lightbearer was?

If anyone wants the solution they are welcome to email me: alric@blueyonder.co.uk

I don't have (or want) a website, but my page on Amazon will tell you as much about me as is relevant:
https://www.amazon.co.uk/Alan-Richardson/e/B005ERRP8E/ref=ntt_dp_epwbk_0